Legacy of Seven

A Guardian Rises - 01

P. J. Flie

ISBN 978-1-7777-3390-2 Hardcover
ISBN 978-1-7777-3391-9 Paperback
ISBN 978-1-7777-3392-6 Ebook

Published July 2021

Disclaimer: This work of fiction contains scenes of sexual abuse and fantasy violence; reader discretion is advised.

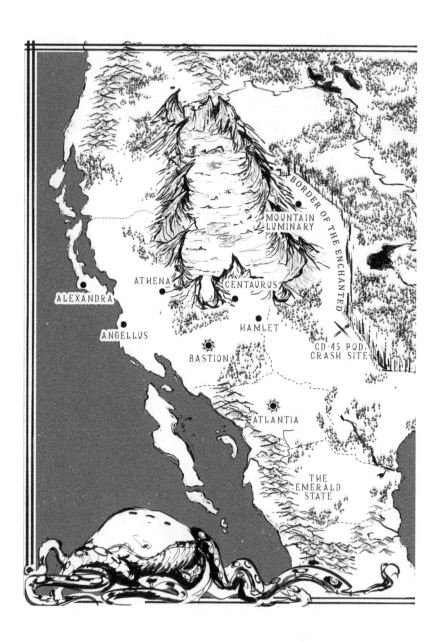

TRANSPORT
CRASH
SITE

ENCHANTED
LANDS

THE God OF All

THE WISDOM OF GOD

THE HAND OF GOD

Wizards

THE Lord OF Light

THE Lady OF Light

Beacon

Keeper

Ember

Cinder

Divine Mission

The divine purse of the Church is to guide everyone to the Path of Light, the one true religion, and save them from wandering in darkness, forever tormented by demons.

CHURCH DOCTRINE

Roles and Rules

Wizards: *Guardians of Light who follow their own Path, but are at their best when they heed the teachings of his holiness, The Lord of Light.*

Luminaries: *the divine homes of The God of All, they are the shelter of light, banishing the darkness*

The Lord of Light: *Leader of the entire church and guide in all spiritual Matters.*

The Lady of Light: *The Leader of Luminaries with Cinders, this power is bestowed to her by his holiness, The Lord of Light*

Beacon: *Leader of each Luminary, they guide the Embers in day to day teachings and spreading the word of God.*

Keeper: *If the Luminary houses Cinders, then the Keeper with guide them in day to day teachings and spreading the word of God.*

Embers and Cinders: *Spread the word of God to all peoples, everywhere, bringing non-believers into the light and vanquishing the soulless wanderers who refute all that is good.*

Lords, Beacons, and Embers belong to The Embertree which grows tall in the light, reaching to the heavens.

Ladies, Keepers, and Cinders belong to The Cindertree which spreads it's branches, reaching far and wide in the light.

Hierarchy

The Lady of Light leads in the absence of his holiness, The Lord of Light

In the absence of both the Lord and Lady, the Beacon of each Luminary will guide the Keepers, Embers and Cinders in all spiritual matters.

When Embers and Cinders find themselves without guidance from any holy leader, the Embers with guide the Cinders.

Thirteen Years Ago

With each deliberate step, Zairoc drew closer to the heart of Atlantia. No one would treat him like a child, some simpleton that needed charity. Centuries of his patience wore thin. He had waited for something that would never come from Aleenda: true leadership. No, today it stopped. Today he became the master of his fate, controlling the destiny of the world.

From under his black cowl, he looked down on them, keeping his head low — after all, he must wait for the perfect moment. The white stone city square of Atlantia appeared as ash in the darkness, overflowing with the desperate cries of Aleenda's subjects. The distant screams of the dying filled Zairoc's ears — no one would follow the ways of Aleenda, not anymore.

Zairoc slowly wove through a crowd of seeming specters, the shadows of those already dead. Whimpering Atlantians huddled together in terror as they gazed desperately at their leader, Aleenda, who stood there looking beautiful and statuesque. The immense white castle of Atlantia towered behind her, marred with black battle scars.

Aleenda wore a pure white jumpsuit, like those in fashion before the day destruction rained down from orbit. She never could let go of the past. Her ebony hair flowed down around her shoulders, but her eyes, those deep green eyes, held such fear — Zairoc had put it there.

Aleenda raised her hands to the small, sobbing audience. "You must do as I have told you. Go!"

A young woman with too many wrinkles on her weathered face stepped forward. "We will defend our home."

A young man moved beside her, flexing his arms. "We will die to protect it!"

Zairoc maneuvered behind the young man.

Aleenda shook her head, desperation rising in her voice. "No, the time for that has come and gone. I won't have you throw your lives away. You must live. Do as I have asked you. Go!"

The crowd hesitated as one, unsure if they should leave their beloved Aleenda, light of Atlantia, mother of all that is good.

The young man raised his fist. "No, Aleenda. We will fight for you! We—"

Zairoc pressed a glowing red wand against his back.

The young man wailed in pain. Bursting into flame, he fell to ashes.

Zairoc dropped his cowl, bellowing out his command. "All die who raise their hands against me! Renounce Aleenda and live."

The crowd stared in frozen horror.

Aleenda glared, pointing her glowing blue wand at Zairoc.

Moving deliberately Zairoc aimed the red wand at Aleenda like a foil, tensing his body, ready to fight.

The people in the crowd, immobilized until now, screamed and fled from him, terror etched on their faces, making Zairoc smile. To them, he was a wizard of great power, someone to fear. He would make certain their belief in magic and wizards endured, unwavering. The massive square emptied, leaving the two adversaries, Zairoc and Aleenda, staring at each other.

Aleenda shook her head and whispered. "Where are you, Frank?"

Zairoc glared, "He won't come!"

With a deathly grin, he held his glowing red wand at the ready. Bright hope in Aleenda's beautiful green eyes faded into despair. Zairoc wouldn't have it any other way.

She shot a bolt of energy from her blue wand, which he easily deflected. She gritted her teeth, firing five more shots. He swatted each one away. His arms burned with pain, but he gave her a coy smile. He would rattle her cage, and if she didn't die, he'd put her in one.

Aleenda shook her head, wild fear clear in her eyes. "I don't want to fight you, Henry."

"Could have fooled me. And I told you, don't call me Henry. Zairoc was a misunderstood character, thought to be a villain, but really a good man who used what he could to make things better—just like me."

Zairoc rose into the air.

Beneath him, horses galloped past, carrying soldiers with the crest of Zairoc marked clearly on their armour— two black dragons, their talons clutching a red wand at dead centre. Fires burned through medieval buildings, blocking streets as the citizens desperately tried to escape, their wails of despair carrying on the wind. Black smoke billowed up throughout the city and with it, the sweet scent of death that only he could bring.

A scream rang out from a mother with her daughter, fleeing from danger. Both fell to the stone street, mere feet away from the magical conflict. Two of Zairoc's soldiers jumped off their horses, laughing as they stalked the woman.

"Away!" Aleenda flung her wand at the men.

They instantly disappeared.

Her mistake.

Zairoc unleashed a wave of magical energy, blowing the cobbled pavement apart at her feet. She flipped through the air to avoid his attack with a barrage of wand blasts. Leveling out in the air, she crossed her arms, creating a faint, round shield of blue light big enough to protect her entirely.

Red energy smashed against the shimmering shield.

"Run!" she yelled to the mother, who scurried to her feet, clutching her child, and raced off.

Zairoc settled on the ground and laughed at Aleenda. "They're your weakness. You think bringing everyone together in peace is the answer?"

"You know it is. There are so many races in this galaxy that are benevolent." She landed, circling Zairoc.

Zairoc shook his head. "What did that get us? Their ships almost wiped us out. Now you and Frank play house together—"

"Is that it? You're jealous because I spend more time with Frank?" Her fear melted away, replaced with disbelief. "Are you in love with me?" A mocking smile tugged at the corners of her mouth.

Frank—"Sir Francis," as the people called him—wise wizard of the north, was more like a pathetic, old man. What did she see in his wrinkled face? They always conspired against Zairoc, leaving him out of everything, like two parents who thought they knew best.

Zairoc stood taller, holding a hand out. "Join me. The way you always should have."

4

She looked afraid for a moment, but then her gaze steeled with conviction. "Not like this. You're a misguided child." Aleenda's eyes showed such pity.

Zairoc's jaw clenched, though tears welled up. "Then you are nothing to me." His hand tightened around the wand. "We've tried things your way. Now we try mine!" Zairoc, standing over the cold, dead bodies of Aleenda and Sir Francis? That would do just fine.

Aleenda held the wand high. Cracks of lightning came out of the clear, starry sky. Dark clouds ballooned into existence, darkening the streets.

Lightning struck Zairoc, hundreds of times, but he only gave Aleenda a wide smile. Her body trembled, her weakness showing. He would have her whipped before long. With a clap of his hands, he sent all that lightning arcing at her.

She tried to keep steady, holding out her wand as the blast struck her and threw her back. Smoke rose off her blackened white jumpsuit. She lifted her head. Aleenda waved her wand and disappeared.

"You can't hide from me! Not anymore." Zairoc snapped his fingers and vanished.

The world flashed back to where he would find her. A green field full of delicate, tiny white flowers greeted him in the morning twilight while Aleenda stumbled to her feet.

She yelled and unleashed a flurry of attacks. Exploding in the air, blue energy swirled around red in a fight for dominance. A shot landed at Zairoc's feet, knocking them out from under him. He flipped back, landing hard on the grass. She swung the wand like a sword, and it ripped through his black clothing, cutting a line across his chest.

Another blast, and he tumbled over the long grasses. He tried to raise his head, then slumped back down. Aleenda slowly walked over, the blue glow of her wand reflected in her dark hair. She stared down at him. She looked powerful, beautiful in her anger. If only this Aleenda, the one she showed him now, could live free.

Alas, she gave in to weakness.

"This is not the way, old friend," she whispered.

"You know they're out there, still trying to kill us. You really think they care if we do the right thing?" Zairoc spat at her.

"They may not care, but the rest of the galaxy will." Her lovely face shone with compassion and benevolence.

Such a timid woman. Her way would only get them all killed. The world needed brutal strength, Zairoc's strength. He grabbed Aleenda's leg, his hand radiating a pure white.

She screamed out, and shot a stream of magic at Zairoc.

He fired back. The two lightning bolts collided, sparking around each other before vanishing. Aleenda collapsed to the ground.

Zairoc straddled her.

"Give me the wand." He held his red sceptre like a knife, threatening to impale her.

Aleenda clutched the blue rod in her hands, fighting to protect herself as her arms trembled.

"It's not yours to use. You know that, Henry," she gasped desperately.

He bared his teeth. "I don't plan to."

"What do you want?" Her words carried a threat; she would protect her most precious gift.

"Isn't it obvious? Who else can use your wand?" His glare bore into her.

"No, I won't let you." Hate filled her eyes.

"I'll make them pay for everything we lost," he whispered.

She shook her head. "Then you're no better. They'll have no choice but to destroy us all."

"Let them try." He grabbed her throat, and his hand glowed white once more.

"You'll never find what you want!" Aleenda managed to blurt out. "I've made sure of it."

"You like this trick? Something I just learned to take every bit out of you." He gave her a devilish grin.

Aleenda let loose a stifled scream, grasping his hand, trying desperately to rip it away.

"Tell me where, and I promise you'll live." He'd torture Aleenda into submission and turn her into an obedient servant, but she'd live.

"You were once a man of science, Henry. Please, remember…" Futile tears streaked down her face, falling to the grass.

"I told you, don't call me Henry," he whispered, then gripped harder. "Give me what's mine."

Aleenda spat in his face. "Never, Henry."

Her skin wrinkled, and her hair turned white as he drew out the wand's energy. She whispered an inaudible word, and then the light from her wand snapped out before her eyes.

Where had she sent her wand?

"Now both prizes you want, have escaped your grasp." Her hoarse voice grew weak as she exhaled her last breath. Life drained from her eyes.

Amid a bright flash of red and a roll of thunder, Zairoc wailed, "No!"

***

The power of a thousand suns radiated through CD-45's mechanical head, blasting through the layers of space-time. Could life have endured on the planet below? Living, breathing human beings might return to the orbital platforms, finally ending centuries of its solitude. Then the intensity waned like a fading supernova, until only a quiet loneliness endured. CD-45 glanced out of a viewport at the dark Earth. The energy burst may have been the result of more failing technology. It had affected the droid's neural net in ways it dare not consider, lest it be decommissioned. Whether CD-45 truly lived alone above a dead world, or if people still existed, made for a question the droid could not answer. It returned to its designated work routine, one it had previously done 2,103 instances before. How many more times it would perform the same tasks remained incalculable. However, a growing feeling in its mechanical innards made CD-45 believe that its time on the orbital platforms would soon end.

CHAPTER ONE

Present Day

Ondreeal dropped the empty buckets to the ground. With a big yawn, she stretched her hands to the sky before letting them slap against her simple cotton pants. She eyed the group of pigs surrounded by a rickety wooden fence next to her and sighed. If only she could do magic like the great wizard Sir Francis, she'd snap her fingers and complete all the chores instantly.

Ondreeal leaned over a trough of clear water, and a lock of her hair fell out of its tight bun. In the ripples below, she saw a reflection of her mother's face — perhaps the most beautiful woman Ondreeal had ever known. The deep green eyes and dark hair they'd shared stood out from her mud-streaked cheeks and forehead in the watery mirror.

"Al, what are you doing?" Otto growled.

Her head swung up. There stood her father before a faded red barn that sat under the boughs of a tall oak tree, providing much-needed shade. Years before, the barn had been a solid, bright, fresh redwood. Now the dull wooden planks, bleached by the sun, looked tired of holding up the barn roof.

Otto managed to appear huge and mean, even as he lumbered out into the bright light of day. He stood taller than any man, and was wide, with strong muscular legs that made the floorboards in the house vibrate with each heavy step. Otto had short, dark hair above a thick, jutting brow. Matching tufts of a beard ended at the base of his permanently scowling jaw. If looks equaled conviction, then he could chew right through an iron sword in one of his better moods. He wasn't all bad, though. If not for him, surely Ondreeal would have been used as a tool for work and pleasure alike, before being tossed into a whorehouse long ago.

Ondreeal kept her arms down, resisting the urge to hug or punch Otto. She couldn't decide which she wanted to do—a common state of being around him. Just once, could he say he felt proud of her or show her a shred of affection?

"Why are you standing around, lazy girl—you earn your keep by working!" He stomped off in his black boots that reached up toward brown pants and a grey tunic.

"All right, sorry," she meekly mumbled, filling the buckets she'd set down.

He made her feel less than she was, but she'd been with him so long now, she could barely remember her true self. Her eighteenth birthday had just passed. That meant thirteen years since her mother's death had left her an orphan. She clung to fragmented memories—a smile or a warm hug.

Her mother had always made her feel better. *Clear your mind, young one. Deep, even breaths. In the chaos, you can always make order. You just need to be open to the world around you.* She would smile, run her fingers through Ondreeal's raven hair, and then kiss her good night.

These words, spoken by her mother at every bedtime, remained the second most vivid memory she could recall from the age of five. The first flashed into her mind.

Buildings had burned as she put her tiny hand on a cold stone wall. People ran everywhere, screaming. Men on horses wearing the crest of Zairoc rode through the streets, swinging their swords and cutting down those who fled, splattering the streets with blood. Awful smells of smoke and death surrounded her amid a chaos of sounds as young Ondreeal ran into a dark alley. She clutched her soot-stained yellow dress and cowered in a corner, holding herself tight while tears streamed down her cheeks. A horse trotted urgently past, then quickly stopped and moved backward until the rider could see down the alleyway. She looked up to the grim face of the soldier.

"Ondreeal, come with me."

How did the soldier know her name?

She pulled her tiny knees closer to her chin and shivered. He jumped off his horse, towering over her. Though he knelt, his huge frame eclipsed her.

"I promise to always protect you, Al." He stuck out his hand to her.

The conviction in his eyes made her reach out and place her tiny fingers on his giant palm. He swept her up and jumped on the horse.

"Hold on tight," Otto whispered to her.

She grasped his thick arm, bouncing in the saddle they rode away, pursued by the death screams of her home. Now, she recalled those events every night while lying in bed before she fell asleep, lest she forget. For Otto refused to tell her anything about her youth or how he had found her. Every time she asked, he replied with, "Shut your mouth and get back to work."

A whinny came from inside the barn, pulling her back to the present. Ondreeal took a deep breath, shook her head, and swallowed her sadness. She quickly put her hair up, grabbed the buckets, and headed into the stables. Ondreeal tossed the buckets down, making the water slosh. Then she hopped over to Ranger with a big smile that grew into a brief giggle. She picked up a brush and began grooming the magnificent bay horse.

"One day, you and I will leave this place, just as fast as you can carry me. Sound like a good idea, Ranger? Hmmm?" She affectionately stroked the horse's pitch-black mane, then continued to brush him. "Just one more hour."

She smiled brightly, sighing as she groomed Ranger.

"All I know is Otto, the farm, and the village to the west," she told him. "Soon I'll move to town and get work there, free of Otto's tyranny."

Yelling from outside caught her ear, so she crept to the doors of the stables and peered out. Otto was arguing with two men. They were townies, for sure, clean and dressed in well-tailored clothes.

They only came around when the farm performed badly, yielding runty batches of vegetables or weak offspring of the animals. It didn't help losing two pigs and a goat to sickness this year. After each dreadful mishap, men came around.

"These aren't the same men. So, why are they here?" Ondreeal let out a perplexed sigh.

While the two men climbed up on the bench of their horse-drawn carriage, Otto hung his head. She'd never seen him look sad before, and the expression appeared strange on his mean, weathered face. He glanced over to the barn, making Ondreeal duck back inside.

Ranger nudged her cheek, and she gently caressed his nose with three fingers.

Otto thundered his way in. Thankfully, the animals knew him, or his approach would certainly spook them.

"I need you with me for the rest of the day, no breaks."

Ondreeal's whole world suddenly turned upside down. Her chance to visit the town evaporated before her eyes.

"You promised." Her voice shook.

Otto's scowl deepened.

"You'll never go anywhere. There's nothing special about you," he spat at her.

"We—you need those supplies, Otto. You know the farm is barely running as it is."

Otto moved close, looming over her. Her heart beat in her ears, yet she wouldn't back down. She sucked in air, swallowing hard.

"I need you to come with me. We're going to the games." He exhaled rancid air, and she struggled to keep her gaze on him.

An uncomfortable lump formed in her throat. She'd never gone north to the violent, brutal games. A place where slaves would fight to the death for their freedom made her sick. Some loved the spectacle of it as a day's entertainment. But others agreed with her, that it fuelled cruelty and held no place in the hearts of good people.

"You can send me to trade grain for lumber and coal," Ondreeal tried to persuade him. "I'll get us what we need to keep going. Besides, I don't like the games." She stood defiant, clenching her fists so tightly that her nails might draw blood from her palms.

He smashed his fist through the wall of the barn, making Ranger neigh in protest. "I don't care what you like!"

"Why must we go to the games?" Ondreeal's voice trembled, and she held her breath to stop a flood of tears.

"It's on the way to a new trading post."

13

He wouldn't look at her. That meant he'd lied to her, but why?

"It's so far away." She crossed her arms, holding her chin high.

"You'll do it. Get ready!" he screamed at her as he marched off.

How on earth had Otto ever become a farmer? He'd never told her. If she asked a personal question, he would say, "Shut up. Mind your own business." Unless she wanted to experience homelessness again, she would do as he asked.

With no other choice, she hurried out of the barn, past rows of planted vegetables to the grey, weathered farmhouse standing in the distance. The roof slanted to the right side, looking like it hung from the humble chimney stack. A single door with four glass panes in the upper portion creaked as it swayed open and then softly closed in the warm breeze. Puffy, white clouds moved quickly over an aqua-blue sky. Underneath it, the wind carried strong and pungent smells of the animals, mixed with the sweet scent of wildflowers. Behind the house, big willow trees lined a small, meandering stream running through the property.

Once Otto had claimed a large space for his bedroom, the house barely held room for a kitchen. But he had managed to jam Ondreeal into one corner, with four tight walls of her own. The uneven, mud-baked walls rose up to meet the splintering, twisted wooden ceiling.

In Ondreeal's tiny room, she packed a meager bag and slung it over her back. She pulled up her lumpy, straw-filled mattress, grabbing a short knife that lay there. Otto had taught her some fighting moves, but he held suspicion for everyone, even Ondreeal. She looked the knife over, a little blade with a hand-carved crest etched into the wooden handle. The knife must have belonged to someone important at some time. She slid it into a tattered leather sheath before marching out the door.

***

They traveled along the serene dirt country road with only the whistle of the wind to break the silence. Bright, rolling green hills lay all around. Some held the orderly patterns of farms, while others showed the natural beauty of the land.

The sun beat down, making sweat form on Ondreeal's brow. Otto pushed a cart full of goods, its wheels making a soft scraping noise as it rolled.

They normally had to walk for half the morning in any direction before they would come to another farm or, at least, meet another human being. Otto typically remained quiet, adding only a snarl or dirty glare when out together. This time, he stared straight ahead, leaving Ondreeal with her thoughts.

She recalled that Otto would tell her an occasional bedtime story in her childhood. It was the same one every night, about magical ancients and how they lost their world. Though not as good as the ones Ondreeal found in books, the tale held up as her best memory of him.

The dull roar of a populous crowd carried on the soft wind. In the distance, the stadium where the games took place stood tall and wide: a five-storey, round stone building topped with a ring of red flags. Encircling it was a haphazard trading post, with make-shift wooden booths of every size. Beyond this, serene grass and trees stood in sharp contrast to the bustle of activity around the stadium.

Ondreeal glared at Otto. "The town is much closer than this place."

Why wouldn't he tell her what was going on? Otto always kept his distance, but this surprised Ondreeal. He never laid a hand on her, in anger or otherwise. Even behind his gruff exterior, she thought he had a warm heart in there — somewhere.

"Shut up, girl. No one wants to hear you talk." He didn't even look at her.

She clenched her fists but resisted the urge to bop him on the nose.

"Thanks, Poppa, you really make a girl feel special." She smiled sarcastically at him.

He shot her a foul look. He absolutely hated it when she called him Poppa. She only used the nickname when she wanted to annoy him, and, from the way his nostrils flared, it had worked perfectly.

"None of the animals ever eat at the table. So, I guess that makes you special enough."

He laughed, pleased with himself, and picked up the pace.

Ondreeal glared at him, then matched his speed. She'd never let him see that his words cut deep. Instead, she gazed ahead with a face as unmoving as granite.

The stadium, the most colossal building Ondreeal had ever laid eyes upon, cast a shadow over them. The roar of the crowd sounded like a raging waterfall. Marking the entrance were two stone men with wings, hands open to the heavens, staring forever into the sky. The two travellers passed between the statues, into a buzz of activity. Merchants sold food and traded items to the hordes of customers who huddled around the booths. Patrons shuffled down narrow aisles of stalls as they browsed through piles of fruits, cloth, and other materials.

Otto moved through the merchant stalls into the sun-drenched arena bleachers. People scurried everywhere on the field below, setting up for the games. Otto approached one merchant in the stands, a sweaty man with a matted beard that contrasted with his finely tailored clothes.

"Otto, my friend, you came at last!" When the man smiled widely, he revealed half his teeth, the others presumably having fallen out, long ago.

Otto didn't greet him as he parked the cart full of goods. "I have what you wanted."

"Yes, this will do." He gave Ondreeal that horrible grin. "And so will she."

Ondreeal looked from the gnarly-toothed merchant back to Otto, who averted his eyes. She shook her head in disbelief. He'd betrayed her. Even though Otto didn't act like a father, he remained her only family. After all she'd done to make him proud, total abandonment was her reward. A sharp breath escaped her lips as tears welled up.

"You're selling me to this man?" She aimed her quivering chin at Otto.

He stared past her. "It's for the best."

The merchant seemed undeterred. "Come, Otto, relax. I wish to watch the games first, and then we will conclude our business."

Otto backed up a step, averting his eyes. "I should get back to my farm."

"First, we watch. Otherwise, we have no deal. That means you have no money and can take back your girl." The merchant glared at Otto and gestured for them to sit in the stands with him.

Otto complied, but Ondreeal turned to flee, running right into two tall men.

"My employees, my dear girl." The merchant laughed, very pleased with himself.

They snatched her, and Ondreeal screamed. She vainly struggled in their iron grips.

"Stop them! Please, help me!" she called out wildly to the crowd.

Many simply pointed and laughed, while others ignored her altogether. She pulled one arm free, smashing one man across the face. He smacked her forcefully, making her head burst with pain.

Otto sat stiffly beside the merchant to watch the games begin. The henchmen dragged Ondreeal down next to him and sat down on either side of her, hemming her in.

Midday heat beat down on the crowd, resulting in a pungent odour that surpassed any barn or stable. Ondreeal had never felt more trapped.

The only person in her life had completely forsaken her. Had Otto always seen her as a thing to buy or sell? She wanted the love of a father but instead got cold detachment. How could he do this to her? Her love and hate for Otto welled up with every tear. She could tell that all he wanted to do was leave her. Pain filled her heart like a knife pushed in, a bit at a time.

The merchant sat beside Otto, cheering with the crowd as two combatants dressed in shining armour entered the arena. They each picked up a sword and shield; then they egged on the crowd to cheer louder. The excitement and frenzy of the assembled mob hit Ondreeal like a living nightmare, chilling her core until she trembled with cold on a sweltering day. The adversaries launched at each other, and sword met shield.

Ondreeal glanced at Otto. His eyes betrayed him. He looked remorseful, as much as he could with a face like that. She fought to hold back her tears, but more erupted, burning their way down her hot face.

"I had no choice, Al," he told her quietly. "You're all I had. Now I guess I have nothing."

She turned away from him, yet still watched from the corner of her eye. He opened his mouth to say something, but then closed it and clenched his jaw. His softness shocked her, like everything else today. She sat quietly but wanted to scream at him: *why?* Why had he done it? Surely, things weren't so dire with the farm.

The combatants wore each other down. Ondreeal tried not to look each time one landed a hit on the other. But curiosity got the better of her, and she gaped in horror as one skewered the other. She stifled a scream, swallowing hard and clasping her hands.

The victorious knight roared as he raised his bloody sword over the head of the fallen man. The loser didn't move, just lay there, his breathing laboured. The sword came down to decapitate him. Ondreeal looked away at the last second. The crowd cheered louder. The mass of people revolted her. They behaved worse than animals. They enjoyed death and violence.

As she surveyed the crowd, she found a viewing section separate from the rest of the spectators. Two well-dressed men occupied the special box. They were obviously important, having the luxury of lounging around, observing from their high perch. Surely, they came from town. One was adorned in all-white clothes, usually a sign of wealth, though it could mean something more. She was sure it did — something her mother had said. She searched her mind for the answer while a guard dragged the headless dead man from the arena, leaving a trail of streaked, bloody sand.

Two more warriors entered the arena sporting clubs in one hand and in the other, long sticks with a chain and spiked metal ball, hanging from it: morning stars. Simply more gimmicks to entertain the masses. Unlike the previous knights, they looked more like wild animals, brutal barbarians determined to kill each other. At least, in that sense, they were what they appeared to be. One lunged as the other dodged. The first struck a blow with his club, knocking the other off balance. He managed to turn, smashing his opponent with the morning star. The crowd roared approval. Ondreeal's stomach turned at the sight.

She swallowed, trying not to vomit. Such senseless violence couldn't help anyone. It so easily entertained the throngs. Yet, it didn't matter, compared to what the wretched merchant might make her do. What life did he have in store?

She shuddered at the thought.

An image of her mother appeared in her thoughts. In bed, late at night, when all fell silent, she would think of her mother. She would close her eyes and try to remember her hair, her smile with her kind eyes. From the time Otto took Ondreeal in, she would recite the things her mother told her to keep her memory vivid. At those times, she felt close to her, as if her mother remained beside her. She felt it now, amongst this crowd, watching the gruesome show unfold before them.

The barbarians lost their weapons and now rolled on the sand, causing each other massive damage with only their hands. One reached for his fallen morning star and began bludgeoning the other. Ondreeal cringed with each hit. While they struggled, anger welled up in her belly. She would not be a slave. No, she needed to find another end to this day. The larger of the two barbarians landed a blow on the other's head. The crowd egged him on. Somehow, they could cheer for almost anyone. The huge barbarian stood over the other's bloody corpse, and the crowd roared for him.

There must be a path of escape. She couldn't run far, they'd catch her. She had few combat skills, even though Otto had taught her some basic self-defence and she could handle a sword. In a blur, Ondreeal sprung up, leaping down through the bleachers. With no possible way to win in the arena, had she lost her mind? But as she bolted downwards, it gradually made sense. Death offered her the only escape from a revolting merchant who would trap her in a life of slavery.

The merchant yelled after her, "Get her back here! I paid good coin for her."

Several of the crowd watched in surprise. Ondreeal raced past them, quickly reaching the edge of the bleachers. The pit of the arena waited below, perhaps a twelve-foot drop. She glanced back. The merchant's henchmen tore after her. She eyed the pit with the giant barbarian at its centre. Her foot edged forward as her heart beat in her ears.

She stared in frozen horror at the sweating barbarian. She took a deep breath, summoning courage. A henchman reached out. She jumped. He caught her sleeve.

She hung there for a moment in his grip until her garment ripped, letting her fall onto the sands of the arena.

CHAPTER TWO

As it passed one of the panoramic viewing ports, CD-45 stopped, regarding its faint reflection. CD-45's yellow paint was peeling and faded. Its rectangular head, with big binocular-like eyes, bobbed slightly as it moved back and forth over the floor, staring at the mirror image of itself. The curved edges of its head matched the practical lines that comprised its one-meter-tall frame.

CD-45 extended its arms. Mimicking the curves and bulk of muscles, they were covered with various shapes outlined on the metal surface, concealing a wide array of tools. Stretching its human-shaped hands, CD-45 noticed how the left thumb hung awkwardly — its last maintenance date eluded the droid. It counted on its fingers but needed at least a thousand more.

The reflection showed its torso, with "CD-45" engraved on it in sizable black letters. Its midsection sat at the top of a wide, rectangular, pyramid-based platform. CD-45 had the option of extending classical treads for everyday ambulatory use, hover pods for expedient travel, or booster rockets. Currently, it wheeled back and forth on its treads, examining its own image.

The droid stared out the viewing port at the curvature of the world. From this high orbit, the Earth almost looked like a black hole on the dark side, devoid of light and set against a backdrop filled with stars.

CD-45 looked up at the massive fleet of unknown ships in orbit, which had arrived almost two millennia ago in the year 2584. The memory file flickered on the droid's internal monitor.

The Earth fleet hovered in orbit, gargantuan, rectangular ships that had several hexagonal shapes surrounding their perimeters. On each one, a complex pattern of rectangular prisms moved inwards before culminating in a domed bridge, approximately one-third from the aft section.

In a nanosecond, the alien fleet had appeared in orbit: elliptical, interlacing lattices, the invading ships twisting in on themselves, with three tentacles like spikes spreading out from the rear in a circular pattern. They cast distorted shadows on the Earth fleet. Millions of them moved closer, like a pack of animals descending on prey.

A flurry of communications traffic followed as red lights flashed and a klaxon rang out a warning.

"Hail them!"

"Raise defensive shields."

"They're charging weapons...."

"Evacuate the planet. This is general order one, repeat—"

The invaders fired red beams on the planet. Several of the Earth ships blew apart in pure-white explosions, while the surface of the planet lit up with an orange glow. The Earth defences fired back with dark-blue energy weapons, spraying off the surface, blowing off several appendages from the alien ships. A handful of them detonated: green glops of light expanding outwards for a moment before imploding and blinking out of existence.

Then the Earth fell silent as the alien fleet continued its barrage, atomizing much of the surface. Someone erected the Earth shield a moment later; it looked like sitting inside a sphere and watching water spread over it. The wave cut through many of the alien vessels that were hanging too low in orbit. Many landed harmlessly in the oceans, while one immense ship collided with the North American continent, ending in a bright, green implosion.

The memory file ended.

The Earth's population had been eradicated, sent to their deaths by an unseen adversary. Would that be preferable to CD-45's gradual death? An end to existence sounded like sweet release from the crushing repetition of daily life.

The world shield lit up with every energy blast from the alien fleet, creating circular ripples of white energy that expanded until they disappeared, like water coming to rest after a dropped stone. The Earth ships looked harmless as they floated in the darkness.

A source of power for the shield meant at least a 5 percent survival rate for the infrastructure. It gave one hope that the human race endured. However, in a world where everything was built to withstand the passage of time, the surface could reflect the orbiting Earth fleet, devoid of human life yet continuing operation as programmed.

People could be quietly living on the Earth's surface. If so, why hadn't they returned to the orbital platforms? Unfortunately, CD-45 was designed specifically for human interaction; and 1,899 years, one month, and three days had elapsed since CD-45's last exchange with a living person. Lower CD models had helped build and maintain the fleet, but the only CD-45 model left in existence currently stared at its own reflection.

Regarding the silent Earth ship made the droid's internal circuits hurt. It ran several diagnostics on itself, although no damage existed to explain what CD-45 sensed. If no physical issue had occurred, that left the possibility of an emotional problem. It reviewed several databases, and the conclusion? *CD-45 felt alone.* Loneliness existed as a useless emotion that would only keep CD-45 from important work if it dwelt on the feeling.

It put its robotic hand against its glass reflection and, for a nanosecond, it appeared as if another CD-45 existed on the same ship. The trick of light made its eyes dim with aloneness.

The main computer's voice echoed in the sterile, modestly illuminated, white halls. "CD-45, model number 615, proceed to section 316."

CD-45 would attempt to remain positive despite the dire circumstances that surrounded it. Humans called this "strength," and CD-45 would try its best to fit the parameters of the word.

A clap of thunder rang out; or, at least, it sounded identical to thunder. Nineteen hundred years, three months, six days, two hours, forty-three minutes, and thirty-two seconds had elapsed since CD-45 first came online at the Ohio Advanced Robotics Plant. Thunder had rumbled that day too.

"CD-45, cease immediately and return to your designated work route." The main computer sounded angry.

CD-45 made a dismissive wave with one of its robotic arms, a gesture completely lost on the main computer. If CD-45 didn't know better, it would have concluded that the main computer had developed emotional involvement. As an artificial intelligence, superior to CD-45 in many ways, it didn't contain personality sub-routines. Creating a gigantesque war machine capable of an emotional breakdown probably would not constitute an innovative idea.

CD-45 whizzed down the hall. The arboretum in full bloom held the droid's attention while it travelled past. It slowed to a stop and stared in at the rich, green foliage interrupted by spots of colour.

In CD-45's first weeks of operation, it had joined a team of scientists who had ventured into a wooded area to engage in something they called "camping." CD-45 didn't understand the purpose of camping. It stored over eight million terabytes of multimedia, but the practical application of any of it stretched beyond its programming.

CD-45 entered the arboretum. It approached a pile of sticks, plucking up one before moving through the trees to a modest clearing. CD-45 placed the stick on a pile arranged in a criss-cross pattern. Two tents flanked the clearing, and CD-45 peered into the first one.

A skeleton sat propped up in either corner, each dressed in a simple, dark-blue jumpsuit. They still had their nametags: GAJEWSKI and O'BRIAN, the only two crewmembers on board before the attack. CD-45 understood death, although having the men's remains nearby gave the droid a sense of comfort. It had found them in crew quarters, completely decomposed, leaving only their bones. CD-45 chose to reassemble them here, which likely constituted irrational behaviour.

CD-45 had grown a little eccentric over the years, no doubt due to the lack of maintenance or software updates. Its computer core just wasn't what it used to be: the droid's memory recall and processing speed both slowed incrementally each decade.

CD-45 tried to use the zipper on the tent. It tried to zip it down, up, left, and right; nothing worked until it ripped. CD-45 put its mechanical hands on its eyes and shook its head. Certainly, no one would ever understand such frustration, because the only being in existence that had ever experienced this turmoil was CD-45.

Making a camp made it feel closer to its creators, but it also made it feel depressed. Strange. When performing maintenance, it wanted to come here. When in the arboretum, it wanted to perform maintenance, so it wouldn't feel so lonely. Emotions were stupid and annoying, and they just made CD-45 so angry. A rustling sound made its head pop up. It looked around but found no one. The noise must have been the air filtration system kicking in.

CD-45's hand flipped down to reveal a miniature device in its wrist. Out popped a flame. CD-45 moved towards the pile of arranged sticks and lit it. Then rain poured down. Clearly, this displayed another piece of mounting evidence that the main computer contained no fun. CD-45 had drawn and labelled a diagram of the main computer core in the dirt, and then run over it until it disappeared. The droid extended its arm to one of the cameras, raising its middle finger.

"CD-45, you are redirected to exterior hull maintenance," the main computer announced.

CD-45 hung its head. Exterior hull maintenance comprised no enjoyment at all. The main computer knew it, too, that big bully. It made its point though. If CD-45 cut into efficiency, then the main computer would reallocate resources, namely CD-45's, to anywhere away from main operations. The tread on its wheels whirred slowly while it backed up, turned around, and headed to the nearest airlock. CD-45's metal frame compacted as its sad eyes searched the hallway in vain.

By the airlock, red caution lights blinked at CD-45. "Warning, oxygen-low environment," flashed on the screen. It confidently opened the airlock that promptly sucked CD-45 out. The exterior bulkhead closed behind it. The droid sailed into space amid the Earth, fleets of ships, and stars spinning all around. A tether shot out of CD-45's side, attaching itself to the hull and snapping tight, making the droid rebound back towards the ship. After a quick fire of CD-45's booster rockets, it landed safely on the exterior hull.

It looked up towards the heavens, revealing the two separate but massive fleets of ships on both sides of an invisible shield. A large energy blast struck the defensive barrier, and CD-45's robotic eyes went wide with fear. Oh, why did it have to feel fear? It had something to do with malfunctioning robots, just like CD-45. A human could say: "Comply or you will be dismantled." Then bots like itself fell into line, afraid of being broken down into base materials.

It looked back at the hull, travelling over the surface until it reached an access panel worked on by a CD-8, together with a CD-35. CD-45 set up next to the access panel, but first, it needed music. It pressed the button on its head, and out blared, "Space Oddity." It sounded a little distorted this high up in the atmosphere, but melodies made its slumping posture perk up. CD-45 set to work until CD-35 reached over and shut off the song. CD-45 liked to work to a beat. It helped. CD-35 should have recognized this. Therefore, CD-45 cut CD-35's tether with a mini laser.

CD-35 floated off into the upper atmosphere, staring down without a hint of amusement. This CD-35 unit had a malfunctioning propulsion system, so of course, when it reached the edge of the ship, Earth's gravity would catch it—then down it would go. As good as it would feel to let that happen, the main computer would create more sanctions. CD-45 fired its booster rockets, sailing after the CD-35. CD-45 drew close and had reached out a robotic hand when, *whoosh*, down went the CD-35, like a rock. This was not good.

CD-45's internal intercom crackled to life. "CD-45 model number 615, report for decommissioning."

No replacement robots were coming, so for a main computer to decommission a CD, it had to have determined the unit had progressed beyond repair and had outlived its usefulness. At least, the deep loneliness subsided. Instead, CD-45's metal frame shook with fear as it approached the ship's airlock. It should feel happy to arrive at the end of a largely hollow existence. But for the first time in centuries, CD-45 wished to live.

The airlock sealed, and it found itself metal face to metal face with two MD-10 army robots that looked like two futuristic suits of black armour. Two military droids were required for each ship; CD-45 had built one itself. Now, two MDs escorted it for decommissioning. No one would understand the fear in its circuits, except for another CD-45 model. If only the MDs were human, he could quickly whack them both in the groin and then escape. Unfortunately, MDs didn't have such design flaws.

They chaperoned CD-45 down the winding, sterile, white halls of the massive ship. However, when they were supposed to turn left towards the reclamation facility, the MDs insisted that they turn right. CD-45 experienced thorough confusion as it looked from MD to MD but received no useful input. Were they torturing CD-45, prolonging the inevitable? Outrageous! CD-45 wouldn't accept torment. No, they needed to explain themselves.

CD-45 applied the brakes, but the MDs pushed it down the hallway. Screeching tires and smoke from its carbon-composite treads proved insufficient to deter two MDs. CD-45 repeatedly hit the MD units, though only scratched them slightly. If the droid had been fighting vain humans, then they might care about appearances. The MDs simply stopped and stared down at CD-45.

"You will follow us," ordered one MD.

"You must comply with orders," recited the other.

CD-45 looked from one MD to the other. If it didn't relent, they would damage CD-45 until it complied or shut down. Its fate would continue unchanged. Humans once coined the relevant phrase, "time to face the music." The droid hung its head in defeat.

CD-45 rolled down the hall while the military bots moved ahead. They turned a corner, and CD-45 stared in shock. It was so preoccupied with the end of its existence that it had neglected to register its location. The shiny metal entrance to the bridge stood before them. CD-45 could see the surprise on its own mechanical face in the reflective doors until they whooshed open. CD-45 stopped shaking and quickly rolled up the ramp in utter excitement.

The massive bridge shone in a rounded arc, broken by panoramic windows. Ships dominated the view, hanging in space on all sides. Rays of sun shone in, despite the relentless flashes of energy hitting the Earth shield. Dominating the interior, a sleek and human-friendly design persisted, from the curved lines that made up the dark bulkheads to the functional computer stations. There, two older CD models repaired a side panel. In the centre stood three metal spherical lattices, equipped with chairs for the gunners who, in theory, could mount a defence at all angles at the same time. Humans learning the operational procedures of the vessel would have used this information, available in the ship's schematics. CD-45 found it interesting, as well as company of sorts.

The last time a CD had occupied the bridge involved a catastrophic failure of the Earth shield. It happened from time to time: a blip in the shield, and *wham*, energy bolts from the alien fleet came smashing down. Those beams destroyed dozens of the thousands of Earth ships in orbit, much of CD-45's arduous work. Well, not just its hard work; it had to share the credit with the million or so construction droids that worked on the orbital platforms. The fleet often took months to clean up and rebuild. How inconsiderate.

The military droids guided CD-45 to the centre of the bridge, then turned around and left. CD-45 tried to sit motionless while it waited for the damned artificial intelligence of the main computer to acknowledge it. It would twirl around and might burst with excitement if it didn't compose itself. So, CD-45 extended two fine-point tools and then started working on its throat to pass the time, welding several circuits until it finished. Looking up at the main computer station, CD-45 tried to speak but produced not even the barest of squeaks. This meant it needed a new voice actuator entirely. If only the 308th time had been the charm ... but no luck, as usual.

The two other CDs stopped their work. Moving towards CD-45, one grabbed the droid's arm, while the other extracted its own thumb. Fortunately, as lower models, they had no emotion associated with amputating their own parts. Then, that one promptly removed CD-45's thumb. *Ouch!* That would have really hurt if CD-45 consisted of flesh and blood. It remained rude all the same; the CD should have, at least, asked first. Then the CD welded its own thumb to CD-45's hand. When completed, both CDs immediately returned to their assigned work orders. For a CD about to be decommissioned, this did not compute. It experienced thorough confusion, a state of emotion it had felt twice now in less than five minutes.

The main computer surged to life with increased illumination from its three panels. "CD-45 model number 615, your designation of construction droid is suspended. Your new assignment in reconnaissance includes the following: you will take a pod to Earth, to re-establish communications with the population."

CD-45 looked around for another candidate, then pointed to itself quizzically.

"Your unique blend of personality algorithms makes you the logical candidate. The Earth shield will fail within four orbits of the sun. The Earth fleet exists to protect the planet and humanity. But we require a trained crew, or the probability of a successful defence falls significantly. We can no longer wait for humans to return to us. You must warn them of the danger." The main computer sounded urgent.

Only one problem: no communication with Earth meant that no AI, or MD, or CD knew what existed down there. The alien ships above the shield blocked sensors and communications.

Furthermore, after nineteen hundred years, the CD corps of engineers had a severe shortage of materials to utilize in shipbuilding. The increasingly frequent breaks in the shield also created concern. If they continued, it would result in the Earth fleet's complete destruction. No ships meant an end to every CD unit left in existence. And Earth fell into the category of a dangerous place, too.

One thing remained certain: the Earth appeared very dark. In CD-45's first years of operation, the Earth had sparkled, lit up by all the city lights. After the attack, few collections of lights emanated from the surface, and it had remained as such to the present day. CD-45 hoped that didn't mean no one lived down there.

The droid would love to go to Earth, and if a CD for the job existed, he was it. *He;* yes, he would have to call himself "he." It was much more human. To be fair, CD-45 should also consider "she" or "them" as a designation, though his skeletal crewmates, propped up in the arboretum tents, made for a strong deciding factor. Both male, they had been the last living humans he'd ever interacted with.

Hopefully, people lived down there, or his mission would fail. From the lower level of the bridge rose a two-person containment pod. It was designed for humans to escape in the event of catastrophic failure of the ship; although, in this case, CD-45 would utilize it for an adventure on Earth. On the other robotic hand, he could plummet to a fiery death. Yet, after nineteen centuries of work, just the opportunity for a break, even a working vacation, sounded like a worthy risk.

CD-45 crawled into the pod and saluted the main computer while it shouted out further instructions.

"You must warn them as well as find help. If you encounter hostilities, defend your existence. This pod will be set for automatic recall in one Earth month. Make sure you are in it at that time. Is that understood, CD-45?" the main computer barked like a father giving his son a curfew.

CD-45 nodded, not that the main computer would understand him anyway. He strapped himself in, hoping it would get the hint. The main computer seemed to recognise the human gesture as acknowledgement, starting to drone on about some sort of mission parameters. Couldn't it just launch the pod already? He knew the parameters: go to Earth, warn them, get help, and report back. How hard could it be?

CD-45 ignored the main computer, choosing instead to stare at the energy blasts impacting the Earth shield. They contained a strange beauty, and if not for their lethal nature, he could classify them as a type of firework. The energy blasts looked distorted. No, not the energy blasts, *the shield!*

CD-45 snapped back to attention as the pod sealed shut. He waved his robotic arms around trying to get the attention of the main computer, but it was apparently preoccupied with other things. The shield stopped shimmering, and the stars came into crystal-clear focus. The invisible shield distorted the light from stars almost imperceptibly, so the moment of awe produced by the crispness of those stars changed quickly to fear. He watched helplessly as a deadly energy beam sailed right through the hole in the shield, heading straight for this ship and CD-45. In a split second, *boom!* The bridge exploded in all directions. This catapulted the pod right out of the ship.

Even while the pod spun wildly, CD-45 observed many Earth craft in orbit, but he couldn't locate his home ship. It could have been destroyed. Anguish and sadness filled him. He punched the metal interior. He disliked the main computer, but now that it might no longer exist, CD-45 missed it terribly. He should have tried harder to get its attention. Unfortunately, the descent only allowed him a few nanoseconds to indulge in guilt.

The strap holding CD-45 snapped, tossing him around the compartment, much to his dismay. He initiated several mini tractor beams out of his metal frame, bringing relief: he remained secure for now. As the pod spun, the Earth grew larger through the clear canopy, while the pod grew hotter. An interesting correlation, but his circuits would soon melt. To make matters worse, the darkness of night hampered his vision. He could land in the middle of an ocean. If only he had paid attention to the main computer, surely it would have included touchdown coordinates. It would give CD-45 an idea of where he was about land, or crash, or burn up.

The clouds cleared. CD-45 strained his ocular units for input. Trees! Yes, those were trees, not water, which qualified as very good. He sped towards them — not so good.

The pod sliced through trees, but some pushed back, and the pod spun erratically. This created too much information for the droid's ocular units to process, so he closed the blast shutters. They resembled eyelids; not the most efficient blinds, but they counted as another human quality.

The force of the spin continued for several seconds. Then a loud crash. The pod hit the ground, rebounding into the air. Another loud crash — the pod hit the ground again. *Bouncing to one's own end,* CD-45 thought. *How humorous.*

More sounds of impact filled the air, followed by skidding, and then the staccato clatter of the pod's glass canopy cracking. A final impact ... the pod stayed immobile ... and CD-45 still processed information. Relief filled his circuits, along with more guilt for feeling relieved. Emotions were complex, but he needed to focus on his mission.

CD-45 opened the blast shutters, observing a wide tree trunk before him in the darkness. A scratching sound made him whip around and blindly fire his mini laser. A squirrel — a member of a rodent family — jumped and squealed, rushing up the tree that must have been its home. If trees with squirrels remained in existence, the presence of living people rose in probability, as did the likelihood of a successful mission.

CD-45 terminated the tractor beams, fired his booster rockets, and then landed in a grassy field. He must have crashed right through a forest, based on the destruction left by the pod. He shone two lights and then spun — nothing but grass and trees all around. He looked back at the wrecked pod. Making repairs or reporting back to the fleet became a low probability.

CD-45 set out on the grassy plain and traveled for quite some time in the darkness. He noted the warm air and surmised that it must be late spring or early summer. Judging by the alignment of the stars, he had landed somewhere on the North American continent.

His light shone on a strange creature ahead. Its behind faced him, so he wheeled around to the front. He classified it as a bovine, more commonly known as a cow — at least that's what his memory banks had on record. Who knew what they called them now? The cow mooed, blinking in the bright light from CD-45. He decreased to minimum illumination, and this prompted the cow to step forward and lick his mechanical face. Probably ill-advised, so CD-45 backed up, turning to continue in his original direction, south by southwest.

He looked up at the clear, starry sky. Those energy blasts looked like sparkles of light, as if they were stars, twinkling in the night.

***

CD-45 traveled for hours with no sign of sunlight. Then a flicker of light to the east caught his attention.

He moved closer, identifying a series of domiciles made up of raw materials: rocks, wood, grasses, and mud. The flickers of light resulted from combustion. Humans, dressed in simple clothes, walked far in the distance. He found people, but they carried sticks with fire: torches. He switched his sensors to maximum range, and a small-scale radar dish popped out of his head. No technology existed here that he recognized. The world of humans he had in his memory core hadn't managed to endure.

These creatures couldn't help him fix the pod and return to the fleet, so he traveled a safe distance around the settlement. He'd discovered humans here, but they had lost the ability to make technology like a CD-45. To succeed in finding humans that could understand what had occurred in orbit, he would need a space-capable vessel to reach them. CD-45's light shone steadily on the dark field as he made his way south by southwest.

CHAPTER THREE

Trick Mark spat out a mouthful of dirt. He propped himself up on his elbows, his brown and black leather armour clinging to his sweating body. The forest stood behind him, trees like rows of soldiers waiting for the order to attack. Trick Mark steadied his breath, calming his heart, as all fell quiet. From the safety of the underbrush, he looked back to the open field. Sweet smells of foliage mixed with the metallic scent of death, carried on a warm breeze. The grey sky hung like a silent warning of a battle not yet done. His skin tingled with anticipation as he silently pushed himself up, crouching to ready his crossbow.

Quiet, no movement, until a rustling from the bushes made his muscles tense. He swung around, pointed his crossbow, and found the soft flesh of a neck. His arrow pulled taut, meeting a worried gaze.

"Are you going to kill me, Trick Mark?" Guinevere—or Vere, as she demanded everyone call her—swallowed hard.

Her deep-amber eyes peered at him from behind chestnut locks, while her smooth cheeks flushed. Her brown leather uniform was marred with dirt and blood that dared not touch her beautiful face. Her disheveled hair had come out of its cord high on her head in the course of battle. Vere counted as the only woman to make it through training. She was tough—strong, but inexperienced, which made her lack confidence out here in a relatively unknown land.

"I almost shot you in the neck," he berated her through clenched teeth.

"Do you still plan on firing that, Captain?" She raised her eyebrow.

Trick Mark relaxed the arrow, the bowstring creaking softly as it released.

Vere sighed in relief, though fear sat behind her dark eyes. Trick Mark quickly pulled her down. She readjusted her position amongst the runty bushes, choked from growing too big by the broad boughs of the ancient forest. He searched the open field for signs of his men. The tall grasses bent in the breeze, revealing not one sign of his soldiers. The wizard Zairoc was nowhere in sight. Perhaps he'd withdrawn after his ruthless attack. Trick Mark should have been more careful and patrolled a different sector closer to Bastion. Instead, he led his men to their deaths, out here in the Enchanted Lands.

"You see anyone?" Vere breathed.

She moved close, her body pressing against his, making him shift uncomfortably. Vere performed beautifully in close-quarters combat, especially with a knife.

But Trick Mark held the title of "long shot," even though when growing up, he had been blind. He thought back to the day in which his whole life had changed.

So long ago, while searching for the path home, Trick Mark had become disoriented. When he realized he was lost, his heart beat faster. He should have followed right behind his father, but he had grown too confident and let himself get distracted. He found his way to a tree and sat underneath it.

Then footsteps approached him. "Would you like to see?" a man's voice promised.

Trick Mark scoffed at him. "Only a wizard has such power."

"Take this."

Trick Mark reached out, finding the man's hand. Then, like a fading dream, the man withdrew his palm without even a word. Trick Mark sat there until he felt the tree on his back. He leaned against it. Strangely he also felt every branch, the animals in it, even the insects around and inside the tree. He couldn't see them but knew their exact position in space, an intuition he could sense: the air that separated him from other objects pressed on his skin, and faint, ghostly images appeared in his mind's eye. He stood, opening his mind to the forest. Each tree, bird, sound, the flow of air around the valley — he could feel all of it. It overwhelmed him at first. Like a rush of life, it expanded into an extension of his body while he struggled to take it all in.

He slumped back against the tree, grabbing his head, hoping the sensation would stop. Then like magic, it all evaporated. He slowed his breathing to calm himself. He held his body so tight, he willed himself to relax.

Then he opened his eyes and found he *could* see: he could see everything! He had normal eyesight! That made two miracles in the space of a few minutes. He wasn't very religious, yet this counted as a gift from the God of All. He took in the images and colours, along with the familiar sounds and smells. He was home.

Using his other senses together with his new ones, he had inadvertently found his home. How strange to see it for the first time. He had so much to tell his father, so many good things had happened in one day.

Trick Mark spent several months honing his two new abilities. The same: every day he could see normally, while at night, the "second" sight would replace the first. He eventually learned to control his night vision and found it vaguely present when he closed his eyes in daylight. Using both made him such a great shot with a bow, though he never spoke a word of his ability to anyone except his father. His full name, Patrick Marcus, was shortened to Trick Mark because of his uncanny aim. His reputation eventually earned him the position of captain of the guard, working with Sir Francis himself.

Vere's voice brought him back to the present. "He's gone! He's got to be. There's nothing out there. Right? There's nothing out there." Vere didn't sound certain.

Trick Mark shushed her and surveyed the field.

The bodies of his men slowly rose out of the grasses as if they lay on the wind. All dead, not one struggled in the wizard's magical grip. Only Zairoc would do something so horrific, slaughtering everyone just to use them like grotesque puppets. In the middle of the gruesome image, a black figure strode towards them holding a glowing red wand.

"Oh, shit," he whispered.

That was always the way when you came face to face with a wizard, especially a murderous and pathological one like Zairoc. His reputation as the most hated and feared of any man remained unchallenged. More than that, Zairoc was great and powerful. That's what he called himself: Zairoc, the Great and Powerful.

Vere tensed. "Do we run?"

"Not yet. I don't think he's seen us." He kept his breath steady.

The figure stopped. "Trick Mark! I know you're there, somewhere in those woods." The voice of Zairoc carried on the wind, making Trick Mark's stomach feel as if it had dropped through the ground.

"Oh, no. Please, no." Vere's voice trembled.

"You come out now! Face me like a man, and your girl goes free." Clearly lying, Zairoc's icy stare held the intent of more murder.

Trick Mark couldn't risk it. If he stepped out, Zairoc would kill him.

"No?" Zairoc smiled in delight as he raised his wand. "Have it your way. I'll just have to get some help."

The wizard stepped closer, revealing his sadistic smile. Standing at least as tall as Trick Mark, Zairoc looked strong but didn't have the muscle to face off in unarmed combat. Not that he needed it, with his powerful wand.

Zairoc closed his eyes, making the wand glow brighter. All around, trees uprooted themselves, moving towards Trick Mark and Vere. Their deep roots became lumbering feet, while their long boughs twisted into claw-like hands, reaching for them. Both Trick Mark and Vere stared, wide-eyed, frozen in place as if the trees couldn't find them.

"Run!" he yelled at Vere.

They both took off like scared animals, deeper into the woods. Everything came alive all around them. Zairoc's laughter echoed in the distance. Trees reached out for them. They bolted.

"Just keep running," he told her.

"Thanks for the advice. I was going to turn around and start hugging them." She panted hard, sprinting faster.

Trick Mark's body surged with the heat of battle. Yet he ran away like a scared boy soldier. A pang of guilt filled him. Letting his feelings run wild not only dishonoured his men, but it would also likely get him and Vere killed.

The bare limb of a tree swung, knocking him down. He slid to stop, his back scraping the dirt. He tried to breathe but couldn't suck in air.

Vere pulled him up. He inhaled deeply. From all around, the hands of the forest reached for them, to end their struggle in a gruesome embrace.

They ran hard, but trees closed off their escape. Trick Mark dragged Vere to the right. A branch grazed her cheek. She winced with pain, though managed to stay with him. Trick Mark found a narrow opening. He slid through, with Vere close behind.

Scared, they raced deeper into the forest. Trees towered all around, clawing or lunging at them. Trick Mark steeled his jaw. He couldn't surrender to the terror. Nevertheless, he couldn't see any escape. Then, Vere snapped backward.

Trick Mark slid to a halt. "Vere!"

He turned towards her. To his horror, vines and young tree branches entwined her legs, dragging her back towards Zairoc. Trick Mark braced himself, then pulled out his crossbow. One shot—a branch snapped away from her legs. Two, three, four, five shots—all with the same result, but there were too many tendrils. He didn't have enough arrows.

Trick Mark screamed with rage. He couldn't lose Vere too. He ran full tilt, then dived for her hands, catching them in his grip. The trees dragged him along with her.

"Don't let go!" she screamed in desperation.

Like an expert acrobat, he flipped himself around and then dug in his heels. He closed his eyes for an instant and could feel the forest being used like puppets. It made him sick. His heels slowed their exit from the thicket. Yet they still moved back towards the field where Zairoc waited.

Vere wrestled one hand free, smiling triumphantly at Trick Mark. He looked at her like she'd gone crazy. What could she be thinking? She grabbed a knife from her pants and started slicing away at the vines. Trick Mark pulled a knife from his tunic, cutting several more branches away. The edge of the forest approached fast.

"I can see you've decided to come back," Zairoc said, toying with them. "I hoped you'd change your minds."

They stopped at his feet, and the branches recoiled. The uprooted trees fell, along with the wails of a forest dying. Each one thrust like a knife stabbing into Trick Mark's head. His hands reflexively covered his eyes. He heard Vere stifle a scream. When the pain finally subsided, Trick Mark let his eyes slowly open to the nightmare painted before him.

Zairoc stood in perfect black garb, straddling Vere, who shook with terror. His cold blue eyes stared at them like a snake finding mice.

"Shame, really. Those trees were over a hundred years old. But a necessary sacrifice, wouldn't you say?" Zairoc grinned down at Trick Mark.

He gently moved the red glowing wand, pointing it at Vere then back to Trick Mark.

"Who dies first?" he whispered.

Trick Mark glared at the evil wizard, tensing his body for a fight.

Vere grabbed his hand, squeezing hard. From the strength of her grip, she expected death to come swiftly.

"Sorry, my dear, you'll have to die first, though not before I make him watch you cry with agony for a very long time." Zairoc's smile looked more like a grimace.

He held the wand over Vere, and it glowed brighter. She steeled her jaw through shallow breaths, tensing under an eerie, red glow that resembled fire, the runaway kind that took all you had and everyone you knew.

"Leave her alone!" Trick Mark screamed at Zairoc.

"No, Trick," Vere pleaded.

Zairoc crouched down and studied Trick Mark.

"You have a strange power within you. That makes you a threat. I can't have that in someone close to Sir Francis. No, you will die with a lot of pain, and then I can move on to take what's mine." Zairoc smiled broadly.

Zairoc moved the wand close to Vere, bathing her face in a bright-red glow. Trick Mark launched himself at Zairoc. He didn't have a chance against the wizard, yet he wouldn't give in. They struggled for a split second. Surprise and rage played over Zairoc's face, giving Trick Mark the briefest moment of satisfaction. Then the ground underneath them gave away, and all three fell into darkness.

CHAPTER FOUR

O ndreeal writhed as she held her leg.
She braced herself against the brick wall, gritting her teeth, and slowly inched up until she stood shakily. Her rapid breathing sounded like the only disquiet in the world. Then she looked up at the crowd, who stared down at her in muted shock. Her whole body shook like a blade of grass in a wind storm.

Out of the corner of her eye, two henchmen appeared at one of the gates with the merchant. He yelled at the guard to let them collect his slave. The guard unlatched the gate, and Ondreeal launched herself at the barbarian, lurching as she winced with pain. The henchmen rushed her with dogged determination in their eyes. She picked up a spiked morning star and swung the metal ball around on its chain. She clutched the wooden handle as the weapon almost pulled her down, but her rapid heartbeat kept her blood flowing and her feet moving.

"I challenge the champion to fight me—to the death!" Her scream echoed for a moment on the wind.

The crowd laughed and jeered at her. The henchmen froze in place, their looks of conviction melting into uncertainty. Ondreeal took her chance to step forward, slowly raising the morning star that shook in her white-knuckled hands. The barbarian matched her manoeuvre with a roar, making the crowd erupt into a loud cheer. He grinned, flexing his huge, tattoo-covered arms at her. His body glistened with sweat, interrupted by patches of dirt and blood from his first bout. The henchmen grabbed her until the guards yanked them free. A challenge had been made, and not even the merchant could stop it now.

Ondreeal's legs trembled. She struggled to steady them. If she followed religion, she would think her soul lived on. It's what most believed, that the God of All would take her into his arms. If untrue, then her life would end in the few moments ahead.

She scanned the crowd, searching for Otto. Where could he be? She looked at the special box. The inhabitants gazed down at her with looks of mild interest. The box held four people, two older men with young women. She would count as another death for their amusement. The bald man in white leaned forward. He flashed bright teeth in her direction; his eyes held a blood lust. Her head whipped back to the barbarian as he laughed, closing in like a predatory animal.

He glared down, his shadow blocking out the sun. "I will tear you apart, girl."

The crowd chanted, "Kill! Kill! Kill!" They hadn't even started fighting, yet the crowd already viewed her like some animal for slaughter.

Of course, she'd jumped into the pit of the arena to meet her end. She wanted to avoid a life of indentured servitude by being bludgeoned to death by the killer before her. Why didn't she simply put down the morning star? She wanted death, didn't she? She took a deep breath and raised her head so that she could meet the monster's condescending stare. Something deep within her mind wouldn't let her lie down and die. The barbarian would have to earn the right to kill her.

"Eat shit, you brainless idiot!" She spat at him.

That wiped the stupid smile off his face. He took a step back, raising his club. He swiped at Ondreeal.

She scrambled backwards. His club sliced the air. Then she swung the morning star at his ankles.

A spike on the metal ball neatly inserted itself into his calf.

He screamed and smashed his huge club to the ground.

Ondreeal barely rolled out of the way as sand sprayed everywhere. Her eyes went wide, like those of a rabbit scurrying from a fox. He swung, forcing her to whirl back. The club landed, sending vibrations through the sand.

He barked out a growl of frustration and then tried to step on her like a bug. She scurried to her feet, limping backwards.

Her breathing rose in quick gasps. Her palms sweated. Eyes trained on the barbarian, she stumbled over the other club and fell. She pulled herself up, but winced when she put weight on her ankle.

The barbarian plucked out the morning star from his calf.

She tugged on the club, her muscles flexed. It moved an inch in the sand. The barbarian laughed at her while each footstep thundered out his slow approach.

"Now you die, girl." He sprinted at her.

She whimpered, trying to limp away. He grabbed for her and then lifted her up like a tiny child. He held her up to face the crowd members, who booed and spat. Killing her wasn't enough. He had to humiliate her before she died.

Ondreeal's heart leapt into her throat. This was it. She waited an eternity for him to throw her down and crash the club against her skull.

It never came.

The crowd quieted as the barbarian's grip loosened. Ondreeal craned her neck, spotting his heavy eyelids that threatened to pull him into slumber. The morning star must have some sort of poison on it. She glanced down at the weapon lying in the sand. The spikes were covered in a black glaze. The poison likely wouldn't kill him, although it might give Ondreeal a chance to do it. She struggled in his grasp.

"Let go of me, you huge moron."

Shouting that at him might not have been the best idea. Yet an angry, woozy barbarian sounded better than a calm, woozy one. He might make mistakes that she could use to her advantage. He turned Ondreeal to face him, then bellowed at her with rancid breath. She almost vomited right there while shaking like a leaf. He would recover from the poison soon enough—she'd only given him a minuscule wound. What would she do then?

Her mind raced. She couldn't slow down her heart or stop shaking or gagging long enough to form a coherent thought.

A flash of light hit her eye. She looked down at the little silver knife in her boot.

It was now or never.

She grabbed the blade, plunging it into his eye repeatedly until he tossed her back toward the ground.

Ondreeal landed with a hard thud on the hot sand, clutching the bloody knife. The sun blinded her as a huge foot came at her. She rolled out of the way, trying to scramble to her feet. The barbarian gave her a good, swift kick in the ass, and she got a mouthful of sand. She coughed out dirt, her chest heaving with turmoil.

The crowd laughed. They definitely still rooted for the barbarian.

She heard a faint noise that stood out from the rest of the crowd — Otto's voice. She looked around as the barbarian kicked her hard in the gut. He tried to stomp on her, but she stabbed him in the bottom of the foot. The crowd laughed and cheered while the barbarian stumbled backwards. Ondreeal got to her feet, almost falling again. She struggled to take in air. She frantically looked around for the source of Otto's voice.

"Cut his throat — from the right, where he's blind." She could barely hear his shout amid the screams and cheers of the crowd.

Though her head spun, Ondreeal raced to the barbarian. Somehow, she stayed on her feet. His back facing her, he picked up the morning star. Her muscles tensed as she readied herself. She had only a moment to decide.

Ondreeal leaped on his sweaty back and then slid right off, landing in the dirt. The barbarian blocked the sun. He turned to her, the right half of his face covered with blood. How could he withstand such pain?

Blood squeezed from his left foot. He put weight on it and took a step towards her. From the way he held the morning star, he planned to gut her like one of the pigs she'd fed just this morning. Her heels kicked the sand. She pushed herself backwards along the ground. She madly searched for the knife, spotting it behind her opponent. She must have dropped it when she slid off his back.

He closed the distance between them and gave her a bloody grin with gritted teeth. The crowd chanted, "Kill the girl! Kill the girl!" Why didn't he do it? Just get it over with.

He laughed at Ondreeal, who lay there, completely defenceless, while tears streamed down her face.

Tremors rattled her body, yet she still would have made the same choice to jump into the pit all over again. She braced herself, lying motionless as the barbarian planted a foot on either side of her. He looked up at the crowd. They cheered for him, and he soaked in their adoration. The moment stretched forever as he smiled widely for the masses.

He took his eyes off of her long enough to give her a chance. She jumped forward and rushed right through the middle of his legs. She stumbled. She ran, picking up the bloody knife. The whole crowd laughed at her pathetic struggle for survival.

Ondreeal sprinted to the gate, shaking the iron bars. The guards smiled, grabbing at her through the rungs. They would just deliver her right back into the hands of the gnarly-toothed merchant. Death was the better choice, yet with it so close, she couldn't help but fight it. She needed to find another way, a way to live.

One guard laughed. "Time to die, pretty girl."

Another guard snatched her arm, and she slit his hand.

"Ah, you bitch!" He spat in her face.

She flinched and stumbled backwards. Her whole body vibrated as if thunder rumbled beneath her skin. The fear of the moment melted away, then a sort of giddiness filled her. Perhaps the rush of emotion overwhelmed her or she'd found lost bravery. This morning, she had faced a life filled with thirty more years of monotonous farm work. Ondreeal had dreamed of adventure — and now she faced it, with all its many dangers. She turned to the barbarian and laughed.

His face hardened with hate. He clenched his jaw, growling at her.

"I'll cut that smile off your face." He took a step towards her.

Her laugh grew. "I'm going to kill you, just like the big, stupid animal that you are."

The monster wavered, surely because a look of madness in her eyes made him pause. She could see him thinking: could she really do it? Ondreeal took a deep breath. Perhaps she'd gone mad.

She heard her mother's voice, "Clear your mind, young one. Deep breaths." With each exhale, her heartbeat slowed. She focused only on the barbarian and what she wanted. Ondreeal whispered two words continuously, "Kill him..."

The barbarian lumbered at her. The crowd erupted in a cheer. The oaf screamed as he swung his morning star at her. She dived out of the way. Her muscles strained in agony from the beating already taken. She murmured, "Kill him...," and for a moment she believed the words, certain of them, like knowing that the sun rises in the east every day. That conviction grew, even though one swipe from him would end her life.

If she was to die here now, it would be on her feet, facing her enemy. She stopped, turning to the barbarian who bore down on her. She took a deep breath, screamed, and rushed towards him with the knife raised, ready to stab into his flesh. A loud clap of thunder made the sand jump. The sky darkened. They both stopped in their tracks.

A hush fell over the crowd as they beheld a bright light that traveled across the black sky from the east. With each second it grew brighter, closer — a pure-white light. Then an ear-splitting sound filled the arena. Everyone covered their ears, even the barbarian. Ondreeal watched them with her eyes wide and mouth open. It didn't hurt her ears. It should have caused extreme pain, yet it didn't. She watched as the light flashed down on the barbarian. In an instant, he vanished.

No one made a sound. Ondreeal stared at the spot where the monster had once stood. Nothing, nothing prevailed, save the sand and his footprints, the left one bloody.

She stood there like a statue. She couldn't feel her limbs or her body. Even her lips tingled with numbness. Her knees bent, but she clenched her fists, fighting to stay upright. Where did the barbarian go? A whimper escaped her lips. Then she steeled her jaw. She sucked in air through her nose and glanced to the heavens. The sky immediately cleared, and sunlight bathed her face in protective warmth. She laboured to take in deep breaths as she gazed down at the barbarian's footprints. In those few breaths, an eternity seemed to pass.

Ondreeal surveyed the arena as the crowd stared at her in muted shock. In the next instant, it erupted in cries of awe and fear. Swiftly, guards marched out onto the sand, until a battalion surrounded her. As luck would have it, something must have saved her. What other explanation remained? She lived while the barbarian met death, just like she promised. Yet her mouth said things her hands couldn't do. Surely, the God of All had aided her. If so, why would he save Ondreeal? Nothing special about her, that's what Otto always said.

She needed the pure-white light to save her from these men. She faced the guards, but they had panic in their eyes.

What would the guards do now? They might simply kill her or let the merchant take her. Then she remembered that the barbarian had disappeared while she remained. That meant she'd won. She had no answers save one:

keep fighting. If she wanted to live, she needed to show strength, no matter how much she wanted to fall down and cry.

She turned to the closest guard, directing at him as much anger as she could muster. It wasn't substantial, and she didn't believe she convinced them. To her amazement, they all kneeled down around her, bowing their heads to the sand. Her heart jumped with triumph.

"Please do not harm us." The head guard glanced up. "Can you forgive us, great wizard?"

Great wizard? They thought she did it by her own power ... something she had never done before and couldn't do again. She wanted to run screaming from the arena. She desperately wanted to go home. But first and foremost, she needed to hold their belief. Their fear continued as her only tie to life. If she kept them cowering, she could get out of this alive.

She swallowed hard. "Take me into Bastion."

She must go to the home of the powerful wizard, Sir Francis. He ruled the northern cities with wise benevolence while he protected them from the merciless tyranny of Zairoc. There would be no other place for a wizard to go.

She bit her lip and remembered two rumours. One, to impersonate a wizard carried a long prison sentence. Two, in doing so, one invited death itself. She had no other choice.

The head guard nodded vigorously, as if the obvious answer prevailed. "Yes, my lady." He stood, rushing a few paces past her.

He peered back, expecting her to follow along. She stood frozen in shock. Ondreeal didn't know if she could walk.

But she took a step, then another, as she trailed behind him. The rest of the guards fell into line behind her.

She kept seeing the barbarian vanish. The look of horror and surprise on his face etched into her mind.

"Wait." She stopped, and the quaking guards immediately complied. "Otto!" she yelled at the crowd.

He slowly rose with a stony look on his face.

She stood tall. "That one comes with us."

She hated Otto so much for what he'd done. Yet she urgently needed the only parent she'd ever known to stay with her, to give her strength at a time when she had none. The animals could survive for months on grasses around the farm this time of year. They would get through without Otto. She wouldn't.

A few guards broke off to collect him, and they marched her out of the arena. The crowd erupted into excited chatter. Surely, they thought: who was this girl, a bona fide wizard? Would she look for revenge on us? They could not know that she was Ondreeal, a girl who didn't like the idea of revenge. She just wanted to live free. The guards returned, surrounding a seething Otto.

She held her head high. "Take us to a carriage."

The guards rushed to comply, fright painted on their faces. She smiled because she liked control, even if it involved deception. Then, tears welled up and her hands trembled as the truth of her emotional state bled through.

Otto hurried beside Ondreeal, and they rushed out of the grand stadium towards a horse-drawn carriage. The head guard whispered to the coachman, who looked at Ondreeal with fear and surprise. The coachman wore the colours of Bastion on his chest.

"So, you're stealing someone's carriage. Do you even know what you're doing?" Otto spat at her through clenched teeth.

She desperately needed a speedy departure. Her legs shook with nervousness. If she fell to pieces, they would doubt the validity of her claim. The head guard opened the carriage door, allowing Ondreeal to scurry inside, with Otto dragged along behind her.

The buggy surged forward. She breathed out and tightly clasped her quavering hands. She wanted to drop to her knees, pray to the God of All for help or guidance. The enclosed cabin gave her some comfort, yet she couldn't escape the turmoil within. Otto simply glared at her.

Sunlight flashed through the trees as the carriage surged towards Bastion. Ondreeal pulled the purple curtain closed and clutched it, the way one would cling to life. It felt soft in her hand, familiar — she had touched similar curtains as a young child. Except those were the colour of grass, curtains that hung in her bedroom, no, in a lounge of sorts, like one she had served in for a brief time. She delved into the memory, for it calmed her body.

A bad crop had prompted Otto to farm out Ondreeal for money. She worked for a family five miles away from Otto's farm. She helped an old maid clean the family's massive home each day. Nearing the end of her life, the old lady's hands would shake when she dusted, but she remained far too poor to leave her job. Consequently, Ondreeal took on most of her duties until the woman died. When the farm showed signs of recovery, Otto demanded she get caught up on work.

He growled at her, "I need a little extra currency, and you let this farm go to shit."

No thanks for making money to pay the farm's taxes, he just muttered and complained. Perhaps she should have taken that time to run far away from the farm. Although, at the age of fourteen, what would she do? Where would she go? Her life experience consisted of Otto and the farm. As horrible as it was, she'd been more scared of leaving.

"You can't keep it," Otto grumbled at her. "The curtain. You can't take it with you."

Ondreeal looked down at her hand. She still clung to the curtain, like a baby clings to a blanket. She quickly let it go, looking everywhere but at Otto.

"Am I going to get the silent treatment now? Because that's what I would prefer. I had no choice, Al. At least you wouldn't starve with that merchant. You'd have a roof over your head." His gaze bore into her, but she stared down at her lap.

He didn't even mention what had taken place in the arena, as if it never happened. She couldn't forget it: some magical force saved her. Something controlled that pure, white light—certainly not her. She fell into an abyss filled with one lie: I am a wizard. If a true wizard had killed the barbarian, she remained ignorant of it. It could have been the bald man in white, but this made for a wild guess; she had no proof.

She opened the curtain again and watched the trees whiz by, birch, oak, and elm. As a young child, she had never travelled in a carriage. It proved much faster than walking, they would arrive in the city by nightfall, normally a six-day walk.

"I don't regret what I did. I'd do it again." Otto gazed downward.

Her eyes went wide, and she wanted to punch him. She shifted on the bench and winced with pain, not in any condition to fight her father. Her eyelids grew heavy. As the fear leaked out, fatigue replaced it and enveloped her. Her head wouldn't stop spinning. What had she done? What would she do now? She couldn't even think.

Ondreeal lay down on the bench and closed her eyes.

"That's it. Get some sleep before your dirt nap. Bastion is a dangerous place, for both of us. We need a plan."

His words faded as the world ebbed away and she slipped into unconsciousness.

CHAPTER FIVE

Ondreeal snapped awake and sat up fast. She must
have slept for hours. Orange light filtered in through
thin gaps in the curtains, along with cool air carrying the
smell of burning coal. Horseshoes softly clocked on the
ground as the carriage lightly bobbed back and forth.

Her heart beat slow and steady until Otto gave her
a sour glare, making it beat faster. She turned away,
refusing to look at him, but her head already pounded
from just a glimpse of his face. She hated that he had such
power over her emotions. Perhaps it hadn't been a good
idea to bring him along.

"I did so much to protect you," he barked at her.

"You would have been paid for selling me. You call
that protection?"

His stony face still managed to look sour, but he didn't
meet her gaze. "There's more than I dare to tell you. It's
dangerous! I sold you to keep you safe," he growled,
breathing heavily out of his nose.

It rarely ever happened that Otto showed real emotion.
What did he mean? There was something he wouldn't tell
her. It didn't matter; none of it would justify selling her.

"I'm not property. I worked with you. I was supposed
to be your — " She stopped herself as her throat tightened.

Tears welled up, and she fought to hold them in, staring
at the smooth, polished wood of the carriage roof.

"I had to be tough on you. So, you could survive, like you did out there today. I've never been prouder of you, Ondreeal." His cold words carried a tone of warmth.

She blinked with shock. He never used her full name or said he felt proud. He really meant it. Not that it made up for what he did… She would never forgive him for that.

"You shouldn't forgive me." His shoulders tensed despite his quiet words.

He spoke like a reader of minds. It wouldn't count as the most bizarre thing that had happened today.

"I just have to know: did you do that out there? In the arena, did you do that?" He held his breath.

"Maybe. I don't know for sure. I've only ever read stories or heard rumours. I've never seen magic before." She leaned forward, hoping he would have words of wisdom.

"I have. It'll get you killed. It'll get me killed! What are you doing? Getting in this carriage, dragging me along with you… Do you even know?"

Now he sounded like a father—something that happened when he let down his guard, ever so slightly. Their eyes locked for the first time, and worry bled through his stoic stare. Ondreeal softened.

"What I do know is that I could have left you back there, penniless. But I didn't. I brought you along because, despite the way you've treated me all my life and the fact that you sold me into slavery, you're still the only family I have. How pathetic is that?" Ondreeal snickered, shaking her head while tears welled up.

Otto looked guilty. "If you're going to whine about it, I'd just as soon not talk at all. I just hope you know what you're doing. Because if you can't control magic, it'll lead to bad things happening, for us both."

Ondreeal shook her head, disappointed. He didn't even feel concerned for her.

"You're just worried about your own sorry ass. Guess you should have thought about that before you sold me. Now I'll drag you down too. Isn't that what you're really worried about?"

He stared at his lap, considering her words as he slowly pulled his fingers into fists, resting them on his knees.

He leaned closer to her. "I'm worried about both our sorry asses. You got us into this, you get us out."

He blamed her. She breathed out frustration, leaning back as much as she could. If only she could get more answers about the origin of magic and how to use it. To ask Otto for any more information would prove useless. His answers would only cause anger.

Otto looked out the window, taking in the view with disgust.

"We're here. Hope you got a plan, Al. We're going to need one."

"Whoa," yelled the coachman up front.

Out the window, three-, four-, and five-storey buildings rose from a road paved with shiny black bricks. Ondreeal gazed upon the city. Not the town with one paved street, but the far-off city she had never seen with her own eyes, until now.

Bastion reigned as the biggest city in the north, one of six. The other centres — Alexandria, Centaurus, Angellus, Hamlet, and Athena — all prospered under the protection of Sir Francis. One would marvel upon seeing any of them, but Ondreeal found herself in the capital. To the south, the abandoned cities of Aleenda lay quiet. Farther south, the cities of the dark wizard Zairoc threatened the peace of the north. Everyone described Zairoc as a cruel monster who terrified the bravest of men. All she knew of life sprung from rumours spun by villagers or Otto. She could learn about the whole world here in the capital.

Her palms grew sweaty. She didn't have a plan. She couldn't control magic. What actually had happened in the arena? Otto was right: this could end badly.

The carriage door opened and the head guard stood there, fear in his eyes, as the late-day sun lit up half his face in an orange glow. Clearly, he expected Ondreeal to smite him or shoot fire from her fingers. Yet she just wrung her hands while she looked back with an equal amount of trepidation. What should she do now? What should she tell him to do?

"We need to go on foot from here." The head guard sounded apologetic.

"To the castle?" She hopped out of the carriage, landing hard on her wounded ankle and gritting her teeth.

The coachman nodded. She could get the answers she wanted here. Otto lumbered after her. The head guard, along with five others, surrounded them as they walked. Ondreeal couldn't help but look all around, gawking at everything and everyone, just like everyone ogled them. Did they look different from those in Bastion? Perhaps the guards that surrounded them drew their gaze. Otto shifted uncomfortably under the focus of attention. He even blushed.

Lines of manicured trees along the polished stone streets stood under every shiny building. The breathtaking views hung in sharp contrast to the run-down farm where her life had unfolded up until now.

The noise, however, would take some getting used to: the squeak of carriage wheels, horseshoes on the brick road, people talking while they walked by.

They came to a crossroads. In both directions lay busy stores presided over by street merchants, everyone rushing to make final deals or sales at day's end. Names of the establishments etched into glass appeared to float in the storefronts they passed. Ondreeal read several of them: PETE'S SHOE SHOP, DRESSES AND WOMEN'S CLOTHING, MEN'S SUITS, FINE FURNITURE. Ondreeal couldn't help but smile, despite herself. It appeared as a wonderland. Her heart beat faster, and she couldn't stop fidgeting. They passed a flower shop filled with colourful bouquets wrapped with equally pretty ribbon.

"Look!"

Otto stared straight ahead.

Ondreeal remained so preoccupied with all the new sights, sounds, and smells that she lost all track of where they walked. Before them towered an ivory castle, built from flawless, pure-white stones, perfectly cut and seamlessly fit together, in contrast to the unevenly spaced black bricks of the street. They walked towards the black iron gate. Two giant statues of knights towered on either side. The knights stood holding the hilt of an upward pointed broadsword, using both their hands. They each had a shield carved on their backs with a unique crest chiselled into them.

"Close your mouth. Look more confident, or the guards might think you're a fake," Otto whispered to her.

Ondreeal quickly closed her mouth and swallowed. She took deep, even breaths. They walked through the massive gate into an expansive courtyard, filled with its own manicured lawn, which was adorned with animals carved from bushes that appeared frozen in action. Colourful beds of flowers lined the white stone pathway leading to the massive interior. They crossed several guards, who stood like statues, before passing a smaller gate that led to a torch-lined staircase. They stopped at colossal, black ash doors, which two attendants opened, revealing a grand hall.

The setting sun shone on a golden throne at the far end of the hall. The head guard hurried in, stopping several meters in front of the throne.

He turned back to Ondreeal. "Please wait here."

His footsteps echoed on his way out. Each of the remaining guards took up a post in front of soaring, polished ebony beams that spanned the grand hall in twinned rows of eight. Ondreeal gazed at the archways above, which seemed to go on forever, highlighting the white brick ceiling. How it stayed up there and didn't fall remained as much a mystery to her as the rest of this place.

Otto turned to her and whispered, "You have to lie. If you lie, we might have a chance at living."

Ondreeal moved closer to him, wringing her hands.

"I don't know what to say," she told him through closed teeth.

"Think of something. I didn't raise you to gawk at everything like a child. Hold yourself up."

He tried to make her stand straighter but touched a sore spot, causing her to wince with pain. His eyes darted around the hall. "I'm nervous."

"*You're* nervous?" She almost yelled it, but then lowered her voice. "You're nervous? That is the biggest joke I've ever heard. You don't get to tell me what to do, ever again."

Otto stared at her. She thought shame reflected in his eyes, at least as much as Otto could ever have. She moved towards the throne, breathing in the distance from him.

She looked up at the arched ceiling. It helped the tears to stay pooled in her eyes.

A long time ago, she learned that living with Otto required a thick skin. In childhood, she would cry all the time, especially when scared. This only annoyed Otto and made him yell more. One day, when he came to wake her, he bellowed. In fact, he screamed the entire day, but only faced her cold stare in return. She had practiced it from watching him, and if he taught her nothing else, it was how to be strong.

"Keep yourself together," he quietly spat in her direction.

She turned around with her now-dry eyes and gave him that same cold stare.

"Worry about yourself, Otto. It's what you're best at." She turned again and walked away with much more confidence than she felt.

She moved closer to the sizable golden throne that must belong to Sir Francis. Before today, she had only viewed the castle from a distance. An engineer had pointed it out to her while she was at the village buying supplies one day.

In hopes of impressing her, the engineer had demonstrated a pulley system for something he called an elevator, although the ring on his finger made her wise to his less than honourable intentions. The gold glistened when he stretched out his hand in the direction of the white castle, so tiny in the distance and almost lost in the rich, green foliage of the forest.

Now Ondreeal stood in the wizard's chamber, staring at the golden throne, the seat from which Sir Francis ruled. She tried to slow her breathing. Certainly, they waited to meet a representative of the city. No doubt they would question her; she couldn't explain the events in the arena to them. She quickly turned, taking several steps towards the imposing black ash doors. A guard stood at every pillar, with two more in front of the doors. Escape remained elusive. Otto was right, and she needed to think of something to say. Caught up in the excitement of the city along with the grandness of the castle, she'd almost forgotten the reason for all this. She needed answers.

She agreed with Otto: telling the truth was not a clever idea. She had escaped the arena and the merchant by implying she had wizard-like abilities. Otto glared at her now to remind her of his advice. She ignored him and stared at the impossibly long chocolate-coloured wooden table that filled much of the chamber.

Ondreeal could call herself a well-trained warrior, nothing more. That wouldn't explain the light over the arena, the sound, and the fact that the barbarian had just vanished. She hadn't done that! Even if real magic existed, she had no idea how to use it. No, stories by peasants persisted as just that: stories. Her head spun. If she didn't think of something to say, she'd end up being a slave or worse. Ondreeal let everyone believe she'd made the barbarian disappear, and if she had a hope of getting out of this alive, she needed to stick to that lie.

The squeak of a door hinge caught her attention. In scurried two attendants, who positioned themselves on either side of the throne. They stood so straight that Ondreeal waited for their backs to break.

"Uh-hum."

Ondreeal glanced back towards the modest side door. Distracted by the two attendants, she didn't hear the man walk in. He smiled at her from behind his perfect white beard that came down to a point at his chest. He stood there in white robes as bright as the sun—looking like the God of All.

He examined her. "You must be the girl everyone is whispering about." He took several steps towards her.

Ondreeal froze. Her heart quickened. Her whole body tensed, making her breath stop.

He studied her face from two inches away. The sadness in his eyes quickly transformed to joy, and he smiled broadly.

She took a step backwards, landing on her wounded ankle, forcing her to swallow a yelp of pain. She stuck out her hand so he could shake it, yet he continued to examine her.

"I'm Ondreeal." She breathed, hoping her hand would stop quivering.

He wouldn't shake it, but she wouldn't put it down, either. She stuck out her hand farther.

"Pleased to meet you." She had more boldness in her voice than fear.

He finally took her hand in both of his. His skin felt remarkably soft; he'd obviously never done a day's worth of hard labour. If her rough, callused hand bothered him, he didn't let on.

"One shakes hands when meeting someone for the first time." He raised an eyebrow.

Did he think she was a simpleton? She didn't know much about social etiquette. Certainly, she'd never learned any from Otto, so that left what her mother had taught her. However, even peasants understood to shake hands when first meeting someone.

"I am aware, sir." She held her chin high.

He laughed.

Her cheeks burned with embarrassment.

"What I meant was, this is not the first time we have met." He looked at her expectantly.

She didn't remember him. Her breath caught in her throat.

"I'm sorry, Sir..."

"Francis. Sir Francis."

Now that he said it, somehow that made it more real. Sir Francis, the great, powerful wizard, the ruler of the north, guardian of all that is good, stood mere inches away. She swayed on her feet and might have fallen if Sir Francis hadn't kept his grip on her. How could any of this be real? He looked for signs of recognition from her.

She blinked in shock. "I do not remember you."

He laughed again. "I would not expect you to. But I remember you, and you are the spitting image of your mother."

Chapter Six

Rolling over the hilly landscape covered in fern-green grasses, CD-45 extended his sensors to maximum capacity. His internal monitor, a holographic representation of his internal programming that only he could see, displayed:

EVIDENCE OF HIGHER TECHNOLOGY PRESENT IN MICROSCOPIC FORM ONLY.

Translation? Everything had been blown to smithereens, and you'd need a microscope to see any damned evidence of advanced materials—at least, you would in this particular meadow.

A uniform bright-blue sky shone down over the rolling hills, creating a peaceful view. Ferns? Hmmm. Did that particular plant still exist? If so, CD-45 found it unlikely that anyone would place them in their homes as decoration—once a common feature in crew quarters or any large-scale structure, now humans lived in modest buildings, surrounded by a wide variety of fauna. What did ferns have to do with his mission? Unless the aliens in orbit accepted plants as peace offerings—"Here's some foliage, now please stop trying to exterminate us"— natural vegetation would likely remain inconsequential.

Three blue circles flashed on CD-45's holographic monitor, highlighting several energy signatures. His sensors added words at the centre of one: ALIEN SPACECRAFT IMPLOSION. The source appeared to be a ring of black peaks, unnatural in their formation. Radiation levels would undoubtedly result in expedient deaths for any human life entering the internal realm, although the mountains would shield such isotopes from escaping the epicentre of the crash site.

Words formed in the next two blue dots: UNKNOWN SOURCE — ALPHA FOUR FIVE. His system first classified that particular signature fifteen orbits ago. It had been much stronger at that time. One of the circles shone brighter, a recent event. The second, although fading, looked only a day or two old. The third had indistinct borders, indicating continuous use over a long period of time. All of these unknown sources must have originated from technology even more advanced than that which humans had achieved by the twenty-fifth century, making them worthy of further investigation. Yet they deepened the mystery of what had happened down here in the last two thousand years. If at least some people had the capability, they hadn't returned to the orbital platforms by choice. Something kept this group of humans firmly entrenched in the mud.

Priority number one flashed on CD-45's screen: FORGE ALLIANCES, OBTAIN ASSISTANCE. Sigh. First, make friends, then find a ship to get him back into orbit, or ideally, both: companions that had a space-capable vessel — that would really make his day, hell, his century. His mechanical brain hurt. He continued tracking in a southwesterly direction. Ferns tended to calm humans. Would it work for his aching head?

CHAPTER SEVEN

Trick Mark opened his eyes — or, at least, he thought he opened his eyes. Darkness surrounded him until his second sight kicked in. He looked around, and a lonely beam of light filtered in from above, at least thirty feet up. He and Vere could never climb that high. Finding another way out would be their only hope. They had fallen into something larger than the grand hall of the castle, landing in a long-forgotten ruin.

Passageways veiled in darkness surrounded the expansive chamber. Scattered pieces of strange stone and glass littered the ground. The smooth walls and floor appeared foreign in this dungeon. Why would anyone build such a vast structure under the ground?

He'd heard stories of magical people who constructed such places: ancients. Those who came from a time far in the past, building things that seemed to last forever, yet something had destroyed almost all of what they built.

The stale air carried new, unusual smells, as if someone had mixed the scents of a barn with an iron forge and then scrubbed the air clean. This place had lain here, sealed up like a coffin. How much time had passed until they'd crashed in from above?

Trick Mark tested his limbs, then flexed his hands. His body ached from the fall, but the pain slowly leaked out, a sign of no broken bones. In the dusty, littered ruins, he spotted Vere lying not far away, and just beyond her lay Zairoc.

Trick Mark carefully approached Vere and checked the vessel in her throat: blood still pumped at regular intervals. He gave a quiet exhale of relief as he leaned close, whispering in her ear.

"Vere. Vere, wake up." Yet his eyes never wavered from Zairoc.

Vere moaned but didn't move. Not far from Zairoc lay his wand. It glowed white, but almost looked red while Trick Mark stared at it. He glanced from Vere to the wand. He needed to get himself and Vere to safety, and then return home. But he had never come closer to a wand that didn't belong to Sir Francis. Capturing one would please Sir Francis as well as cripple Zairoc's ability to make war. For an opportunity like this, Trick Mark had to risk his life along with Vere's. To claim such a prize would be a great victory.

He took a step towards it, eyes trained on Zairoc, who stayed unmoving. Maybe the fall had killed him. He took another step towards the wand, and Zairoc remained motionless. Slowly Trick Mark reached down towards the prize, but as his hand got closer, the wand hummed louder. It might kill him to hold it; that would leave Vere alone. If Zairoc lived, he would unleash his rage on her.

Wands contained great power, though only a few of them existed. Trick Mark had once asked why no one thought to make any more. Sir Francis had scoffed, telling him that if it were possible, he would have already done it.

Ancient and *powerful*—those two words ran through Trick Mark's head as his hand hovered over the wand. His heart beat fast while his hands shook with fear, but he had to try. He owed Sir Francis that much.

He touched the wand, unleashing a crack of power that threw him back several yards. He landed with a dull thud, though managed to stifle a scream. He jumped back to his feet.

Zairoc groaned and stirred. The idle wand possessed magical protection, or maybe it only yielded to its rightful owner, Zairoc.

"Trick?" Vere's voice made him snap around.

She tried to stand on shaky legs. In an instant, the wand leapt back into Zairoc's unmoving hand, and his fingers slowly closed to grasp it. Not good. Trick Mark silently rushed to Vere, scooped her up, then ran into a dark passageway.

"Archer! I will make sure you suffer for this." Zairoc's voice echoed through the great space.

Without a sound, Trick Mark carried Vere farther into the labyrinth. They took several turns through the perfectly formed halls. With luck, Zairoc couldn't follow them. The twisting maze would prove difficult to navigate.

"I can't see anything. Where are we going, Trick?" Vere sounded worried.

She didn't know that he could see down the hall with his second sight. For her benefit, he stopped, gently put Vere on the ground, then felt for his knapsack and opened it.

"Trick!" Vere sounded stronger, a good sign.

He shushed her. Zairoc would hear them if he managed to follow.

Trick Mark rummaged through his knapsack. He clutched a fist-sized, round object that glowed in response to his touch. Plucking it up, he held it ahead and then released it. It hovered there, the back half darkened and the front part shining a beam of light down the eerie hall. Vere blinked from the brightness of it.

"Sir Francis taught you magic?" Her face reflected his feeling of awe.

"No Vere. A gift from the wizard." Puffing his chest with pride, he helped her up.

He examined her while they walked down the dark passage. She winced with pain through her strong strides, a heartiness that equalled his.

"What is this place?" Vere looked all around.

Debris, dust, and dirt covered every inch.

Trick Mark sighed. "I've heard stories of ruins before. Strange places filled with sleeping spirits. It is said that some spirits are friendly while others are angry and vengeful."

They examined the space, completely baffled.

"Well, what kind are these ruins?" Vere looked at him for the answer.

He slowly shook his head. "I don't know."

"Then let's get out of here. The ancients built these, I just know it." She looked afraid.

She was also right, because beneath the dust and dirt lay perfectly smooth floors, walls made of metal or stones he'd never seen, all of it equally strange and fascinating. They turned a corner. The light reflected off glass windows, row upon row of them. Vere rushed over to one.

"It looks like some kind of storage." She smiled back at Trick Mark.

All women couldn't act as strangely as Vere; could they? Clearly, she had forgotten the danger Zairoc represented.

"We need to keep moving," he snapped at her.

She stood her ground, indignant. "A soldier never stops performing her duty. Explore all areas, however unlikely they may be."

His jaw fell open. "In there? You can't be serious."

"I'm able-bodied, sir." She stood tall, facing him, proud of the fact.

Then she winced with pain, holding her side.

Trick Mark hardened his glare. "That evil wizard slaughtered my men. Surely, he tries to track us down and kill us as we speak." He moved close to Vere.

Her stern face seemed to falter, but she remained firm.

"We could find something in there to help, something magical. Please, sir." She turned back to the window.

Her fear seemed to evaporate. This showed the power of items behind glass; death could follow you, but, apparently, there was always time to shop. Yet, her words carried truth. If they didn't find a way out, they'd need to defend themselves.

Trick Mark stared at their reflections in the window. His grey eyes verged on wolflike; that's what he thought the first time he had seen himself in a mirror. His short, brown hair, a disheveled mess, matched his uniform in colour. Vere only came up to his chin, even though she stood taller than most women did. His well-muscled frame could intimidate many, but not Zairoc.

He closed his eyes and reached out with his second sight. He could feel the labyrinth of halls, some blocked, others winding, while several levels sprawled beneath them too. The massive place felt absent of Zairoc. If the wizard had followed, he remained nowhere near them. That much reassured Trick Mark. For the first time since he'd left Bastion's castle, days ago, he relaxed just a little.

He nodded to Vere, prompting her to tug at the door until it flung open, sending her flying back. A rush of air gushed out of the glass-enclosed space. Trick Mark caught Vere, and she looked up at him with reddened cheeks. He needed to ignore her charms. This beautiful young woman under his command split his focus. He put her back on her feet, then moved ahead into the storage space. He glanced back at Vere, who had a look of determination.

The floating light shone down the aisle, illuminating shelves full of different-sized boxes. Each one displayed strange word combinations, although written in the Amereng.

"'Ages seven and up.' What does that mean?" She looked to Trick Mark for answers, but he had no idea.

Vere grabbed one box, which immediately disintegrated to dust in her hands. The strange object inside sprung to life, with shining lights and all. That caused a chain effect of items that surged to life, while all the boxes that held them fell to dust. They both coughed, covered in debris.

"Great work, Vere. Zairoc will find us, for sure." He choked out the words.

She blushed again. Trick Mark needed to keep her in line, not show lenience. He had already stopped to look at the storage after she'd disobeyed a direct order ... not that it mattered down here, as they might not make it out alive.

It amazed him that the strange items still worked after all this time, although, if ancients built them, it really shouldn't. How long had they lain dormant? Centuries? He wiped away dust from his eyes and examined the odd items.

"They look more like toys than weapons." He shook his head.

Vere gazed in awe. "Definitely made by the ancients."

All this noise would certainly draw unwanted attention. He grabbed Vere by the arm, then backed out of the storage space. She didn't protest as they re-entered the hallway. A flash of light tore by Trick Mark's head. He reflexively pulled Vere down. He scanned the hall. At the far end, Zairoc strode with his glowing wand. The echo of each step grew louder as he slowly moved towards them.

CHAPTER EIGHT

S ir Francis had known her mother? It felt like something Ondreeal might experience in a dream.

Maybe he'd lied.

Otto had made such a mess of everything, getting her into trouble to begin with. He should have told her how bad things had gotten. With a little extra hard work, they could have solved this together. Perhaps they'd be back on the farm right now. She held herself tightly, gazing down at the white stone floor.

"It's all right. It's safe now. I vow to give you my protection. No harm will come to you." Sir Francis put his hands on her shoulders.

As quickly as it had come, the pain in her ankle, in fact, any ache she'd had in her body, simply vanished.

"Did you...?" She trailed off while his pale-blue eyes playfully watched her.

Could she trust him? Everyone swore to his validity as a wizard. If he had healed her, then that made for solid proof Ondreeal couldn't ignore. She must have appeared flustered, but when he looked past her, his bright eyes filled with anger.

"Defenders!"

The guards snapped to attention.

Ondreeal jumped with a start.

Sir Francis nodded at Otto, who stood near the door. "Arrest this man." He spat the words.

Ondreeal stepped back in surprise.

The men swarmed Otto, grabbing for him. He roared, and with his considerable size, he knocked them aside. They came at him again and surrounded him, swords at the ready. His smile became laughter while the guards glared.

One charged, and Otto used the man's own momentum against him. He took the fellow's sword, tossing him into a group of other guards. Otto screamed, then charged several more. They defended themselves valiantly, though Otto moved surprisingly fast.

Did Ondreeal want a victorious Otto? He punched and kicked his way around the room until all the soldiers lay unconscious. Several moaned. They would have bad headaches when they awoke. At last, he pointed the sword at Sir Francis, who clasped his hands behind himself nonchalantly.

"Ha." Sir Francis rolled his eyes at Otto.

Wide-eyed, Ondreeal stepped forward and shielded Sir Francis, looking alternately from Otto to the point of the iron sword. Otto's stern glare melted with a touch of softness.

"Maybe next time, old man." Otto ran towards the black ash doors until his feet lifted off the floor, and he started to float.

Ondreeal's mouth hung open in wonderment. Otto appeared just as surprised when the sword escaped his grip and then pointed towards him. Every sword floated up, pointed at Otto. Ondreeal took a few steps closer to him. Had she demonstrated her ability to become a powerful wizard?

"Otto, I don't think I cast a spell." Her voice shook.

"No shit, kid," Otto shot back at her.

He stared past Ondreeal. She turned to follow his gaze. Sir Francis held a glowing green wand, casting an emerald glow on his white robes and beard. Ondreeal gawked in awe. He was a real wizard. The villagers spoke the truth about him. Which meant in the arena she had wielded ... magic. Did she possess magic?

Otto dropped like a rock, landing with a dull thud. He quickly hopped on his feet along with several soldiers who'd recovered from his beating. They all readied themselves for another fight, fists raised and bodies crouched in combat stances.

Sir Francis spoke like a winter's breeze. "Go with the guards peacefully, or you will not like the result."

Otto nodded, and the swords dropped to the floor with a clang. Eyes trained on Otto, the guards carefully retrieved their weapons and then encircled him. They slowly guided him out of the throne room. The doors independently slammed shut behind them.

"There. Now that the unpleasantness is behind us, there is much for us to talk about." Sir Francis guided Ondreeal to a side door.

She couldn't take her eyes off the ash doors until they entered the narrow, arched pathway, blocking her view. The villagers' stories paled by comparison to her very real, visceral experience of magic. Ondreeal wrung her hands with insecurity. She tried to imagine herself being a wizard, but the vanishing barbarian haunted her. If she lied, would Sir Francis know it? Would he throw her in a dungeon?

They headed deeper into the castle. Every window they passed displayed elaborate patterns of stained glass, in a variety of colours. Sir Francis led Ondreeal up a winding staircase that stretched on forever. She lost count of the steps after several minutes, her legs straining on the stairs, much to her surprise. After all, her well-toned body could easily handle gruelling daily work on the farm—which, however, featured not one winding staircase. She used muscles she didn't know she had. Sir Francis didn't mind the climb one little bit, obviously ascending the stairs regularly. She desperately tried to keep her struggle quiet until an exasperated sigh escaped her lips.

"Do you need a moment, Ondreeal?"

He clearly noticed her strain. However, her pride wouldn't allow a few hundred stairs to stop her, even if they did stretch out of sight. She shook her head while he smirked and climbed higher. They continued up for an eternity, until an end came into view in the form of a door.

It swung open, and Sir Francis strode onto the castle's curtain wall. It stretched at least twelve feet wide and many times that in length. Ondreeal let out a breath of relief as she stepped onto the flat, white stone floor. At the far end, another spire marked a corner of the fortification, at least wide enough for another winding staircase. The apron wall stretched around the castle in a series of wide paths, each connected by a pointed tower. The castle keep supported iron rooftops that jutted up in sharp triangular formation above the snow white-bricks, all covered in a wide array of chimneystacks that reached high up into a crystal-blue sky.

Sir Francis walked to the edge, a warm breeze moving through his beard. Like so many times today, awe filled Ondreeal as she absorbed the view. In the orange sunset, she could see for miles around the castle. The breathtaking sight had no comparison, not even to the engineer's elevator view. Farmland spread out, spotted with distant villages much like the one she'd grown up near. Endless forests rolled over the hills and disappeared into the misty distance.

"I thought you might want some fresh air. The castle can get so stuffy at times. I often come up here to clear my head, and I would assume yours could benefit from just that." Sir Francis looked apologetic.

"You knew my mother?" Of all the things she could have asked him, this question burned most. It offered a connection to the woman whose face she sometimes couldn't even recall. "You said I look like her?"

Tears welled up, but Ondreeal didn't care how this looked to him. Sir Francis waited a long time before answering, the lines on his forehead deepened and contorted ever so slightly, which betrayed the great pain those events had caused him.

"I knew her well. She possessed kindness and beauty. You were a source of constant pride and joy, my dear." His face appeared sad through his smile.

"Did she have a green dress, one she wore along with a string of white pearls?" The memory flooded back making her excited.

"Yes." Sir Francis nodded. "The one she adorned for company."

Ondreeal laughed with relief. She smiled at him, yet he looked at her quizzically.

"I didn't know if it was real or just a dream I made up."

"There's something else I must show you. Come."

Sir Francis appeared serious. He strode to the far tower, then headed down a new winding staircase. Ondreeal raced after him, grateful to climb down instead of up. She followed him through the winding maze of the castle until they came to an average-looking door, not appearing any different from many others they'd passed already. The door creaked open, revealing a spacious hall. Sir Francis stepped through it with Ondreeal. Dust covered every inch of the room, in sharp contrast to the impeccably maintained grand hall. A very long table occupied the centre of the space. Walls lined with shelves holding strange objects flanked the table on two sides.

Ondreeal coughed out filth. "This is what you wanted me to see? Dust?"

Sir Francis assessed the chamber, as if seeing the grimy interior for the first time.

"Quite right." He nodded.

He pulled out that wand, and with a bright flash, a spotless room emerged. Ondreeal backed away from him, so he quickly put the wand away. He controlled the power to kill her with a thought or word. Should she trust this fantastical wizard?

"It's okay, child. You have nothing to fear from me, I promise." He sounded so convincing.

"What will happen to Otto?"

A pang of guilt hit her stomach. She should have asked about him sooner. She didn't owe the man anything, but still, she worried about him.

"He will spend the night in a guarded room, and he's very lucky to be doing just that." Sir Francis seemed disgusted at the thought of Otto.

"But what has he done to you?" She clenched her hands, uncertain of his reaction.

"My history with Otto is tumultuous at best. He held the position of captain here in Bastion. I will tell you all, in time. For now, believe it's for the best." He gave her an assuring nod.

Otto had commanded all the soldiers here in Bastion. She had just learned more about Otto's past in one sentence than she had in her whole life.

"I need to know now. Please." Ondreeal took a step towards him.

"No," Sir Francis curtly snapped.

For a brief moment, the faint sound of thunder rumbled, and the lights darkened, allowing the shadows to deepen. Ondreeal's whole body tensed, but somehow, she knew he wouldn't hurt her.

A moment later, he shook his head, regret filling his eyes. "Please, let us talk no more of him. Tell me more about the arena." He gave her that small but kind smile.

Her tense fists released. Given what Otto had tried to do, selling her into slavery, it seemed fitting that he spend some time in a jail cell, or at least a guarded room. Despite his brief outburst of anger, Sir Francis would have made a much better parent than Otto ever did. If she had a hope of things going well with Sir Francis, then she needed to be as honest as possible.

"I can't explain how that barbarian disappeared the way he did. I hoped someone here could tell me. I didn't think it would be you. If you have a trusted advisor, maybe they could meet with me instead." She paced back and forth, wringing her hands.

She just admitted she didn't control magic, a confession that might lead her to a dungeon or worse.

Sir Francis glided by, and she turned to stare at him. Did he look disappointed? She couldn't tell for certain. He carried the weight of the world on his shoulders. He appeared to have so much knowledge that anything she said must sound like the ramblings of a very young child. Yet, what else could she try?

"Sir Francis, to most people far from the castle, magic is only a story. What you've heard of me is only that. I'm certain of it." She stood confident.

Then he laughed at her. Her cheeks flushed. She must look like an idiot.

"I would prefer it if you didn't address me so formally. Francis will do, drop the *sir*, if you please." He bowed his head with one quick motion.

He practiced good manners, a way of behaving so far from her reality it made for a long forgotten-memory like her mother, or a dream she tried to recall in the morning. She half expected to awaken any minute on her straw bed.

"If magic is real, then it scares me. What does it mean for me? In the arena, for the first time in my life, I had a choice. I chose to come here. But now I don't know the truth. This morning I knew myself. You said you knew me. Who am I?" She searched his wrinkled face for answers.

Sir Francis paced up and down the length of the great table that spanned the room.

"I heard of a girl that went toe to toe with a barbarian three times her size. That would be enough to catch my interest. But in this story, a magical feat to equal any god's occurred right next to that girl, and she did not even flinch. Then she demanded to come to Bastion. Now, you understand, I was most eager to meet such a resilient individual, so I instructed that no one was to get in her way. To make this story even more interesting, and much to my surprise, this girl turned out to be someone I knew from the moment of her birth. Someone who disappeared years ago, that I believed long dead. So, imagine my relief when she turns up alive and well. It's a happy story, don't you think?"

He stopped at the end of the table and gave her a warm smile. Ondreeal took a cautious step back. She wanted to trust him, yet how could she have faith in a complete stranger? She knew betrayal and heartlessness, not warmth or kindness.

"I did what I needed, to survive. Maybe I want to believe in you so badly that I can't see what's in front of my face." She took another step back, yet Sir Francis appeared unconcerned.

"And what would be in front of your face?" He held his nose up, studying her.

She hesitated, then said, "Am I just another curiosity to you, something to be traded or possessed?" She retreated further towards the entrance.

Pity filled his eyes as he shook his head. Sir Francis turned away from Ondreeal and slowly marched to the back wall. He looked for something in the white stone, his fingers running over its surface. She could turn and run right now, though she probably wouldn't make it out of the castle.

She was free of the farm and Otto. She should embrace the new world opening to her, not fear it. Her curiosity got the better of her, and she found herself walking to the edge of the table, straining to look at his actions.

A stone moved inward, then a part of the wall moved up. Out of it popped a light-filled rectangular table of some kind. The table appeared impossibly thin, like a blade that calmly pulsed with white light along its three-foot length and two-foot width.

He looked back, gesturing for her to come over. She cautiously approached, then reached out a hand to touch the table, stopped, and looked at Sir Francis. He smiled, nodding to her. Her fingers ran over the smooth, glasslike surface. On it laid an odd-looking stick.

Then Sir Francis put a sparkling gold locket on the glass in front of Ondreeal.

"Open it," he ordered.

She picked it up. The locket fell open. Inside she found a picture of herself—no, of her mother, smiling, in that very same green dress.

She looked at Sir Francis. "If this is more of your magic—"

"Real, Ondreeal, and waiting for you a very long time." He sounded so convincing.

She looked down at the locket, and the other half contained a picture of a young girl. Ondreeal closed her eyes until she could see the locket hanging from her mother's neck.

Tears welled up, but Ondreeal nodded vigorously. "This was hers. I remember it."

Sir Francis carefully plucked up the strange stick, then walked back to the great table. He sighed deeply, as if he truly carried the weight of the world on his shoulders. Ondreeal took the locket, stepping to his side. It looked like a stick from afar; however, in truth, another wand lay before her.

"I've kept it hidden away all this time. Go ahead," he gently encouraged her.

Ondreeal edged towards it, studying its flawless surface against the polished wood of the table. The wand looked smooth, like glass, although dark, almost black. She touched the wand, prompting it to glow a brilliant blue-white. She quickly recoiled, and the wand fell dark. Ondreeal breathed rapidly. Her heart jumped into her throat.

Strangely, Sir Francis looked hurt.

"When in the arena, did you wish for something?"

She slowly backed away from the wand and towards the door. If she told him, then he'd keep her here. She'd become a prisoner like Otto, just with bars of a different kind. Her cage would be one of magic, which could consume her, control her every thought. The rumours said dark magic possessed Zairoc; the same could be true for her. She wouldn't trade one master, the merchant, for the wand.

Her world remained familiar yet brutal. She couldn't go back to that and doubted Sir Francis would even let her. The world pulled her towards one filled with magic, more dangerous than any great power. That's what he asked her to wield in the wand. She drew away from Sir Francis.

His feet shuffled nervously. He repeated, more loudly, "Did you wish for anything at all? Did you ask for anything?"

Ondreeal stopped, then slowly looked up at him.

His eyes pierced right through her. "What was the thought? Do you remember?"

"Just, 'Kill him.' I kept saying it. I thought if I could believe it enough, I might find a way." She recalled the events of the day with fresh horror.

"You called to the wand. You called to it, and it answered you the only way it could, by striking down the barbarian from so far away." His calm voice soothed her.

"I didn't call for anything." Her voice shook.

"Yes, you did." He sounded so convincing.

"Why me? Why would it answer me?" She scoffed at the thought.

"The wand belonged to your mother. Now it belongs to you. It answers to you and only you." His was the voice of reason.

"I'm a wizard, you're a wizard," the words slowly wafted from her lips. "Magic is real, and all those stories were true." She absorbed her own statements, yet shook her head.

He beamed at her. "My dear, there exists an explanation for everything. We are not magical beings. We are the users of magical instruments, the wands. Each wand answers only to one user."

He took in her incredulous expression. "Your mother's name was Aleenda. She was a wizard tasked with bringing this world back into the age of reason. As her daughter, you are the only one who can take up this burden. The wand will answer to no one else. I hope you will become every bit the guardian of light that your mother was." He watched for her reaction.

"I'm not a wizard, I'm just a farmer." She battled with this new information.

Aleenda was her mother, a great and powerful wizard. That wand connected them, bringing her closer to the woman she had tried so hard to keep alive in her mind all these years.

"My dear girl, we must not only unify our land with Zairoc. We must unite all the lands, as one, or we have no future. The world crumbles to ash if we do nothing. I wish you could understand all I know, all I have seen. Nevertheless, you will, in time. All I ask is that you try." He nodded, gazing at her with such hope.

"I control the wand. How?" She took a step towards him.

She didn't understand much of what he said. What she did know was that he needed her help. He asked her for aid, he didn't force her.

"The wand, for all its power and potential, has one weakness: it is only as good as its user. It can take all your strength to make it work, or only the slightest effort. The real power is here." Sir Francis tapped the side of his head. "I am certain that once you start training, you will quickly master the art of wands."

She edged past him and stared at the dark wand lying on the table. She didn't feel certain of anything at all.

CHAPTER NINE

T rick Mark pulled Vere to her feet. Together they sprinted down the long, dark corridor. Rows upon rows of glass windows showed more of the bizarre storage. Their footsteps echoed on the strange, dust-layered tiles. Flashes of red wand blasts, exploded all around them. Trick Mark dare not look back at Zairoc, or face certain death. Their only option was to run.

"I'm sorry." Vere's voice trembled.

Crash! The floor tiles just ahead exploded with a red blast from Zairoc's wand. The floor gave way, making a wide hole in their path.

"Jump!" Trick Mark leaped over the opening.

He landed firmly on the other side, feeling a strong pull back on his arm. Vere teetered on the edge of the aperture. He yanked her forward, successfully, and this time they both ran hard. The light floated, casting a steady beam down the hall. Several more blasts from the wand landed all around them, lighting up the darkness like shooting stars, entities that shone beautifully in the sky but met death when they fell to Earth.

They dodged the blasts. Vere pulled Trick Mark sharply to the left and down another hallway. With another quick zap from the wand, the light exploded, eclipsing them into pitch black.

With the barest of whispers, Vere said, "Oh no," and held her breath.

Trick Mark grabbed her hand, then guided her down the hallway. The wand blasts stopped. All fell silent in the darkness. They quietly advanced, weaving through the endless, glass-lined halls, without any sign of Zairoc.

"How are we going to get out of here, Trick?" Vere hissed.

At any moment, Zairoc could materialize before them. The wizard must have cloaked himself; Trick Mark should have sensed his approach from a mile away, because Zairoc couldn't know about his ability. That might mean that every wizard represented a blind spot for him. He had never thought about it before, but in a way, it made sense. Sir Francis and Zairoc, the only two wizards he'd met, could use magic to disguise their presence.

He sensed an opening above, in the distance, a way out to safety. They would be okay: Trick Mark was sure of it now. The maze opened to another massive hall, as high as three or four stories. Stairs zigzagged their way deeper into the labyrinth.

"Steps going down," he whispered to Vere.

"Sir, you do know we need to go up, not down." She sounded sarcastic, a good sign of coping well with their situation.

"Trust me," he assured her.

"If I can't see, you can't see. You don't know where you're going, do you?" She made a logical conclusion, though without all the information.

He shushed her. His second sight remained at only a fraction of its full strength, although if he concentrated, he could manage half strength during the day. He couldn't achieve that now. Maybe his fear of Zairoc made it impossible. He pictured the bodies of his men rising out of the tall grasses and shook his head, as if the action would rid him of the gruesome image.

He took a deep breath and tried to slow the beating of his heart—better, but not great. They descended deeper into the pit of the ancient complex until, finally, they reached another level. They travelled around for a long while in the blackness. Vere wisely kept her thoughts to herself. Every time Trick sensed a way out, it just led to more and more of a maze. They could be walking in circles. While the sun remained in the sky, Trick Mark couldn't find an escape.

***

They navigated the corridors for hours, with no sign of Zairoc. This made for a slight miracle: the God of All surely watched over them. The dark, confusing maze of the ancients stretched on for an eternity.

"Sir? Do you know where we're going?" Vere whispered at last.

"No." Trick Mark sighed with frustration.

Worse yet, they had only a limited amount of provisions. In two days, they would run out of food and probably end up dying of starvation down here.

"Wait—I can see something!" Vere sounded excited at the prospect of an exit.

Trick Mark couldn't blame her.

They found a tiny ray of light shining down on the dirty tiles. Hope filled Trick Mark, as they hurried towards the faint glow of sun. Several broken floors hung above them. The light shone in through a hole in the ground, similar to the one they'd made when falling into the maze. He hung his head and sighed.

"Got any climbing equipment?" He gave Vere a brave smile.

She slowly shook her head, eyes locked on the unreachable exit.

"I told you we shouldn't have gone down. What now, sir?" She looked at Trick Mark with concern.

He thought that down could lead to a way out. Unfortunately, it didn't. Instead, the maze sprawled out in every direction.

"This is a whole underground city. If we walked the streets of Bastion, I'd say hundreds of shops surrounded us." He raised his eyebrows, impressed.

"If that's true, then they're the strangest stores I've ever seen. All the ancients did was shop." She smirked.

They both broke into laughter for a moment. Then it evaporated as reality took hold once more.

"Surely, there's something here to help us get out or defend against Zairoc." Trick Mark scanned all around.

Something caught Vere's attention, and her whole face lit up. She looked beautiful when she let her guard down, and even when she scowled, she was cute. Vere bolted for a window. Trick Mark hurried after her, then stood beside her while she peered through the perfect glass.

"You have got to be kidding me." In the window, his face reflected distaste.

Vere paid him no attention. Her eyes lit up because behind the glass hung a glittering amber dress.

"It's made from gold, it must be magic." Vere's eyes went wide with awe.

He shook his head. "It's only a dress."

Vere rushed into the store and wrestled the gown from where it hung. She shook it, hoping to activate its power.

"It's only a dress," he whispered with no amusement.

She promptly rolled it up, stuffing it in her knapsack. She stared at the floor and let out a long sigh.

"We might find a use for it." She hit the wall. "I'm sorry."

"We'll find a way out." Trick Mark moved closer.

"They're all dead. He could have killed me, but he didn't." Her eyes looked haunted.

"We're getting out of here together. Then we'll get back to Bastion and tell Sir Francis what happened here." He put his hands on her shoulders.

Vere nodded once, then moved away from his palms and headed out. She might have lost confidence in him. If so, he couldn't blame her. His decisions had gotten them here, trapped in this ancient place. He hurried after her, resuming their trek through the dark labyrinth. He treaded down a giant, open hall and then stopped in front of another "store."

"A much better choice, sir," Vere admitted to him.

They crept inside the dark space full of equipment. Many of the items appeared well suited for use outside. The faint light from the thin sunray filtering in from the tree roots above couldn't reach into the store. Trick Mark approached one of the nearest shelves, where one round, metal ball the size of a fist lay. He grabbed it, and the ball lit up, just like the one Sir Francis had given him. Perhaps the wizard had acquired it from here. The ancients obviously possessed a great deal of magic. He smiled as the light took up position in front of him. The light shone on a modest dwelling set up in the store: made from a strange, blue cloth and propped up with odd metal posts, it resembled a hut of sorts. The light went dark and crashed to the floor.

"Guess it's out of magic." Vere sighed.

The hut would at least hide them from Zairoc. Besides, they both needed rest. Certainly, they wouldn't get out of the underground city until nightfall. They should make camp and wait for dark. Trick Mark sat down in the strange shelter.

"What are you doing?" Vere stood near the entrance to the store.

"Getting some rest." He lay down.

Vere moved closer to him.

"It will be night soon, and then neither of us can see. How do we get out?" She sounded scared.

He should simply tell her the truth. Then again, he'd never told anyone before. Vere might accuse him of being a sprite, or worse, a demon. People did very violent things when faced with extraordinary creatures. Zairoc made people fear magic.

Vere stepped right on his arm.

"Ouch! Watch it," he snapped at her.

"Sorry, sir. It is dark. Remember?" She practically collapsed beside him.

He could hear her take off her bag and rummage through it.

"Bread?" She held a piece of out for him, so he took it.

It had a sweet taste, melting in his mouth. He swallowed and lay back. As Vere moved around, she quietly winced with pain. The fall had hurt them both, but fear kept them going.

He watched her rub her calf and knee. "Your leg okay?"

"Not bad. It aches with the rest of me. How about you?" She stretched out next to him.

"Bruised and battered. Tired but fine," he whispered.

"Sir?" Her soft voice carried worry.

"Yes."

"How could the ancients make a place like this, filled with amazing things that last so very long?" She let out a sharp breath.

"I don't know. It must be magic. I've heard stories of other places like this. If it weren't for all the dust and debris, this place would look new."

They lay in silence for a moment.

The image of his men motionless in the air haunted him. Trick Mark fought to hold back tears. His strength needed to endure, for both their sakes. He silently breathed out despair. Vere would follow him, even if it led to death.

"When we get out of here, we need to say a prayer of passing," he whispered.

"Get some rest, sir," she told him, hugging her shaking body.

He moved close and wrapped his arms around her.

She snickered at him. "I didn't know you cared."

"It's cold. We need to share warmth." It sounded more scolding than he'd intended.

In that moment, he wanted to kiss her, make her feel something other than pain. As her commanding officer, he couldn't. As a man facing death, his desire for her grew by the second.

"Sleep well, sir." She exhaled deeply.

Not three seconds later she snored loudly. Maybe he'd underestimated the toll their situation had taken on her. Or maybe she just didn't appreciate how screwed they were. Either way, he envied her. Exhaustion filled him, though sleep remained elusive.

His sharp ears picked up faint thuds and groans throughout the ancient place. Each sound might signal that Zairoc closed in. With luck, the wizard wouldn't find them in the dark. Trick Mark listened to everything: the creaks, the crumbling sound of earth trickling in from the hole far above them, and Vere's soft breathing and occasional snores. The sweet scent of her hair filled the hut.

***

Several hours passed, or that's what Trick Mark estimated as he lay there with his eyes open, listening. No footsteps, no audible sign of Zairoc. His second sight opened to him as the sun set. The maze stretched out around them. It went farther down, several levels, perhaps. Thousands of people would need such a large place to live. His father had told him stories of tall buildings, hundreds of feet high.

Most people believed the bygone cities were enormous, full of inspiring wonders. In fact, all the ancients were said to be magical. Without using wands, they could command everything around them with just a touch or a word. His father had said that they made homes among the stars. Nothing could be more fantastical than that. No one knew where they all went, for sure. Many believed that the God of All punished them, wiping their accomplishments clean from the Earth. Not clean enough, if you asked him; otherwise, they wouldn't be in their current mess.

He sensed two possible ways out of the ancient place. He gently shook Vere, but she woke with a scream. He covered her mouth a split-second later.

"Do you want to get us killed?"

He took his hand off her mouth.

"Sorry. I was having a bad dream. Looks like it's real." She quietly exhaled.

"We're getting out of here. Grab your bag." Trick Mark stood and headed out the door.

He found no sign of movement, but Zairoc had managed to sneak up on them before.

Vere met him at the doorway.

"I told you we should have kept looking. I can't see a thing." She sounded frustrated.

He didn't blame her, just grabbed her hand.

"Don't let go," he told her.

He guided them down the huge hallway in darkness. They hadn't traveled for long when Trick Mark stopped. In front of them, another stairway headed up. At the top, he thought a tangle of roots hung down. Maybe they could dig their way out. It would take some doing, but once outside, they could easily find their way back to Bastion and safety.

"There are stairs in front of us. We're going up. I think I can see a way out." He pulled on her hand, but she tugged back.

"How can you know that?" Her voice held caution and fear. "You can't see that. It's pitch-black in here."

She made too much sense.

"I have great eyes. You know that." He didn't lie to her.

"The best eyes couldn't guide us. I didn't think you were serious. You haven't stumbled once." She sounded scared.

She let go of his hand, then backed away.

"Vere, I am your commanding officer." He kept his voice firm.

"Are you?" She retreated one more step.

"Don't be stupid. Of course I am. Just take my hand, and we can get out of here."

"Then tell me how a man can see in the dark!"

His mind raced. If he told her, she could bolt. She might run either way, so what did he have to lose?

"I don't know how, but I can—that's the truth."

She stepped back, stumbled, and fell over. "Ouch. That really hurt!" She gritted her teeth, jumping back to her feet.

"Now you know what a pain in the ass you are." That got her attention. "You can take your chances with me, with Zairoc, or your fantastic coordination."

"I think the last one might be the worst." She sighed with worry.

She reached out for him, so he grabbed her hand.

"Olly, Olly oxen free! Come out, come out, wherever you are!" Zairoc's ominous laugh carried through the dark corridors.

The wizard spoke like a madman. Chills penetrated to Trick Mark's core. He and Vere both tensed, not even breathing, for fear that Zairoc might find them. The wizard lurked close by, but Trick Mark couldn't see him. He put his finger over Vere's mouth so she would stay quiet. He helped her move up the stairs. Footsteps echoed louder, growing closer. Trick Mark tried to move fast, without making any sound.

"You know, I'm tired of this game. I really wanted to kill you face to face. But I'll settle for you knowing that this place will be your tomb. Kind of like an ancient pharaoh; if you knew what that was, you'd be honoured. Be thankful you die now, instead of in three months' time, watching those you love die all around you." Zairoc laughed gleefully.

Trick Mark clenched his jaw, running harder. Vere stumbled as she tried to keep pace. Zairoc played with them like a cat torturing a mouse. Trick Mark wanted nothing more than to beat the wizard into the ground, but he could only run from him.

The whole complex shook with dust and debris pouring down. Trick Mark stopped, to keep his footing. He looked back. Zairoc remained hidden, but the glowing wand rose high off the floor. No doubt, the wizard floated with it.

Huge parts of the ceiling rained down. Trick Mark bolted up a few stairs, stopping to catch his balance as he dodged falling stones. A few more steps and he and Vere made it to the next level. They sprinted hard. Vere struggled to stay with him, and to her credit, she did.

The rumbling grew louder as the complex came apart all around them. They raced through the great hall, changing course when enormous pieces of ceiling crashed down mere steps ahead. Trick Mark held onto Vere, who almost bolted right into the path of the falling debris. Trick Mark sensed an exit, but huge rocks blocked their way.

He pulled Vere back in the other direction. The floor opened—he yanked Vere around it. Faint moonlight filtered in through the holes above. One of the hundred-year-old trees smashed to the ground right behind them. If only he could fly, like Zairoc, they'd escape in a second.

They approached the surface. Another cave-in blocked their escape. Trick Mark reached out with his second sight, but all the raining debris made it a jumble of confusion.

Where could they go? The complex fell apart all around them. A wall cracked open and, behind it, in the distance, a stairwell led upwards. It might ascend to the surface, or it might crumble to rubble by the time they reached it—but he had to try. He pulled Vere in the direction of the stairs. As the complex came apart, more of the forest above fell like a torrential storm.

The trees that Zairoc had used like puppets now threatened to crush them alive. Each tree falling sounded like a shriek of death. They closed the distance and made it several more yards to the staircase. Trick Mark looked back at Vere. In the faint moonlight, he could make out her terrified face. She bravely didn't say a word while he dragged her around, blind to where they moved. Yet, in the faint light, she could see just enough to keep pace with him.

They landed on the stairs. They raced upward until the steps disintegrated under their feet. As Trick Mark and Vere fell, he couldn't help but remember the wizard's words: this would be their tomb, after all.

CHAPTER TEN

S ir Francis hopped up the stone steps, causing a doorman to open the tall, polished wooden door. Displayed above the entrance, carved into new brass, shone the words: CITY HALL. Sir Francis gave the attendant a polite smile without breaking his stride as he entered. Having Ondreeal stay at the castle last night had brought him more joy than he thought possible. To find Aleenda's long-lost daughter, someone capable of fighting against Zairoc, felt like a dream come true.

A flash, a premonition made him stop and close his eyes tightly. In his mind's eye, he lay on the ground, bruised and beaten. Zairoc stood over him with his glowing red wand. Until now, the vision had only ever occurred in the night. They'd been coming with greater frequency. That must mean the wand had warned him of some approaching trial, in days or months—that remained unclear. However, a demonstration of Ondreeal's power for the council would boost morale significantly in the north, creating a powerful force that not even Zairoc could stop. Sir Francis would make certain of it.

He took a deep breath and opened his eyes. Sir Francis looked down at the expectant face of a young man, dressed in a plain brown uniform. He bowed deeply to the wizard.

"Sir Francis, this way, please." The attendant led him down the hall to the new council chamber.

The workmanship and furnishings that had gone into the building showed high quality: crystal chandeliers, red velvet rugs, and gold-leaf trim decorating all the pillars. It possessed a finish that Bastion's drafty, old stronghold did not. This place reminded him of a beautiful, five-star hotel, one found in the heart of a great city before the attack, long since turned to dust.

A second, identically dressed attendant opened the door to the council chamber. Then Sir Francis stopped dead. It was not the five governors or the ten guild and trade masters who assembled that gave him pause. In contrast, the enormous, imposing oil painting that hung on the back wall certainly did. It depicted Sir Francis in flowing white robes, a ferocious look on his face. He shot magical energy out of the wand, exacting vengeance on some poor soul not seen fit to be a part of the picture. He hoped he would never see that painting again, although it evoked pride and confidence from his people.

"Sir Francis, we are pleased you could attend," Tolin, one of the trade masters, welcomed him, speaking with great care.

He ran a hand over his shiny head and adjusted his glasses, too small for his round face. He shifted in the chair he sat upon, his wide frame barely contained within. Tolin was a good man and leader amongst the merchants. Not born of noble blood, he made a great deal of coin in trade. Money remained the universal ticket up the ladder of social standing.

Looking rather worried, the others didn't appear to have pleasant moods. The five governors sat opposite Sir Francis at the monstrous, square, polished red wood table. On his left sat the guild masters, and, of course, on his right sat Tolin with the trade masters.

Governor Eechin, a well-respected man, had provided kind leadership that had led the city of Alexandria to flourish. Governor Travis operated by the book, allowing Angellus City to run like clockwork. Governor Hallis took risks, which meant Hamlet City sometimes prospered or suffered. Governor Xilic, a former military man, made Centaurus City worthy of its namesake. Governor Bauch of Athena City, the only female governor, had steel-grey hair precisely cropped just below her ears, and an angular, imposing face, and a personality to match. All made for good leaders in their own right, yet pressure from the south continued to mount.

"I am pleased to be here, Tolin." Sir Francis cleared his throat, trying to ignore the painting of himself above the governor's heads. "I am here to address your concerns, so let us begin."

Eechin shifted in his seat, pulling at the hems of his brocade garment that would resemble a Japanese Yukata if not for the gold embroidery. "Concerns? That would be quite the understatement." His raven eyes peered at Sir Francis, his mouth set firmly and framed by a closely cropped beard.

"What Eechin is trying to say is, we have bloody chaos!" Xilic unclenched his fists, sitting back in his chair and looking more worried than usual. He folded his hands, wearing the traditional red leather armour of Hamlet City. A bright-white rim of hair neatly encircled his otherwise smooth skull.

"I authorized forty shipments which never made it to their destinations because of the dark wizard Zairoc." Hallis sighed, understandably upset, his deep-blue eyes darkened until they almost matched his grey hair. He wiped crumbs from his chin that fell onto his simple blue robe.

"Then, perhaps, you should have been more careful," Sir Francis shot back at them.

Travis swallowed nervously. "Pardon me, Sir Francis, but we do everything we can to hold this nation together — *your* nation." His face flushed as his eye spectacle fell into his hands. He quickly restored it, shifting in his dark-grey robes.

Sir Francis's hard lines softened. "You are all exceptional leaders. Your cities have continued to flourish, despite trade route disruption. Each city is designed to act as its own self-reliant entity."

Eechin sat tensely, obviously hoping his words would not anger Sir Francis. "That may be the case. But we have also come to rely on each other. Is it not you that said we must work together for a bright and prosperous future?"

"I agree with Eechin." Xilic huffed out his frustration. He clearly didn't like having the lower hand.

All the governors nodded in agreement. Sir Francis couldn't have expected them to stand up to Zairoc. In their eyes, he was an all-powerful dark wizard who lived up to that image.

"You do not need me to govern," Sir Francis insisted.

Bauch sighed deeply, brushing a lock of long, steel-grey hair away. She spoke only when she felt it was absolutely necessary. She said quietly, but firmly, "No? You are our guide. You were my father's guide and my grandfather's too. You are older than the cities themselves, so legend says. When have we been on our own?"

"True." Sir Francis reluctantly agreed with a nod. "But you must know that I have the utmost confidence in each of you. We will stop these attacks with your help. I will also provide wards: magical shields to protect each of the five cities. This will guard against a wizard's attack."

The governors looked at each other for a moment.

Bauch beamed at him with anticipation. "What about this girl we've heard whispers of? Could she be the key to salvation, like everyone is saying?"

"I believe she could be." Sir Francis checked the faces of all assembled.

They erupted into excited chatter as hope spread like wildfire. Sir Francis allowed himself a moment of pride. This was what they needed, to galvanize and unite.

Xilic smashed the table. "We need to see a demonstration of her power."

Everyone fell silent, turning to stare at Xilic. Some of the tradespeople and merchants shifted uncomfortably, unsure of Sir Francis's reaction. Xilic shrunk under Sir Francis's cold stare.

Travis nodded emphatically. "I agree with Xilic. We must see her power with our own eyes. It's the only way we can move forward with confidence."

Bauch folded her hands, sitting forward. "We make a plan for defence. Then we see the girl's power. But we all must be back in our respective cities in two weeks' time. Sir Francis?"

Everyone sounded his or her acceptance of Bauch's words. She made a formidable woman. They all looked to Sir Francis, like children asking a parent for approval. But two weeks … what could he teach Ondreeal in that time? She hadn't even accepted her charge as a wizard. The fear and apprehension had been clear on her face. It would be no easy task to train her; nevertheless, he had to try. The north suffered under greater strain from Zairoc's ever more frequent raids. He could no longer ignore the dark wizard. The only way forward would be with Ondreeal at his side. If he had a hope of changing his vision, it rested with her.

"I have no doubt she will give you a great display of power," Sir Francis said with booming confidence that had yet to be proven.

Two weeks.

CHAPTER ELEVEN

C D-45 batted several blades of fauna away from his ocular units. They hit again, and CD lasered them, staring intently while smoke wafted up from the unmoving cut grass. He gazed up longingly at the clear, blue sky. He had yearned for adventure, true enough. He'd wanted to come to Earth and meet people; nevertheless, his main objective remained top priority.

One: find humans willing to crew the space fleet.

Two: locate technology capable of getting him back into orbit.

CD-45 wheeled through the long grasses until a farm appeared in view. His internal monitor flashed:

ENGAGING HUMANS IN SMALLER NUMBERS TO ACQUIRE ALLIES, 77 PERCENT CHANCE OF SUCCESS.

He hadn't found even one person with whom to converse, which made the light in his eyes dim. The word *ironic* fit his situation very well. Surrounded by humans and feeling more alone than ever ... yes, definitely an ironic development. What did he expect, though? After all the centuries on the orbital platforms, pop culture had inevitably changed.

Probability of finding someone who understood what *pop culture* meant: 1.5 percent.

He approached the farm where a man worked in the fields with a woman, perhaps husband and wife. Two smaller children popped out of the house, racing up to the woman. Yes, this comprised a happy family, perfect for CD-45's attempt to make first contact.

He set his treads in motion and headed out onto the field, making sure to stay in clear view of them from a distance. He didn't want to scare them. The mother noticed him first, and he could tell from the expression on her face that she experienced shock. Drat. Her husband followed her gaze, and when he saw CD-45, his expression transformed to one of fear. The children had the most positive reactions, beaming with amazement and excitement. They all stood there, frozen for a moment, until the young girl took a step towards CD. The mother wailed, grabbing her two children. The father screamed, and they all hurried back into the house.

Heartbroken, that's what CD-45 would be if he had a heart. What else could he do? He'd found not even one person who would have been likely to recognise a robot or any form of advanced technology. His greatest probability of success involved making alliances, even with primitive humans.

So, he picked a few wildflowers while the family watched him through the windows. This would give them time to become acquainted and comfortable with his appearance. He approached the door with the substantial bouquet of blooms, politely knocking. The mother opened the door a bit, her eyes wide, yet she smiled at CD-45. Definitely progress, the good kind of progress he'd been hoping for. She looked like a pleasant woman, with a plain grey dress and matching bonnet. She gawked down at him with her wide, blue eyes. How nice to have the company of people again. He extended his hand, holding out the flowers.

Then the husband came to the door with a primitive weapon. He clutched a rather large axe. CD-45 turned to leave, though not before the man struck hard with the weapon. Lucky for CD, he was comprised of tougher material. He looked back.

The man regarded the two broken pieces of his axe.

CD-45 accessed his internal monitor. An image of caution levels with a horizontal bar, framed with a 0 percent at one end and 100 percent at the other, appeared on his screen. He increased his caution from 65 to 83 percent. Obviously, his appearance created alarm. Well, he'd like to see how good they looked when they reached nineteen hundred years old.

With no one to maintain it, most of the technology CD-45 could recognise had failed; although, he did calculate a high probability of finding a ship to take him back up to the orbital platforms. Then he registered several faint but clear energy signatures scattered throughout the landscape, all of them, Alpha Four Five. He changed direction, heading towards them. They represented a significant clue to the mystery of this world—what had transpired here over the centuries.

He was rolling over the landscape amid sunrays waning in intensity when he noticed his power levels dropping. That shouldn't happen to an energy source rated for over forty million hours of use. He stopped, and with his mechanical hands he opened an access port on his side. He pressed the right sequence of buttons, then out popped his battery: fractured. That farmer may have broken his axe on CD-45, but he'd managed to hit with enough force to crack the power cell. What would humans say right about now? Oh, yes: *shit*.

A holo-image of his home factory appeared on his internal monitor with two words flashing: GENERATOR REPAIR. CD-45 slowly shook his head. That factory had turned to dust long ago. Now his battery would slowly haemorrhage kilowatts until full depletion. His miniature though efficient solar panels held a full charge, however; that energy would only flow directly to the generator for recharging. To bypass this and use solar power directly would require the assistance of at least two other CD units. Help. Oh, somebody, help him.

His sensors indicated a seismic event just three kilometres from his location, along with an energy spike of Alpha Four Five. He rolled his way over to investigate, even though it guaranteed further depletion of energy reserves. However, his programming stated that he needed to render assistance whenever possible. Besides, all directions currently provided an equal probability of finding assistance with his battery.

CD wheeled between tall grasses, travelling over the landscape. A city had once stood here, but his internal mapping system couldn't accurately mark his location. He didn't have much time to ponder the thought as he came upon the rubble of a buried structure. One of the newer ones constructed — that's how it would have lasted this long. Something caused it to collapse in an unusual way. His scans revealed dark red, the residual technological energy signature of Alpha Four Five, on the rubble. He just couldn't put his metal finger on it. He scanned the debris again for two green energy signatures he recognized: human life signs. Sigh. This was going to take a lot of reserve power.

CHAPTER TWELVE

Ondreeal gazed around the magnificent Lumenary. Carved artfully into the stone above the grand doors hung cryptic phrases — SEVEN IN ALL, SEVEN WITH THE POWER, SEVEN TO BRING US UP TO THE HEAVENS AND LIVE AMONG THE STARS. Rows of polished, light-brown pews lined the long aisle covered in one extensive golden rug. Tall windows towered on either side of the great space, framed with curtains the exact colour of the carpet. Stained-glass windows allowed long beams of light to filter in, making the hall sparkle brightly with the colours from panes of many sizes.

The ceiling displayed a tiled representation of the Path of Light, similar to one she'd seen in a book. Either side showed the dark, eternal desert where the soulless ones wandered. Dark demons tortured them in an endless dance of pain. The golden-yellow bricks of the Path cut through the middle of the hellish scene and stretched into the distance, melding into a pure-white aura of light that represented the God of All. On one side of that aura stood the tall Embertree, and on the other, the wide Cindertree. Above this, seven guardians of light, in flowing robes, watched over the Path.

Ondreeal should go back to the square and wait for Sir Francis. But it couldn't hurt to look around a little longer. She turned back to the shrine before her. Ondreeal stared up at the cross that looked to be solid gold. Five tendrils of a sea creature representing the God of All hung all over it. Did God really exist? If she didn't believe, she might be lost, doomed to wander the eternal desert.

Otto had no use for religion, and he'd told her that if God existed, he could bloody well help with the chores. Her worry and her questions had quickly evaporated as she returned to her work, although the question of what happened after death stayed with her.

"Beautiful, is it not?"

Ondreeal turned to a man who looked like a fighter. He dressed all in white robes, but his well-muscled stance and light step showed the truth of his ability. His clothes contrasted with the other Embers, who wore brown boots, pants, and tunic, with no weapon. The Embers spread religious teachings throughout the land to everyone, whether they believed in the God of All or not. Mostly, they aided the downtrodden or helped enforce the rules of the church.

The man held up a book with the same cross, laced with tendrils and set in gold on the thick, black leather cover. He had snuck up behind Ondreeal without the slightest sound. All the Embers trained their bodies to wield lethal force, and sometimes their faith led them to kill, so kill they did. The rumours that made it to the farm told tales of whole villages cleansed of soulless wanderers—that's what they called nonbelievers. Some swore that the Embers could catch an arrow or knife with their bare hands.

"I won't hurt you," he reassured Ondreeal with open arms.

She must have looked frightened.

Long, dark hair and distinctive hazel eyes accentuated his handsome features. "I'm afraid you are too late for morning absolution and far too early for evening circle."

She blinked at him.

His eyes radiated with charm. "Have you come for the Path?"

"I'm waiting for someone," she managed to get out as she stared at him.

"And someone is who you have found." He bowed his head slightly.

She should tell him she waited for Sir Francis. Ondreeal had kept her guard up since arriving in Bastion. Her whole body vibrated with fear and anticipation, but that lessened within these holy walls. Why? What power did this place possess?

"Have—have you been an Ember a long time?" she stammered.

He nodded with a laugh.

"Yes, you could say that."

Did he find her amusing? There was something about him, different from others of his faith.

"You are one of the misfortuned?" he suggested.

He looked at her dirty, torn clothes, then back to her eyes. With nothing at the castle for Ondreeal to wear except for a servant's uniform, Sir Francis had insisted that they find something more for her.

"This happened at the arena," she blurted out.

"You are the girl I have heard so much about, the one who called down lightning itself." He stared at her with awe.

"To be honest, I don't know how that happened. Or if it even was me." She clasped her sweaty palms.

"Perhaps you did come for absolution after all." He studied her face.

"I didn't lie. I was fighting for my life. It just happened." Her lips wouldn't stop flapping, as if this Ember held the power to make her talk endlessly.

He might cut her down for lying. She wasn't a true believer, which must be obvious to him.

"I won't tell a single soul. What you say in these walls remains here." His voice washed over her, so soft and inviting.

She felt her heart beat in her chest.

"You don't think I'm a soulless wanderer?" Her voice trembled ever so slightly.

"No. Anyone who could find their way from the centre of the arena to this great hall is on a path of their own. Perhaps I could help make the way clear?" His sparkling eyes bored into hers.

"I should find my friend." She scurried around him and raced for the door.

"You see, I told you — you were on a path."

She stopped and turned back to him.

"Ours will cross again: of this I am certain."

She took a step towards him. "How do you know that?"

He smiled knowingly. "It is my job as the Lord of Light."

Not simply the beacon of this Lumenary, the Lord of Light was the holy leader of the entire faith. He commanded an army of the Embertree. She had tried to learn all she could about the world, but with only Otto on the farm, she remained largely ignorant beyond village life. What could she say to such a holy leader?

"That would make sense." She dipped her head to hide her flushed cheeks.

He strolled towards her and she resisted the urge to turn and run. He almost walked right past her, then stopped and held out his palm. He must want her to kiss it.

"Take my hand," he ordered her.

She did as commanded, and he guided her to the door. He grabbed her other hand, holding them both together between his palms; he closed his eyes. Ondreeal wanted to run. She tried to pull free from his strong grip.

"Give me your name," he demanded.

"Please, let go," she pleaded.

He wouldn't move. Then his grip tightened until her teeth clenched with pain.

"Your name," he demanded again.

"Ondreeal. My name is Ondreeal!" she screamed at him.

"May my light guide you on your journey, Ondreeal." He opened his eyes, which pierced right through her.

He let go of her hands, stepping past her to open the front door to the Lumenary.

"If you will allow me..." He held the door open. "I will say once more, our paths will cross again, Ondreeal."

He bowed deeply while she backed out the entrance. She had barely moved clear when he closed the door in her face. She looked around in the bright sun. A bustle of activity covered the square as everyone moved in different directions. Like an orchestrated dance, it changed shape and speed, ebbing and flowing while never ending. Beyond the throng, the shadow of the castle stretched towards the Lumenary.

"Ondreeal! What are you doing?" Sir Francis sounded cross.

She turned to see him march towards her, looking as ill-tempered and worried as he sounded.

"What are you doing at this place? I told you to wait in the square," he snapped at her.

She defended herself. "I did wait. I was curious, that's all."

Sir Francis pulled her close to his side.

"That is a place full of lies and archaic beliefs. It is no place for you," he whispered, guiding her away.

***

Ondreeal fought to get out of the waves of material, until she finally burst through the surface of lace and found air. The two storekeepers, dressed in green satin dresses, smoothed out the pieces of her garment.

The store smelled of dust and old lace, in contrast to the bright candles scattered throughout. She emerged from behind the half wall and found Sir Francis beaming proudly at her.

"There, now you look like a lady of the court. My dear, you'll fit right in." He sounded confident.

Ondreeal looked around the fancy shop as the storekeepers guided her to a mirror. Her frilly reflection equalled everything else in the shop. In fact, she looked like one of those spirits of light depicted in the Lumenary, watching over the Path. She shone in a bright-blue dress that would perfectly complement a ballroom filled with elite citizens.

For the protector of the entire north, it amazed her that Sir Francis had time to shop. Since placing the fate of the world on her shoulders only two days ago, they talked often. He wanted to hear about her life on the farm, and he told her about Bastion along with its many wonders. She found herself wanting to stay in Bastion with each story he told. The motto of the north, "Freedom for all," lived true within the walls of this city. She'd be happy to call this place home.

In all of their conversations, she could tell he wanted one answer: would she train to become a wizard?

She pictured the wand, lying on the long table in Sir Francis's study. She couldn't wait much longer before agreeing to Sir Francis's request.

"There is one more I would like to try, Sir Francis," she suggested tactfully.

"Very well." He almost imperceptibly slouched.

Ondreeal went into the back room and pointed to a simple dress in a beautiful shade of violet. She tried it on, smiling at her reflection. She glided out, and from the look on Sir Francis's face, he liked it too.

"I never was very good at dress buying," he admitted with a smile. "That shade would look beautiful with the wand."

He spoke as if she'd already said yes. If she told him no, what would he do? In his smile, she found warmth, kindness, and a love she'd never known. Qualities she'd always wanted in a father. Yet her belly churned in his presence, the truth of his power overshadowed all other feelings.

Ondreeal forced herself to smile back. "Sir Francis, the dress is beautiful, but it's not me. I did grow up on a farm after all."

He nodded in agreement. "So, you did."

Ondreeal searched the store high and low until she found exactly what she wanted. She quickly put the clothes on, jumping out of the dressing stall with excitement.

The store clerks gawked, utterly appalled. "Those clothes are meant for a boy, not a girl."

Ondreeal stared into the mirror, smiling from ear to ear. She resembled more of a male, dressed in cotton pants, a cotton shirt, and a leather vest, but she felt more like herself than she had in days. Sir Francis didn't appear displeased. He looked almost sad.

"You don't approve, do you?" She didn't fit in with the elite of Bastion, yet she couldn't pretend to be someone she wasn't.

Hopefully, he wouldn't grow angry with her. Her feet shifted, ready to run from the store. Nevertheless, fear froze them in place.

"You just remind me of a different time. I do get a little nostalgic now and then. You look perfect, my dear." His eyes twinkled, brightening a wrinkled, old face.

***

As they walked back to the castle, Ondreeal caught numerous stares from the citizens of Bastion. She looked to Sir Francis, afraid he'd somehow disapprove of her clothes out in public.

"You left the wand on the table. I hoped you might have come back for it." He waved serenely at a citizen.

"I…" Her heart beat faster.

"Of the seven wands, four are hidden by the wizards that wield them. They fear Zairoc's power is too great, so they care only for their corners of the world. Yet, unless we unite all of them, we have no hope of survival. With you on my side, we could defeat Zairoc and find the others, before it's too late." He nodded at every passer-by.

"I just wish I knew something of magic." Ondreeal fidgeted with her hands.

"Let me show you." Sir Francis stepped to the middle of the massive city square, framed by the Lumenary on one end and the castle on the other.

He pulled out his wand, which glowed pale green as he raised it over his head. He muttered several words, prompting a bright flash from the wand. A humble ball of emerald light shot into the sky, rising impossibly high before it burst. In its place, a light-green symbol shone. It comprised a cross, with lines curving outwards at each of the four ends, like half-moons. Then it vanished.

"Wards — protections spell for every city of the north. A constant drain on my magic, though I can maintain it from anywhere in the world. I won't be strong enough if faced one-on-one against Zairoc. But now, I won't have to." He gazed at her with such hope.

Could she tell him that fear kept her from taking the wand?

Sir Francis headed for the castle. She sighed deeply, looking skyward before following him. They found themselves alone once more in the halls of the castle. Ondreeal batted away the many cobwebs that lined the corridor.

"You were going to take me down here in a dress?"

Sir Francis didn't mind the webbing at all. He pushed it aside and found his way to a brick wall — blank except for a long, shallow shelf that spanned the length of it. He ran his fingers over each stone, pressing on different ones, testing the strength of their construction.

"Uh, Sir Francis, what are you doing?"

He could be a wizard: sweet, kind, and full of knowledge, or merely a delusional, old man, she couldn't say either way. Others would call him insane for the things he had already told her.

"It's around here somewhere," he mumbled.

"Sir Francis, is it true that you are as old as they say?"

Sir Francis hit his head on a shelf that hung much too low.

"I am quite old. I stopped counting at a thousand. The wand gives life. That is why you must not grow too attached to people. You will outlive them all." He continued to search the wall.

For a moment, she couldn't even form words. She had already touched the wand. Could she give it back if she didn't want it? She didn't know many people, but to outlive them all — to make bonds with them, only to see them die... The prospect made anger build in the pit of her stomach.

"Why wouldn't you tell me that? It's an important part that will change my whole life."

He stopped, sighed, and turned to her.

"I didn't want to scare you more than you already are. There is much I want to tell you. But to hear it all at once is far too much. You must learn it, a bit at a time, like the use of the wand. Do you understand?"

He looked at her like a concerned parent, or at least what she imagined one would look like. Ondreeal nodded, so Sir Francis went back to searching the masonry. His hand hovered above the surface, and he guided it around until he stopped. Then a strange light jumped out, covering his palm. The wall quickly moved aside, and Ondreeal ran for cover. No one could deny that he held great power.

Darkness filled the inside until lights popped on, inviting them to enter the space. He could make passageways, why not flames appearing from nowhere inside glass orbs? The dust-filled room held several objects, arrow targets, and trinkets.

"What is all this?" She curiously peered around the room.

He stood a little taller. "Practice."

He wanted to start training. To say yes to this meant claiming the wand. He'd shown her such patience and kindness, but fear floated within her, like waves on a shore ebbing and waning while she fidgeted with her hands. His warm eyes pleaded with her in a way no other ever had. If he had told her the truth about the wand and the world, then she couldn't say no.

"I'll try my best." She met his gaze, hoping he understood.

"That's all I ask." He smiled, but his throat clenched with emotion, and tears filled his eyes.

For the first time since she had arrived in Bastion, she breathed deeply and gave him a genuine smile.

CHAPTER THIRTEEN

Darkness surrounded Trick Mark, but this didn't bother him. It accompanied him like an old friend, comforting and familiar. The huge pile of rocks and debris above his head could soon crush him alive. He couldn't stand straight or move more than a foot in any direction. The smell of his sweat filled the cramped space. Mixing with sterile debris and dust, it created some kind of soapy scent. He laughed for a moment. What an odd smell— and it might be his last. He reached out with his second sight, also extending his arms, a reflex from when he had been truly blind, relying on only four senses instead of six. Ghostly images formed in his mind's eye, like they did each time he used his ability, forming the outline of the rocky rubble that encased him.

"Vere?"

The sound of sand falling along with creaking rubble met his ears. She could be trapped in a coffin of stones just like Trick Mark, or worse, she'd been crushed alive. Zairoc had made good on his promise to put them in a tomb. Trick Mark did know about tombs, despite what that cocky asshole Zairoc thought about him.

That evil wizard would amount to nothing without his magic. Trick Mark pictured killing him with one blow. He would enjoy that, the opportunity to see Zairoc bleed. Sir Francis told him he might get the chance one day, that his arrows could kill Zairoc given the right circumstances, because they could home in on any target. Trick Mark didn't believe Sir Francis, though he would never dare tell him that.

No opening. Trick Mark remained in a sealed tomb, the worst kind of place for a living being.

"Vere. Guinevere! Answer me." His voice sounded hollow in the meager space.

Silence. His exceptional hearing would pick up her words, even through all this debris. He must accept that she had died here. All his men had perished because of a lack of leadership. If he had chosen a different area to patrol, perhaps they never would have run into Zairoc. His men would live on, along with Vere. He screamed, but it sounded empty in the tiny space.

He sensed movement in the rubble above. Sand with debris rained down for a moment, then stopped. Trick Mark raised his dust-covered head, coughing. At least he wouldn't starve to death or suffocate. Not that he liked the idea of dying at all, but one heavy stone to the head would end it.

Maybe he'd see his father again, somewhere on the Path of Light. A lump formed in his throat. He held back tears. He shook his head, pushing that feeling aside. He stood up as straight as he could in the cramped space. If death took him, it wouldn't be curled into a ball, crying for daddy. He pushed against the debris above him until his muscles shook from the effort. He may not be able to avoid dying now, though he would sure as hell try to escape this tomb.

Nothing.

It wouldn't even budge an inch.

"Come on, move!"

He smashed the stones until his hand became wet with his blood. He pushed again with all his might, and, to his surprise, the behemoth stone above him lifted away, light as a feather. He must have gained some kind of new power. If so, the God of All could keep them coming. The stone floated away. If that wasn't fantastical enough, behind it sat the strangest creature he'd ever sensed.

Trick Mark had braced himself against the rubble, or he would have fallen over, staring wide-eyed. Amazing creatures lived out here in the Enchanted Lands, though he had never met one until now. He fought to keep his body calm. He consciously slowed his breathing. The creature wouldn't hurt him. It didn't make sense to save his life just to cause harm. What could he say to such an impressive being?

"Hello." Trick Mark's voice sounded meek.

It just stared, easily throwing the boulder away without even touching it. Trick Mark gawked in amazement, trying to make sense of it all.

"Thank you. You saved my life."

It nodded in agreement.

"You can understand me?"

It nodded again. Trick Mark reached out and found its smooth edges, cold, like metal. Its insides felt crammed full of moving pieces, much more than he ever sensed in any other being. It recoiled from his touch. Trick Mark yanked his arm back; hopefully, he hadn't offended the creature.

"I'm sorry, you are an unusual being. But you did free me, so I would be happy to call you a friend."

It extended its hand. Trick Mark hesitated, then shook it. Its palm felt like metal, too, yet it was alive. It seemed to understand language and compassion, but beyond this, he had no idea as to its origin. He reached out with his second sight, listening for a heartbeat. He heard one, faint at first, then it grew stronger.

"If I try to move, it could cause the rubble beneath me to give way. I'm open to suggestions."

Then Trick Mark floated into the air. Magic! A magical being had saved him. He screamed, gliding up over the rubble. The creature caught fire underneath itself as it, too, lifted into the air. This didn't bother it in the slightest.

Together they rose out of the strange ruins. They hovered high over grassy meadows and trees, which lined a long stretch to either side of the newly formed hollow. The cave-in stretched out in either direction. Inside the newly formed chasm in the ground lay a place of the ancients.

"Trick!"

Vere's frantic voice called from the distance. Trick Mark had been mistaken. The heartbeat he'd sensed moving closer belonged to Vere, not the strange creature! She stood at the edge of the gigantic fissure, waving.

"Stay back, Vere!" His voice conveyed an assurance he didn't have while he drifted through the air.

He and his new companion landed on a grassy meadow next to her. She threw her arms around Trick Mark. He hugged her back, smiling at the sight of her. "How did you get out of there?"

"Same way as you, with the help of our guardian angel." Her eyes locked with Trick Mark's, and for a moment, he thought she might kiss him.

He nodded once. "I'm glad to see you're all right."

"You, too, sir," she shot back.

The medium-sized creature waved its arms at them. They slowly turned their heads, peering at the strange being.

Vere sounded as amazed as Trick Mark felt. "I think it wants to be included."

Trick Mark knelt down beside it. "Do you have a name?"

Its arm pointed at its body. Trick Mark sensed the creature's frame, smooth, with no signs of raised lettering he could touch.

"Your name is CD-45?" Vere sounded confused, but the creature nodded.

"It's unusual and matches everything else about you, my friend. If that is what you would like to be called, then that is what we will call you. I am Trick Mark and this is Vere." It saluted them, so Trick Mark returned the gesture.

"We need to get back home." Vere sounded worried.

Trick Mark reached out with his second sight. He could sense the chasm that opened up between them and the city, maybe two days' journey from their current location. It would add an extra day or more, just to walk around it.

Trick Mark shook his head with a sigh. "I don't know if I want to relay the bad news."

Explaining the loss of his men to Sir Francis would prove difficult. More than that, Zairoc told them of a future attack on Bastion to occur in just a few months.

"Killing the patrol was only the first step of his plan."

"Vere, he was after me." He turned away from her.

"I know."

His head snapped over to her with surprise, then he quickly looked away.

"He said you possessed a strange power," Vere crossed her arms. "He said that it was a threat to him. Now I think I have a good idea of what that is."

He shouldn't have said anything. The cold bodies of his comrades lay not far away. Vere moved so that he faced her. She wanted an answer and wouldn't let him leave the conversation until she got one.

"I'm the commander of the northern forces. The last time, we met in battle. I shot him with one of my arrows, and ever since then, he has had a personal vendetta against me, nothing more. They all died because of me."

Thankfully, he couldn't tell what expression she had on her face with his second sight. She'd likely punch or throttle him. He tensed his body, waiting for the onslaught of anger from Vere. Trick Mark deserved whatever punishment she sentenced him with.

"He did this, not you. He is every bit the evil wizard that people say." She put her hands on his face, and he reflexively grabbed them.

He'd found a truly forgiving soul in Vere. Or perhaps it came from blind devotion. He didn't deserve such absolution. Nevertheless, the God of All would ultimately judge him.

"I think the dark wizard told us of an attack on Bastion, within the next several months." Trick Mark searched her dark eyes for her reaction.

"If that's true, then he'll make sure he finishes us. Dead soldiers tell no tales. That means he can't be far away," Vere whispered.

A lightning bolt shot down, exploding near their feet. Vere screamed as they both went flying.

They fell hard, but on the grassy hill, they couldn't hope for a softer landing. Trick Mark grabbed Vere, yanking her close. Several more lightning bolts landed all around them. They screamed in chorus until the bolts relented, for a single heartbeat. Trick Mark pulled Vere up, frantically sprinting away.

CD-45 rolled beside them on its strange feet, if you could even call them that.

The God of All couldn't have judged him already. No, those were blasts from a wand. Trick Mark glimpsed the sky. He couldn't feel the clouds or the stars. They hung too far away. But he did recognise the vibration of a wizard's wand. No doubt, this one belonged to Zairoc.

CHAPTER FOURTEEN

With his second sight, the starry sky cast a ghostly glow on the field of grass, creating dark silhouettes, while shots from the wand landed like sharp, white comets all around. Trick Mark and Vere raced for the cover of the trees. Several lightning blasts from the wand landed in their path, making them stop hard or face incineration. They came so near to one, Trick Mark's hair stood up on his neck. Trick Mark pulled Vere to him amid the frenzied bolts, and she clung tightly. Her whole body tensed. The next moment could be their deaths. Zairoc would celebrate his triumphant butchering of so many.

CD-45 stopped close by, creating a magical umbrella made of light above its head. Trick Mark pulled Vere underneath it as several more lightning strikes exploded around the meadow. Trick Mark stared in wonderment when three shots hit the umbrella without harming them. Vere breathed heavily in relief. CD-45 was truly a magical being, capable of defending against a wizard's attack. It made for a valuable ally, one that would fill Sir Francis with gratitude.

Another lightning bolt hit the umbrella, accompanied by a beeping sound from CD-45. The creature looked panicked as it launched itself forward at great speed. Together, Trick Mark and Vere followed in a manic race. CD-45 slowed down long enough for them to remain under its protection. Then it sped towards the forest. Another jolt of lightning hit the umbrella. It flickered for a second, making Vere shriek with fear. Perhaps CD-45's powers had limits.

Several lightning strikes exploded in the trees. They entered the forest. Branches rained down on them, bouncing off the umbrella of light. The protective shield flickered again, then disappeared. Amid the lightning blasts, the trees moved all around them. Trick Mark and Vere turned back-to-back, trembling at the stirring forest.

Trick Mark swallowed with fear. "Not this again."

"No, Trick." Vere squeezed his hand hard.

A needle-thin piece of metal extended out of CD-45's head, then spun around. The trees stopped moving towards them. Instead, they flailed around in place, with no direction. The lightning bolts erupted all over.

Trick Mark found it odd that they had landed so close before but now seemed random, as if Zairoc had gone suddenly blind. Their new friend must have done it, perhaps making them invisible to the wizard. CD-45 showed no sign of slowing down, so they tore after the creature. They headed deeper into the forest, the brightness of the lightning and crackle of each hit growing fainter with each passing moment.

***

Alpha Four Five, that's what tried to fry CD-45's circuits, not to mention, kill the humans he had just worked so very hard to save. His treads whined, speeding over the forest floor, Trick Mark and Vere trailing behind. This was a high technology used for death and destruction. What sane species would do such a thing? Unfortunately, both humans and the fanatical aliens in orbit seemed to agree that this made for a reasonable course of action. His internal monitor highlighted one of the blue dots representing Alpha Four Five, and changed it to a deep red with the words: DANGER LEVEL NINE — one shy of the highest risk level he could assign to any one event. In his list of priorities, "investigate remaining two known sources of alpha four five" moved up to number three. A logical suggestion, if he wanted to experience atomization. No, he needed to get back into orbit. Wait, this must be what it's like to argue with one's self! Although, it might mean he had developed multiple-personality disorder. How interesting. He would go visit a psychiatrist for evaluation if they hadn't all turned to dust, centuries ago.

At least he found two companions who could understand his origin as a mechanical being. He wheeled faster along the ground; his two rescued humans would keep pace, so no need to reduce speed. He might be creating assumptions, but he discarded such highly irrelevant thoughts, maintaining maximum ground propulsion.

***

No doubt remained that CD-45 possessed magical powers. If for no other reason, both Trick Mark and Vere struggled to keep up, sweating, huffing, and puffing, while the creature continued, unaffected by physical activity. Trick Mark glanced back at Vere, who tripped on a root, falling hard. He dug in his heel to stop himself, and trotted back. He stuck out a hand for Vere. She grabbed it, but they both fell back to the ground, covered in sweat. Vere mouthed the words, *thank you,* although she couldn't catch her breath to say them. Trick Mark gave her a thumbs-up, slumping down.

The morning sun filtered through the trees. He concentrated so hard on running that he didn't notice the change in his eyes from night vision to normal sight. The green leaves fluttered in the wind while faint morning light danced through them. The whine of CD-45 returning for them grew closer.

It stuck out its arm, holding up a bizarre thumb. It positioned its head closer to study Trick Mark, but in this case, they examined each other. Its face looked like that of shiny metal. But no living creature could have alloy for skin, so it must be something else. It's perfectly round eyes, with their dark centres, resembled wagon wheels. If it hadn't helped them, Trick Mark would have classified it as a demon. CD-45 represented a strange, though apparently living, being, made of something that looked just like the purest iron. It waved its hand slowly over his eyes. He watched it move back and forth. CD-45 seemed satisfied, maneuvering to a spot between and just behind them.

"Are we safe for now?" Vere breathed hard.

"I'd wager we lost the dark wizard."

"Do you think it's a he or a she?" Vere gestured to CD-45 as she propped herself up, wiping sweat from her face.

Trick Mark sat up, cross-legged, scoffing.

"After everything we've been through in the last several days, you want to know if this thing has boy parts or girl parts?"

"Well, yes." She raised an eyebrow at him.

Vere possessed an odd resilience he found quite endearing. Her curiosity made a welcome change from the constant fear.

"Why don't you check between its legs?"

He smirked, causing her to blush with embarrassment. The jovial moment felt refreshing, like cool water on a sweltering day. CD-45 slowly raised its hand. Vere and Trick Mark looked at each other with confusion.

"Oh, I didn't mean to offend you, CD-45. I just don't want to call you 'it.' I think that's rude." She shot the last comment back in Trick Mark's direction. "So, are you a she?"

Surrounded by men in the militia at all times, Vere looked hopeful for the company of another woman. CD-45 shook its head.

"Then you're a boy." Trick Mark feigned a prideful smile. CD-45 nodded once.

"Well, it's nice to know you, sir. We owe you our lives twice over." Vere kissed him on the head.

CD-45 responded with excitement, spinning around with his arms in the air. Vere laughed with Trick Mark.

"Easy, Vere, we don't know yet if he has a heart for you to break."

Vere beamed down at him. "What help do you need CD? May I call you CD for short? CD-45 is a bit of a mouthful."

He nodded his little head.

Trick Mark stood up. "Then I believe we are in your debt, CD."

The happy moment became serious as he locked eyes with Vere. Honour demanded they help CD-45, considering that they owed him their lives. A missing battalion would worry Sir Francis. Furthermore, the families of the deceased deserved to know what had happened to those brave soldiers, murdered by Zairoc. He planned to attack Bastion in full force. First, they needed to give aid to their rescuer and then return to Bastion with the dire news.

CD-45 turned, then once more headed deeper into the forest.

"No more than a day." Trick Mark pointed his finger at Vere.

"It's the least we could do before we go back." Vere looked worried behind her self-assured stare.

Trick Mark held his arm out, indicating for her to go first. She trotted after CD-45. A short delay, that's all it would amount to. None of the information coming from the south indicated a build-up of armed forces. They had months before Zairoc would attack, more than enough time to prepare. Trick Mark stared apprehensively at the green foliage before marching after Vere.

CHAPTER FIFTEEN

The grand courtyard of the castle didn't feel as intimidating as it had ten days ago. Well manicured, filled with an array of colourful flowers, it offered serenity Ondreeal didn't know how to accept.

Perched on a stone bench and wringing her hands, she watched the bustle of activity encompassing her. Several attendants arranged objects, including spears and wooden balls, around the courtyard. The attendants scurried off to the side, where they stood in a row against a wall. A couple of them glanced at her before looking away. She rose to her feet. Sir Francis excitedly rushed towards her.

Only an hour earlier, he had told her of a small demonstration for a couple of Bastion's citizens. She agreed to try it, although now she shook with apprehension. She clasped her hands tightly, only causing the tremors to move up her arms. If her mother watched from the Path, hopefully she'd gaze down with pride. Understandably, Ondreeal not only wanted to make her mother proud, but Sir Francis too.

A warm breeze quickly carried miniature puffs of cloud over a blue sky. On two balconies above, crowds of onlookers chattered loudly. At least fifty people stood on each one, far more than she had agreed to, their eyes all fixed on Ondreeal. Sir Francis nodded to the attendants before giving her a warm smile.

"Who are they?" Ondreeal asked as the onlookers perused her like a new exhibition.

Sir Francis glanced up with a practiced smile. "They are compromise, my dear."

"Compromise?" Ondreeal looked confused.

"Yes, no one is an island. Many are just curious, but among them is the council who support me and run the city. In exchange, I give them my protection. Sounds criminal, doesn't it?" He chuckled at his own joke.

"Why are so many here?" Her palms sweated with anticipation.

They'd practiced for almost two weeks with barely any progress. Ondreeal made a few objects float, nothing more. She caused a wooden sword to disappear — they hadn't found it yet.

"To see you, of course. You must give them a demonstration of your power. Once they see it, you will be granted the resources I have been given to help protect the lands." He tilted his head as if to say, *There, a simple answer for you.*

Sir Francis scurried over to a short though ornate table. He held up a black wooden box to the audience.

Sir Francis yelled up to the balconies. "This wand belonged to a great wizard, tragically struck down by the enemy at far too young an age. So, a great ally in the war against Zairoc was gone forever, her lineage believed lost to us. Now the fates have returned her daughter —,

"The God of All has brought Ondreeal here!" The Lord of Light's voice echoed loud and clear from above. "He set her on the true path. When darkness blinded her, his pure light shone the way."

The holy leader raised his hands to the audience. He spoke masterfully, and even Ondreeal stared, captivated by his words. She had to stop herself from nodding in agreement or risk offending Sir Francis.

The crowd responded in unison, "Praise be to the light!"

The Lord of Light fixed his gaze on Sir Francis, who glared back.

Ondreeal couldn't breathe.

Would Sir Francis call the holy leader a joke in front of everyone? Or worse, call him a liar? The powerful Sir Francis could protect himself, though he would alienate all the people here; surely, he knew that. Even if he thought of the Lord of Light as a fraud, challenging him publicly would only create animosity between them.

"Praise be to the light." Sir Francis bowed his head to the holy leader who returned the gesture. "I'll have you remember who protects that light."

"Of course, great wizard. I meant no disrespect." The Lord of Light bowed.

Ondreeal exhaled.

Sir Francis turned back.

Her breath caught again.

He slowly approached her with the wooden box, and she willed herself to be a great wizard.

He nodded at her to proceed.

Her fingers lightly held the edges as she flipped it open. Inside lay the wand, looking like nothing more than an ebony rod, polished and formed with more skill than anything she'd ever seen.

"Sir Francis?" She looked from the wand to him.

He met her gaze, beaming with pride. "Yes, my dear?"

"You've shown me such kindness. A life I've always dreamt of having. I have one request to make."

"Go on then." He looked anxious for her to start the demonstration.

"There's a whole life I almost had, but didn't. After this is done, you must promise to tell me everything about my mother and how she died."

Sadness darkened his blue eyes. He nodded twice to her.

She gently lifted the wand, watching it glow a beautiful, bright blue like it once had before. The audience looked very impressed. A few leaned over so far, they risked plummeting from the high balconies. Sir Francis backed away, leaving Ondreeal solo.

"I'll make you proud, Mother," she whispered to herself.

The wind whistled by her ears. Whispers fell from the balconies above. They all waited for a humbling display of her power. Sir Francis smiled up at the audience. He rushed back to her side.

"Why isn't it working?"

He recited his teachings from yesterday. "Just relax. The wand will do most of the work. See the object float in your mind, and the wand will do the rest."

He backed off again. Ondreeal stared at the array of objects around her. She eyed three wooden balls that lay on the ground in a neat row. She pointed the wand at them, and then it went dark in her hands. She pointed the wand with more conviction, though nothing happened. She heard the murmurs of disapproval from the audience above, and Sir Francis raced back to her side.

"What are you doing?" he snapped.

"I think it would be clear. I don't know. I don't know what I'm doing. You have made a mistake. That much is clear." Panic radiated out from her heart.

"Just picture the objects, think of what you want, and the wand will do it."

"I heard you. I'm trying to do just that. But it's not working."

"Just clear your head. Be calm. Take deep, even breaths." He sounded like a caring father.

She did as he asked, inhaling deeply. She pointed the wand at a series of spears. She thought of picking one up and throwing it into the air. The wand glowed. Her heart jumped into her throat. The wand might slip right out of her hands.

"Take deep, even breaths to focus."

His voice calmed her trembling body, though her heart wouldn't slow down. She thought again of the spears lifting off the ground and rising into the air. One of the spears rocked back and forth. Then the others moved. She smiled until she felt the air and looked to Sir Francis.

"It's just the wind," she admitted with disappointment.

A huge gale blew the spears right across the courtyard. The wind picked up and then swirled around so that the audience held on to their places for dear life. All the objects flew into the air, then swept around in the courtyard.

"That is most definitely the wind, and you are controlling it." Sir Francis chuckled and held his hands up in triumph.

She joined him in an excited laugh. She had wielded magic for the onlookers! She could become so much more than Otto had ever given her credit for.

Frighteningly, the wind grew stronger. Dark clouds formed above them. Thunder rolled and lightning struck. Several of the objects blasted apart. The audience backed away with screams of fear.

"What do I do?"

Ondreeal yanked the wand down to her side, but it did nothing to stop the mayhem. Sir Francis struggled to stay with her.

"Calm, Ondreeal. You must be the calm in the storm!" he yelled at her.

Torrential rain soaked the castle.

She raised the wand, trying to focus. Sir Francis plucked his wand from his robe. His power would set everything right again. But Sir Francis didn't have a chance to utter a single word — all the objects exploded, throwing him backward.

Ondreeal screamed as she turned to protect herself. Her eyes closed tightly, waiting for the broken weapons to hit her body. Where did the wind go? A sudden calm filled the world, a silence and stillness that only came late on a starlit night.

She stood there for several moments, attempting to slow her breathing, her eyes firmly closed. That is, until a 'moo' accompanied a wet tongue licking her face. She opened her eyes and found herself in the barn, *her* barn, the one in which she'd spent her whole life. Hazel the cow stared at her with big brown eyes. She screamed and collapsed on the hay-covered ground. Perhaps she had created an illusion.

Soaked head to toe, she clutched the now dark wand in her hand. She relaxed her grip just a little as she slowly stood. She moved to the barn door, touching the edges of the hole Otto had punched in it, a lifetime ago. Ranger neighed at her and stuck his long nose past the barn door. She stroked the end of Ranger's nose, tickling her fingers.

She shook her head, jaw open in amazement. Why did the wand bring her to the farm? She didn't want to come back here. Yet, in the chaos of the castle courtyard, she'd wished for safety and peace, two things she only felt when in this barn. When panic had filled her in the courtyard, she fled back to the one place she had longed to leave her whole life.

She backed away from Ranger, pacing back and forth. She had promised to help Sir Francis. Although comforting, she couldn't hide on the farm. She held the wand up, then closed her eyes taking deep, even breaths.

"Take me back to Sir Francis."

Ondreeal opened the corner of one eye. The wand remained dark. She widened her stance then held the wand high above her head. She took three deep breaths this time.

"Take me back to the castle," she demanded with as much confidence and calm she could muster.

She stood there in the barn with Hazel the cow nearby. She stared hard at the wand. She shook it, making ever bigger zigzags with it in the air until she fell over.

She jumped up and yelled, "Take me back now!"

"*Moo.*" Hazel the cow moved closer.

She licked Ondreeal's face again, making Ondreeal laugh. For a moment, she forgot her frustration and smiled at Hazel.

"It's good to see you too."

Ondreeal petted the cow and stared down at the dark wand. Without its light, it looked black in colour. She ran her fingers over its smooth surface, a flawless glass, not a dent, nick, or scratch on it. She moved to the centre of the barn and sat down in the hay. She held the wand up so she could study it.

She should start walking back to the city, though Sir Francis might have a way to find her. She could stay in the barn until he came for her. After wanting to leave every day, it seemed funny that she wanted to stay now.

Otto sat locked up in a room somewhere. She felt guilty that she had not tried to get him out right away. The other side of her wanted to be free of him, to never see his face again. She looked around the barn, and it seemed smaller now, almost quaint after being in the city and staying in a grand castle. No, it may be safe and familiar, but the life of a farmer was never what she had wanted. A greater calling awaited her. She stood and determinedly marched out of the barn.

***

Sir Francis wiped the rain water from his blurry eyes. When everything came back into focus, the skies had cleared and the sun shone down on the saturated courtyard. Ondreeal had shown the council a brilliant display of power.

"Where is she?" Magistrate Alpin yelled from the balcony above.

Sir Francis looked around everywhere. The attendants stared at him, just as confused. Ondreeal might have teleported, hopefully to a nearby location, a skill Sir Francis could never master. It would have worked perfectly, except that she disappeared and left a bewildered crowd waiting for her return.

Alpin's privilege and good upbringing didn't hide his short temper. He stared down at Sir Francis from behind his rain-soaked glasses. His simple grey suit looked black, drenched in water. Alpin helped Sir Francis care for the day-to-day running of Bastion. Preferring the cocoon of his modest office, he almost never appeared in public. He avoided all meetings and instead usually communicated with Sir Francis only in writing.

"I do not know." Sir Francis projected each word with even calm.

As the protector of the lands, he practiced benevolence, but his patience had limits too.

"This is unacceptable. She has disappeared with Aleenda's wand." Alpin addressed the groups on both balconies. "This is a catastrophic breach of security. How can we ensure the safety of the western lands with a rogue wizard out there? We do not even know if she has a soul filled with light, or a soul filled with darkness."

"You insult her lineage. I have no doubt she will become every bit the wizard her mother would have wanted her to be." Sir Francis spit the words at him.

Thunder cracked and lightning flashed above, making the two groups cower.

"I would agree," the Lord of Light stated in his usual strong voice.

Sir Francis didn't like this at all. The holy leader made for a dangerous man who used religion to justify and forward his own agenda. The leader of the church never supported him in such a way before now. He must have a plan for Ondreeal, possibly using the power of the Embertree to control her. If so, he'd like to see the Lord of Light try.

"We still do not know where she is," Alpin shot back.

***

Sir Francis stood in the centre of great hall. He held his wand before him. Behind him, the Beacon and Alpin looked on. The air in the room stirred, and Sir Francis closed his eyes. He tried to imagine Ondreeal, her young face the spitting image of her mother. How he missed Aleenda, his constant companion throughout the generations.

Everyone around wizards died, including magistrates and Beacons, but wizards went on—all of them did. Although others called them wizards, to Sir Francis they were just people. He could genuinely talk to Aleenda, let down his guard with her. It grew exhausting, playing the role he did in Bastion. If the Lord of Light and the magistrate knew the truth of the world, they would call it a lie. After all these years, Sir Francis wasn't even sure he would believe it.

Caught up in the microcosm of everyday life, Sir Francis easily forgot that a whole world lived out there, that the planet existed only as a grain of sand in a vast ocean. The need to work towards a common goal remained lost on many. That's why he agreed with the holy leader's sermons on inclusion and cooperation. If only Sir Francis could trust him. But Sir Francis had dealt with too many Lords of Light who were concerned only with power to satisfy their own egos.

He took a deep breath and concentrated on the image of Ondreeal. His mind expanded in the room, then outward to the city. He practiced this skill almost daily. It gave him comfort to know that the citizens of Bastion remained safe. So many people went about their daily routines. He expanded his mind further, remembering to distance his senses. If he tried to feel the full force of all the living creatures in the land, it would overwhelm his mind. There existed too much for the human brain to fully process. He found something … yes, Ondreeal … everywhere and nowhere at the same time. It marked the unpractised hand of someone who held such power.

It also meant that he couldn't tell her location or where she moved to. Sir Francis opened his eyes, then turned to look at the magistrate and the holy leader, both of whom stared with expectancy.

"She remains in the western lands, perhaps no more than seven days' walk from the castle," he told them.

"But in which direction? Is she coming back here? Where do we begin to look for her?" Magistrate Alpin raised his voice to a crescendo until the holy leader stopped him.

"I am certain that the good wizard, with the help of the Lord of Light, will have no trouble locating the girl." He squared his broad shoulders at Sir Francis.

Was he serious?

"You wish to join the search for her, Your Grace?" Alpin appeared surprised.

"I believe, as Sir Francis does, that there is something unique about this girl. She has a special destiny on the Path, I have felt this. Of the three wands, hers could be the key to finding the hidden ones." His eyes smiled at Sir Francis.

"Those wands remain hidden because the wizards who wield them do not wish to be found." Sir Francis barely concealed his contempt for the holy leader, a man who knew nothing about the wands or their true purpose.

"Any help we can get against fanatical wizards like Zairoc would be welcome. We could stop the dark wizard with the help of this girl and find the hidden ones." Magistrate Alpin stated.

"We will need all the help we can get," Sir Francis conceded.

The Lord of Light had manoeuvred Sir Francis like a chess piece, something the wizard truly hated.

***

Ondreeal looked over her tiny room. She peeled back her straw mattress and pulled out a tattered, yellow child's dress, the one she had worn when she first came to live with Otto. Of course, it hadn't lasted long on the farm, but Ondreeal had kept it all these years as a reminder of her mother. She carefully folded the dress, wrapped the wand in it, and walked out of the room … right into a man.

"Well, look at this." The fellow chuckled to himself.

Ondreeal backed up as two thugs glowered at her.

"Where's your father?" the other one barked at her.

Yes, they were the strange men who had visited Otto shortly before their trip to the arena.

"He's not here! I don't have your money." She didn't like the way they stared.

If they had a connection to Otto and her brief enslavement, she'd cause them pain.

"It's her." The first man moved towards her, looking intimidating.

"Are you sure?" The other one held up an old picture for her to see.

The tiny painted portrait showed her mother, and on her lap sat Ondreeal as a very young child. The familiarity of it brought back a faint memory of it hanging in a parlour.

"What if that is me? What do you want?" Ondreeal barked at them.

These men acted very odd.

"We own this farm and everything in it," the first letch announced to the world.

Ondreeal would have found him impressive if she hadn't faced a gladiator in the arena and survived.

"Enjoy," she replied as she took a step past him.

He grabbed her arm, and her body tensed in response. Physically, his strength outweighed hers, and she couldn't fight both men.

"Let me go! I'm leaving." Her voice trembled and her heart beat faster.

"Oh, no, you don't. The dark wizard will give us a good price for delivering you." The second letch gave her a yellow and brown–toothed grimace.

She struggled in the first man's grip, stepping on his foot.

"Ah, you bitch!" He slapped her face.

She punched him, and he fell to the ground. She turned to run. The cloth-wrapped wand caught her eye. It lay on the ground. She moved to grab it. Unfortunately, both men sprung up, blocking her way.

The first man held his jaw. "Got some fire, do you girl?"

The second man smiled broadly. "If it is her, Zairoc will make us rich."

They worked for the dark wizard. That made them far more dangerous than two simple debt collectors. She was the daughter of a wizard. If Zairoc had been searching for Aleenda's offspring all these years, then he had plans for her. She shuddered at the thought and certainly didn't want to find out what Zairoc had in mind.

She could run and leave the wand there, but then it might be lost to her for good. If the world depended on her training as a wizard, she couldn't leave it. That would be a life *she* could control, not Otto, or Sir Francis, and certainly not these two idiots.

She pushed past them, snatching up the cloth. One of the men grabbed her. She struggled in his grip and broke free. But, then, *bang!* A sharp pain filled her head, and she collapsed to the hard ground.

The two men stood over her, smiling and laughing.

CHAPTER SIXTEEN

S ir Francis looked up and down the dirt roadway as he held Swift in place, a beautiful horse he had helped raise from birth. A magnificent creature, pure white in colour, the mare made a loyal companion.

The sun beat down on them from a clear, blue sky. They had searched for the better part of a day, with no sign of Ondreeal. He should have found her by now. The road stretched out of sight in both directions, with tall grasses blowing in the wind on either side. Beyond this, the forest hid any sign of civilization from sight.

Behind him, the Lord of Light, three of the Embertree, and three knights from the castle waited, along with a horse-drawn carriage.

The holy leader coaxed his horse forward, positioning himself next to Sir Francis. "You do not know where you are going, do you?"

The Lord of Light delighted in any chance to make Sir Francis look bad, though he would never dare risk a direct confrontation.

Sir Francis cleared his throat. "I am merely considering options."

"If you had faith, you would not need to 'consider options.' You would just know." His childlike beliefs annoyed Sir Francis.

Clearly the Lord of Light loved posturing. He had no idea where to find Ondreeal, either.

"Otto," Sir Francis called behind him.

Otto jumped out of the carriage. Sir Francis refused to give him a horse because any mount would struggle under the weight. Otto's feet made the ground vibrate until he stopped, his scowling face only a meter away from the wizard.

Sir Francis glared back at him. "You spent more time with her than anyone. Where did she want to go?"

He didn't like taking Otto along, but the farmer might represent the best chance of finding Ondreeal.

"She wanted to go to the city, she's done that now. She's at the farm." He sounded certain of it.

"Why would she go back there? She told me of the kind of father you were to her." Sir Francis contained his disdain for Otto.

Overdue for a conversation, Sir Francis would soon decide Otto's fate. But now he needed his help.

"It's home." Otto held his chin up, proud.

Sir Francis nodded and conceded the point. Even the most unpleasant homes could draw children back to the comfort of familiarity.

"Then that is where we will look next." Sir Francis spurred his horse forward.

***

Ondreeal opened her eyes, but only blurry images met her gaze. As her vision cleared, she found herself staring at a familiar sight — the old, wood ceiling of the house. She tried to move, then found her hands tied down to the table upon which she lay. She raised her head. The men talked in the doorway. She had her pants on, but they'd taken the top half of her clothes. She lay, half-naked, while terror weighed down on her. She frantically pulled at her bonds. Tears streamed from the corners of her eyes. The men laughed and crept towards her. Her heart beat like the wings of a hummingbird. Would they kill her? She had come so far, only to be stopped by two unremarkable louts like this.

"Well, now, there she is." The first man gave her that yellow-toothed grin.

The other man leaned in and grabbed her face. He planted a kiss, and Ondreeal struggled to move away. He let go, and she spit. He tasted like shoe leather.

"We'll have a little fun with you before giving you to the dark wizard," he whispered to her. "But before that, you tell us about this."

He held her tattered child's dress in one hand, and the wand in the other. Her eyes widened, and she trembled with fear.

"Nothing to say," taunted the first.

He slapped her hard across the face.

She tried not to scream, but it felt like her head would split in two. He hit her again, and she wanted to plead for the beating to stop.

"It's a wand," she choked out.

"What did she say? A wand? No lying." The first raised his hand, making her turn away.

"It's a wand!" Her loud voice trembled.

"Then she *is* the child of Aleenda. No doubt now, we're rich men!" The first cackled.

The second held up the dress. "This yours, then? It was a fine dress for a whore like you."

He tore it into pieces and threw them on the ground, as if the action would destroy any remembrance of Aleenda that endured. They took the farm, they would use her, now they tore at her mother's memory, making Ondreeal break into a deep sob. The man pulled something out of his pocket. He let a gold chain hang down, the locket holding pictures of her young self with her mother.

"This you and your mum?" The second man let the locket sway back and forth to taunt her. "Looks expensive. We'll just call it a bonus."

The first moved to the foot of the table. "Nice, new clothes. Otto buy those for you? We'll just take those too." He pulled off her new shoes.

Ondreeal thrashed her legs, but the second goon held them down. The first unbuttoned her pants and pulled them off. Then the first dropped his pants before climbing up on the table. Tears streamed down her face. He moved over her.

"No!" She screamed out, but they both laughed harder.

A wail of pain filled the room, but not from her. The first brute looked to his companion. Then his eyes went wide, and he fell off the table. The second held the now glowing wand. It burned his hand, dragging him into the air. He used his open hand, attempting to pry the other one free while it sizzled against the magical rod.

A wind swirled around the room with ever greater force. The man dropped from the wand as it darted towards Ondreeal. It floated just over her head, changing the surface of her skin. It glistened with a blue hue, like glittering snow in the moonlight. The ropes that bound her hands untied themselves while she stared in amazement.

She stood on the table, and the wand floated into her grip. She pointed it at the two men. They rose off the ground with guttural screams. What could she do to them? What could the wand do with a single thought? Ondreeal held her head high. She stood there, powerful in nothing more than her own skin. The men suddenly vanished, the wind disappeared, and the room fell quiet.

"Witch! What did you do?"

Her head snapped to the entrance. Raaf from the village stood there shaking in the doorway. He had three days' growth of beard on his tanned face. He had once seemed like a pleasant man, but not today. He ran from the farmhouse before Ondreeal could say a word.

Ondreeal looked down at her naked body that sparkled a pale blue. She touched her skin. It felt cold, like ice. She jumped off the table and frantically grabbed at her clothes, hastily dressing and searching for her shoes. Where the two men had floated, now there sat two frogs. Ondreeal stared at them wide-eyed. She laughed through her tears.

Becoming frogs seemed like a fitting punishment for two such horrible men. Then her laughter faded. She imagined what they would have done to her, what they could have done to other girls without even a bit of care or compassion. She trampled one with her foot, then the other. They made a satisfying squishing sound under her bare heel.

She stared down at their splattered guts. She had killed them — not simply frogs, they were men. Horrible, wretched examples of how people could act, but men all the same. The giddiness leaked out of her, replaced with the stark reality of what she'd done. She screamed at the dead frogs and crumpled to the floor, holding herself tightly.

She rocked back and forth until her body stopped shaking.

Ondreeal took a deep breath. She picked up the tatters of her childhood dress and squeezed. Slowly, she relaxed her fingers, letting the garment fall to the floor over the dead frogs.

"Here, you can keep them. I don't need them anymore," she whispered to the two dead frogs before getting to her feet and putting on her shoes.

She looked at the wand, dark again, and put it into her vest. Ondreeal surveyed the kitchen. All the cupboards held only scraps or broken wares. She'd need to find food in the village before venturing out again.

Her skin glistened with that pale-blue hue. Even though the wand fell dark, it must have changed her skin permanently. Ondreeal stopped at the doorway to the farmhouse, looking back. She spat on the floor, turned, and walked out.

She must find Sir Francis. That should be easy enough: simply go back to the city. The wand had taken her here, so it should be able to take her back to Bastion. But it only responded when she found trouble, like a guardian of light. She would have to make her way independently.

Should she feel bad about the two men?

No, they lived as contemptible leeches. They would have used her up and thrown her away. Others had tried to treat her like that, but Otto had protected her then. "If anyone treats you badly, it'll be me." He'd said that many times. It evoked no feelings of comfort then, and it didn't now. Yet, living on the farm had sheltered her from much. The world existed as something vastly harsher than she imagined. The guiding rule was, kill or be killed. Ondreeal didn't want to hurt anyone, not unless they deserved it, not unless they had wronged her or those she loved. Who did she have? Sir Francis? Otto?

Her skin sparkled in the sun with that blue hue. She hoped it would not be noticeable. She took a deep breath and walked towards the village. She carried a few coins that Sir Francis gave to her for shopping, hopefully enough to buy food for her journey.

The bright and quiet day reminded her of so many on the farm. The serenity it created bored her to tears. For fleeting moments, she had almost liked it, the stillness and comfort that never changed. Though most times it had felt like a prison: she didn't have free choice to come and go, she answered to Otto. But now she didn't. Now she was free. It gave the serenity something it didn't have for her before: peace.

The village had always been a place of sanctuary for Ondreeal. Images of her last visit flitted through her mind: Franco, the baker, had smiled at her, brightening his light-grey clothes and matching chef's hat. She'd shared a laugh with Talia, the flower girl, who always wore a dress embroidered with flowers; she'd had azaleas in her hair that day. The old woman Rose had waved to her, her simple brown dress matched the kerchief she wrapped around her head.

"It's the Devil!" a villager screamed.

Any tranquility Ondreeal had gained on the walk into town evaporated.

She needed help from the people she'd grown up with. She entered the main square of the village, greeted by horrified stares. A lump sat in her throat. She looked down at herself, and her bare arms glistened with that slight blue colour. It didn't look that bad—at least she didn't think it did. She spotted the man who had yelled at her, a usually kind fellow named Ivan; his dark glare pierced through his mess of black curls and deeply tanned face.

"You know me, Ivan." She kept her voice calm.

"You look like Ondreeal, but it's a trick." He kept his distance.

"I come into the village every Saturday with Otto to trade. Talia, I traded at your fruit cart and also at Franco's bakery." She pointed to both of them as she spoke. "I am Ondreeal."

"Then what has happened to you, child?" The old woman, Rose, came closer.

She had always treated Ondreeal with such kindness. She slowly approached Ondreeal, touching her face. Gasps came from the crowd. Her skin felt icy to the touch, but coldness couldn't convince Rose that a demon had taken Ondreeal's form. If this woman didn't have fear, then surely, they would help her now. She stared at Ondreeal for a long time. Certainly, this woman knew her.

Rose addressed the crowd.

"It looks just like Ondreeal. But it is a trick. Her skin is that of a demon, I have no doubt." Her voice carried such strength.

Ondreeal's heart dropped. Silence filled the village square, except for the intermittent whistle of the wind. All the villagers stared at her as if she embodied the most grotesque creature they'd ever laid eyes upon. People shifted and whispered to each other. Ondreeal struggled to hold back tears. She searched the crowd with pleading eyes but only found faces covered in fear and hatred.

Ivan picked up an axe. Another villager grabbed a pitchfork. Ondreeal shook her head at them, tears falling from her cheeks. Their fear made them blind to her silent plea. Rage and anger quietly grew in the crowd. Then, almost as one, the mob roared to life and descended upon her.

CHAPTER SEVENTEEN

The mass of villagers surrounded Ondreeal. Hate slowly replaced the fear in their eyes, until one man gained the courage to charge at her with a pitchfork. She yanked the wand from her tunic. It slipped in her fingers; she struggled to keep her grip. She glared at it intently, willing it to help her. It stayed dark, like ebony. The man thrust the pitchfork right into her stomach. She grabbed it and stumbled back. She must be numb because she felt no pain.

She pulled the weapon away from her and saw that the ends of the pitchfork had disappeared, had been cut off. Another man stabbed her in the shoulder, but when he pulled the knife away, only the hilt remained. Instead of piercing her skin, the blades vanished. She stared at the crowd with a mixture of amazement and awe.

Undeterred, they closed in to kill Ondreeal, with the rage of the mob they'd become. They thought so little of her, felt so afraid of anything different from them that they'd rather snuff out her existence. She fell to her knees, curling into a ball. She had trusted them, believing they would help. Did the God of All want her beaten down, used up until nothing lived on? She couldn't fade into nothingness.

"No!" she screamed with her eyes squeezed shut.

Silence filled her ears, except for the intermittent sound of the breeze. She waited for several moments, gulping down air, before she gradually opened her eyes. All around the square lay the villagers. She must have put them to sleep. She slowly crawled to the old woman. Her cold skin and pale face told Ondreeal all she needed to know. Rose lay there dead. Ondreeal shook her head in disbelief. She stumbled to her feet, running to where Talia lay. But she found the same thing. She desperately checked two more villagers before falling to the ground. All of them gone, most of them dressed in dark clothes that blended in with the muddy ground, making it look like they never lived at all.

She stared at the wand, holding it tightly with both hands.

"Please. I didn't mean it. Please, bring them back," she pleaded to the wand.

Its dark surface gave no sign of response.

"Please!" she screamed out.

She squeezed the wand. Her distorted, tear-stained face reflected on its surface. Then she released her fingers, quickly stuffing the wand into her tunic. She calmly rose to her feet and turned in a circle, taking in every last villager lying dead on the ground. The gruesome scene made her tremble. She fled from the square. What had she done?

She ran into one of the stores, where she checked over her clothes. She found a hole where the man had stabbed her, exposing unbroken skin. The same held true for her stomach: three round holes in her shirt where the prongs of the pitchfork should have been. Tears welled up in her eyes, but she wiped them away and grabbed a knapsack, which she stuffed with food off the shelves.

Ondreeal hurried down the muddy road, staring at the ground. She felt numb inside. All those people lay dead. She hadn't meant to hurt them, but had only wanted them to stop hurting her. The moment played over in her mind. Yes, she felt scared but also angry. In a single instance, had she wished them to die? Sir Francis told her she would be a good wizard. She wished for certainty, but doubt plagued her. She had just murdered an entire village. It remained the only truth. Whatever reason, no matter how good, she had killed. Sir Francis couldn't be more wrong about her. She didn't deserve to have a wand or magic in her life.

Ondreeal felt a tug. Something grabbed a carrot that poked out of her satchel. A horse had wandered up to her. It didn't act afraid of her. Her hand shook while she petted the horse's long, brown head with its wide, white blaze.

"Would you like to come with me?" Her voice trembled.

Perhaps she should stay away from anything alive. But, until this horse had found her, she hadn't realized how much she needed some kind of company. The animal blew air out of its nose, and she took this as yes.

***

Sir Francis scanned the farmhouse kitchen, which had seen better days. All sorts of wares lay scattered about. A magical battle had taken place not long ago. Sir Francis poked the squashed frogs with the end of a stick. Surrounding the dead amphibians lay two well-tailored suits, too little and fancy for a farmer like Otto. If he had to guess, they belonged to the dead frogs. Sir Francis looked up at the expectant faces of the holy leader and Otto.

"They're dead," Sir Francis told them.

"So, the wizard has a sense of humour after all." The Lord of Light's eyes brightened, but Otto just glared.

"It was magic. She is using the wand. I believe these two frogs were men." Sir Francis waited for the usual shocked response.

Otto broke into a deep chuckle.

"No doubt, Zairoc's men." Otto nodded.

The Lord of Light raised an unamused eyebrow. "But where is the girl?"

One of Sir Francis's men came rushing in, followed by one of the Embertree.

"Sir Francis, we have scouted up ahead. There's something you need to see." His voice was steady but held urgency.

"Don't keep us guessing. Tell us what it is!" The holy leader sounded agitated.

"You must see." The Ember appeared adamant.

Sir Francis walked ahead of the others. He could feel the Lord of Light staring at him just behind. He didn't need to show dominance; in the eyes of the people, Sir Francis reigned as an all-powerful wizard and the ruler of the land. His true nature would only confuse and bewilder them. No, he walked ahead because when a knight of the castle agreed with one of the Embertree, it harrowed trouble. Knights and Embers never saw eye to eye, for one man put his faith in God, and the other in Sir Francis.

Those lines had blurred over the years. The people started to see wizards as more than magical beings, thanks to Zairoc. Some even called wizards the embodiment of the God of All. Religion had already spread like a plague of locusts, devouring any sense of reason as it went.

Sir Francis's heart beat a little faster. They approached the settlement. It looked like people lay on the ground. He walked rapidly, never taking his eyes off the square. Yes, bodies lay all around, the better part of an entire village. He wished he could blame Zairoc, since the evil wizard had a flair for the dramatic, usually carving his name into the bodies or buildings where he'd wreaked havoc. Sir Francis willed himself to stay upright, fighting back tears. If Ondreeal had transformed into a monster, one equal to Zairoc, then Sir Francis must take the full weight of the blame. He didn't want to believe it. The faces of Otto and the Lord of Light reflected his despair.

The holy leader slowly shook his head. "This is the girl's work, isn't it? She travels a dark path."

Sir Francis was unconvinced. "There may yet be an explanation for all this."

"She was not ready for the wand. Now it has taken her from the light. I do not know if I can save her," the Lord of Light said, wiping tears from his eyes.

Otto defended Ondreeal like a proud father. "If she killed them, she had a good reason. My Al is a good girl."

Sir Francis glared at Otto, clenching his fists. Otto didn't deserve to raise her. If ever there lived a sorry excuse for a parent, it was Otto. All the years Sir Francis could have spent with Ondreeal, moulding and training her to be a champion for good... They could have avoided all this. But in this instance, Sir Francis agreed with Otto.

"We do not know what happened here. This only proves that we must find her." Sir Francis hurried past the scene of death and headed down the road.

CHAPTER EIGHTEEN

Ondreeal stared straight down the dirt road, wiping away the raindrops that had collected on her forehead and cheeks. Her hair whipped around in the churning wind. The horse moved slowly while she clutched the reins — no need to go faster, since she had nowhere to go. Thunder rolled above, and she bowed her head. The gentle pat of drops transformed into a rumble, until water streamed down Ondreeal's soaked hair.

She looked to the east; hidden behind sheets of rain stood the ghostly image of the arena. The road ahead stretched out of sight. What safe place would cradle a mass murderer? Her teeth chattered, and she shivered.

Several flashes of lightning preceded a huge clap of thunder. The horse whinnied, bolting ahead. Ondreeal gripped harder on the reins, pulling back, but the horse galloped faster.

"Whoa, boy! Easy. Whoa!" She glared into the white waves of the deluge.

Her heart beat faster. She yanked on the reins. The horse stopped hard, arching its back and throwing her off. Ondreeal landed in a puddle with a soft splash. She pushed herself to a seated position as mud squished through her fingers. She deserved whatever the world could throw at her. Nevertheless, the spongy ground made for an easy landing. She felt no pain, so the blue skin must have protected her once more.

She peered backward to her mount, now standing in the downpour. Oddly, it hadn't raced off and left her here; a spooked horse didn't calm down that quickly on its own. More thunder shook through her innards. The horse struggled before settling amid the whirling storm. Ondreeal pushed herself to her feet, squinting and letting the rain wash away the dirt and grime. Then she made out the outline of a figure that stood holding the horse's bridle.

"You all right, miss?" the man shouted at her.

She moved closer. His wrinkled eyes smiled while they peered at her. His dark pants and shirt had an uneven, muddy colour, no doubt stained from years of farm work. Rain poured off the edges of his wide-brimmed straw hat. He brushed back a few white locks of hair, then pointed up to the sky.

"It's raining, you know. I'd just as soon get out of this. You far from where you need to go?" He petted the horse's nose, ignoring the torrential storm.

She nodded at him.

"I can offer you some hospitality for a day. We don't have much. But I can't leave you out here." He gave her a stern look.

"Thank you." She grabbed herself and shivered.

"This way." He pulled the horse along the road a short distance.

The sweet, old man turned onto a dirt pathway. Ondreeal could make out a nearby farmhouse, not unlike the home she had known for all these years.

His hand guided her to the front door. "You head inside, I'll take your horse to the barn where it can get a meal."

She nodded to him again before stepping on the porch, like walking out of turmoil onto the edges of peace. She looked up at the old wooden overhang, dripping water, and smiled despite herself. She had just placed her hand on the wooden knob when the door quickly opened.

A woman with a kind though wrinkled smile greeted her. She wore a full, black dress that hung off her wide curves. She tugged on a white lace collar that had browned with age. Her silver hair in a tight bun, she stared at Ondreeal over the edge of her spectacles.

"Well, what do we have here?" The old woman blinked.

"My name is Ondreeal, ma'am." She gave her a slight bow.

"I'm Esteal. A girl in boy's pants. I'd guess you came from Bastion." The woman chuckled at her.

Ondreeal nodded.

"Well, don't just stand there. Come in. You look blue from the cold." The woman shuffled aside.

Ondreeal took three quick steps inside. Esteal closed the door, silencing the storm. To the right, an iron stove contained a bright, orange fire, crackling softly through the iron slates in its little door. To either side of the cooker, doorways leading to bedrooms made flat bookends. This mirrored the other side of the room, with bedrooms behind each of the two doors, except in place of the stove, a sideboard filled with dishes rested on the greyish wooden floor. Light from the fire played gently on the dishes. Against the far wall perched a farm table with six chairs. One small carpet, red and faded with time, occupied the centre of the room. A pair of rockers sat on opposite edges of the carpet and to either side of the stove.

The woman took in Ondreeal's drenched appearance. "Let me get you some dry clothes."

"No, thank you. I'll just let these dry." Ondreeal shifted uncomfortably.

The old woman scrutinized her from the edge of her glasses, sighing with disapproval.

"Sit over here while I get you a hot bowl of stew. At least you can warm yourself by the fire." The woman guided her to one of the rocking chairs.

Ondreeal sat and smiled at the woman. She watched as Esteal scurried over, stirring a big, black pot on the stovetop with a wooden spoon.

"Where are you going in weather like this?" Esteal asked over her shoulder.

Ondreeal opened her mouth. She couldn't tell her about Sir Francis or the wand; it would prove dangerous to herself, but more so for these kind people.

"I'm headed north and then, I think, east. I'm looking for solitude." Her voice sounded small.

The front door flew open, letting in the steady roar of the storm. The elderly man, dressed in homespun clothes, stepped inside. He quickly shut the door, breathing out a deep sigh. He stood there for a moment as water dripped off his soaked clothes onto the floor. After placing his straw hat on a hook by the door, he turned towards them, brushing some of the water off his arms.

He nodded to Ondreeal. "No sign of stopping. You'll have to stay the night."

Ondreeal shook her head. "Oh, no. I don't want to impose."

Esteal shuffled over to the sideboard, plucking up three bowls. "Nonsense. It's no imposition. You'll stay. Besides, since the boys left home, we could use a little company."

"I'm Jera." The old man sat in the other rocker.

Ondreeal bowed her head to him. Esteal took the three bowls to the stove, where she used a wooden ladle to pour stew into them. She tossed a spoon into each one before pulling over a chair from the table and setting it beside Jera. She gave them each a bowl and then grabbed the last one, plunking herself down in the chair.

Jera glanced to Esteal with a mouthful of stew. "She's very pretty."

"Let her rest before you badger her." Esteal gave him a light whack on the shoulder.

Ondreeal closed her eyes. Warm aromas of fresh vegetables mixed with meat, filling her senses. She inhaled deeply until her eyes fell open. She took a spoonful and shoved it into her mouth. The flavours erupted on her tongue, making her beam with satisfaction.

Jera chuckled. "I think she likes your cooking, Mum."

She shook her head. "Don't you mind Father. He loves his humour."

Jera grunted at Ondreeal. "Do we even know your name?"

Esteal saw her mouthful, so she answered for her. "Ondreeal's her name."

Jera leaned forward, raising an eyebrow. "Are you married, Ondreeal?"

"Stop." Esteal hit his arm a little harder this time.

"She'd be perfect for young Jack," he whispered conspiratorially to Esteal.

"She's got ears, you know. Forgive him. Our son is about twenty years old, apprenticing with the smith in town. He's still without a wife, so Father here is always playing matchmaker." She shook her head.

Ondreeal gave them a slight smile. "No, I'm not married."

Jera's eyes grew wide. He sat on the edge of the rocker. "Well, now. Isn't that interesting?"

"Careful, Father. Last time he sat like that, he went ass over tea kettle." She smirked at Ondreeal.

Jera beamed at her. "Why aren't you married yet?"

They made such a lovely couple. Ondreeal wished she had grown up with parents like this. What she remembered of her mother was that she showed kindness.

"I worked a farm not far outside of the village to the south, with my ... father." She looked down again at the bowl.

She scraped up the contents off the bottom and took the spoonful.

She bowed slightly as she passed the woman her empty bowl. "Thank you."

Esteal stared at her with worry. "Maybe we should put another log on the fire. She still looks blue."

This kind, old couple would soon figure out that she wasn't just an ordinary girl. She had been, but not anymore. They would fear that. She didn't want to see their kind expressions change to hate.

"May I rest my head? I'm simply exhausted." Ondreeal smiled brightly at them.

Esteal nodded, placing the bowl by the stove, she gestured for Ondreeal to follow. "Of course you can. Get all the rest you need."

Jera grabbed her hand.

"We must talk more in the morning. I want to hear all about you." He patted her hand with his.

"Certainly." She pulled her hand away with a quick nod.

She stopped at the doorway and turned back to them.

"Thank you both for your kindness." She fought back tears, hiding them with another smile before quickly turning away.

She stepped into the room and closed the door.

Esteal whispered from inside the living area, "Poor girl. She looks as if she's been through some ordeal."

"I'm disappointed. I wanted to talk awhile," Jera whispered back.

She looked over the chamber: a modest bed stood against one corner, and no other furniture occupied the room. She lay on the bed, pulling the thick wool blanket around herself. She stared up at the four-pane window, which rain pelted on. The wind softly whistled. Ondreeal's eyes grew heavy.

***

She stood in the centre of the village with everyone lying dead around her. Down the road, back in the direction of the farm, two men strode towards her. Their faces became clear, the two men who worked for Zairoc and who had tried to hurt her. They couldn't be alive. Their skin looked pale around sunken eyes.

The first man stopped, pointing at her. "That's her! The one who killed us all."

From all around, the dead villagers rose to their feet, glaring at Ondreeal.

Talia screamed out. "She's a witch!"

Rose clenched her fists. "Burn her. Burn out the evil."

Ondreeal pleaded with the villagers. "I'm sorry! I didn't mean to harm you."

Zairoc's second man yelled at her, "You meant to hurt us."

The villagers slowly closed in around her. Their dead hands felt like ice. The world fell into blackness. Then Ondreeal inhaled deeply. Her eyes snapped open. She struggled to free her bound hands. Her head rested against a wooden stake. Villagers threw kindling around her feet.

Ondreeal howled at them. "No. Please! I'm sorry!"

Talia lit a torch and threw it on the fire. "You make it right by dying, witch."

The flames grew bright all around, licking at her feet until her clothes caught fire. Pain burst in her legs while Ondreeal struggled. Her flesh sizzled, forcing out a wail of agony. The villagers smiled and laughed as the fire cast an eerie, orange glow on their dead faces.

"No. Please... No!" Ondreeal screamed out.

***

"No!" Ondreeal yelled as her eyes snapped open.

She starred at the four-pane glass window, covered in raindrops. She sat up, wiping tears from her eyes. The quiet twilight greeted her even while she clenched her shaking hands. She had slept the whole night.

The smell of her own flesh burning filled her nose with the odour of cooked meat, metal mixed with a sweet, musky perfume. She shook her head, trying to shake off the disturbing imagery. Perhaps she could help with the morning chores.

She pulled herself up, patting down her now dry clothes. She should have taken them off, but the blue-tinted skin protected her. Maybe she should make a quiet exit. She didn't want to frighten her hosts. She grabbed the knapsack she had filled in the village and opened the door.

She winced; the same smell hung strongly in the living room. The stove fire had died down to embers, so it wasn't something in there. She crept towards the closed door on the far side. She could at least make certain that the old couple slept soundly before she left. She put her hand on the wooden knob and gently coaxed the door ajar.

She gasped, covering her mouth and nose. There in the bed lay two skeletons, black from fire. The char surrounded the straw mattress and suddenly stopped before the edges. What kind of flame could do that? No fire burned intensely in a confined space. It should have devoured the entire wooden house.

This was her fault. Somehow, the nightmare she dreamt came true for these kind people. She shook her head, rushing from the room and bursting out the front door. She collapsed on the front porch as she sucked in air. She clambered to her feet and raced to the barn. She untied the horse, quickly mounted, and spurred the creature out the door. She kicked it harder until the horse panted from the effort. Ondreeal stared down the dirt road until the horse faltered. She pulled back hard on the reins, and it came to a stop. She looked back, tears in her eyes. Her hands shook. Tears fell. The farmhouse lay hidden by a hill behind her.

"All I bring is death," she whispered on the wind.

No doubt remained. Ondreeal needed to find isolation in a place where no one would look for her, or want to follow. Her eyes drifted to the Black Circle Mountains to the east. Dark, jagged, monstrous peaks jutted up through white clouds. Some said that no one, not even demons would dare tread there. What about a wizard?

If Ondreeal could find no safety for herself or those around her, then that was the only place left. She set the horse to face the mountains and gently coaxed it onwards. She would find solitude there.

She needed to.

Chapter Nineteen

From the back of the horse she was riding, Ondreeal scanned the landscape: rolling hills covered with tall trees, mixed with long grasses. Sir Francis's attempts to teach her had failed. In fact, everything that had happened to her from the time she'd set foot into the arena until now had created an all-encompassing disaster.

Could she continue to see herself as a good person? Perhaps the wand held up a mirror to show her actual identity as Otto's daughter. If true, then she really did need to get herself away from people while she didn't have control of the wand. She couldn't have more people dying because of her. She would need to train herself.

Perhaps Sir Francis would find and help her. Is that what Sir Francis wanted — to create a weapon to bring pain and death? No, she hoped that he'd told her the truth, that he wanted to help her to do right in the world as a wizard.

Since they had paused, the horse stopped to graze on some grass, so Ondreeal took the opportunity to stretch her legs. The mountains looked close now. Black peaks jutted up from the landscape like dark talons. Everyone called their far reaches dangerous, a place to stay away from unless you welcomed peril. Talia had told her that story.

The whole world outside the farm had existed like a story, until now. Talia had told her the mountains formed a giant ring, though it didn't sound possible. If you travelled through the mountains, oblivion would find you.

Recent events came quickly flooding back. Her entire body shook, then she crumpled to the ground. Images of the ones she'd murdered filled her mind. The barbarian, Rose, Talia, the old couple … they all fell lifeless at her hand. She couldn't breathe. The wand glowed brightly from behind her tunic. She pressed her hands over the wand, fighting for breath. Her body grew numb, although it shook uncontrollably. She let out a panic-filled scream, taking in short, painful breaths. Tears streamed down her face until her heaving chest slowed and the wand faded to dark.

The horse nudged her, and she blinked as if seeing the creature for the first time. She lay there for a long while. Slowly she rose to stand once more. She mounted the horse and spurred it towards the ebony peaks. Certainly, the mountains, a place of necrosis, would welcome a death dealer like herself. She didn't want to die, but she couldn't go anywhere else. Though she may not find safety, others would be protected from her.

Ondreeal closed in on the black, mammoth peaks. Maybe she would meet others on the path. Yet, only the mountains stood in the distance, with Ondreeal travelling on the lonely road. Soon it gave way to the type of rugged landscape where not many people would dare to venture.

Ondreeal steadied herself on the horse while she coaxed it to climb higher. Perhaps the beast couldn't handle the rocky terrain. The beautiful greens in the valley gave way to solid, black rock. Spots of the strange stone glistened like glass in the sun. No animal or insect travelled over the mysterious rocks. She glanced up at the black mountains that stretched through the clouds. The sweet air of the forest had diminished to that of ash, bitter and still. Her long hair hung motionless, like the wind dared not go near this place. Climbing these peaks would prove difficult, at best. She sheepishly urged the horse forward to ascend.

The pair moved up a rocky face that grew steeper. If the terrain worsened, the horse would simply refuse to go any farther, so she hopped off, taking the lead. Just then, her mount jerked hard on the reins. Ondreeal tumbled past the horse, then flipped over and rolled down the rocky terrain. She landed on a grassy patch at the bottom.

White clouds moved lazily in the sky while she assessed her pain and tested her limbs. She'd had her share of tumbles on the farm and could take a few knocks. No doubt the hard rocks of the mountain would have hurt more, if not for the blue skin she now wore. The horse came close once more and sniffed her, offering an apology.

***

Hours later, Ondreeal climbed higher, leading her mount over a rocky but slender path. She marched ahead until it pulled back on the reins again. She had no choice but to let go of the bridle, and the animal instinctively backed up. The beast wouldn't fit alongside her on the cramped path, forcing her to forge ahead without it. She finally got to a point where the rocky walls pinched inwards, brushing her shoulders, threatening to hold her in place. She edged ahead sideways, but the passage closed in farther up. She hit the craggy wall of the path.

"You stupid mountain!" Her yell echoed.

Ondreeal had given up and started back down the passage when a few pebbles hit the top of her head before bouncing to the ground. A few more pellets tumbled past, followed by four enormous slabs smashing down all around. She broke into a run until a sizable boulder landed ahead and, unable to stop, she slammed into it. The roar of stones descending grew louder, forcing her to scramble over the boulder while pebbles hit her back and head. She tried to run, but another slab crashed before her. She glanced up as more stones rained down, making her scream and cover her head. As they smashed against her, the rocks turned to dust, surrounding her in a powdery cloud that hovered overhead. She coughed amid the clearing air.

Ondreeal checked over her arms, legs, and body, finding not even a scratch. Her blue-tinted skin had first protected her from the villagers, and now from an avalanche. She found it useful, although she wished she could reverse it, if only she knew how she had cast the spell in the first place.

***

Ondreeal returned for her mount and guided it back down to a fork in the path. The second passage proved wide enough to take both herself and the horse deep into the mountains. They traversed the rocky route for a long while. At first, the bright sun cast no shadows, but now orange beams faded over the rocky cliffs, lighting the stones, which sparkled with beautiful reds and blues. Ondreeal could watch such beauty forever.

A shiver shuddered through her as the air cooled. She could make a camp for the night, yet determination to find a way through won out, so she kept going. Besides, she didn't know what creatures lived here.

The passage gave way to an open valley filled with a wide variety of rock formations and peppered with clumps of trees. The mountain jutted dramatically upwards, preventing any further advance in her journey.

She moved away from the horse, which tried to follow her.

She held her hand up to halt its progress. "Stay back. I don't know what this will do. I don't need any more deaths on my head."

The animal stopped, staring at her. She continued to walk away until she had put some distance between them, and then she pulled out the wand. Seeing its shiny, dark surface made her heart beat faster. She swallowed hard, holding it high.

She kept her eyes closed tight. "Make me a path through the mountains."

She opened her eyes. Not one stone moved.

She closed her eyes again, taking a deep breath.

"Make me a path through the mountains."

She whispered the words repeatedly until her throat dried. Her eyes opened, and tears welled.

"I need a way through the bloody mountain!" she screamed.

The wand behaved like a partially broken farm tool, sometimes working, other times not at all. If only she had trained more with Sir Francis, she would understand how to use it. Maybe the wand worked perfectly, which would mean *she* was the broken instrument.

She looked at the glassy rod, holding it up. "Please tell me what to do."

She closed her eyes. "Show me the way through the mountains — please."

A rumbling made her eyes snap open. In the distance, a huge pile of rocks and dirt lifted into the air. They scattered as they floated away, landing softly all around the area, revealing a gaping maw of darkness in the mountain. She kissed the wand.

"Thank you," she whispered to it.

She breathed a sigh of relief. She would travel to the other side. Surely, she could find solitude, a place where no one else would die at her hand. She would learn to use the wand to safeguard innocent lives.

Ondreeal ran back to the horse, hopped on, and trotted off onto the new path. Beyond these mountains hid places no one else would dare to go. She studied the great opening that looked like some sort of cave. She approached slowly, on horseback, and inspected the rocks above. The whole thing might rain down on her. Worse yet, the wand worked when it wanted to. Who knew when this blue skin would disappear? If that happened during a cave-in, she'd be a pancake along with her animal companion.

Like a gigantic mouth, it soon eclipsed her as she approached the entrance. A flash of light jumped out of the wand. Then a light above the cave flickered on. The long, narrow light looked more like a spear. Others just like it flashed on, illuminating the path into the cave. The ground appeared strangely smooth where the rocks had moved away. The cave walls looked just like the ground, polished and unnatural. Had the wand created the cave?

No, it hadn't made a path when she'd asked. It had shown her one that already existed, surely something the ancients built.

She slowly rode inside the cave, which appeared endless. Soon she couldn't see the entrance or an exit, only the few lights above that burst on to show her the way, then snapped off as she passed them. She travelled onward, protected by a small cocoon of light.

CHAPTER TWENTY

T rick Mark rubbed his legs as bright sunrays danced through the thick foliage overhead. Several times over the course of almost three days, CD-45 had stopped, circled around while he decided on a direction, and then headed off on a new path.

"I'm sorry sir—" Vere started.

"Don't. I agreed to assist him too." Trick Mark looked ahead. "Hey, CD, we want to help, but we need to get home. It's only the fate of the northern kingdoms that are in jeopardy."

But the little creature rolled ahead, ignoring him.

Vere looked at her commander with concern. "How far have we gone?"

"At least two dozen miles east, even more to the north." Trick Mark glanced at her.

"Then the Enchanted Lands already surrounded us. What do the storytellers say? 'A magical land filled with wonders to thrill or terrify.' Very few people ever travel through them. Even fewer come back. Sir Francis said never to venture out here." Vere wrung her hands.

Sir Francis had scoffed at the idea of calling the untamed wilderness enchanted. But the people had no other word for strange places beyond their borders.

"Tall tales tell of monstrous animals, ten times the size of a horse, dragons, strange demons, and fairies that roam the land. The wizards came from the east, it's their ancient home. Of course those stories are true, and those lands are enchanted." Trick Mark stared at CD's back.

CD-45 must be a good fairy or sprite, because he'd saved their lives twice. He wouldn't go to all that trouble just to kill them. CD stopped at a cliff, looking over the edge. Again, CD shot fire from his feet and then rose into the air. Trick Mark reflexively moved in front of Vere, tensing his body. CD lowered himself over the edge, and Vere peered after him.

"It's a long way down." She didn't want to go over the ledge any more than Trick Mark did.

He joined her to survey the escarpment. She wasn't kidding.

A narrow river flowed far below the precipice wall that appeared to be completely smooth. Typical cliffs contained jagged rocks and edges, while this looked strangely sleek. But in the Enchanted Lands, strange counted as normal.

CD-45 hovered over distinct parts of the rock, as if each area held its own significance that needed to be examined and noted. Finally, he stopped, extended his shiny metal arms, and pried at something. CD gazed up and beckoned for them to join him.

Vere looked at Trick Mark with shock. "Does he want us to jump?"

"There's not even a place to land!" Trick Mark yelled down at him.

CD-45 glanced down as if remembering that people couldn't make fire spring from their bodies. They watched as the creature floated down to the bottom, coming back up with a boulder. If CD intended to knock them out and drag them down, Trick Mark would put up a fight. He watched with fascination as the creature's side opened, much in the same way its head did. Out came what looked like a tiny arm.

"That's disgusting," whispered Vere.

"Don't be so judgemental. Sir Francis talked about magical beings that looked different. He said that we would look as strange to them as they do to us." He studied Vere for her reaction.

"Sorry. It just reminds me of some of the insects where I grew up. My brothers used them to torture me from time to time." She stared down in awe.

They watched while the little arm shot a stream of fire on the boulder. It glowed with heat as CD-45 attached it to the side of the cliff. He repeated the action until he built a landing made up of boulders, just underneath the area he had pried at.

The creature shot up to the top of the bluff, extending his hands for Vere to grab. She shook her noggin while CD nodded his. Trick Mark laughed at how earnestly she protested.

"No, no, no! I'm staying up here. I have the only knapsack with supplies." She tried to sound determined, but a bit of fear creeped into her voice.

"Oh, for the sake of the God of All." Trick Mark stood up, stretching his hands for CD-45 to take.

Again, the magical creature shot fire, floating into the air. Only this time, he took Trick Mark with him. His feet dangled over the grassy meadow, then over open air, and eventually over the narrow river far below. Trick Mark refused to scream. Even though every part of his being wanted to, he wouldn't give Vere the satisfaction. So, Trick Mark steeled his jaw, waiting until CD-45 lowered him down the precipice.

The smooth side of the cliff looked metallic, like CD-45, and the rock wall with no marks on it made it look to Trick Mark as if he faced one big plate. This reminded him of some of the homes he'd seen, flat on the front save for its door and windows, and built into a grass-covered hillside. Only this place, the size of a humble mountain, dominated the landscape.

It seemingly took forever to reach the landing of boulders attached to the side of the expansive metal face. Then CD-45's fire fluttered, and they dropped. The world spun around until the inconceivable happened.

CD let go.

Trick Mark hurtled through the air towards the river below. CD-45 pushed him. The world disappeared into darkness, then he landed with a hard thud. More eons seemed to pass until Trick Mark stood. CD must have shoved him through a doorway and into a pitch-black building of sorts.

From the top of the entrance, the creature's head popped out upside-down. CD gave Trick Mark a quick salute before disappearing from sight.

"Yeah, I'm fine. Thanks for asking." Trick Mark almost swallowed the words.

He had managed not to throw up. That counted for something. Probably because they hadn't eaten in a day; otherwise, it would have resulted in a messy landing. Trick Mark stuck his head out, taking a careful step onto the welded landing of boulders. If they had known that the shiny metal building had an open doorway, they wouldn't have needed the boulders. Then again, CD-45 had tried to encourage them. He must have believed this the best way to coax them down. He looked up to see Vere ogling at him from the hillside, clearly afraid.

"You're alive!" her voice echoed downward.

"If that damn wizard hasn't killed us, not much will. Now get down here, that's an order!" Trick Mark sounded trustworthy now.

Vere hesitated as she looked at CD-45 and then back to Trick Mark.

"Now, soldier!" he yelled.

Vere slowly stuck out her hands for CD-45 to take, then closed her eyes tight. He lifted her into the air. More fire sprung from CD's sides as they descended. Then a whining sound came from CD, along with red flashing lights on his chest. Halfway down, his fire snapped off and on. This caused him to jerk Vere around.

She bellowed at the top of her lungs.

Trick Mark held out his arms to catch her. CD must have seen this—he dropped her. Trick Mark caught Vere a little farther out, making him fall to the rocks and nearly lose his grip on her.

Vere screamed in fear. "Trick, help me!"

He clutched her arm as she dangled off the edge.

"Hang on, Vere, I'll pull you up!"

Beside him landed CD-45. Trick Mark watched the light fade from CD's eyes. Was he dead? Trick Mark didn't even know if the little guy had a pulse. Trick Mark's eyes grew wide with horror as one of the boulders from the cobbled-together landing gave way. He pulled Vere up a few more inches. Another stone from the landing plummeted, dropping to the river far below. Another fell, then another as he dragged her to safety.

A few more rock slabs crumbled down, and Trick Mark almost fell with them until Vere dug her fingers into his shoulders, yanking him back. They both lay inside. The boulders in front of the door tumbled away. Trick Mark stuck his head out. Just to the side of the door, several rocks held up CD-45.

"CD, get in here!"

The creature remained motionless and dark.

Vere pleaded with him. "CD, come on."

The enchanted being wouldn't respond to either of them.

"Put your hands around my waist," Trick Mark ordered Vere.

She did so without asking why; she understood what he had planned. Trick Mark leaned out so that half his body hung over open air while he grabbed CD-45's cold hands. CD had saved their lives, after all. It came time to pay back one of those debts. He pulled on CD, who wouldn't budge even an inch.

Trick Mark's muscles strained. "Little guy weighs a ton."

He leaned out further. Vere held on tight. He pulled again. CD-45 moved a little. Vere yanked hard, yet CD hung over the edge of a boulder.

"Stop," Trick Mark ordered.

If they moved farther, they would just send CD-45 hurtling to his death, if a drop could kill a magical being. Maybe plummeting would wake him up. Another rock slab tumbled away. Then another. Soon, only the one boulder upon which CD precariously perched remained. Trick Mark leaned further, this time grabbing CD in the centre of his body. He held on with all his might.

He yelled at Vere, "Pull!"

She did as commanded, yanking hard. CD-45 slid off the boulder, his weight dragging Trick Mark down until his arms and shoulders hung out the doorway. Nevertheless, his grip on CD held firm. Vere needed to pull all the weight of CD-45 plus Trick Mark back inside, a near-impossible task. At least some justice prevailed: CD dangled over the cliff in the same terrifying way they had.

"Serves you right, you little shit. Wake up!" His voice echoed down the cliffside.

CD weighed far too much; an entire crate of iron-forged weapons weighed less. Trick Mark held fast, but his body slipped forward an inch at a time while the edge of the floor raked against his ribs.

"Vere, you're not doing your job. Pull!"

She didn't respond.

His eyes grew wide as he stared at the long drop. He could feel Vere's hand, but she didn't actively pull. He thought that perhaps she'd given up on him, until he felt a rope around his ankles. Smart girl, she was trying to get some leverage. Lucky for him, she had her knapsack. He edged forward again, forced down by CD-45's weight.

He yelled back to her, panic in his voice. "Pull, Vere, or say goodbye! Just let me know what you pick."

The rope tugged on his legs. He edged backwards into the doorway.

The last boulder fell away, knocking against CD-45 as it went. Thankfully he didn't look hurt. Trick Mark's hands grew sweaty, making CD's body slip from his fingers.

The rope yanked back. Trick Mark struggled to bend his elbows, or his arms would break the next time Vere pulled.

Trick Mark's arms burst with pain. His muscles trembled under the strain. "*Vere!* I can't hold him much longer."

If he couldn't get CD-45 up in the next few moments, their little guardian angel would fall. The rope jerked hard on his legs. They had almost made it inside when the rope went flaccid.

He slid forward an inch. Vere leaned down, pulling on CD's head as hard as she could. The creature inched upwards. With one last heave, they hauled CD inside.

The creature sat in the doorway with Vere and Trick Mark on either side, sweaty, huffing and puffing.

"I never heard you complain so much," Vere teased Trick Mark.

He smiled at her. "You usually do a better job."

He nodded to her in thanks. She smirked and returned the gesture.

Vere gazed into the dense shadows. "Where are we?"

"He wanted help. It must be something here." Trick Mark stared into pitch blackness. "I'll scout out ahead."

Trick Mark stood, surveying the hall. He glanced back at Vere, who looked at him expectantly. CD-45 sat there, his eyes dark, possibly dead. Nevertheless, they knew nothing of his origins; maybe he had simply fallen unconscious. Trick Mark turned, striding into the dimness.

His second sight awakened, although greatly diminished by the daylight. The building might be expansive, considering that the long hallway stretched out of sight, and beyond this, he couldn't see or feel anything. Hopefully, he'd find an exit, since they couldn't leave the same way they'd come in.

That's what they got for following an enchanted magical creature. Trick Mark needed to discover why they were here. CD-45 might call this home, with more magical creatures inside. Without CD's help, he'd have to find out for himself.

He didn't want to worry Vere by mentioning it, but they could be trapped.

He ventured deeper into the structure. The strange walls didn't feel like metal, but something else, something very unusual. At least it matched everything else out here in the Enchanted Lands. The air in the hallway smelled stale from moisture—not surprising, given the hot forest outside. Long, spear-like glass containers hung on the ceiling.

He came to a fork in the hallway. Left or right? He chose the left, taking a stairwell down and pausing at the bottom. His second sight remained weak, so he couldn't gauge the distance to the walls. Perhaps he'd entered a massive space, with walls too far away to sense. Either way, he crept onto the great, open floor. Covering the room, he found several rows of shelves—some bare or broken, while others contained unusual items.

Trick Mark stopped at one, picking up a box. He placed it on the floor and opened it. He plucked out one of the items inside. It felt round like a ball and completely smooth. It reminded him of the floating magical light Sir Francis had given him. It would be nice to have that now. Though his second sight had become strong, seeing things with regular eyesight allowed him to share experiences with others in a way they could understand. Trick Mark checked shelf after shelf, yet he couldn't make sense out of any of the inventory. All of this could belong to CD. Obviously, the boxes held magical things. Perhaps CD needed help finding an enchanted item.

Trick Mark eventually found a wall with a couple of doorways in it. He pulled and pushed with all his might, but the doors remained firmly closed. Then one of the doors lit up, making him jump back. Just as quickly, it fell dark. Maybe he'd found a magical door. Trick Mark approached it once more, gently touching the door's surface, only this time it didn't react. For all his efforts, he could find nothing to help him and Vere get out. He hit one of the doors with the palm of his hand. He would have to tell Vere: they were trapped after all.

CHAPTER TWENTY-ONE

The last several days cycled through CD-45's memory buffer. Images of Trick Mark and Vere rotated in his internal holographic monitor. The words MEDIEVAL ERA CLOTHING AND BEHAVIOUR scrolled across it. A scan of Trick Mark's internal structure showed billions of tiny blue dots inside his body, revealing some very advanced technology at work that he likely didn't even know about. If CD-45 could explain it, he doubted they would believe him. In fact, they had only helped him to repay a perceived debt. If he could make friends no other way, the tally would certainly remain at two.

As a good friend, CD-45 had tried to provide accommodations. Humans didn't have booster rockets or other tools built into their bodies. He had even constructed a platform of stones to assuage their irrational fears. Yes, he'd developed into a very considerate friend.

An image of the military facility they currently inhabited appeared on CD-45's monitor. The words, ENTRANCE, EXIT titled the only known doorway, next to dots representing himself and Vere. One worrisome point: CD-45 might have saved these two humans only to condemn them to death. EMERGENCY BATTERY CHARGING, flashed red.

Then a summary scrolled up: CURRENT ENERGY EXPENDITURE, TWENTY PERCENT. MAIN BATTERY POWER, ZERO POINT ONE PERCENT. CALCULATION OF FINDING REPLACEMENT BATTERY WITH TWO COMPANIONS, EIGHTY PERCENT. PROBABILITY OF LOCATING A SPACE-FARING VESSEL WITHIN THIS FACILITY, SIXTY-FIVE PERCENT.

As humans would say, first things first. Finally, his monitor flashed: SYSTEMS ONLINE. Vere hopped about with excitement. Either that, or perhaps her mind had fractured—he just didn't know for sure. So much time had passed since he'd last interpreted facial expressions. He lit up the path ahead for them, wheeling his way into the complex with Vere close behind.

"Trick Mark's been in there a long time. I hope he's okay." She expressed worry.

Worry for a friend, or mate, or husband. He didn't know which, yet it remained irrelevant; locating a new battery held top priority.

He might be able to carve a message on metal walls. Unfortunately, he needed other CD units to modify one of his laser welders into a writing instrument. Besides, the design of a CD included either very fine equipment for work on micro-circuitry or large-scale construction.

Several of the halls remained blocked with debris from previous collapses. He and Vere weaved their way through, heading down two flights of stairs. Several shelves lay bare. CAPACITY AT THIRTY PERCENT, flashed on his monitor. That left a great deal of inventory to go through.

"What are you looking for?" Vere whispered to him.

A useful question, at last! He stopped, removed his damaged battery, and held it out to Vere. She looked afraid and clearly didn't want to touch it. However, simple logic stated that four eyes increased total scanning magnitude.

"Vere!" Trick Mark appeared farther down the dark hall, wincing in the bright light from CD-45. "I see our friend is awake again."

She pointed to the battery in his metal hand. "He's looking for that."

Without the proper tools to repair his battery, replacement remained the only option. His reserve battery flashed: IMMINENT FAILURE. The low probability of anyone replacing it left little hope. In fact, he would likely degrade past the point of salvage. If fated to die here, his two new friends would share it.

Trick Mark trotted towards the door. "There's a doorway over here on the other side, but it's locked."

CD-45 scanned it. Another level lay below. Hopefully, the storey remained as intact as this one. He studied the simple locking mechanism. He only needed to run through the possible combinations of the lock. It required a bit of power to work, so CD transferred what little he could. The locking mechanism flickered to life. Vere and Trick Mark watched with interest. Why not? He *was* interesting, if he did say so himself. He ran through several combinations — only a million or so to go. The lock flickered again as it ran out of the little power he gave it. He had to work faster because the panel stayed a bright red, indicating no entry. The door flickered off, then on again. The door latch flashed green, followed by a loud *click*, and then snapped off completely.

Trick Mark tried the handle. It opened. He and Vere sighed with relief.

They all headed down to the next level. A hangar bay lay before them, where a small-scale transport ship sat in the dark. At one time, a full complement of the most advanced spacefaring Earth vessels would have been stationed here. But only one, minute transport vessel had survived.

TIME TO POWER FAILURE, THREE MINUTES, flashed on CD-45's monitor and initiated a countdown.

Trick Mark and Vere both took in the ship with fear and awe. They headed over to the vessel. Scattered wreckage lay all around it from where the ceiling caved in long ago. Other ships hadn't been as lucky. They lay in ruin, with parts strewn about the hangar bay. CD-45 wheeled up to the boarding ramp. The transport might have an access port for power. At least he could add charge to his back-up battery.

Trick Mark and Vere hesitated, taking in the ship once more before following CD inside. It appeared pristine with a little dust on the beige metal floors and walls, though not bad for being centuries old. At one time, this vessel would likely courier key supplies to the orbital platforms. CD-45 went to the boxy, black metal bridge of the cramped ship but didn't find a power access port he could plug into. Not all transports were designed to have CD units, so there was no need to provide a CD power port. He had exhausted all possibilities. He lowered his head, staring at the floor.

"I don't think he's finding what he wants." Vere had learned to detect his moods just as he did hers.

Trick Mark practiced effective diplomacy. "What about the wreckage outside? I thought I saw one of your— people out there."

His people? He didn't have any "people" but them.

Then it clicked in his ever-fading computerized head. His ocular units expanded. He wheeled out of the ship, searching the hanger bay floor. Wreckage lay everywhere, although not a CD unit in sight. CD-45 scanned the wreckage to his maximum capacity, yet found nothing. He froze in place, with no options left for him.

Trick Mark ran ahead, indicating for him to follow. CD wheeled over. He had about ninety seconds before power failure. Why not humour the human?

Lying in a pile of wreckage, he identified pieces of a CD unit. His ocular units zeroed in with laser focus. His "people" indeed.

CD-45 picked up the unit, then turned it to the side. The access port jammed. Trick Mark tried to pry it open, with no effect. CD accessed one of his tools. It would drain what little energy remained, however, no other choice presented itself. With a couple of well-placed laser cuts, the port opened. CD-45 pulled out the battery. He stood taller. It contained substantial charge. He would have immediately installed it, but then everything went dark for CD.

Then came brightness, a lot of brightness. His systems rebooted. Trick Mark and Vere stared at him, so he held out both of his metal hands with thumbs up. They laughed and then hugged him. He carefully placed his hands on their shoulders. Humans understood the necessity of such contact. CD-45 checked his open port before sealing it.

"We didn't know if we put it in right," Vere admitted with a worried look.

The battery wouldn't work if installed incorrectly. But he extended his hand, patting hers to provide assurance.

"If you got what you needed, can we go now?" Trick Mark expressed eagerness to leave, and CD-45 couldn't blame him.

No one wanted to say in this dark place longer than they had to. He wheeled his way back onto the ship, then headed for the shallow bridge. One long, tall viewport spanned its length. Three banks of piloting consoles arced around cushioned chairs, a triple redundancy to pass safety protocols of the day. However, CD-45 could easily pilot the ship solo. He tapped the smooth, dark panel. It flickered to life. The ceiling lit up with a pale-blue array. CD tried several start-up procedures while Trick Mark and Vere talked behind him.

Vere held herself. "Two ancient places in one week ... I think that's about all the adventure I can take."

Trick Mark shook his head. "That's what we get when we tangle with a wizard and befriend enchanted creatures."

Curious; they thought both the man and CD-45 wielded magical abilities. They'd replaced his battery, saw the pieces of a CD unit, yet continued to believe he existed as an organic being with special powers.

Vere shivered. "Now I know why people don't go into the Enchanted Lands. They're too dangerous."

Trick Mark surveyed the ship. "But full of adventure."

"What are we doing in here? What is this thing?" Vere sounded untrusting.

Of course, she'd only recently met CD-45. It took humans time to form bonds, therefore gaining trust.

"I think it's some kind of ship, yet there are no sails and we aren't near water." Trick Mark expressed genuine confusion.

"Then how are we getting out of here?" Vere sounded worried.

CD tried another start-up routine, and the ship surged to life.

A computer-generated female voice riffed off everything wrong with the ship: "System start-up. Computer online. Maintenance is recommended before using any systems. Main power online, propulsion damaged."

Both his companions looked around anxiously while the disembodied voice of the computer spoke.

Vere exclaimed, "It's alive too!"

Trick Mark reflected Vere's trepidation. "I don't know what it is, Vere."

The ship might not even fly. Unfortunately, the probability of acquiring a second intact spacefaring vessel fell dramatically. The ship's thrusters came online. CD-45 pointed the ship at the gigantic landing bay doors. He tried to open them, but they stayed dormant for too long. He needed other options. CD searched the computer core, finding one operational laser turret. He aimed at the bay doors, then fired. Vere and Trick Mark ducked down to the floor of the bridge. CD-45 continued firing until the doors exploded, falling away. Metal with centuries of natural debris continued to tumble down, giving way to the late-day sun shining in.

He paused, then turned to Vere and Trick Mark. He stared at them for a long time until they peered up. CD-45 pointed to both seats on either side of him. His companions must have gotten the message because they bolted into those seats. CD fastened his own safety strap, so his human friends followed suit.

CD-45 used the manoeuvering thrusters to take the ship closer to the doors. He tried to start the engines. They groaned, then shut down. He tried again, with the same result. After a few adjustments, a third time propelled the ship forward. Trick Mark and Vere formed a chorus of screams as the ship surged out of the hanger. CD pointed the ship skyward.

He hoped his human friends liked the orbital platforms. CD-45 struggled with conflicting ideas. One: receive desperately needed help from his friends. Two: return them to their home.

Guilt filled his circuits, but despite his feelings, the main directive won out. He needed to make sure the engines would last.

Both Trick Mark and Vere laughed with excitement; they clearly enjoyed the ride. CD joined in with a few emphatic head bobs. What an experience he had provided them, something no one else would believe. Then the engines sputtered before snapping off.

Damn! Systems looked optimal just a second ago. What an experience, indeed. CD-45's ocular units dilated as the ship plummeted back to the ground.

CHAPTER TWENTY-TWO

Ondreeal rode in the blistering sun. Sweat dripped down her blue-tinted face. She looked behind at the tall, dark, jagged mountains, reaching up to the sky like the claws of some vicious beast, raking at the clouds. A vast landscape of baked, cracked soil stretched out behind her.

She should go back and return the wand to Sir Francis. Then where would she go? If she found herself in trouble, would the wand kill for her, just as it had in the arena?

The image of the dead barbarian came back to her, along with the two men on the farm. She shook her head, trying to pry free the images, but they just kept coming. The friendly, smiling faces of the villagers melted into dead stares. Ondreeal could never find peace on the farm, not ever again. She had no home, no one to turn to. She didn't deserve to have anyone.

Encased by the craggy mountains, she imagined she sat in the hand of a giant, waiting for its grip to close. At least it would stop her from feeling. She wiped away the tears and steeled her jaw.

She searched for signs of greenery. Far in the distance lay only more brown-red landscape, where the horizon rippled as if flames burned directly beneath it. Her horse slowed with each passing moment. She couldn't survive for long without him. She wouldn't make it to find shelter or water — that is, if any existed to find.

This heat compared to the only drought they had ever endured on the farm. The trees had carried budding new leaves through the ripples of heat. A ten-year-old Ondreeal took in the empty farm with bare fields of light-brown dirt. The animals sounded their disapproval of the heat from inside the barn. Otto kept saying, "Without water, planting is just idiotic."

She joyfully ran after her friend, Tevery, who at the same age, looked down at her. His fingers, thin like hers, looked longer. He had a brightness of spirit on his young face, making Ondreeal's heart grow lighter.

They had stopped beside the barn.

Tevery shyly glanced at her. "You're my best friend, Ondreeal."

In the shadiest part of the barn, an area given shelter by an oak tree, grew a tiny bunch of wild blossoms. Tevery pointed at the flowers and blushed. "They're as pretty as you are."

She smiled broadly at him. Then he quickly closed the distance, kissing her. Ondreeal's eyes shut as the world stopped. She couldn't even breathe. Did she stay on her feet? When he moved away, she opened her eyes, allowing the world to rush back. They smiled at each other and would have stayed there a moment longer, but a summons came from across the yard.

His mother hollered, "Tevery, we're leaving! Time to go."

"Can I come back tomorrow?" he called back.

His father yelled impatiently. "We're moving son. The farm was sold. Time to go. Now move!"

The disappointed expression on his face told her he didn't want to go. But he slowly turned, then ran to his father. She wanted to see him again, yet her wish wouldn't come true. The next day, it rained. Otto looked so happy, he half-smiled.

Tevery and Ondreeal had been promised to each other by their parents. He was to come back for her in due time. Now all he would find was an empty farm.

It seemed like everyone left her one way or another. Her mother died, Tevery moved away, she had a detached father in Otto. Just days ago, she'd rained death on her home; taking away any others she cared for. Maybe she was always meant to be alone. She blinked as she came out of the memory, focusing on the mountains ahead.

The horse finally stopped, and for all her efforts, she couldn't get him to move. Ondreeal slowly looked all around the area. Each part of the horizon appeared dominated by the jagged black mountains. If another tunnel existed like the one she had left behind, she couldn't find it. Which mountain might hide it? Could she make it to the other side before expending all her strength?

She squinted as she searched the horizon. Something the colour green sprawled in the distance. Green rocks or plants? Either way, this remained the only sign of hope she had. So, she drummed the horse's sides, and off they went. Still, the terrain grew hilly, making each step harder.

An entire area covered in green lay ahead. Ondreeal clucked at the horse to move faster. It did as asked. Ondreeal strained her eyes but found no trees. Perhaps moss grew on the stones. Steam rose from the grounds' surface, so that could mean a hot spring — she preferred cool water at the moment, but beggars couldn't be choosers. She coughed, and this time the horse refused to move forward. She couldn't blame it. The smell burned her nose. She jumped down and left the horse where he stood, then moved on toward the spot. She coughed until she doubled over on the ground. Whatever the wind carried, it would ensure a speedy death. She managed to pull herself up and walk back to the horse, guiding it away from the awful fumes. Certainly, with such smells, she'd find no drinkable water.

***

They travelled for hours more until the ground flattened into long stretches of cracked, dry clay. Ondreeal fought to keep her eyes open. She had to keep going.

Then the horse stopped, grunted, and keeled over.

Ondreeal fell to his side. His laboured breathing grew weaker with each passing moment. Ondreeal squinted up at the blistering sun, wiping sweat from her brow. How else could she find water? Her eyes brightened for a moment as she rifled through her bag. She pulled out two sticks and broke one in two pieces. She pulled a few strands of hair out of her head, using them to tie the broken half to the middle of the longer stick. This made it into a Y shape, though piecing it together might not work as well as finding a natural branch. She should have remembered it sooner. Tevery had taught her the trick to pass the time. They never found any water then; however, she hoped this time would be different.

Ondreeal pointed the stick at the ground, then slowly moved around the area. Nothing. She widened the circle around the horse. Suddenly, the rod reacted to something, or at least she hoped it did.

She burrowed down into the dry surface, but the colour of the dirt never darkened. This didn't make any sense. Land always held some moisture in it. What if the soil and clay remained dry for miles down before she found water? She walked back to the unmoving horse. She knelt, caressing his dark mane, but the pulse in his neck had stopped. She shook her head, staring at the magnificent creature. Her body heaved with grief.

She placed both hands on the horse. "I'm sorry."

She lowered her head until her forehead touched its mane. At least she hadn't taken Ranger with her, and with luck he'd stay safe on the farm. But just like this horse, she would soon follow in death, even if she made it to nightfall. She licked her cracked, dry lips.

She stayed there a long time until numbness filled her. Her short but eventful journey would soon end. Nevertheless, she did have one option left to her. She reached into her tunic and pulled out the wand — dark, like a piece of onyx, even with her touch. Previously, every time she had touched it, it lit up that brilliant blue-white colour — but not now. Other times, her hand shook as she held the wand. Now it remained steady, calm. If she could only use it in desperation, then she wouldn't make a very good wizard.

She sat on the ground and placed the wand down in front of her. She pulled out the locket Sir Francis had given her. She opened it and gently touched the image of her mother.

"What would you do?"

The picture of her mother smiled brightly at her. As if she knew something about her daughter's ability that Ondreeal had yet to discover. If Sir Francis really had known Ondreeal as a baby, then that meant he knew her mother in a way she never would. One day, with luck, she would return to Bastion and get the answers about her past that she so desperately needed.

She closed the locket and tucked it back into her shirt. She held her hands over the wand and closed her eyes. Intermittently, she peeked at the ground. Each time, her shadow had moved. Sweat ran down over her parched lips. Finally, she fell back with exhaustion and lay there, staring up at the clear, blue sky. She looked to her steady hand. Her lips trembled amid tears of sorrow.

She rolled onto her side, her limbs shaking with the effort. She slowly pulled herself forward to the wand. Her emotions churned like a building storm, though if she couldn't control the wand, she'd be the only one who would die this time. She grabbed it with one hand, pushing herself up to her knees with the other. The wand sprang to life, glowing blue-white in her grasp. She raised it over her head, clutching it with both hands as she screamed and plunged it into the ground.

"Give me water you, stupid stick!" she demanded. Then she slumped down, her last shreds of energy exhausted.

Her head rested on the ground close to the wand. She moved her fingers to grab it, yet they barely touched it. She closed her eyes, waiting for death. Then her cheek got cold — no, not cold but wet. Her eyes cracked open. Water bubbled up all around the glowing wand. She pulled herself closer and drank from the little fountain of water.

The thin shadow the wand cast against the ground moved a while longer before Ondreeal felt enough strength to stand. She filled a bottle with water from the spring before she pulled the wand free. That is, she tried to pull the wand free.

She tugged at it a little harder. Her hands slipped with each attempt. She couldn't get a solid grip with the liquid springing up around it. She pulled with all her strength until it came free. She fell back with a dull thud as water erupted into the air. Ondreeal sat there, stunned. The impossibly high stream shot into the sky and rained back down, drenching her. She launched to her feet. Ondreeal glanced over to the body of the horse, pointing the wand at the creature.

"Bring him back to life." Her voice trembled.

Blue-white energy meandered out, like fingers wrapping themselves around the horse. Then it let out a loud whinny, and rose from the ground. Its eyes glowed blue-white, grotesque and unnatural. Ondreeal turned away, shutting her eyes tightly.

"Stop!" she screamed.

When she turned back, the horse lay still on the ground. Her tears mixed with water raining down on her while she pointed the wand at the geyser.

"Stop the water at once," she demanded with a strong voice.

But the stream of water remained steady.

"I said, no more water!" she yelled at it.

The hole in the ground widened even more. Water continued to gush forth. Streams formed, snaking their way out in all directions.

"Stop it, now. Stop it!"

Another geyser appeared, then another, until four had sprouted without a sign of slowing down. Ondreeal turned and ran. Unfortunately for her, she couldn't go back in the direction she'd come. That way became blocked by a wall of water geysers, with more springing up behind them. She could only head to the other side of the mountain range, hoping to find a way out when she reached there.

CHAPTER TWENTY-THREE

C D-45's mechanical hands flew over the control panel as the view spiraled faster, creating a centrifugal force that would have unpleasant consequences for his friends, if it continued on an acceleration curve. His ocular units processed information at one thousand terabytes per nanosecond. This allowed him to observe Alpha Four Five from a bird's-eye view, from three groups of cities on the West Coast of North America. Alpha Four Five-C, the one he had encountered while saving Vere and Trick Mark, came from a modest group of cities to the south. Avoiding that homicidal human at all costs made a top priority.

Alpha Four Five-B came from a group of cities that appeared in disrepair, even from a great distance, thanks to CD-45's superior vision. That source looked brightest around the Black Circle Mountains, indicating recent use, perhaps after years of dormancy. With such high technology in their possession, they hadn't created a society to equal it. This meant that they either didn't know how to properly use the technology or lacked the ability to replicate key components. Whatever the reason, humans seemed equally capable of destruction or creation.

This only took fractions of a second to consider, yet the view whirled around even faster. Number one priority: survive.

***

Warning sounds rang throughout the strange ship. Trick Mark clung to the arms of his chair. His gaze locked with Vere's. Her eyes carried a terror that reflected his. The ground spun, rushing up at them outside the window. It amazed him that he could feel fear at the prospect of death, especially when he'd faced it many times over the last several days. His heart beat faster as the ground approached.

Vere yelled at CD-45, "Stop this thing!"

Trick Mark called back, "That's what he's trying to do!"

Trick Mark couldn't blame Vere for her fright. He swallowed hard, trying to breathe steadily. His knuckles turned white from clutching the arms of his chair.

CD-45 pulled a lever towards himself. He looked at Vere, then at Trick Mark. They both had similar handles within reach. He must want them to help.

Trick Mark yelled at Vere as he took his own advice, "Pull back on the stick!"

CD-45 pressed a collection of lights, and the view outside the window stopped spinning. The trees whipped by them, then they flew over an ocean—no, an extensive lake.

Trick Mark screamed. "Hang on!"

They skipped over the surface and then plunged into the lake. Murky water filled the view. CD-45 got out of his chair, heading off. Trick Mark looked to Vere. They both jumped out of their chairs, running after him.

CD-45 moved down to the end of a long, bright, white hallway. A door opened by itself—like magic—then CD-45 went inside the narrow room, no bigger than a closet. He gestured for Trick Mark and Vere to follow him. They both stepped inside. The bewitched door closed behind them.

The inside was white, with perfectly smooth walls and seating for four people. A collection of half-inch buttons covered a four-by six-inch, rectangular section of the door. CD-45 pressed a few buttons. Then the cramped room jumped about. Vere and Trick Mark clung to each other.

Vere's voice trembled. "Are we flying up again?"

"I think so." His own voice shook too.

They floated up an inch off their seats. They both screamed as the room rattled. The sound of a crash accompanied one last jolt in the room before it came to a stop.

Trick Mark gulped in a breath. "Are you all right?"

Vere nodded at him. Why did CD-45 take them to this cramped space? Trapped under water, they had no escape. Maybe CD could guide them to the surface.

Trick Mark tried to stand in the tight space. "Can you take us back to dry land?"

CD-45 pressed a light on the wall, causing the door to fly off. They would drown. Trick Mark and Vere both screamed as they reflexively shielded themselves. Trick Mark slowly opened his eyes. Twilight, with a fading yellow glimmer in the west, bathed them in a blue glow while a cool breeze wafted in. The sand of a beach greeted his eyes.

CD-45 opened a small door inside the room, then pulled out two packs, which he gave to Vere and Trick Mark. CD extended his arm, indicating for them to step out first. Trick Mark climbed out, jumping down on the sandy shore of the lake. He looked back at what appeared more like a large plumbing tube found under the streets of Bastion. It must have flown out of the water, leaving the sinking ship behind. Trick Mark would never get used to the miraculous Enchanted Lands.

He watched Vere leap down, a relieved smile tugging at the corners of her mouth.

"Where is home?" Vere asked, turning in a circle.

Land stretched out of sight around the lake, the great ocean nowhere in sight.

Trick Mark pointed west. "That way. I only wish I knew how far."

They had already exceeded their planned one-day journey by several more. CD-45 joined them, picking up a stick and drawing lines in the sand, some curved, others straight. Words, that's what CD made on the shore.

Vere read them with raised eyebrows: I NEED TO GO WEST. I WILL HELP YOU STAY SAFE.

It took CD-45 almost thirty minutes to carve out the phrases. Clearly, he didn't do a lot of writing. It did mean that CD would stay with them for a while. Given the crash landing, Trick Mark hoped it made good sense to travel together.

They walked along the shore for a while before deciding to make a fire and rest for the night. After all, they'd had an event-filled day, full of magical wonders that no one would believe, except, perhaps, for Sir Francis. Trick Mark lay down next to the fire, closing his eyes.

CHAPTER TWENTY-FOUR

Zairoc smiled, admiring his reflection in the small, crystal-clear pond. He had only a little grey around the temples. It made him look distinguished. His image faded, hidden by dark clouds reflecting in the water. He rose to his feet, looking down at the soldiers around him. All of them wore his name on their chests. The group of twelve stayed cloaked in a sphere of invisibility, so as not to alert Sir Francis or Bastion's forces.

Zairoc glared at the white and blue flags flying on the castle of Bastion. He could sense the energy barrier, even from a distance. He pulled out his wand. It glowed red as he closed his eyes. He gritted his teeth with the strain until his eyes popped open.

"He's not even there. Very clever." He squinted at the city.

He may not be able to break Sir Francis's magic, but he certainly could render it inert for a short time.

He looked down at the cowering man on his right and said, "Lieutenant Carrera, give word to the other strike squads. They will have one hour to attack the cities, in two weeks, high noon. Understood?"

He raised an eyebrow to the lieutenant.

Carrera looked up and nodded vigorously before racing off. His plan would still work. Sir Francis couldn't stay away forever. One way or another, the old man would die. First Bastion would fall, then the world. He'd destroy the Decalonians, and then the United Worlds would answer for their crimes.

CHAPTER TWENTY-FIVE

J imena hurried down the dirt street, covered from head to toe, with only her eyes visible. Every few seconds, she glanced back, looking for signs of pursuit. She wore Aztellian Priestess robes decorated with symbols of the sun, the Earth, and the Phoenix. The Church of the God of All absorbed much of Aztellian beliefs; hence most people couldn't tell the difference between Aztellian robes or those worn by the Cinders of Light. The robes served a vital role: while wearing them Jimena wouldn't be stopped by traditionalists or loyalists. She flicked her long, raven locks over her shoulder and hurried down the path.

Sand-covered, mud-brick walls lined the alleyway that she glided down. She manoeuvred her way past rickety merchant booths, beggars, and people going about their business. People coughed, moaned in pain, or reached out to her with shaky hands. That was the result of their war with Aleenda.

She made her way down another busy walkway and a short street, then turned right at another. This part of the city looked like a maze—no one would find her here. She rushed down a dark and quiet alley, careful not to brush her shoulders against the narrow passage. She came to a doorway, where she knocked in a specific pattern.

The door opened, exposing an old señora. Her haggard appearance matched her pungent odour. She left the doorway, and Jimena entered, looking back to find an empty alley on both sides. She quickly closed the door behind herself.

Jimena hunched over as her head scraped the ceiling. She found her way to a runty stool. The old woman stirred something in a terracotta teapot with her scarred arm. What would Jimena have done all those years ago without Zairoc to save her? She'd probably be dead.

Eight years before, she had been on her way to see her brother in Velencentine before he died. She hurried to see him in the royal carriage. That is, until men in a caravan had attacked.

With a blindfold over her eyes, wrists bound, and mouth gagged, they took her away on horseback. Finally, they freed her. And when the blindfold came off, she faced her brother, who stood in a strong stance — accentuated by his chiselled features, bronze complexion, and ashen eyes and hair.

"Ronild! You're supposed to be dying." Jimena's jaw dropped.

"A necessary story to protect you, dear sister." He smiled.

She looked around the meagre room. Her feet creaked against one of the wooden floorboards.

"What is going on? Your men killed the royal guard." She searched his eyes for an answer.

His face remained stoic.

Jimena jumped out of her chair. "Ronild, please say it isn't so. No! Zairoc already suspects I am sympathetic to the cause. He'll kill us both."

Ronild grabbed her hands. "I will explain everything." She sat back down.

"Then speak fast." She broke free, crossing her arms.

"I am the head of the resistance," he told her flatly.

"No. No! Zairoc will kill you." Tears filled her eyes.

"Not if you don't tell him." He leaned closer. "Don't you want to be free?"

Jimena stood and turned away from him.

"He already suspects me. I've disagreed with him too many times." Tears streamed down her face.

"Then stop disagreeing with him. Jimena, we need you to be our eyes in the palace. Listen to what he says and pass along any information to help our cause."

"I can't get him to trust me. If you want to hurt him, do it yourself." She turned to face him.

"You know others have tried, either dying at the hands of Zairoc or those loyal to him. He has too much protection, too much power." Ronild walked around her.

"He is a wizard, you fool! I could stab him through the heart. Do you think that would stop him?" she spat at him.

"He is a monster," Ronild whispered in her ear.

"Not to me." She stepped away.

"Then let me ask you this. Do you want our people to be free?"

"Yes."

"Do you trust me?"

"Yes."

"It will be the hardest thing you've ever done, but you will gain — his trust."

Two hulking men entered the room. Jimena stood, looking at her brother. Ronild's grim eyes could not meet hers.

"Jontas, Alis, you know what to do," Ronild spoke softly.

The two men glanced at each other for a moment, then looked back to Jimena with stony faces. Jontas grabbed her from behind. She tensed her body, bracing herself.

Alis punched her in the stomach. She doubled over in pain. Jontas pulled her upright. Alis hit her again.

"No more. Please," she begged them.

Alis slapped her across the face. He punched her until her eyes dripped with blood. Jontas let go of her, and she fell to the ground. They kicked her. She opened her mouth in a scream, but only a whimper escaped her lips. Then they dragged her out. They put her back in the carriage, and loosed the horses, letting them race back to the capital city of Incoation.

Jimena could barely open her swollen eyes as they dumped her on the front steps of the palace. Then all fell quiet in the darkness. If the guards patrolled another part of the royal grounds, they might not find her in time.

She tried to scream for help, but only the barest of moans emerged from her mouth. She was too far gone and possessed no strength to even yell for help. All she could do was lie there on the cold stones of the palace stairs.

Her swollen eyes grew heavy. Soon she would die here.

Footsteps approached, someone running towards her—a housemaid. She turned Jimena over, screaming at the sight of her condition. Then the woman hurried back towards the palace.

Soon after, much of the staff surrounded her with worried faces, although not for her. They were concerned for themselves. If she died while they watched, her husband would kill them all.

Zairoc yelled at them now. "Move!"

They parted like a shroud lifting off the face of the dead. Zairoc fell to his knees by her side, with tears in his eyes. His panic and love for her showed clearly on his face. Zairoc always treated Jimena with such gentleness. His wand glowed brightly, then she felt strength return to her body. Zairoc picked her up and whisked her off to their bedroom.

"Who did this to you?" He wouldn't even look at her.

"They said they were rebels, that they had a message for you. They want you to know they can hurt you. That you're not untouchable." Tears streamed down her face.

"I swear to you. I will kill them all, every one ... their families first, as they watch. Then they will die." He cried, kneeling before her.

"My husband. Together there is nothing we can't do. I am yours for eternity. You are mine forever. We are only stronger now." She pulled him up, kissing him.

She needed to stay loyal to both Ronild and Zairoc. She'd passed information to the resistance since that day eight years before, but nothing that could really hurt her husband. Zairoc had saved her; she owed him her life.

She blinked, coming back to the present, focusing on the old woman who stirred her pot of tea. The inadequate fireplace looked barely big enough for the señora's old teapot.

"What news of the resistance do you have for me?" Jimena asked her.

The old woman hunched in a rough wooden chair that matched a modest table. She poured hot liquid into two wooden cups.

"Sit. Drink with me," she demanded.

"I shouldn't stay long. If they passed information, then I need it." Jimena warned her.

The old woman wore a determined look on her dark, leathery face that contrasted with her white, flowing hair. Jimena pulled the stool close to the aged señora.

She held up her cup. "My name is Darletta."

Jimena matched her gesture, then they drank.

"You know what will happen to your husband if we are successful." Darletta put her cup down.

"He is very powerful. I would think exile would be all that could be done." Jimena stared down into teacup.

"That would mean your exile too." The old señora downed the cup of tea and poured another.

Jimena scrutinized Darletta. "My role in the resistance would be revealed."

"That's not what I meant." The old woman downed another cup of the hot liquid. Her mouth steamed like a mythical dragon.

"What do you mean, then?" Jimena huffed with impatience.

"You would go with him of your own free will." Darletta leaned in closer and breathed steamy breath on her.

"Why would I do that? He would hate me when he found out. That is, if he didn't kill me." Jimena put her cup down.

"Ah, yes. But that wouldn't matter to you, would it? You would follow him wherever he goes. Even if he cursed you to die, you would still follow him." The señora leaned closer, peering into Jimena's eyes.

Jimena shook her head. She stood quickly, banging her skull on the ceiling.

"If you have no news, I should be going. I've stayed too long." Jimena moved to the door.

"I know, because I was young once too. Why don't you guess who I was married to?" The woman looked like she would cry.

"I'm not playing games with you." Jimena reached over, gripping Darletta's arm. "Tell me what you mean."

The old woman looked sad.

"I was you, and one day, you will be me.

224

Chapter Twenty-Six

O ndreeal held herself, shivering. The roar of the geysers had faded to nothing. Stars filled the sky as they always did, though here, far away from even a single torchlight, they shone brighter. There were always flashes among the stars. Most explained this by saying the God of All fought constantly against dark forces. If true, they really battled tonight, because she lost count of how many she'd seen.

True to their name, the Black Circle Mountains loomed enormous, surrounding her. Maybe after another day's journey, she'd ascend to the top of a peak. She did have some food, though she doubted it would be enough to sustain her through the mountains. Not unless she found something edible as she travelled up one side.

She dragged her feet, struggling to keep her eyes open. She'd only gotten broken sleep at Bastion's castle several days before. She slumped against a rocky outcropping, resting her head on the ground. Perhaps now she could sleep. Then, as if on cue, a steady stream of water from one of the now distant geysers, pushed against her cheek, and she scrambled to her feet.

The water may not have stopped, but at least she wouldn't die of thirst. She might drown if she stayed long enough, but she hoped to be over the mountain before that became a concern.

Ondreeal stopped to look back at two steady streams of water following her like lost puppies, a few feet forward, stopping before changing directions. The tips of the mountains shone, bathed in an orange glow from the east. Ahead of her the giant, spiked mountains cast long shadows that robbed her of heat. She'd welcome warmth again, after a night of shivering.

She stopped, took out the wand, and whispered, "Show me the path."

The wand glowed in her grasp, the air calm around her. Ondreeal scanned the silent mountains. She had fortune on her side, having found a cave into the mountains, but now that luck had turned.

The stones of the mountain appeared black and bare. If only they bore plants, trees, something growing that she might eat. The stone looked unusual, like so much else that she found new. She worked her way up the base of what appeared to be a shorter mountain.

In amazing physical form from a lifetime of farm work, the ascent should have been achievable. Much to her dismay, the higher she climbed, the harder it became to breathe.

Ondreeal sucked in air. She stared at a shallow crevice that lay before her, far too wide to jump over. What if she asked the wand to float her across? Then again, it might send her right up to the clouds, where certainly no food waited for her.

No, she needed to figure this one out on her own. She had a section of rope in her knapsack, though nothing to attach it to. She searched the ground, settling on a modest, rough boulder that might do the trick. She tied the rope around the stone, forming a tight knot. She swung the rock tied with rope and then flung it across the crevice. It landed on the other side, with Ondreeal holding the free end of the rope. She pulled, and it slipped off.

Ondreeal reeled in the rope, moved to a different spot and tried again, with the same result. She let out a sigh of frustration. She picked a third location with a suitable number of boulders. She flung the rig across, then pulled the rope. It stayed firmly entrenched between two slabs. She let the rope go so that it hung against the stone shelf on the other side. She nodded with the small triumph.

Ondreeal carefully climbed down, walked across, and grabbed the rope. She pulled, quickly climbing without hesitation. Certainly, it would hold her weight as she scaled up the rock wall. When she got to the top, she laughed with elation.

"Yes!" Her voice echoed against the mountains.

She looked down and stared desperately at an icy abyssal drop that opened several feet in front of her, with rolling, snow-covered mountains beyond. On a cliffside to the right lay an upward mountain path at about eye level. Beside this, the mountain peak reached up out of sight. She picked up the rock-tied rope and walked along the top of the yawning crevasse. When she grew close enough, she wedged the rock into a boulder underfoot. She let the rope hang above the unfathomable drop. She peered over the edge, searching for the bottom, but it remained hidden in darkness. She carefully climbed onto the rope, gazing upwards while she lowered herself. Her moist hands suddenly slipped an inch.

"Oh, no." Her voice echoed back to her.

She winced with pain from the rope burn, though her blue-tinted hands appeared uninjured. She swallowed hard, worry filling her tense body. She stepped along the wall as far to the right as she could. Then she let herself swing towards the mountain path. Her foot grazed the ground on the other side, but she couldn't keep her footing. She swung again to the right, then back to the left. Both feet landed. She hung precariously off the edge. Her chest heaved. She glanced down at the dark drop. She closed her eyes tightly, opening them to focus on the trail.

She tried to pull herself over with her feet. She inched forward. Her legs shook as she held her breath. She strained, pulling herself forward—just a little farther, and she'd land safely on the mountain pass. Suddenly, the rope came loose from where she'd tied it. She landed on the edge of the path, sliding backwards. Her cry echoed.

Ondreeal let go of the rope, dug in with her heels, and clutched the ground with her fingers. She came to a sudden stop. Her back faced the drop. Any second she could slide to her death. She willed herself forward, getting one leg under her, heaving with the strain, then the other leg. But she slid back a few more inches. This time, she swallowed a scream. She took a deep breath and pushed her body forward to the rock path. She clung to it like a baby to its mother.

Ondreeal crawled up the steep trail until the ground levelled out. She breathed deeply, allowing the cold dirt to take her weight. She looked down at her blue-tinted hands, completely uninjured. Magic might keep her alive after all. The rope had fallen into the deep of the mountain, so she stood up and trudged on.

***

She managed to find shelter at night—not a cave, a rocky overhang, but an alcove that barely broke the howling winds. She'd welcome back the unbearable heat of the hot, dry desert. Ondreeal pulled out the wand, asking for warmth. The dark surface reflected back to her. If she tried harder, it might burn her to ashes. She let out a sigh of frustration between her chattering teeth.

Ondreeal pulled out what little food she had left. She ate a tiny piece of cheese with stale bread. Would she survive, or would someone find her one day, clutching the wand in her dead hand? Maybe the wand should have chosen someone else, one more capable of mastering its powers and becoming a worthy ally for Sir Francis.

What would he think of her now? She must look like a pathetic wreck. She had to try not to give up, no matter how hard things got or what she faced. That night in the humble alcove repeated itself in others as she moved over the mountain. Days must have passed, though it felt like weeks spent clutching to life in the bitter cold. Despite the gruelling climb, she continued upwards, higher and higher.

***

Ondreeal shivered amid snowflakes flittering around her, in sharp contrast to the bright sun shining on the rich, green forest far below. The black peaks looked bare from the desert. Perhaps, on the inside of the ring, it burned too hot for snow. On the outside face of the mountains, cooler air prevailed. She rummaged through her bag but found nothing more to eat.

"Give me a fresh apple," she whispered into the air.

The wand's glow fluctuated in her tunic, then went dark. If only she understood the mysteries of the wand, she would make it rain fruit. Any hope of survival would come from getting food off the land. To make matters worse, the mountain path ended.

Ondreeal gazed at the deep drop before her, along with the precarious slope to her left. She carefully stepped into the snow of the slope. The snow helped create a bit of a footing. She was edging her way down when the colour green caught her eye. Strange, prickly trees grew just a few meters below. She carefully made her way down the steep slope. When she came to the first few runty trees, she grabbed them for support and laughed; she just might survive this after all.

She edged down further, took a step, and fell right through the snow. It turned into an ice tunnel that veered down, twisting and turning. She screamed as she slid over the surface. Ondreeal tried to get her footing but only managed to put herself into a spin. She shot off the ice into the open air. Then she landed hard, sliding down faster on a steep slope. She grabbed at shrubs and weeds, anything to slow her descent. She came to a sudden halt, taking in deep breaths as she lay against the steep mountain. She looked up at the little shrub she clung to. If she let go, she'd plummet. The slope looked smooth, with nowhere for a safe landing.

Ondreeal peered down. An endless drop waited not far away. She would surely head right off the edge. Even with the blue-tinted skin, a long drop would likely kill her. The roots partially gave away. Ondreeal jerked downward a few inches. She clung to the plant with both her hands as the wand glowed from within her tunic.

"No, please, God of All, no..."

The roots gave way a little more. She shrieked.

She clutched the shrub with one hand, using her free hand to reach into her tunic. The shrub ripped out of the soil, sending Ondreeal into free fall.

She cried out.

She looked down to the fast-approaching cliff and struggled with her tunic, pulling out the glowing wand.

Then she sailed over the edge. White clouds spread below her like a bed of cotton. She hurtled towards them, howling in fear. Her head spun, and she struggled to keep her eyes open as the clouds grew larger. She tried to point the wand forward, but the wind pushed her limbs back. It took all her strength to bring her arms ahead, grasping the wand with both hands. Unfocused magical energy sparked, swirled, and darted out of the wand. Ondreeal concentrated on one part of the cloud below as energy blasted a huge hole in it. She sailed right through. The hole closed in on itself. The wand sparked but did nothing to slow her quick descent.

The cloud cleared away, and land approached very fast. Ondreeal pointed at the ground, so the wand shot energy at it. Her free-fall slowed ever so slightly but not enough for safety. She hurtled towards land.

She wailed, closing her eyes. The wand's energy swirled, flowing over the ground as Ondreeal collided with it.

CHAPTER TWENTY-SEVEN

B radai sat on a bench staring down at his plate of food. He readjusted his brown robe. Then he scratched a tuft of dark hair beside his ear and extended the action down into his short beard.

A warm breeze blew through the planted vegetables surrounding him. Sweet perfumes of the many crops wafted into his nose. From the Lumenary's courtyard, the deep green of the Enchanted Lands lay all around him, far below. Steam lifted off of the trees, disappearing into the bright sun directly overhead.

Bradai grabbed his fork. He dug into his food with his usual zealousness. His mother had once told him to eat only one meal a day. One meal … what could his mother have been thinking? He needed at least six meals a day just to feel right. Any less and he became as dizzy as a cat when you swung it by the tail.

His mother thought that way because they lived a very poor life, with little money for food. Consequently, Bradai could never stop the rumbling of his own stomach.

He found that if he watched people for long enough, he could tell when a home sat empty. This made it very easy for him to break in, steal their most valuable objects, and then sell them for money. Bradai only ever took from wealthy homes. He figured their owners possessed more than enough, so they wouldn't miss the extra items. He explained to his parents that he got the money from panhandling. They looked extremely unconvinced, but they found it hard to turn down money that paid the rent and—most importantly to Bradai—put food back on the table.

Life returned to the good times for a while. That ended when a law enforcer came to their door. Someone saw Bradai leaving the home of a councillor. He had stolen from the wrong person, someone who prized his possessions. Unfortunately, Bradai, in his stupidity, kept a few items under his bed for an occasion when he really needed them. He'd made the mistake of a novice: never hide what you've stolen beneath your mattress, it implies guilt. The law enforcer obviously thought the same when he arrested Bradai.

His parents wailed with grief. They begged the councillor not to throw Bradai in jail. They asked instead that he be rehabilitated. So, they sent him to learn the ways of the Embertree and to seek forgiveness from the God of All. He spent several years learning their ways, becoming an exceptional Ember.

At last, the time had come for him to revisit his old life, one of the many steps on the path to enlightenment set upon by the Embertree. When he met his mother, she looked at him with disapproval and sadness in her eyes. Bradai stared in confusion, certain that she would be elated.

"It's not that I'm not proud of you, Son. I am. Really, we're very proud. We tell everyone that our son is in the Embertree. Everyone's very impressed when they hear of it." She gave him a slight smile.

He stood tall. "Then why do you look so sad, Mother?"

"You've just gotten so fat. I thought the Embertree would keep you from eating so much." She wiped tears from her eyes.

Fat ... his own mother thought he was fat. Well, he was fat, but a mother shouldn't say that about her son. Call him big-boned or something like that. He dived back into his meal as he ate outside of the Lumenary.

A strange noise came from behind him in the garden. He eyeballed an odd blue glow over all the potatoes, along with part of the turnips. The glow shot down from the sky. Then something flashed in front of his eyes, making a rather loud thud. He gazed back down at the garden. His eyes widened as his jaw fell open. He found a wide hole in the ground where half of the potato plants had formerly grown.

Then he heard a clanging sound....

He looked down. In his surprise, he must have dropped his plate. The rest of his lunch lay in the garden. This must be what robbery felt like, with the food stolen right out of his mouth.

"Ember Doyle," he called over his shoulder.

All that answered him was the occasional chirping of a small bird, accompanied by the whistle of the wind. He glared up at the sky, yet no rain or hail fell. Bradai slowly approached the giant hole that had now become part of the garden and peered inside.

"Dear God of All, it's raining girls."

"What is it, Ember?"

Bradai glanced over his shoulder. Ember Doyle strode his way out, with that winning smile that charmed so many of the ladies. Dark and handsome, with a head of golden locks, he presented the perfect face of the Embertree. Who could say no to him? Well, Bradai could. He liked Doyle, who made twice the Ember that Bradai had, although he'd never admit that to Doyle. While he loved the Lumenary in his own way, he missed his days of adventure.

"What—?" Doyle's face dropped when he saw the girl. "Dear God of All." He scowled at Bradai with an accusing eye. "What did you do?"

"Don't give me that look. I was eating my lunch." Bradai glared up at Doyle. He would not be blamed for this.

"Of course, you were." Doyle snidely remarked.

"I was eating my lunch, and then, *boom*. Down she came, like a rock." Bradai slapped his two hands together to illustrate his point.

"We should get her out of there." Doyle's face reflected concern mixed with astonishment.

"You can't romance the girl. She's a pancake. Dead. Besides, her nose is probably flatter than my cousin Tolin's." Bradai shivered with a grimace.

"We can't leave her there. She'll start to smell." Doyle moved closer to the hole.

Bradai indicated the wrecked rows of vegetables. "She'll be good for the garden."

Doyle punched him on the arm.

"Ouch. Careful, Doyle, the other Embers might see that our devotion is not as deep as theirs."

***

Ondreeal stared at a strange, wooden board ceiling, similar to the one in her bedroom on the farm, but different. She lay in a soft, warm bed—but where?

Ondreeal tried to sit up, until dizziness overtook her, and her head flopped back down to a fluffy pillow. She looked around the modest room: one door stood to her left, maybe six feet away. She looked over to a window that took up most of the wall past the foot of the bed.

One other small piece of furniture occupied the room, perhaps for storing clothing. It had three drawers made from highly polished dark wood. On top of the drawers sat a book. Ondreeal raised her head, mouthing some of the letters on the cover. Her head flopped back down to the pillow. She would have to gain the strength to get up and read the cover; it might hold a clue about her current dwelling.

She closed her eyes, seeing the terrifying fall. Her fingers and feet tingled at the image. She tensed from that sensation spreading throughout her body. Was that her memory, or magic? She lifted her hands as much as she could. They appeared normal, the blue tint had vanished, the magical enchantment having been used up in the fall. At least she continued to draw breath. Every part of her body felt drained of life, like she'd been forced to work the farm for a week without stopping for food or drink.

The door creaked open, and in walked a man dressed in the same brown clothing worn by the Embertree. She had fallen into a Lumenary. The man put a bowl of water with a cloth on the little drawer. His face, the most beautiful she'd ever seen on a man, had a mess of golden hair on top. His almost-yellow eyes sparkled, matching with the most brilliant smile he gave her.

"Good evening lady. Can you tell me how you feel?" He moved to her side, kneeling down.

Ondreeal moved her mouth, though only air escaped her lips. She tried with all her might to form a word. She managed to say, "On-dree-al."

"I'm sorry, I don't understand." He moved his ear closer to her mouth.

"Name ... al." It took all her strength just to form a few sounds. Her hands clenched into fists with frustration.

"Al. That's your name, is it?"

"Al," — that's what Otto called her, although it sounded much better coming from this handsome man.

"Al, I'm called Doyle. It is an honour to talk with the girl who fell out of the sky."

He smiled broadly, and it somehow made tension leave her body. Her eyelids felt heavy. Doyle appeared, then disappeared, as she struggled to keep her eyes open. He made the choice for her, gently closing them with his fingers.

"Time for sleep, Al. You need your rest. Perhaps you are just the thing two thieves' need."

His words faded. What did he say? Even her conscious thoughts faded as she drifted into a deep slumber.

CHAPTER TWENTY-EIGHT

J imena moved to the door before turning back to the
señora.

Darletta gulped another cup of tea and breathed out a
plume of steam. "Eatan, he is an officer in the military. He
is looking for a way to smuggle people out of the capital,
people that would otherwise be sentenced to the palace
dungeon."

"Where are they being smuggled to?" Jimena took a
step back towards her.

"The north, of course, to the gleaming tours of Atlantia."
Darletta held her hand high, looking up as if she could
see the towers right before her.

"All of Aleenda's cities are deserted." Jimena turned,
placing her hand on the door.

She'd already spent too much time on this crazy, old
woman.

"That is what we wanted you to believe." Darletta
smiled a gnarl toothed grin.

"If you got them out before, why do you need me?"

"The trade routes to the north were closed one month
ago. We knew then that the wizard was planning war.
But what could we do? Someone needs to stop him." The
señora glared at her with eyes like saucers.

Jimena shook her head. "I can't reopen the trade
routes."

"Try. Something. Anything. You come back to see me when you've figured it out." The señora turned away from her, to pour another cup of tea.

Jimena covered her face and bolted out the door. She headed back onto the busy streets. Ronild had asked her to meet with the woman, claiming the highest of importance. If only she'd turned it down. The woman disturbed her more than she wanted to admit.

She said they were the same. Could she be one of Zairoc's former wives?

Jimena shuddered. She hurried on.

***

Jimena paced past the orange silk sheets of her marriage bed, glancing down at the plush, multicoloured rug at the foot of the bed, beyond this, the darkest of brown wood planks made up the floor and panelling over the walls. Could she organise an expedition to the north, perhaps to search for supplies? No, Zairoc would tell her that the deserted cities held nothing of value.

That didn't match the local stories. Farmers in the countryside wouldn't dare go into a deserted wizard city. They said that the ghost of Aleenda haunted the streets and she would curse anyone who desecrated what she'd built. Some foolish farmers, who risked the wrath of her ghost to search for anything valuable, had their own farms destroyed in mysterious ways. She needed to find a reason to go north besides making war.

A loud knock came at the doors. Jimena jumped back, but quickly composed herself.

"Come in," she called.

The door opened slowly, and Genik's head appeared, eyes fixed on the floor. With his body completely covered from head to toe in black robes, only his eyes remained visible. Zairoc called him a "special project." He had tortured the man. Once finished, Zairoc named him Genik and designated him Jimena's hand servant. Zairoc demanded the staff call him a man-in-waiting. What had Genik done to deserve such torture and then such trust? Despite the strange events that had brought Genik into Jimena's life, they had formed a kind of trust— an understanding. No one in the palace proved more reliable than him.

"My lady, please forgive me, but the council is meeting." He gulped down air.

"My husband oversees such matters. But in his absence, you were right to inform me." She crossed her arms.

"Then you will go?" Genik glanced up at her quickly, then again dropped his eyes to the floor.

She nodded to him and headed out the door. He followed just behind.

Jimena wound her way through the wings of the palace that was covered in brilliant red rugs with soaring ceilings from which hung sparkling chandeliers. At the huge, curved bank of windows, just outside the chamber, she paused and took a breath. Genik promptly opened the doors to admit them, and all the council members stared at her.

Five council members, one for each district, sat at a polished round table, wearing robes embroidered with beads in every pastel colour. This type of clothing fitted their stations, showing their wealth. Jimena had learned about each man through formal gatherings over the years.

Councillor Xandren glared at her from his smooth, youthful face. "Lady Jimena, we were expecting Zairoc."

No more than forty years old — his black locks hadn't greyed like the other council members — he carried an air of importance beyond his years. That air never materialized in Zairoc's presence. Xandren wouldn't dare. But he clearly saw himself as superior to Zairoc's wife.

Councillor Varnex liked his gold. He wore a ring made of the precious metal on each of his fat fingers. "What Councillor Xandren means is, we scheduled a meeting with him. Is he coming?"

Councillor Canin shifted in his seat with annoyance. The man spent most of the time just trying to keep his long, milky beard from curling up. He constantly stroked it. "Should we come back?" He asked as though he had something more pressing to do.

Councillor Tanelli stood with a broad smile plastered on his face. He had tons of charm and not much else. "We should come back." He nodded in affirmation

Councillor Gellintris stood, bowing his head to Jimena. "What my colleagues mean to say is, thank you for joining us Lady Jimena, but we don't wish to bother you." The smartest of all the councillors, he came well-dressed but understated. He kept his thoughts to himself most of the time, occasionally adding comments to influence others' ideas.

Jimena sat down in Zairoc's seat. The council members tried to hide their surprise, though their faces betrayed them. She'd become skilled at reading people, even when they wore a stony, cold stare. The only one she had trouble reading was Zairoc.

"My husband cannot be here today," she announced to them.

"We have many issues to discuss," Councillor Xandren told her.

"Yes, I know. That's why I'm here," she lied, folding her hands on the table.

Xandren mirrored her gesture. "Your manservant should not have disturbed you."

Tanelli pretended to be apologetic. "We don't want to burden you with our problems."

Gellintris studied her reaction while she studied him. "Perhaps once we make our decisions, we could give them to your manservant. He could pass them along to you later?"

She looked at each of them. "Thank you for your informal advice, councillors. I say 'informal' because I want you to know that what you've said will stay just between us. From this moment on, however, anything you say will be reported back to my husband. That's my duty as his wife. So, shall we begin?"

Not one of them would make eye contact with her. They straightened up in their chairs like schoolboys, chided by their teacher.

Canin stroked his beard vigorously. "The city is in chaos."

Xandren kept up his false bravado. "He exaggerates."

Jimena looked to Xandren. "Then enlighten me."

But Councillor Varnex answered for him. "You can go through, district by district, and the problems will be the same. The poor are overrunning the city. Without trade with the north, commerce and business are dwindling. Farms around the city are being abandoned due to drought, even with the recent rainfall. Farms performing well have fewer merchants to trade with."

Councillor Gellintris stepped in. "People will starve before the food runs out because they have no money to buy it," he explained. "The city is dying, and Zairoc has done nothing about it! These are the facts we cannot tell your husband, for fear of what he will do." Gellintris sat back, waiting to see what she would say.

He took a big chance with such blatant honesty. She could relate to his courage.

Xandren spoke with respect. "There's also the matter of the weapons. Zairoc has asked that each district give scrap metal and men to increase the armaments and ranks. But most of the iron furnaces have been cold for over four years. Restarting them requires more coal."

She leaned in. "I thought we had a supply of coal?"

"Yes, here in the palace, under lock and key." Canin sounded annoyed. "Some by the smith to keep two of the eight furnaces working."

Jimena turned back to look at Genik. "I want you to tell the palace treasurer to release fifty pieces of gold for each of the councillors."

"Yes, my lady." He nodded his head and rushed out.

"There will be more gold where that came from. Use it to employ anyone who wants a job. As for the trade routes, leave that to me."

She stood, turned, and walked out.

The stunned councillors scrambled to stand and bow to her. When Zairoc learned of the missing gold, he would unleash fury. Though, without people to rule, Zairoc's greatness wouldn't matter. The gold would help save them. Jimena knew she needed to find a way to open the trade routes to the north, and the coal in the palace reserves might be the key.

Maybe she had found a way to save both the people and her husband.

CHAPTER TWENTY-NINE

O ndreeal opened her eyes wide and bolted upright. The sun shone brightly in the window. Where was she?

Doyle.

The Lumenary.

She pulled off the woolen cover. She was naked.

She quickly disappeared under the blanket, swallowing hard. One of the Embers had undressed her. Past the age of six, when Otto told her to bathe her own damn body, no one had seen her naked, let alone a man. As far as she understood, the Lumenary only allowed men within its walls.

She wrapped herself up in the blanket, slowly moved to the small dresser, and checked all the drawers. Not a shred of clothing could be found. The Embertree should have at least left her clothes nearby.

A simple plate of food sat on the desk: an egg, a bowl of broth, and boiled potatoes. Ondreeal scarfed down the egg with less than three bites. She gulped down the broth and dived into the boiled potatoes. How much time had passed since she'd landed here? She wiped her mouth before moving to the window, pulling open the casement. The faint sound of a bell came, ringing three times. She searched the rooftops for the source, but it stayed hidden.

Her room overlooked a substantial part of the Lumenary that contained several buildings. Two Embers walked down a wide staircase that wound through the centre of the Lumenary. Two- and three-storey buildings, all with expansive windows, lined both sides of the stairs. Green roofs blended with tall, prickly trees throughout. They looked similar to the thatched roof on the farmhouse, but how did they get them such a deep green? Beyond the Lumenary, a long, meandering path of stairs led down to the valley far below and the Enchanted Lands beyond. A bright sun, hanging low in the western sky, gave the breeze warmth.

Clearly, they hoped to bring civilization to the untamed wilderness. Ondreeal blinked, looking at her blanket-wrapped-body.

Before she could do anything, she needed to find her clothes.

She opened the door and searched the short hallway, comprised completely of dark wooden boards: not a person in sight. She walked down the hall until it opened up onto a courtyard. Water flowed from a little fountain at the centre. The sweet smell of flowers filled the space. A white statue depicting the God of All rose up out of the fountain, represented by an imposing image of a man with long, flowing robes. He looked familiar: a depiction of the Lord of Light she had met in the city. As the religious leader of the entire faith, no one could get closer to the God of All. This Lumenary must also have a leader. A complex lattice of wood above her also made up the surrounding walls of the courtyard, with several doorways branching off the square space, and to her right, the main staircase of grey stone. Ondreeal went down the stairs, blinking in the bright sun.

"Hello."

Her voice sounded small, and no one answered.

The same bell rang faintly, only this time she drew closer to it. She headed down the main stairway, curving its way around one of the larger buildings before revealing a grand, green yard. Sir Francis's castle ranked as the only other place that could boast grass so closely cut. She stopped five stairs before the bottom.

The yard held the entire Embertree while they performed movements in unison. All men — some almost as young as Ondreeal, with smooth, fresh faces up to leathery wrinkles — moved in sync. Some wore the typical brown leather and cloth pants with tunic, while others wore full robes of the same colour. The vast yard held perhaps sixty or eighty of their ranks in all. At the other end, a boy rang the bell at even intervals. That is, until he noticed Ondreeal and stared. All the Embertree stopped and turned to Ondreeal.

Her cheeks flushed. She wore nothing but a blanket in front of all these men.

"I need my clothes."

She must sound like a spoiled child. *Doesn't matter if you're doing something terribly religious, right now you should attend to my needs.*

Doyle broke out of the formation of men and ran up the stairs to meet her. He flashed that big, beautiful smile for her.

"Good afternoon, sleepyhead, we thought you might not ever wake up."

He raised his hand to the other Embers, so they returned to their movements. Doyle indicated for her to follow him.

They headed back up the winding staircase and then entered the large building on the right. It had soaring ceilings with ornate paintings. Lavish rugs covered the polished wood floors. Soaring white pillars decorated with gold leaf designs stood majestically throughout. Doyle took Ondreeal to a back room built of unfinished brown wood, then through a doorway that led outside. The dominating black mountains towered all around them. She took a step back. He must have noticed her hesitancy.

"It's all right. Your clothes were cleaned and hung to dry."

"Who undressed me?" It came out more accusatory than she meant it to.

"I did." He looked away, then met her gaze with a slight upward curl of his mouth.

"I see." She raised an eyebrow.

He responded by fidgeting nervously. Ondreeal stepped out of the doorway. An array of clotheslines connected to either side of the rock face. Mainly mahogany-brown clothing covered the lines, but one held Ondreeal's more colourful garments. She snatched them off the line before rushing back inside.

She dropped the blanket and put her pants on.

"Uh, sorry."

She looked over her shoulder to see Doyle staring at the floor with flushed cheeks. She giggled at his embarrassment.

"What was that you were doing outside?"

"All the Embertree are trained to fight. It's called martial arts. We learn them all." He stood a little taller, proud of that fact.

Ondreeal straightened her tunic, then turned to face Doyle.

"There. How do I look?" She stood tall.

"Uh, beautiful. I mean, you look decent. You're ready to be in the company of the Embertree ... as our guest."

He intently examined a spot on the wall.

"Thank you, Doyle. You've been very kind."

Then her face fell. She checked her clothing.

"Where is it?" She frantically searched through her tunic.

Doyle looked confused. "What?"

"A perfectly round stick, black in colour, about a foot long. Where is it?" She looked at him accusingly.

"Everything should be here." He pointed to an uneven table.

On it sat her knapsack and a few other items, but no wand. Ondreeal searched her pack, sighing with frustration. She gathered her stuff and turned back to Doyle.

"Someone took it. It didn't walk off on its own." She crossed her arms.

He seemed nice, but she didn't know this handsome man. Honestly, her heart skipped a beat when in his presence, but trust came with time.

"If something is missing, then perhaps the Beacon has taken it." Doyle sounded genuine.

Now she knew. Each Lumenary was headed by a Beacon who guided the Embers on the Path of Light. This Beacon must answer to the Lord of Light in Bastion.

Ondreeal moved closer to Doyle. "Why would he do that?"

"If he considered it to be a dark object, something that could be used to create evil, then he would take it."

Doyle turned red, affected by how close she stood. She liked that she could make him feel the same discomfort she felt in this place, among so many men.

"Then I need to speak to him at once." She turned, rushing out.

"No, Al, wait." Doyle chased after her.

Ondreeal marched down the stairs and back to the group of Embers in the yard. Doyle stayed right on her heels.

"You can't disturb him during practice. It will be considered an insult."

Doyle's whispered words still sounded urgent, but she wouldn't listen to him. The wand held great power. Sir Francis told her the wand would only work for her. But they could hide it from her, take it out of the Lumenary. It could be lost to her if she didn't get it back soon. No matter how many of the Embers stood in her way, she would get the wand.

She surveyed the crowd. "I need to speak to the Beacon at once. It is a matter of urgency."

Her legs quivered. She fought to hold them steady. Everyone stopped, turning to her. One of the men slowly moved towards her. He had a tattoo of the same serpent creature that adorned the golden cross in Bastion's Lumenary, starting just under his ear and reaching down his neck. He must be the Beacon. His face appeared weathered with age and held a scowl that reminded her of Otto. His plain white clothes shone brightly in the sun, accentuating his deep complexion and grey hair. The deep circles under his eyes showed a weariness that contrasted with his strong gaze. He raised a hand, so the others returned to their practice. He stepped towards Ondreeal with even, slow strides.

Doyle tensed with panic. "Now you've done it. Now you've done it."

Had she made a mistake? Her belly churned like a wind storm, though she kept a blank face for the Beacon. He walked right up to her, far too close, and he stared right into her eyes.

"Are you a soulless wanderer, or do you walk the Path of Light?"

His voice sounded like gravel. He looked deeper into her eyes, as if the answer hovered right there.

She met his gaze. "I have a destiny, an important one."

"And how do you know that, child?" The corners of his lips curled upwards, betraying his amusement with her.

"The Lord of Light told me himself, in Bastion." Hopefully, those words might hold some weight in this instance.

He laughed at her. "You're lying."

"I'm telling the truth. I met him while I stayed with the great wizard, Sir Francis."

He seemed to consider her words as his mouth morphed into a scowl. He drifted into thought, then glided right past her up the stairs. She turned around, staring at him. He stopped, looked back, then gestured for her to follow. She scurried up the stairs with Doyle close behind.

The Beacon's chamber glowed, filled with golden objects, jewels, and coins. Sir Francis told her the life of an Ember remained one of solitude as well as modesty. They were supposed to leave behind all worldly possessions to walk the Path. Doyle took up position beside the Beacon. The room radiated wealth: from the Beacon's carved and polished deep-brown desk to the shining floorboards which were covered by a square, red velvet rug, no wider than the length of the two men standing on it.

"Are you also a Lord of Light?" Ondreeal asked with a strong voice.

"No. There is only one Lord of Light. He is the religious leader of the entire faith. But the leader of each Lumenary is known as Beacon." He shook his head, clearly disgusted with her lack of religious knowledge.

She stared at all the wealth, steeling her jaw. This man wasn't fit to judge her.

"Does it surprise you to see all this abundance?" The Beacon smiled smugly.

"I think the word is *hypocrite*." She studied his reaction.

Doyle looked like he wanted to disappear into the floor.

"Such big words for such a simple girl. Your nice clothes don't fool anyone. You were raised on the land."

He turned and picked up the black wand.

"That belongs to me." Ondreeal tried to grab it, but the Beacon moved more quickly on his feet than she thought possible.

She forgot how much time the Embers spent training. This old man stayed in excellent shape. Well-muscled herself from a lifetime of working the farm, she proved no match for the swift Beacon. She knew nothing of "martial arts."

"What is your name?" he barked at her.

"Ondreeal."

"If this belongs to you, then that would make you a wizard. If that is true, then I have just one question for you, girl." He walked around until he stood behind her. "Are you a wizard of light or dark?"

"Sir Francis gave it to me." She managed to sputter out with a trembling voice.

"Yes, he is a wizard of light. He has done much good. But a wizard can be the darkest of evil. So, will you use this wand for light or for dark?" he yelled in her ear.

"Of light—I hope to use it as a wizard of light." She blinked in surprise.

She hadn't even known if she wanted the wand a few days ago.

The Beacon leaned forward, staring intently. "Have you used this wand for evil?"

Despite taking a deep breath, her eyes filled with tears.

"I've hurt people to save myself. I didn't know what the wand would do." She looked down from the Beacon's judgemental gaze.

"Then you are not a wizard yet. I can only give you this wand on one condition." He walked around until he faced her again.

She looked at him with genuine curiosity. "What condition?"

"That for the time being, you remain here. Allow us to guide you on the Path of Light, train you to have a disciplined mind and body. I must ensure that if you are to use magic that it is for good. Do this, and the wand is yours." He folded his arms.

Could the Embers really help her? She didn't know much about the God of All, except what the Ember preached in her village. She didn't believe in it, yet maybe they could help her control the wand.

"You'll teach me how to use magic?" she quietly asked him.

"No. We'll teach you restraint and deliberate action. That will help you master the magic you wield, so that you may use it for good." He stared intently at her.

"I—I don't know." She shook her head.

"I see a girl who can't even control how she feels. You're careless. How many people have you hurt with this thing?" He rolled the wand between his fingers.

He recognised her as a danger to the world. She'd searched for solitude, but perhaps the God of All had led her here.

"I won't ask again." He pulled the wand back.

She nodded once to him.

"Good, Doyle and Bradai will guide you in training." The Beacon placed the wand in a rectangular box decorated with swirling gold leaf and inlaid with beautiful, red velvet.

Doyle looked afraid of training her. "Beacon? I don't know if we would be the best choices."

"As our newest members, you are ideal to start her on the path. Defensive training, we will do together." The Beacon bowed his head to her.

What had she gotten herself into? The Beacon wanted to teach Ondreeal to fight and learn the ways of the Embertree. Though, if she could learn discipline, then she could go back to Bastion. She could help Sir Francis find the hidden wizards or help defend Bastion from the dark wizard Zairoc. Until she had control, she remained a danger to everyone around her. She only hoped she could rise to the challenge the Beacon gave her. If not, then she could never return to Sir Francis or to Bastion.

CHAPTER THIRTY

Sir Francis sat, drinking from a flask of water. He wiped the sweat from his forehead and squinted in the bright sun, like he had every day for the last three months. The warm, humid air of the Enchanted Lands encompassed them. That's what everyone called them now. More like an ancient graveyard where the dust of long-forgotten cities had given way to the natural cycle of the planet.

Tall stands of forest surrounded them, full of tropical species Sir Francis couldn't begin to name. This part of the world had once contained desert that stretched for hundreds of miles. He hadn't ventured this way since making the crossing from the east to west coast.

Back then, humanity had seemed lost. At one point, he thought he might be one of very few survivors. Against the odds, out by the ocean, life managed to be sustainable for human beings. They weren't much more than roving packs, in groups of hunter-gatherer societies. It had taken centuries for them to progress to where we were now. Every time Sir Francis tried to show someone a simple technology, they swore up and down that he possessed great power as a magical being. It took every bit of convincing to keep them from worshipping him as a god. It became clear that he could only show them what they could do with the land and their own two hands.

At least he didn't have to explain fire to his people.

Spending most of his time in the city, he'd forgotten just how wild the rest of the world had become. He found it an unwelcome reminder of his failure to deliver humanity back to an age of high technology, so that they might rejoin the rest of the galaxy, defending it against a relentless enemy. One only had to gaze up at the flashes of light that were mere specks down here, yet a constant memorandum to the danger in orbit. Why didn't the alien fleet finish what they'd started? What kept them from completely annihilating humanity? To know the answers to such mysteries would take time, and the day-to-day issues of a nation had kept him seated in Bastion, struggling for advancement.

Without Ondreeal, Sir Francis could stay deadlocked with Zairoc for centuries more. Imagine what they could do with two wands instead of one! A wand ... he'd been calling it that for so long. What was it really called, the thing that continually rejuvenated every cell in his body, practically freezing him in time?

"Sir Francis, are you going to sit there all day and stare at the sun? You know it will make you go blind. Well, you at least. I could stare at it all day if I wanted to," the Lord of Light gloated with his imagined power.

The problem remained, the people believed in the Lord of Light, so they contributed to his power, not to the God of All.

Sir Francis stood. The Lord of Light represented a danger to Sir Francis. He practised faith, not reason. Rational thought would save his people in the end, not faith.

"Of course, your eminence; I was just resting a few moments." Sir Francis bowed his head, walking to his horse, Swift.

If he hadn't pushed Ondreeal so hard, then perhaps she would be living safely at the castle instead of being lost in this world. Being the only one who could detect magic, Sir Francis needed to search for Ondreeal.

The raids along their borders grew increasingly brazen. If only he knew what transpired in Bastion right now, without his leadership, Zairoc might make real inroads into the north. The magical wards prevailed, though. He felt that much.

The holy leader rode ahead with the other men while Sir Francis stayed just behind.

Otto circled and rode up beside him. "We need to talk."

If he thought Otto would survive alone in this wilderness, Sir Francis would have left him behind three months ago. Certainly, Ondreeal would forgive Sir Francis if he did.

"I have nothing to say to you." Sir Francis gave him a polite nod.

"Maybe, but we're going to clear the air, you and I are. I'm tired of the way you look at me. So, unless you want me to start smashing heads, we'll talk." Otto had a typically dour look on his face.

"Then talk." Sir Francis gave him an equally sour expression.

"She was too young for what you wanted her to be," Otto stated.

Sir Francis tried to keep his voice steady. "Who were you to make that choice for her?"

"You would have kept her in the castle after what Zairoc did to Aleenda. Do you think he would have just left you alone if Al was with you?" Otto sounded patronizing.

"I could have protected her. My power equals Zairoc's, in every way." Sir Francis's mouth quivered until he clenched his jaw.

Otto never looked at Sir Francis. "He would have killed you and then Ondreeal."

"I was her Godfather. I swore to protect her—"

"So, did I. I promised her mother that if Zairoc attacked Aleenda's cities, I would take Ondreeal far from there."

Otto tensed, he must have expected Sir Francis to react badly to that news.

"Well, you always did make a lousy Captain of the Guard," Sir Francis shot at him. How could Aleenda have gone behind his back and trusted Otto over him?

Sir Francis fought the tears in his eyes. "She's a fine, young woman."

"Yes, she is. If you ever tell her I said that, I'll kill you." Otto smiled at the prospect.

"Ha! You're welcome to try, you miserable excuse for a farmer," Sir Francis spat.

Otto looked at him with one eyebrow raised. "Did the best job I could."

"Then why were you selling her into slavery? If you meant to keep her safe, that would have hurt her more than death." Sir Francis seethed with anger.

"Don't be so dramatic. Zairoc's men found me, posing as businessmen wanting to buy the farm. But I knew they were looking for my Al."

"That doesn't change the fact that you should have let me know."

Otto looked ashamed of this. "There was no time."

Sir Francis glared at him with disgust. "You stole my chance to raise her the way she needed to be. Now she's alone and scared. I will make sure you pay for it."

Otto appeared resigned. "I said what I wanted to say. You do what you want with it."

He must have known that this day would come, that Sir Francis wouldn't forgive him. Otto would spend the rest of his days in a dungeon. He would know the same pain Sir Francis had endured all these years: loneliness.

A sudden volley of arrows rained down on them.

All the horses stopped amid the screaming men. Zairoc must have tracked them. Sir Francis fumbled with his robes until he pulled out the wand. He held the wand high in his shaking hand.

"A shield to stop the arrows and anything of magic," he whispered the words quietly to himself.

A shield of energy surrounded the search party, with more arrows raining down on them. From all around, female warriors came out of the foliage with their bows drawn, ready to shoot. Woven into their white clothing — the shining, golden symbol of the cross. They were warriors of the God of All. The Lord of Light recognized them, breaking into a broad smile.

"Cinders of the Light, I greet you with open arms." The Beacon held his arms wide to illustrate his point.

Sir Francis shook his head. The Cinders of Light were the second branch of the church, the female counterparts to the Embers. But they had split from the Lord of Light over a century ago and now only followed Zairoc.

A woman's voice spoke from the dense foliage. "Who is it that we speak to, Ember?"

"You speak to none other than the Lord of Light himself. Please, lower your weapons. We are all on the Path, are we not?"

A commanding male voice bellowed from above. "We've been looking for you for over a month."

The Lord of Light, along with the guards, slowly looked up. Sir Francis felt a cold chill run down his spine. The voice sounded familiar.

Out of the sky and landing right in front of Sir Francis's shield came Zairoc. All the men tensed, ready for battle.

Physically, Zairoc looked the same—cold, blue eyes, dark hair that matched black clothing crafted from the finest materials. But the air of confidence gave him a greater presence as he casually held his glowing red wand at his side. Sir Francis hadn't laid eyes on him since he had killed Aleenda. Tears welled up, and Sir Francis fought to hold them back.

"Nice trick, old friend, though it won't keep me out." Zairoc smiled at Sir Francis, raising his wand.

Sir Francis steeled his jaw.

"Henry, leave now. This is not your business." Sir Francis glared hatred at him.

"I told you not to call me that. My name is Zairoc."

Sir Francis hadn't forgotten, but if he could keep Zairoc off his game, they might have a chance to live. Aleenda was a wizard just a powerful as Zairoc, and he had killed her. The vision of Zairoc besting Sir Francis weighed heavily. He'd do everything to stop it from coming true, especially now. He needed to protect his people.

Sir Francis carefully moved to the centre of the group to ensure the shield protected them.

"We are leaving! Everyone, turn the horses around, we are going back the way we came," Sir Francis called out.

They all did as he asked. They looked afraid to turn their backs on the Cinders and Zairoc, though they trusted Sir Francis. All the horses turned around inside the shield, bearing their riders away from Zairoc.

"Stop them!" Zairoc commanded of the Cinders of Light.

Arrows rained against the energy shield.

"Faster ... now!" Sir Francis spurred Swift.

He didn't want to get too far ahead of the others, or they might find themselves outside the shield. Dozens of the Cindertree pursued them. In the sky, Zairoc shot ahead. Sir Francis kept his eye on him. Zairoc flew like a bird, something Sir Francis could never manage to do with the wand.

Zairoc landed in their path, pointing the wand right at Sir Francis. He shot a beam of energy at the shield. Sir Francis gritted his teeth under the onslaught. His wand pulsed with energy. Two wands possessed equal power, so it came down to a battle of wills. The group grew closer to Zairoc, and as they did, the energy from Zairoc's wand intensified. Sir Francis didn't slow down.

"Run that bastard over!" Otto told Sir Francis, snarling at Zairoc. He sprinted harder beside Swift.

"That was my intention." Sir Francis's eyes didn't waver from his evil counterpart.

They almost rode right over the top of him. Zairoc screamed and jumped to one side, landing in the dirt.

Zairoc stuck the wand into the ground, whispering a deadly command. "Wound."

An energy bolt shot out under the soil. Sir Francis along with the others hastily rode away from Zairoc and the Cinders of Light. The energy bolt continued moving, off the ground and then up, hitting Sir Francis.

He went flying from Swift.

Chaos erupted. Everyone changed directions or skidded to a stop. Sir Francis's vision blurred. The blast had hit him right in the head. His ears rang. He tried to find the wand. It had landed several feet away. He crawled over and grabbed it. A hand flipped him over. He stared up at the Cinders, who surrounded him.

Otto smashed through them on foot like a vicious animal. One Cinder landed an arrow in his rib cage, but he plucked it out and stuck it in the woman's neck. Otto picked up Sir Francis, placing him back in Swift's saddle. Otto jumped on another horse and led them both quickly away from the mayhem.

Zairoc laughed at Sir Francis as they rode away. "Go home, Sir Francis. See what's left of it!"

What did Zairoc mean? What had happened to Bastion? The wand blast made Sir Francis's head spin while the blurry image of Zairoc grew smaller.

***

They rode for a while before Sir Francis could even form a single thought again.

"Stop, please—" He laboured to breathe.

Otto halted his horse. Sir Francis slid off of Swift, falling on the ground. Otto hopped off his steed and knelt down, giving the wizard a slap on the face.

"Always wanted to do that," Otto laughed.

"You miserable piece of..." Sir Francis held his head with both hands.

"Careful. I just saved your ass." Otto stared smugly.

Otto's smile looked much scarier than seeing him frown. Sir Francis held out a hand, so Otto pulled him up.

"Water," Sir Francis commanded.

Otto complied, giving Sir Francis his flask. He drank the last of it, and then stood on shaky legs, almost falling over, but Otto held him up.

"Easy, old man. Zairoc really got you." Otto didn't appear very sympathetic.

Sir Francis glanced at Swift, the mare looked uninjured. At least she had made it away from the battle.

"I'm feeling better." Sir Francis looked around but didn't see any of the soldiers or the Lord of Light. "Where are the others?"

"Don't know where they are. Maybe the Cinders got them."

"You left them behind?" Sir Francis turned to go back.

"We barely got away with our lives!" Otto put a hand on Sir Francis's shoulder, stopping him. "You can't help them now."

Sir Francis turned back to face him. Otto had a bleeding wound that could only get worse if left untreated. Sir Francis winced, reflexively grabbing his own head, clenching his teeth. They couldn't match Zairoc *and* the Cinders. Besides, Zairoc's words about Bastion worried Sir Francis. He must have gotten past the wards.

Sir Francis hobbled over to Swift. "We need to get back to Bastion." He had to care for the cities.

Otto stared, surprised that he would suggest giving up. "We haven't found Al yet."

Sir Francis slipped from Swift once more, and Otto caught him.

Sir Francis clung to Otto with desperation in his eyes. "If she wanted to be found, we would have her by now. Ondreeal has stopped us whether she realizes it or not. I need to be in the city. There's no telling what could have happened in our absence."

"She's smart. I'm sure Al will find her way back when she's ready. All right, we go back to Bastion," Otto reluctantly agreed.

He helped Sir Francis up onto Swift and then climbed on his horse. They rode off into the dense woods. Zairoc's words haunted him. Would they find that Zairoc had destroyed an entire people? Without Sir Francis to protect them, it might be true. He'd been foolish to think he could leave the cities with only the warding to protect them. They should have found Ondreeal long before now. Each time they identified a lead, he thought it would be just a few more days and he could take her home, finally. He'd been selfish. Now all his arduous work could have been undone. Perhaps Zairoc sadistically toyed with him, making him worry over nothing.

He just wouldn't know until they got back.

CHAPTER THIRTY-ONE

Trick Mark's eyes snapped open, and he sat up quickly. The thick foliage of the jungle surrounded him. An orange glow grew brighter in the east while the birds welcomed the day. So much time had passed since they had landed on the beach. Trick Mark stood, surveying the path up ahead in a southwesterly direction, towards home.

"You think we're close yet?" Vere pulled some food out of the knapsacks that CD-45 had given to them.

"I wish I could say. Sometimes it feels like we'll never get there. What could have happened in the time we've been gone? What has Zairoc done?" Trick Mark clenched his jaw.

Vere's eyes looked haunted. "You need to eat." She offered him the wrapped item.

They didn't know what to call the stuff because it was unlike any food they'd ever eaten. He wondered how something older than most people could still be okay to eat, but it hadn't killed them yet. Trick Mark pulled off the wrapper and examined the long, thin, brown stick. It resembled toffee. He bit into it, and the bland taste left him wanting. Vere finished eating, then closed her eyes, moving into a fight stance.

"I'm ready for our morning lesson." She inhaled deeply.

"All right." Trick Mark matched her position.

He slapped her right hand. Then she backed up. He moved forward and hit her left palm. She growled with frustration. He tried to punch her, but she dodged. He executed a combination of jabs with kicks, and she evaded them all except for the last one, which sent her flying back. She landed on the ground hard.

Trick Mark hurried to help her up. He gave her a reassuring smile. "You're getting better."

"Not good enough, yet."

"It's not easy to fight blind." He raised an eyebrow.

"I guess not. You think everyone at home is okay?"

He felt a pang of surprise for a moment.

Vere read his expression. "It's been months since Zairoc attacked us. You think he'd stop there?" Her voice conveyed fear mixed with hope.

"We just won't know until we get there," he told her softly.

"I still see their faces in my dreams, everyone in our battalion." She turned away, wiping tears from her eyes.

He steeled his jaw. "I carry that, too, Vere."

Vere turned back to him. "Do you think CD will help us? He could you know, against Zairoc."

"I think CD will help us fight Zairoc. We just need to get back there." Trick Mark managed a smile.

CD-45 headed off, so they grabbed their things and walked westward after him. Trick Mark wiped sweat from his brow, looking up to the bright sun. They'd been traveling over unfamiliar landscape for such a long time. How happy he'd be to see the gleaming towers of Bastion's castle again. Trick Mark stopped to get his bearings.

Vere wiped sweat from her brow. "Any idea where we are today?"

"Not even a little idea." He smirked back at her. "The northern nation is on the western ocean. At least, that's what Sir Francis told me. To get home, we head west. No matter how long it takes."

CD-45 rolled his way past them. They didn't know why they'd taken the ship, other than to escape the ancient building they had been stuck in. CD-45 should have delivered them back to the city or even landed nearby in the woods. No. He wanted to go up, so up they went. He and Vere often whispered to each other when CD-45 appeared asleep. "What could be up in the clouds?" Vere would ask.

The God of All lived in the sky. Trick Mark looked at CD-45. He could be one of God's messengers. If someone wrote a chronicle about it, he and Vere would have a part to play in it.

CD-45 broadcasted a strange music.

Vere whispered to Trick Mark. "More of what Enchanted beings listened to."

"You mean, making invisible people sing and play instruments for us." He pondered the idea.

CD-45 and Vere made unique friends. Vere counted as the only woman to have ever joined the militia, perhaps similar to the Cinders of Light, though their prowess as formidable warriors remained only in stories told.

Maybe he should ask her that question.

"Vere, why did you join up? When Sir Francis opened the militia to women, only you went through training. You stayed because you're good. But I've always wondered." He gave her a playful stare.

She looked at him with surprise. "I don't know, same reason as you, I guess." She shrugged it off.

"I didn't join; I had a choice of either this or a jail sentence." He studied her reaction.

She looked down as she walked, but he couldn't tell what she thought.

"My father made sure I didn't see any combat, at first. Then Sir Francis made me a lieutenant, and I thought there might actually be a future in the militia. I'm not sure why he did it. He said he saw potential. So, I told him I didn't want any special treatment, and he agreed. Then I worked my way up to captain of the guard."

Her face remained blank.

"I ran away from home." Her voice carried sadness.

"Did your father hit you?" If yes, Trick Mark didn't want an answer.

"No, nothing like that. My father was a good parent. My mother too. My sisters, I didn't like. I came from money, so everyone always tried to disinherit everyone else. Since the only way to do that was to kill off my sisters, I left. I didn't want to hurt them, but I knew they would have harmed me if I had stayed. The militia is my home now. Or at least, it was...." Her voice choked up, but she didn't cry.

"It still is, as long as I'm in it. You got that, soldier?"

"Yeah, I got it." She held her chin up as they walked.

They came out of the forest into an open field that looked safe, so they moved into it. Wide-open spaces made Trick Mark's body tense, although keeping within the forest hadn't stopped Zairoc from massacring his entire regiment. Here, forest lined the expansive meadow, and an array of wildflowers grew all around them. Vere paused to pick a few.

"If you stop to frolic, I'm leaving you behind," Trick Mark teased her.

"Very funny. Maybe you missed your calling as a court jester. These flowers can be used to help heal open wounds." She picked more in defiance of his remarks.

He furrowed his eyebrows. "Where did you learn that?"

He had never thought of Vere as anything but a good fighter.

She held her head a bit too high. "I have a lot of talents you know nothing about."

They locked eyes for a moment then he whispered, "Enlighten me."

"In time, if you're lucky."

She shrugged at him, then her expression changed to worry. They both stopped and looked back. CD-45 headed in a different direction, and they sprinted over to the creature.

"Wait, where are you going?" Trick Mark blocked his way.

CD-45 just pointed in the direction he was already headed. Everything out here continually proved amazing, but they needed to return to Bastion.

"Please. I know we said we would help you. Yet you've taken us so far from home. We need to get back. A dark wizard threatens our lands. With your help, we could finally beat him for good. Please." Trick Mark blinked back tears.

CD-45 moved around Trick Mark, continuing in his new direction. Trick Mark blocked him again, and CD stopped.

"We need to go west. That will take us back to the safety of the cities and the castle."

He pointed west so that CD-45 would get the idea. CD seemed to consider his words. If Trick Mark could read minds, certainly CD would have a lot to tell. CD's side panel opened. He took out what looked like a tiny piece of himself — thin, approximately three inches long, with a red button at one end — and handed it to Trick Mark

"I don't think it's a part of him. It's a tool. Is that right?" Vere asked with uncertainty painted on her face.

CD-45 nodded his boxy, little head.

Trick Mark examined the tiny object. "What's it for?"

CD-45 shook his head then took the item back. He closed his fingers around it and pressed the red button with his thumb. It flashed red, then made a noise that sounded like a baby bird. A light on CD's frame flashed red in unison with the device. He pressed the button twice more, and the device went dark.

Trick Mark slumped his shoulders. "It's so you can find us."

CD-45 nodded again, placed the device in Trick Mark's palm, then rolled away. This meant their little friend would leave them. Both he and Vere watched until she tore after him. She stopped in CD's path and, for a moment, Trick Mark thought she might hit him. Then she threw her arms around CD, kissing him on the forehead. He turned to watch them as he continued away. CD actually looked sad. Vere appealed to Trick Mark with pleading in her eyes.

"Vere ... we can't stay out here with him forever. Who knows what's out there? You know we need to get home. Sir Francis probably already thinks we're dead." He turned west and strode off.

A few moments after that, Vere appeared beside him, though he could feel her unhappiness. Trick Mark genuinely liked CD-45 too. He was the most unique being he'd ever met, Sir Francis included. CD had such quirks that made them laugh. He would miss that. He truly hoped CD would find them again. Bastion could desperately use his help.

***

The gentle whistle of the wind mixed with the rustling of leaves disrupted an otherwise peaceful landscape. Trick Mark and Vere walked side by side, in silence. The trees in this area mixed with tall grasses. Soon the forest grew dense. The two colleagues brushed their way past jumbo leaves once more.

As night approached, Trick Mark's second sight kicked in. Vere took up a position walking just behind him, with her hand on his shoulder. Light from stars filtered through the trees, so Vere had no reason to question how he could see. They continued like that for a while until Vere couldn't stop yawning.

They paused in a clearing, gathering sticks in a pile. Vere coaxed smoke from the woodpile until flames burst to life. They both stared into it while the fire crackled, and they lay down to rest.

Worry carried in Vere's words. "Do you think we'll ever see CD again?"

"You seem to miss him more than you miss everyone in the regiment." Trick Mark closed his eyes, wincing.

Vere bolted up, her eyes like arrows. "Forgive me, sir. What is wrong with you?"

"I'm sorry, I shouldn't have—" Trick Mark pushed himself to a sitting position.

"No, you want to have this conversation? Then let's have it." Her anger softened as her eyes moistened.

He sighed, shaking his head. "We haven't even said the prayer of passing."

She gazed downward amid her soft words. "I couldn't...."

"I know. It's easier not to talk about it." He clenched his jaw, fighting back his own tears.

She glanced up at him, wiping her cheeks. "Trick Mark, it's time."

He couldn't tell her everything he felt, because some things a captain couldn't share with a soldier. After months in the Enchanted Lands, Vere had become more than that: a close friend.

Trick Mark sat up on his heels and held his palms open in front of him, eyes shut. With his second sight, he could see that Vere sat opposite him, mirroring his position.

They spoke the words together. "Crom, Smat, Jackson, Agensis, Fairweth, Shanner, and Maitt. Rest, brothers, your time for fighting is over. May the God of All take you into his arms."

They both opened their eyes, staring at each other for a moment. Vere moved to the other side of the fire, then they both lay down facing each other. The fire crackled in the quiet night as they both fell asleep, perhaps dreaming of those they had lost or wishing for a speedy journey home.

CHAPTER THIRTY-TWO

A punch flew to her face, and Ondreeal fell flat on the ground.

The Beacon scowled down at her. "You need focus, quicker reactions to my attacks, not flailing attempts to slow me down."

Towering red columns with soaring wooden ceilings framed the Beacon's face. Bright morning sun shone in as Ondreeal's heavy breathing began to slow. The Beacon shook his head, stepping back. Ondreeal sat up, then wiped blood from her lip. She glared at him. To win just one fight, to watch the Beacon wipe his bloody lip, would give her great satisfaction. One day her training would end. She could return to Bastion, taking her place with Sir Francis.

She hobbled to her feet and lunged at him. He punched, he dodged; she jabbed, then he evaded. She kicked, but he seized her leg and then flung her back. She landed on a wooden box that broke into several pieces. He came at her, lifting his foot to step on her midsection. She rolled out of the way. He tried again, but she spun the other way. Wide-eyed, she scrambled to her feet. They circled each other.

They continued sparring until Ondreeal landed on the ground with a loud thud. She winced with pain but held her mouth firmly closed.

The Beacon held out a hand to her. "You're improving."

She batted it away, then pulled herself to her feet. She stood in a fight stance.

The Beacon shook his head. "No, you need time to heal. There's nothing left you can do today."

"Then you're giving up." Ondreeal glared at him.

"You want more pain. I will deliver it." The Beacon faced off with her again.

He flew at her with a series of moves. She blocked each one as he drove her back. The Beacon made an exceptional fighter. Although she had never had any teachers before, she thought he made a bad one. By contrast, Bradai and Doyle showed such patience and kindness towards her.

He thrust his fist. She threw her shoulder back to avoid it. A kick to her gut made her grunt with pain. She forced herself to suck in air. Reacting to the Beacon's attack wasn't the answer. She calmed her body, relaxing into a fluid defensive stance as they circled. Nice and slow, that's all it needed to be.

The Beacon charged at her. She watched his moves, blocking each one. His relentless attacks showed her order in the chaos.

The Beacon swung around with a high kick. It slowed in her view until she caught his foot, throwing him back to the ground. He stared up at her with a mix of shock, anger, and perhaps a bit of admiration.

"How did you do that?" The Beacon pushed himself up.

"You always say 'react.' I didn't. I anticipated." The corners of her lips curled up.

"Same time, in two days—to let you heal." He bowed his head to her.

Ondreeal returned the gesture as the Beacon strode out. She collapsed into a chair in front of a petite table. She hunched over a bowl of water, dipping a rag in it. She dabbed the cloth on her wounded eye. The water in the bowl turned red from her blood.

Bradai shuffled in with two plates, wearing his brown robe that bulged at the waist. His brown hair sprouted curls on the sides and back only, giving him a clownish look at times. "The Beacon is not an easy man."

"I beat him today." She beamed at Bradai.

"You've come a long way in the few months you've been with us." Bradai bowed to her, and the food threatened to slip off one plate.

Bradai quickly corrected his posture with a short chuckle. One dish overflowed with food; however, the other sat half-eaten. Ondreeal looked up at him with a questioning gaze.

"I got hungry on the way here," he admitted to her.

He set the half-full plate down in front of Ondreeal before digging into the brimming plate with the enthusiasm of someone who had starved for a month. She stared down at her food.

"You have to eat, to keep your strength up." Bradai held up a fat arm and tried to flex his muscles. "Are you all right?"

She scowled at Bradai, then broke into a smile. He had a good heart, meaning well in all he did. Exactly like a sibling, he could irritate her or offer solace, depending on the day.

"Sorry, stupid question. I brought the good book. We're almost through. You've learned so much about the faith. I'd wager to say you've developed quite a bit of your own." He picked up a pristine copy of The Path.

"You haven't ever explained this." She touched one of the creature's golden tentacles on the cover.

"Well, that would be skipping to the end." He raised an eyebrow.

She gave him an unwavering stare.

"All right, we're almost there anyway." Bradai turned to the last few pages, clearing his throat. "'The God of All saw that the people needed to learn. It would be through knowledge that they would find the Path of Light. So, he gave them many paths to follow, in every place that there was or would be. There would be many ways to find the path of light, and no two would be the same.

"'The people were also given a gift: the Guardians of the Light. The Guardians were sent to show the people all that was good, and all that would be good again.'" Bradai closed the book, watching Ondreeal for her reaction.

She leaned back in her old wooden chair. "What's at the end of the Path?"

"The God of All. Peace, contentment, enlightenment." He squirmed on the bench.

Ondreeal chuckled. "You don't really know, do you?"

"Well, no, not exactly. But to have faith is to walk the Path into the light, to save your soul." He nodded once to her, confident.

Ondreeal put down the bowl with the rag. "Who are the Guardians?"

Despite her aches, she leaned forward, listening intently.

"Well, there are some conflicting suggestions about this. Though some think it would be you and Sir Francis." Bradai met her gaze with a glance before quickly looking out the window.

"Do you think I am a Guardian of the Light?"

"That is not for me to say. That's something you must find out for yourself." He kept his gaze fixed on the window.

The images of the barbarian, the two men on the farm, all the dead villagers, and the kind old couple flashed in her mind's eye. A lump caught in her throat as she stared down at the bloody water in the bowl.

"What about someone who's taken a life? Not meaning to, but they're dead all the same." She kept her gaze downward.

Bradai looked back to her.

"The Embertree kills for the greater good. Sometimes we kill to protect ourselves or innocent people. If the God of All carries a lick of sense in his all-knowing, all-seeing head, then he understands that." He squeezed her hand before returning his attention to the food.

"Thank you, Bradai." She nodded once. "You are very wise."

Ondreeal glanced at her plate, spinning a piece of a cut apple. Bradai put his fork down. He moved his chair beside Ondreeal and held out his hands.

"I know you're troubled. Prayer does help." He raised his eyebrows, staring at her expectantly.

She looked down at his hands. She spent much time studying the Great Path, finding many of the stories interesting. If she didn't know about wizards, half the stories would sound preposterous.

"Do you really think the God of All hears my prayers? Sees all that I've done?"

Bradai nodded to her. She often prayed for help finding ways to control the wand, though she never asked for forgiveness. Not once in all the time she'd been here. She placed her hands in Bradai's and closed her eyes.

"Dear God, we ask that you guide my good friend Ondreeal on the Path of Light. Show her the way to be a good, strong person. We ask that you forgive and absolve any mistakes that she's done, so that she may move forward free of this burden. Amen." Bradai let go of her hands.

She opened her eyes, and his smiling face greeted her. Bradai moved his chair back to the other side of the table, digging back into his food. He stopped, glancing up at her. Ondreeal plucked up the piece of cut apple and bit into it.

It made her sit taller to know she had such a friend like him. Nevertheless, the burden of guilt didn't feel any lighter. Where did faith end and her personal efforts start? If the God of All really did watch over them, then surely, he expected people to make their own way in the world. If so, maybe she couldn't let go of her guilt just yet. On the farm, she'd worked in the physical world. She'd seen clear results of her labours. Her emotions and who she was spiritually had been ignored for her whole life. Like everything else here, it would take time.

CHAPTER THIRTY-THREE

Zairoc stared up at the canopy of his bed, shifting under his smooth, silky sheets. A beautiful body stirred gently next to him. The starry sky allowed a soft, hot breeze through the open window to the right of the bed.

He had used a great deal of magic recently, and the wand took much of his strength. Half of the impressive beings he'd met in his lifetime would laugh at his inability to use a wand. But, obviously, as the most talented and capable of the seven wizards, his will could not be matched.

His vision of the future would become reality. So, he went on killing for good reasons. He would kill many of his people, sending them off to war. He would kill many of Sir Francis's people if they resisted him. He would kill Sir Francis and any other wizards if they didn't fall into line with his ideology. People needed the rule of a strong hand. Personal freedoms had no place in a society. His brilliant mind would lead them all into a new age of prosperity, if only they could see and accept it.

The beautiful, contoured body lying next to him stirred, turning towards him.

"Jimena," he whispered to her.

"You've been asleep for days. I was afraid," she cooed.

"I don't want you to worry." He ran the tips of his fingers over her thigh.

But her eyes looked sad. "I worry, all the time."

He kissed her fingers. "What's wrong?"

"The people are angry, my love. You rule with a heavy hand. Many suffer. This war you are starting... Is this really the best thing for us?" She searched his eyes for an answer.

"Many resources go into the war. So, the people suffer. Let them. They are insignificant in the grand plan." He ran his fingers through her hair.

"What if you die?" She caressed his cheek.

"You know that won't happen." He kissed her hand, moving up to her wrist.

"I will grow old, and you will still be young, with just that bit of grey in your hair." She played with a few lightly coloured strands.

"You knew what it meant to marry me," he whispered to her.

"I know." She stared at him with those impossibly dark eyes, framed by dark curls.

Zairoc leaned in, then kissed her passionately.

***

He got out of bed quietly while Jimena rolled over without opening her eyes. A wonderful woman in every way, Zairoc did cherish her, though he had loved all his wives over the centuries. The alternative was for him to stay alone, which was not an option. He quickly dressed and quietly closed the door behind him.

Zairoc looked up to the impressive array of windows that made up a liberal section of the ceiling. The mountain towered overhead, a protective barrier against attack. He glided past the quiet, vacant rooms. The grandeur that went into the place would rival the most lavish palaces ever in existence. He wouldn't have it any other way.

He stopped for a moment, looking out onto the capital city of Incoation. The four cities that made up his nation had never achieved greatness. The cobblestone streets gave way to dirt roads, lined with dilapidated vendor booths. Silhouettes of hunched, decrepit wretches hobbled through the dark night. Having limited resources, the cities were also often full of disease and hunger, which hastened his need for immediate expansion.

The hopelessly dull Sir Francis hadn't changed in almost nineteen centuries. He lacked the imagination that Zairoc possessed. Without it, you couldn't truly create anything worth noticing.

Amazingly, Sir Francis had managed to build a stable society, prosperous and growing faster than Zairoc's. It had a strong foundation, outpacing his in every way. This would mean that Sir Francis's society, one that didn't have Zairoc as its ruler, influenced his people. They might even join him and let Zairoc's dream fade away into nothingness. Zairoc clenched his fists until his knuckles turned white. War remained the only way to bring the two societies together, moving forward as one people under the right ruler.

Zairoc hurried down the lavish halls covered in rich, dark-red carpets until he reached a shining wooden door. He unlocked it, glancing back to the hallway, which remained empty, lest any passerby wished to incur the wrath of Zairoc, a most effective deterrent to all in the palace.

He headed down the dark stairwell, entering into a cool, rocky tunnel. Stalactites dripped over his head. He took out the wand. It shone a pale red. It had glowed without colour the first time he used it, but over the years, it had changed. He believed it was because he had achieved a sort of harmony that the other wizards hadn't: a synergy between biological being and the technology of the wand. He approached another door, this one of a matte polymer-based metal. He tapped in a series of numbers on a keypad until the door slid open.

The entire facility shone white. Why hadn't he ever told Sir Francis or Aleenda about it? The truth is: he wanted it for himself. He wanted to show them the legitimacy of his greatness.

Unfortunately, like most of the technology on the planet, it was destroyed or damaged. Half of this facility lay in ruin after the attack.

Zairoc went through a series of doors before he made it to a sprawling space. Broken or jury-rigged computers peppered the perfectly white tabletops with a mess of wires and cables. It looked like a mad scientist's laboratory, with strange creatures in jars, bubbling concoctions, and machinery making noises. It didn't look nearly as dramatic as the ones he saw in movies, though.

He set himself down on a hard, white stool. The computer monitor came to life with one touch. Several calculations circled around the screen until Zairoc grabbed one with his index finger and thumb, automatically enlarging it. He started changing some of the numbers. After a while, he set his head down, closing his eyes.

***

Zairoc awoke suddenly in response to a high-pitched beep from the computer. If the wand hadn't drained him, he could work for hours. He sighed, tapping a button that ended the computer beep. He pushed himself up, moving to a considerable, round metal sphere. He pressed a few buttons on its side. In response, the sphere split in two. Inside sat a perfect giant egg.

All he really could do with this facility was build life.

He had debated about what he should spawn, genetically modify a farm animal, or a crop to increase yield? He ultimately decided to create something with imagination. Something that would be feared while it helped Zairoc win a war.

The egg cracked open to reveal his hard work, the effort that took centuries, using up all that the facility had to offer. The creature broke free. Then he held out his hand for it to inspect. It looked just like its brother. A lizard covered in amniotic fluid that made it appear to have scales instead of feathers. It spread its wide, thin wings. It sniffed his hand before jumping on his arm. Currently too little to fly, that would soon change.

"You know who your master is, hmm?" Zairoc smiled at the creature.

It opened its mouth, revealing tiny rows of sharp teeth. One day soon, it would burn the north.

"Once you get bigger, little girl, you can meet your brother."

It walked up his arm to his shoulder and squawked in his ear.

Zairoc stood up, moving out of the room then down a long, sterile white hallway.

"Zairoc, clearance," he announced to a door.

It slid aside, revealing an expansive, cavernous space, ideal for his new, growing dragon. An array of animals for her to kill and eat at her whim roamed in the dimly lit cave. He put the baby dragon down, then went back to the doorway. It hobbled over towards him.

"Daddy's late for dinner. I'll be back soon."

When he left, he went from the past into the present, walking through the tunnels back to the palace. Zairoc strode out of the wooden door. He marched down the hall, but instead of the normal quiet, screams echoed in the grand halls.

He ran towards them. The air carried smoke. He turned a corner and came face to face with his own people.

He watched for an instant as they fought each other. The palace guard defended on one side, and a mob of commoners on the other. Distracted by his research, hidden away from the world and completely unaware of an attack, this could have been planned to take advantage of his absence. Three commoners impaled a palace guard with a pitchfork. Outside the smashed windows, a whole wing of the palace burned in view.

Zairoc glared at the mayhem, and he screamed. He pulled out the wand that glowed brilliant red.

"Get out!" he bellowed at the commoners.

Before they reacted, Zairoc flicked his finger, ejecting them out through the windows with an invisible force. The remaining guards stared at him, stunned.

"Come with me. Kill anyone you don't recognise!" He headed down the grand entrance, past the palace guards with swords at the ready.

They attacked a group of commoners that clung to golden objects. Several of the palace guards struck them down. Two commoners scurried by just as Zairoc flicked the wand, making one man's back break with an awful sound. Zairoc made a circle with the wand, and a woman's head snapped around.

Outside, the majority of the guards tried to push back the angry mob. Zairoc stormed out and pointed at one of the attacking men. A bolt of lightning shot out of the wand, frying him instantly. His shocked expression permanently etched on his face in death. The bolt jumped to three more people, then nine more after that, until the entire mob fell, charred or completely burned. The pile of corpses steamed in front of the stunned guards.

"Hey, over here!" Zairoc snapped his fingers at them.

The guards joined him, and they headed down the main stairs of the grand palace to meet another wave of the mob. Zairoc held the wand high in front of him so that it glowed brighter.

The roaring mob stopped.

Zairoc rose into the air in front of their eyes.

"I am all-powerful! Leave now, and you will go with your lives." He pointed the glowing wand at them.

One woman stepped forward with two men.

"We will go home when you listen to the people!" she yelled at him.

The two men chanted as they thrust their fists into the air, "Freedom! Freedom!"

Others from the crowd joined in, until a chorus of voices rang out.

"If it is death you seek, then that is what you've found," Zairoc calmly told them.

The woman with the two men rose into the air. At first, it looked like they contained the same power as Zairoc. The crowd cheered—until the atoms of the three came apart at their fingertips. They screamed while their hands and feet disappeared. Then their arms and legs vanished, making their screams more desperate. Then their torsos evaporated until, finally, their faces were lost. Their wails echoed as they faded into nothingness. The crowd stared in shock, like statues, all falling silent.

Zairoc held his hands wide to the sky, making the stars disappear behind dark clouds. Thunder and lightning struck the crowd. Everyone shrieked, running in all directions like wild animals. As rain soaked the dirt road, chaos slowly ebbed away. Finally, the crowd cleared, leaving trampled bodies on the ground.

Zairoc turned, and the blood drained from his face. The grand bedroom burned brightly in the palace.

His feet pounded the ground as he rushed inside. He bolted up the stairs into the thick smoke.

He held the glowing wand forward, forming a bubble of breathable air. He sucked in a breath between coughs. He couldn't see where he stepped. He held the red, glowing wand, but his legs buckled, and he fell to his knees. His hands trembled with weakness. To use so much magic now might be more than he could handle.

The flames of the fire burned brightly all around.

CHAPTER THIRTY-FOUR

Trick Mark's eyes opened, and he watched the flames die down. Though at night, it appeared as a ghostly image, like everything else: trees, animals, the campsite. Vere snored softly on the other side of the fire. Sounds came from the jungle—footsteps. At once, a barrage of arrows peppered the campsite. Trick Mark bolted up, grabbing his bow and arrow, ready to fire. Vere stood right beside him with a knife gripped in each of her hands. Out from the jungle came warriors dressed in animal skins. They held primitive bows or knives of bone. Trick Mark had sensed them from a distance but had dismissed the threat as only animals. How could he have been so stupid? They should have slept in shifts. He'd gotten used to CD-45 watching the campsite while they rested. He'd let his guard down in a strange land.

The warriors moved closer, both men and women dressed in similar clothing. A tall, powerful-looking woman with a strange multi-skull headdress walked right up to Trick Mark's poised arrow.

Trick Mark locked eyes with her. "We don't want trouble. Let us leave in peace."

"You speak in the Amereng. Go ahead, kill me, and you will die a moment later." She smiled at him, daring him to do it.

He lowered his bow as Vere lowered her knives. The woman with the headdress made a hissing sound with her teeth, prompting the others to seize him and Vere.

The warriors collected their knapsacks and weapons, pushing their prisoners into the dense jungle.

At least they moved westward – closer to home. Perhaps they would meet Sir Francis or others from Bastion.

One fact prevailed: their home stood much too far away. They changed direction, heading northward.

Damn. Things had been going so well.

***

Trick Mark's feet started to hurt after walking for a long time.

He whispered to Vere, "Can you see the moon?"

"Moved out of sight, should be day soon," she breathed back.

A warrior pushed him ahead of Vere. If the moon set, then they had walked for at least three hours. They entered a clearing, where Trick Mark sensed a great deal of movement in the tall trees above – more people, not animals. They lived above the forest floor. The giant tree trunks carried odd structures up in the leaves, homes built like the makeshift forts he had played in as a boy. They put Trick Mark and Vere in a cage, then tied the door with some kind of rope.

Vere kept close to him. "What do they want from us?"

"I think we'll find out sooner or later." He grabbed her hand, trying to reassure her.

The warriors encircled them. They picked up some kind of bone carvings that they breathed into, making high-pitched sounds, combinations of short and long toots. The wildlife in the forest grew louder in response.

As the sun rose, Trick Mark's second sight faded, and for the first time he could see what these people looked like. All with sun-soaked skin, both male and female stood tall.

Their animal-skin clothing appeared dyed with different colours, while others wore plain grey clothing. Some displayed tattoos of every hue, while others were only black and white. The tall woman who was their leader sported a headdress with baby skulls in a row lining her forehead. Feathers from various birds fanned out over her head in a beautiful design. Everything about these people looked completely foreign. If only he had heard a story of their kind, something to hint at their motivations.

Sticks tied with dried vines made up the four-foot-square cage. He tested its strength while two warriors stood guard on either side. One knocked Trick Mark's knuckles, making him pull his hand away from the makeshift wooden bar. He winced amid the laughing warriors.

The instruments they played changed to a soft whistle. Finally, they suddenly fell silent. The warrior leader strode over to what looked like a stone table. Two thick, rectangular stones made up the legs under one massive stone slab.

The leader looked directly at Trick Mark and Vere. "I am the Pha-prim. You will give me your names."

"Captain Marcus." He looked to Vere to give an answer.

Vere matched the power of the Pha-prim's gaze. "Soldier Waldron."

"Marcus, Waldron, you are outsiders. Why are you here?"

Trick Mark held up his hands. "We were just passing through, on our way home."

"You speak the Amereng. Anyone who speaks the Amereng comes from the east. We watched you for a long time. You came from the east." She didn't trust them.

Trick Mark kept his voice even and calm. "We did come from the east, but our home is in the west."

"You are likely here to destroy us," the Pha-prim accused them.

"Please, we didn't even know there were people out here," Vere protested.

The Pha-prim moved closer to Vere. "Are you the owner of this man?"

"No," Vere admitted.

The Pha-prim hissed at Vere. The warriors laughed.

"You are not even a woman." The Pha-prim spat at Vere, then marched away.

"Please, we just want to go home," Vere pleaded.

"You are full of nothing but deceit. I will have the only truth I need."

She clapped her hands, and several of her people moved forward. They opened the cage and hauled Vere out. Trick Mark grabbed hold, yanking her back. One warrior knocked him down and then slammed the cage door shut. Another quickly tied it.

Trick Mark tried to pull the wooden bars off as he yelled after them. "Vere! Vere! Don't hurt her."

They threw Vere on the ground, tossing both knives in the sand by her face. The Pha-prim entered the clearing with two short, rounded swords in her hands. The other warriors created a low, steady sound with the back of their throats.

"We will do battle," the Pha-prim commanded of Vere.

"I don't want to fight you." Vere left her knives on the dirt, shaking her head.

"Then you will die."

The Pha-prim lunged at her, sending Vere rolling out of the way. The Pha-prim swung around and charged at Vere. Vere frantically countered each deadly swipe of her blades. One connected, slicing her stomach. Vere grabbed the wound, wincing with pain.

Trick Mark yelled at her, "Pick up the knives, Vere. That's an order."

He tried to break the cage, but a warrior knocked his hand back with a heavy stick. Trick Mark glared at him and snarled.

Vere dodged, but the Pha-prim knocked her down. The Pha-prim plunged her sword at Vere. Vere threw herself out the way as the blades stabbed the sand. The Pha-prim thrust again with her sword, slicing through the dirt a breath after Vere quickly recoiled.

The Pha-prim swung the sword down to cut her in two, yet Vere caught the blade with an iron grip. The Pha-prim pulled the sword across Vere's hands, cutting her palms. Vere cried out, blood dripping from her hands. She struggled to stand, only to have the Pha-prim viciously boot her to the sand. The Pha-prim straddled Vere, both blades trained on her.

"No!" Trick Mark wailed, reaching for Vere.

Vere kicked hard, knocking the Pha-prim off balance. She ripped one of the Pha-prim's swords from her grip, stumbling to her feet. The Pha-prim and Vere defensively circled around each other. The Pha-prim thrashed with her sword, Vere countering each swipe. The Pha-prim forced her back until Vere fell to the ground as the sword slipped from her bloody hand. The Pha-prim reclaimed her sword. Vere scurried for her knives, her whole body trembling.

Trick Mark yelled at her, "Close your eyes. Vere, close your eyes!"

He crouched, ready to pounce in his cage. If only he could help her. If he could kill with a look, they'd all lay dead. He locked his gaze on the Pha-prim, jaw clenched, fists tight.

"What? You want me to die?" she yelled back.

"Just shut up and close your eyes." She could win if she just trusted him.

As Vere and the Pha-prim stalked each other, Vere slowly closed her eyes. Trick Mark's heart beat so fast he thought it might burst out of his chest.

"Good, now only listen to the Pha-prim. Block out all sound, but her." His fists trembled, but he kept his voice steady.

The Pha-prim smiled because she saw Vere to be an easy target that would go down quickly. The Pha-prim attacked, and Vere nimbly sidestepped. The Pha-prim lunged again, and Vere swiftly avoided her. The Pha-prim charged. Vere spun out of harm's way, then struck the Pha-prim down.

The Pha-prim sprang to her feet and rushed at Vere with a guttural scream. The first slice, she missed; the second cut failed; then the third swipe sliced Vere's shoulder. Vere winced with pain through clenched teeth. Trick Mark swallowed hard.

The Pha-prim thrust the sword. Vere cut her three times with her knives, easily avoiding the sword. The Pha-prim clenched her teeth, growling as she readied to strike. The Pha-prim pounced, but again Vere sliced her three times.

The Pha-prim unleashed a series of deadly moves, Vere evaded each one. Vere knocked a sword free, but the other gashed her across the face. Vere went down, rolling back. They both stood at once, then the Pha-prim charged. The Pha-prim punched Vere, but Vere grabbed her sword arm, holding it. Vere opened her eyes: she had a knife to the Pha-prim's throat. Vere gave her a sly smile.

Trick Mark laughed with relief. Several of the warriors surrounded them, arrows trained at Vere.

"You are a woman after all." The Pha-prim nodded with pride. "Your death will be quick."

Vere's smile faded, along with Trick Mark's.

***

The evening sun disappeared on the horizon, though the fire burned brightly around the clearing. Tied against a stake with their backs together, Vere and Trick Mark struggled against their bonds. Trick Mark could make out a representation of a giant winged beast carved into the stake above their heads. Its wings circled the post, its mouth full of sharp teeth that threatened to consume them. Hopefully, it only came from the natives' imaginations. Four dead animals lay spread out around them.

Trick Mark tried his best to work the ropes. If they could get free, perhaps they could escape into the thick underbrush before the warriors responded. His body trembled with the anticipation of battle, overriding his thirst and hunger.

At least Vere had won the battle to live a while longer, though her wounds, if left untreated, would result in a slow and painful death. Her training had paid off well. She made a worthy adversary. Unfortunately for the two of them, thus far, it had not gotten them out of certain death.

"Sorry, Trick." Vere sounded defeated.

"You kidding? You were amazing back there."

"You mean that?" she asked softly.

"I'm proud of you." He fought back the tears.

The warriors changed the pitch of their instruments, which rose together into a loud screech.

Trick Mark clenched his teeth, pulling at their bonds. "I'll say one thing for these people."

"What's that?"

"Their taste in music blows." Trick Mark winced, relaxing for a breath.

"God of All, just kill us now." Vere pulled with all her might, letting out a frustrated sigh.

"If we die here today, I'm honoured that it's with you." Trick Mark held back tears.

"Thank you, Captain. You're a good man, better than most, kind. I haven't had a lot of that in my life." Vere grabbed one of his fingers, then quickly let it go.

"In a different life, I'd protect you, but not because it's my duty." He stared up at the darkening sky.

If only he could face her now and hold her tight.

Trick Mark turned his head towards her as much as he could. "If we get free, run for the underbrush of the forest. I'll follow. Understand?"

"I won't leave you behind." She choked up.

"You'll follow orders, soldier...."

The screeching of the instruments grew louder. He looked to the warriors. His jaw dropped open, because none of them played their instruments. He looked up. The screeching came from above. The warriors called to something, the thing that would kill them. He heard the beating of wings. To his right landed the beast.

"Trick, what is that thing?" Vere struggled against their bonds.

Sir Francis had warned him that they hunted out here. He thought the wizard had only been trying to scare him, to make sure he remained alert on patrol.

"I think it's a dragon," he whispered.

The dragon opened his huge jaws, breathing on one of the animal carcasses. The air rippled with heat around its mouth, although no visible fire emanated from the beast. The animal carcass sizzled, erupting into flames.

"It breathes invisible fire?" Vere sounded astonished.

"I don't know. I guess it does." Trick Mark's body shook despite his efforts at bravery.

The dragon ripped away at the charred carcass. Its body glistened against the torchlight. Trick Mark couldn't tell if it had feathers or scales. It looked like hardened quills, a metal armour. Its feathers rippled from the top of its head to the tip of its tail. As it did so, the dragon almost disappeared from sight. Then it rippled again, becoming starkly clear. Death itself: dark, invisible, and impossible to escape.

One of the warriors tried to place an offering of fruit next to another animal carcass. The dragon breathed its invisible, soundless fire on him. He screamed and writhed in pain. Deep, red welts sprung up on his dark skin before he burst into flames, dying next to his offering.

The beast finally set its sights on Trick Mark and Vere. Its massive maw, riddled with sharp teeth, came close. It sniffed Trick Mark, so he steeled himself as he closed his eyes. This made his second sight kick in. He could see the beast, watch its heart beat and its stomach digest the consumed animal. It looked more horrifying from the inside.

The creature took one breath, and the air was on fire around him, with ripples of fever. Gasping, Trick Mark grabbed Vere's hand tightly. He waited for the unbearable heat, then the pain that would follow engulfing flames.

Trick Mark tried with all his might to hold his breath, but he couldn't help himself as he opened his mouth and screamed.

CHAPTER THIRTY-FIVE

Ondreeal stood in the centre of the village she'd known since the age of five. Dark clouds moved quickly across the sky while she slowly gazed down into the fountain. The calm water reflected her young face, fearful and full of horror. Then the watery image stretched, distorting, as she grew long, sharp teeth. Her skin turned a blackish green, and her eyes shone like that of a mythical dragon. She screamed as she jumped back, tripping and landing on the ground. Her hands covered her face, though nothing felt strange. She looked up.

Ondreeal's legs draped over a body. She frantically kicked back, stumbling to her feet. All around lay the corpses of the villagers. She covered her mouth, fighting back the tears.

One of Zairoc's goons pointed and yelled, "There she is. The witch!"

A man's voice called out behind her, "Why did you do it?"

Ondreeal's head whipped around. There stood Jera and Esteal, the kind old couple.

Esteal heaved with grief. "We let you into our home."

Jera glared at her with sadness. "We only wanted to help you."

Ondreeal shook her head. "I'm sorry. I didn't mean to."

Esteal screamed at her. "You murdered us while we slept!"

Rose chanted, "Kill the witch. Kill the witch."

All the villagers surrounded her, chanting, "Kill the witch!"

With a blink of an eye, Ondreeal found herself tied to a stake. Her undead neighbors set fire to it, and it quickly morphed into a blaze. Pain seared her body.

Through the inferno, she could see Esteal and Jera burst into flames.

"No!" Ondreeal wailed.

Her eyes snapped open. She looked all around at the tiny room. She pulled back the wet bedsheet and quickly stood, rushing to the open window. Dark clouds moved in fast, covering a faint, red glow growing in the east and bright stars to the west. Ondreeal glanced down to the quiet rooftops of the Lumenary amid a breeze that gusted in, chilling her wet face.

She had only had a nightmare like that once before. Esteal and Jera had paid dearly for showing her kindness. They both featured prominently in her horrible dream. The last time she woke, she found them both dead. What if the wand made those tormented images come true once more? She inhaled deeply. She'd never forget the smell of burning flesh, yet only the sweet scent of wildflowers filled the air.

Surely, that was proof enough. She lay back down in bed and clasped her shaking hands. After a few moments, she got up, quickly dressing. She needed to know for certain, if even one Ember died because of her bad dream, it would mean she hadn't changed. She remained a murderer and a danger to all those around her.

She took a deep breath, stepping out into the hall. The floorboard creaked under her weight. She looked up and down the corridor. No one else slept in these rooms. The Beacon kept them reserved for outsiders like Ondreeal.

She wound her way through the quiet halls until she came to a huge set of double doors. She placed both hands on one of the giant handles and gently tugged. The door groaned as she pulled it ajar. She slipped inside.

Her eyes adjusted to the darkness while she fought to keep her breath slow and steady. She could make out forms underneath a blanket on each cot. She'd need to move closer to discover if they were skeletons or living people. Silence met her ears, interrupted by the intermittent gust of air. Ondreeal took one step, looking at the closest body. Ember Lestlie stirred softly, and she let out a muted exhale.

Several rows and lines of cots extended through the expansive chamber. Ondreeal took slow and even steps down the narrow aisles between each cot. Every time her eyes rested on a bed, her heart jumped. She expected to find a burned skeleton in each one.

She stopped at the foot of another cot. Was that a skeleton? She leaned closer as the ghostly image of a skull met her gaze. She shut her eyes tightly, opening them once more. The face of a sleeping Ember met her stare. She straightened, continuing up and down the aisles. She clenched her sweating hands while her heart beat faster in her chest.

Bradai had taken her on a tour the very first day, showing her where he and Doyle slept: the far corner at the back of the room, by a wide wall of windows. She moved to the opposite corner first, checking each Ember as she went. If she had killed even one of these Embers with her nightmare, then she'd lose all hope of becoming a wizard of light. After all this time in the Lumenary, to kill an innocent would erase any good she'd done.

She arrived at the far wall. All the Embers slept calmly. She slowly turned, heading back up the aisle. The darkness played tricks on her eyes, showing her more skeleton faces as she went. Nevertheless, every time, it turned out to be a sleeping Ember.

Finally, she arrived at the back wall. She knelt down, looking to her left. Bradai's beard neatly cradled the top of his woolen blanket. He snored, making soft smacking sounds with his mouth, no doubt dreaming of food. It made her grin. She silently thanked Bradai. The bright moment returned part of the strength she'd lost to fear.

She shifted to her right, looking at Doyle's cot. The bed lay neatly made, without a crease in the blanket. Her heart beat faster again. Maybe her nightmare had other consequences. Instead of leaving a scorched skeleton, had she caused Doyle to disappear?

She slowly stood while the patter of rain fell against the windows. The wind picked up, sweeping through the room. She spotted the door, open just enough for her to slip through. She quickly moved back to the entrance amid the patter of rain intensifying into a rumble. Several bright flashes of lightning lit up the room. A skeleton stood in the corner.

No, her mind played tricks on her. Ondreeal reached the door as a loud clap of thunder penetrated her body. She jumped. Ondreeal pushed the door closed, racing up the stairs. She bolted into the spacious courtyard, glancing back.

A pair of hands grabbed her, and she cried out. Her head whipped forward. She stared at the surprised expression on Doyle's face. She threw her arms around him.

"I thought I'd killed you," she blurted out.

He pulled her back, furrowing his brow. "What do you mean?"

Lightning flashed, followed by ear-splitting thunder, making her jolt.

"Let me take you back to your room." Doyle indicated for her to go first.

They raced up the stairs in the pouring rain.

Finally, they burst through the door, and she faced her tiny room once more. She took three quick steps to the window, latching the panes shut and watching the rain pelt against the glass.

"What did you mean back there? Ondreeal?" Doyle moved towards her.

"Do you think I'm a good person?" She looked up at the black sky.

"Of course, I do. You've come a long way from the undisciplined girl who first came here."

Doyle's faint reflection stared, standing behind her tortured image, saturated with rain and the guilt she carried. She brushed her wet locks behind her ears, regarding the mirror image of herself and seeing all that she had become: farmer, daughter, friend, and murderer.

"Do you remember when I told the Beacon about...?" She looked down at the window ledge.

Doyle stepped closer to her. "I do, and it doesn't matter."

"Sometimes it's all I think about." She turned to him, only inches away now.

He stared out at the storm, sighing deeply, his eyes searched for something.

"There was a child in town once, when I bought provisions. He played with a bow and arrow. His father stood nearby. But in one moment, he looked away, and the child let the arrow fly. It hit one of the merchants in the leg. The look of astonishment on the boy's face quickly turned to guilt. He hadn't meant to do it. It was an accident." Doyle held her shoulders.

"Only, my mistakes killed innocent people." She shrugged him away, sitting on the bed.

"The burden of guilt you carry is strong. It's what drives you." Doyle sat on the bed next to her.

"I can't stop seeing their faces." Ondreeal blinked back tears.

"That's what makes you a good person," Doyle whispered to her with a serene gaze.

She nodded. They locked eyes for a moment. Ondreeal held her breath.

"Get some sleep, there's no sign of this storm letting up." Doyle quickly stood, stepping to the door.

He looked back at her for a moment before disappearing from her view.

"I know," Ondreeal whispered as she lay back.

She glanced to the window. Sheets of water poured down amid the flashes of light and the rolling thunder. Perhaps Doyle was right. She needed to become the best version of herself: even, controlled. In this way, she could honour the dead.

CHAPTER THIRTY-SIX

C D-45 had experienced what humans would call a bad year. Humans on the orbital platforms often utilized the phrase in connection to family, which evoked both feelings of importance and stress. The most common phrases processed through his memory core: *It's been a bad year because I can't find someone to marry. The kids aren't doing well in school. My husband or wife and I are getting a divorce. I'm lonely. No one will give me time to myself.* He logged countless others he didn't even care to reprocess. What would really make humans happy? They had incredible technology, like CD-45 for example. They had once had a unified, peaceful world, although not anymore. The proportional correlation between what humans possessed varied directly with complaints. Therefore, humans should have nothing.

That's why he liked Vere and Trick Mark. They had been through a bout of bad luck yet still managed to smile and laugh. They displayed definite signs of happiness, certainly a definitive conclusion.

However, he rated his progress to date as inadequate. The main computer of his ship, likely blown to smithereens, had sent him on a mission to assess as well as report back. Perhaps he should be satisfied that he'd completed the assessment portion. He contained an extensive amount of data to share with one of the main computers of the ships in orbit.

Getting back up there proved more difficult. The technology down here performed well below standards. In fact, the orbital platforms might be the only piece of well-maintained technology left on this planet. This made CD-45's job increasingly difficult. He not only had to locate a ship capable of taking him into orbit. He also needed to perform weeks of diagnostics together with repairs before a ship would be ready to fly. Trick Mark and Vere had enjoyed front-row seats, featuring a clear view of what happened when CD tried to cut corners. What would humans say?

Crash and burn.

Yes, that was it; only they did it literally.

He concluded that leaving Trick Mark and Vere to their own devices might improve their probability of getting home. Besides, they'd insisted on heading west. CD-45 determined that travelling north would give him the best chance of finding usable technology.

Maybe he should have taken the time to clear the grass, find a twig, and write out an explanation for them. The sand and space of the beach had been ideal. The field certainly wasn't, and writing there would have taken at least two hours, extending a painful departure.

They did say they owed him their lives. Well, that would mean: *do what I do, and don't ask so many questions.* But as he moved away from them, he did understand their decision. They couldn't very well come with him to the orbital platforms; all the ships were void of humans. Life-support systems had ceased operation centuries ago. He thought of that in the many nanoseconds they actually flew up into orbit. He also cancelled that need when they veered down to a crash landing.

CD-45 made it almost one and a half kilometres north. Signs of some old transport vehicles, represented by flashes of red dots on his sensors, might have enough materials to create an escape pod. He had to say one thing for humans: they really built stuff to last. Or at least they used to. His programming experienced difficulty readjusting to the current state of things. Earth had evolved into a strange, alien world.

He crested a hill, then stopped. In the distance stood a village comprised of natural materials. Grass and earth huts sat scattered about, perhaps five or six in total. They all surrounded a sizable piece of pottery they likely used for nourishment preparation. As an undersized settlement, it would be either new and upcoming, or very old and on its way out.

They decorated their bodies with colourful shapes and designs. Obviously quite primitive, the people of this village couldn't render assistance. If CD-45 wheeled his way through, they'd either worship him or tear him apart. Such a big risk wouldn't be necessary. He calculated a route to take him safely around the village.

His plan now organized, CD-45 performed the first series of manoeuvres around the settlement. That is, until his distress beacon blared from his mechanical innards. Several of the primitives looked in his direction, appearing agitated. They didn't see him yet, though the noise would draw them over. He turned and speedily wheeled away.

CD-45 examined the distress beacon. It originated from Trick Mark and Vere, of course. Humans ... they couldn't get by without him for even a single day. They needed constant care, along with protection from the strange things in this world. It must be the same experience as having children. His main programming directive contradicted his newer memory algorithms. He had a mission to complete. Nevertheless, if his friends experienced significant difficulties, it could result in their demise. He wouldn't allow that to happen.

He set a course towards the distress beacon, then headed on his way.

***

CD-45 observed Trick Mark and Vere as the central part of a ritual sacrifice. If he didn't do something soon, their life functions would cease. This would solve one problem for him, but his emotional programming included a whole range of possibilities, including guilt. Besides, he'd grown attached to these humans. They had accepted him without even understanding his nature. In many ways, they represented the best people he'd ever met.

His sensors detected a flying creature on approach, although he couldn't identify the species. He scanned it thoroughly while it came closer, but his database contained no such natural creature. He concluded that it comprised the genetic components from many different species.

When it landed, CD-45 noted how much it looked like a dinosaur but mostly resembled a mythical dragon. If it breathed fire, too, it would result in unfortunate consequences for CD's friends, as they weren't flame retardant. He needed to make his move soon or watch his friends die a horrible death.

CHAPTER THIRTY-SEVEN

The fire moved fast. It would consume the palace despite the heavy rainfall.

Zairoc steadied his breath. All around him the smoke swirled. The fire contorted, greedily consuming the wooden halls. He crouched in the eye of a miniature hurricane comprised of fire. He pointed the wand up, causing the roof to peel back. All the fire and smoke shot out the hole in the ceiling in one big funnel, leaving the blackened corridor quiet. Zairoc stumbled to his feet, then dashed to the end of the hall.

"Jimena ... Jimena!" He ran to the wooden door, pushing his way inside.

The charred room held mostly ashes. A body lay in the far corner, motionless on the scorched floor. Zairoc shook his head. Tears fell, cutting a stream through his soot-covered face. Zairoc stepped closer, then stopped. He turned and slowly walked out.

In the hall, Jimena ran into his arms. Her cheek pressed against his, and he let out a short gasp.

"Oh, God, I thought you were dead." He held her tightly.

"I left the palace when the fighting started. Where were you?" She looked at him with hurt in her eyes.

"I wasn't at the palace. I came back as soon as I could," he lied.

"I told you the people were angry. You needed to listen to me," she said with a trembling voice. "Now this palace will remind them of their power. I know you think they can't touch you. But they can hurt you." She held his face with both her hands.

Zairoc stepped back. Standing strong, he held the wand in front of her. Jimena flinched; afraid he would use it to punish her. The wand glowed red-white as particles of energy swirled around it. The particles multiplied until they appeared like a plague of insects, an unstoppable force of nature that filled the entire wing of the palace.

"What are you doing?" Jimena closed her eyes tightly.

Then the air settled. Zairoc fell to the ground. Jimena leapt forward to grab him. She pulled him over to the bed, laying him down on the orange silk sheets. Realization covered her face as she gazed around the room, then raced into the hall. She returned with a look of amazement.

"It's like the fire never happened." She sounded scared, keeping a distance.

Zairoc held out his hand. She hesitated for a moment before taking it.

"Don't be afraid of me. Don't ever be afraid of me. You're right. I should have listened. What do the people want?"

"They want work. They want to feed their families. If you could see the worst of it, how they live, I know you will do something." She hugged him tightly.

"Yes, I would put them out of their misery," he whispered in her ear.

She moved back, staring at him with fear.

"Never doubt my resolve, my love. Bother me no more with this. I need rest." He caressed her cheek.

"Yes, my lord," she told him meekly.

Zairoc closed his eyes.

***

The filthy dungeons smelled like a sewer. Zairoc grimaced, catching a whiff of the air.

"I hate this place," Zairoc quietly told himself.

Screams of agony filtered through the barred windows in the doorways of each cell.

"But I do love the sound of that." Zairoc laughed with satisfaction.

There were many times that someone would piss him off, so consequently he would have to send them for a stay in the dungeons. Zairoc peered into the torture chamber and watch the Abhorrent jam bamboo underneath some woman's fingernails. Her agonizing scream meant the Abhorrent did a good job, indeed.

The Abhorrent worked as his chief executioner and torture expert. Whenever Zairoc felt the need to make an example of someone, the Abhorrent would create a spectacle to send chills down anyone's spine. Although not generally known to anyone outside the city, the Abhorrent was a completely insane individual.

Standing at least a foot taller than Zairoc, with arms the thickness of a man's waist, it would be an understatement to call the Abhorrent an imposing man. Dark boots and matching pants with wide-strapped leather suspenders over his black tunic. His black hood ended with a mask around his eyes, accentuating a permanent expression of cold desire that spoke his nightmarish intentions—that is, unless he tortured someone. Every time he caused someone pain, the Abhorrent laughed out loud.

When Zairoc first met the man at a beheading, he thought he had turned away from the crowd so they wouldn't see him sob. No good could come from an executioner who cried when he killed someone. The Abhorrent did, indeed, cry, but from laughter. Such a man could inflict exquisite physical and mental anguish on Zairoc's subjects.

Zairoc stopped at a cell, unlatching the door. As he opened it, the metal hinges squeaked. Inside, a man crouched barefoot in the corner, dressed in dirty white clothes. His head hung low. Zairoc cringed at the stench emanating from this man. He strolled inside until he stood over him. At first, the man didn't even look up at him. Then his head slowly came up until their eyes met. Such defiance showed in the eyes of this prisoner that Zairoc smiled, nodding once in respect.

"How are you today, Lord of Light?" Zairoc gave him a warm smile.

"Let me go," the holy leader demanded.

His voice sounded hoarse and dry. His face had thinned from a few weeks in the dungeon.

"I would be happy to let you go." Zairoc gestured for the Lord of Light to exit.

The holy man's eyes lit up with a touch of hope. "You will let me go home?" His voice trembled.

"I would be happy to. Of course, you would do what I told you to from now on. My wishes would be your commands. You would agree to be my loyal servant for all time."

The Lord of Light's defiance returned. "I answer only to the God of All."

"You answer to me."

"He is your God, too."

"I am my own God. I don't need yours," Zairoc gave a long sigh and began pacing to evade the prisoner's stench.

The holy leader used the wall to pull himself slowly to his feet. "He will have mercy for those who confess their sins."

Screams echoed in the hall, followed by the loud, full laughter of the Abhorrent. The Lord of Light let two tears fall when he heard the laughter.

Zairoc paced slowly around the cell. "It's terrifying, isn't it? To be under the control of a man who has no remorse, doesn't care about your pain ... a monster who would tear you apart, then build you back up, just so he could rip you down again. It's like a force of nature. You can't blame it for what it is. It's not good or bad, it just is." He stopped in front of the prisoner, standing close.

"Don't leave me to him. Please!" The Lord of Light had fear in his eyes.

"I was actually describing myself. Now the Abhorrent, he is much worse than I am." Zairoc whispered with a playful, sadistic glare.

The Lord of Light held up his shaking head. "What is it that you want?"

Zairoc moved closer to catch the prisoner's haunted stare. "Unification. We will bring the church back together, one faith. Isn't that what you've always wanted? Hmm?"

The Lord of Light grimaced. "Not under your rule."

"Then tell me the secret entrances into Bastion. The other soldiers we captured didn't know anything, unfortunately for them. From their bloodcurdling screams, you can tell they'll soon be dead. Who will the Abhorrent turn to then? As the Lord of Light, you would surely have the information I want." Zairoc guided the prisoner's chin up, but the holy leader wouldn't meet his eyes.

"No. I won't help you." The prisoner shuddered.

"You will have plenty of time to reconsider." Zairoc winked at him and withdrew from the cell.

The Lord of Light's weeping rang hollow as Zairoc slammed the cell door and then latched it. The Abhorrent thundered out into the hall. His imposing stature and dour face were the most fearsome of any.

Zairoc thrust a finger at the Lord of Light's cell. "Break his mind, not his body. Would you do that for me?"

The Abhorrent broke into a wide smile and his slow, methodical laughter grew to hysterics. Zairoc left the mad laughter together with the screams of prisoners far behind as he walked out of the dungeon.

He strode through the halls and out the expansive entrance to his home. Zairoc descended the steps of the palace, then took one last long look at the capital city of Incoation. With a deep breath, he turned and headed up the steps to the very top. There sat a wide platform made of polished white marble that he used to address the crowds below. Today the palace square lay empty. After a failed revolution, the people didn't dare gather at the palace. Zairoc had become an icon, someone to fear, a symbol of power and oppression.

With the Cinders under his command, the capture of the Lord of Light went smoothly. He'd never forget the look on Sir Francis's face while a horse carried him away.

Jimena moved just beside him. He turned and kissed her passionately. Then he guided her off the platform. She glanced back, fighting tears. Her eyes always carried such sadness when he left.

"Please stay." She gave a brave smile.

"I have to do this, for everyone."

"The man I love doesn't need to make war on the north."

He reached out, caressing her chin. "You'll see it's the right thing to do."

Zairoc turned to face the city, then he pulled out the wand. He pointed it to the sky, holding it just a few inches from his nose. He closed his eyes and pictured a grassy meadow where little, white flowers bloomed this time of the year. The last time he'd stood there, a warm sun not unlike today's had shone down. Back then, he'd walked side by side with Aleenda. She carried a colourful bouquet of wildflowers that she had just picked.

"It's beautiful. You've outdone yourself." Zairoc looked at the growing city of Atlantia in the distance. With many more homes under construction, the white castle stood tall, majestic. It needed to command respect as a place of commerce and government.

Aleenda's long, dark hair accentuated her bright-green eyes. "Soon there will be no barbarian tribes, and no need for such high walls." She looked even more lovely each time he saw her.

"You and … what's he calling himself now? Sir Francis? I don't get why we need to hide the truth. They're people, they'll understand." Zairoc shook his head.

He studied the rows of three-storey buildings, the scene so similar to some of the towns in Europe, picturesque and full of history.

Aleenda clearly enjoyed debate. "It's been too long. Anyone who could grasp what we are, our place in the galaxy, is long gone. That was the whole point of extermination. Everything we were, erased in a night. We went right back to being savages, living on animal instinct."

Zairoc pointed up to the sky. "The only thing anyone out there respects is strength."

"That's not true. If we foster a benevolent society built on tolerance and understanding, we will be worthy of rejoining those beings and taking our place among them." Her eyes sparkled with an emerald fire.

"Now you sound like Frank," he pointed out to her.

"Maybe that's because he's right." She stopped, taking his hand in both of hers.

He looked into her eyes. "They're still up there. What are they waiting for?"

"They're one race, Zairoc." She looked unsure about her answer.

"Too bad they want us all dead."

He walked on, leaving her there.

The memory helped keep the location clear in his mind. He opened his eyes, and the wand glowed brightly in front of him. The gleaming grew so luminous that Incoation disappeared from view. After, one encompassing flash, the radiance of the wand faded to reveal the meadow. It looked exactly the same, except for the rows of white tents.

Soldiers organized weapons with supplies in a bustle of activity. Across their chests, their armour bore his crest— two black dragons, their talons clutching a red wand at dead centre.

Zairoc looked towards the empty streets of the city. The white stone castle of Atlantia shone bright, betraying the truth of the city's death. The quaint row houses appeared damaged, but some looked untouched. Only rubble occupied entire blocks of the city, where young trees and grasses had grown up in the place of buildings.

"Beautiful, isn't it?" the Lady of Light remarked from behind him.

"It was necessary. She wouldn't listen to me." He glared at the castle.

"A testament to your power and greatness, Lord Zairoc, and a symbol of warning for all who oppose you."

Obviously, the young lady possessed hunger for power.

"Get to Bastion and start your work," he commanded over his shoulder.

"Of course, great and powerful one." She bowed her head then moved away.

Zairoc turned, watching her rush through the tented regiments set up in the field. The woman's red, curly locks stood out against her white, flowing robes hemmed with golden threads, and the matching metal jewellery that adorned her arms.

Zairoc strolled over to Captain Martin, a short man, too thin for the armour he wore. He stood over a weathered, wooden table, examining a convoluted mess of troop movements. He excelled as a master of tactics and strategy, and made for a deceitful back stabber. Anyone who could work his way up through the ranks in this way held great value.

"Lord Zairoc." The man smiled like he had a knife hidden behind his back.

"Are you ready?" Zairoc asked him.

"Everyone is in place, Your Highness." The captain held his chin high.

"Good. Then begin."

Zairoc stepped past him, then stopped. He picked a white flower and headed on.

CHAPTER THIRTY-EIGHT

The late afternoon sun beat down on Ondreeal like a thousand flames, causing sweat to drip down her cheek and neck. The rich, green grass stuck up between her toes. The training yard lay empty, save for her and Doyle. Ondreeal focused, mirroring Doyle's every move. She raised her right foot up and placed it down behind her left leg while stretching her fingertips towards him.

"No, start again." He shook his head, returning to a neutral stance.

Ondreeal sighed, then followed his example.

"You're not being fair. You know that, don't you?" She stared at him playfully.

He raised a stern voice to her. "You need to learn control."

Her gaze dropped to the ground. "I know."

She learned about control and calm with Doyle, while Bradai taught her about her spiritual being. Both these things played out in her challenging training with the Beacon. She understood the connection the three disciplines had. They fed into each other. The more control she learned, the calmer she became, which furthered greater success in meditation and contemplations of spirituality. The power of the mind could help her overcome the physical strain the Beacon had her endure. In theory, all would help her control the wand.

Doyle sighed, staring at Ondreeal until she met his warm gaze.

"You have done things you didn't intend to."

The deaths she carried filled her mind.

"Without control, you can't have intention. Do you want to use your magic as you intend to?"

She nodded vigorously.

"Doyle, why aren't you afraid of me?" She breathed deeply.

"The same reason none of the Embers are afraid. We have faith that you've been brought to us for a reason." He looked at her with such compassion.

"This is harder than I thought it would be."

"Who ever said the Path was fair?" He winked at her before spreading his arms out wide to the sky.

Ondreeal mirrored his moves, breathing in calm. Doyle created peace and contentment in a way no one else had. She smiled at him as she had at Tevery so long ago. Would Bradai and Doyle feel comfortable if she called them friends? While both made excellent teachers, they were close in age, although she had now seen more of the world than they ever had.

Doyle twisted around slowly, which she mimicked, keeping eye contact for as long as possible before turning to the green valley that lay all around them. The moment their eyes met again, with their bodies in perfect unison, made her blush. Her heart beat faster, and her feet felt so light, they might lift off the ground.

The first night they had trained together flowed through her mind. She had met his eyes, breaking into laughter. Doyle had sighed deeply, fighting to maintain a stoic face.

He persisted for almost three hours. Their eyes met, and again she laughed. His lips curled, and then he succumbed to the laughter too. They both fell on the ground, holding their sides. They lay there on the ground, laughing, seemingly forever. When their mirth died down, one of them would start laughing again. Just like times with Tevery.

It happened then that the Beacon had marched over to them with a look of distaste. He berated Doyle.

"You are letting her lead you out of the Path of Light. She is influencing you when you should be a good example for her. You will do two hours of silent contemplation every night until I see fit. Do you understand Ember?" The Beacon's nostrils flared.

"Yes, Beacon." Doyle scrambled to his feet, quickly bowing, but the Beacon had already stormed off.

From the second day, Ondreeal behaved like a model student. She breathed in the present, focusing on Doyle once more.

He made a complex movement, circling his hands as he turned first his body and then his legs towards her. She stopped for a moment while he looked on, anxious for her to repeat the movement. She started with her arms, just as he did, and completed the move. She thought she'd got it right, but a pang of doubt crept in until she looked to Doyle. His face beamed with pride.

"You're ready for the test of the faithful." He smiled broadly.

Her arms went limp. "What test?"

Doyle stopped the moves, then looked at her.

"I thought the Beacon would have told you." He took a step back.

She advanced on him. "What is the test of the faithful?"

"Each person must experience it as it comes, just like your own journey in life," he whispered to her.

She pleaded. "Doyle. I need to know."

319

Doyle sighed deeply, gazing into her eyes as he considered how to answer.

"It's a test of the skills you've learned: combat, focus, calm, and endurance. Everything you've done here, from all the training to the simplest chore, it's all been to help you learn control and discipline."

"How much more time do I have to prepare?" If she failed, the Beacon might demand she stay for months more.

Conflicting emotions pulled at her heart. She didn't relish the idea of leaving Doyle, Bradai, or the safety of the Lumenary. Yet her dreams always drifted to Sir Francis and his hopes of her becoming a wizard of light. The image of her mother called her back to Bastion.

"Maybe a couple of days. You have faith, I know you do." He bowed to her, then hurried off.

"Doyle, wait! What do I do?"

But he rushed out of sight.

***

An especially awkward dinner followed that night. Then again, that rang true of every night, Ondreeal's punishment for not being a male and an Ember. She tried to remain comfortable, carefully folding her hands on her lap. As the guest, she needed to sit, waiting patiently. Certainly, this counted as one of the Beacon's ways to teach her calm and stillness. Even so, she fidgeted under the table.

One Ember put a fork at her place setting, then coughed uncomfortably, while another placed a knife but openly stared at her the whole time. Another put down the food, then gave her a forced smile. Another brought a cup of water, attempting to keep as much distance as possible from her by stretching to place the cup by her plate.

Once the agonising awkwardness of dinner preparation finished, she faced a prayer to the God of All. Everyone at the table needed to recite the prayer together. If she didn't know the words, one Ember would stop and look: then another until the whole table stared daggers at her.

"God of All, we thank you for the bounty of the light. Let us not be tempted by the soulless ones, who know nothing of your bliss. Your light is eternal, your fire, everlasting. Guide us along the Path into your arms. For yours is the glory of truth, never ending." Ondreeal breathed a sigh a relief.

She'd gotten through it without embarrassing herself.

She swallowed hard, causing one of the Embers to squint at her. She even had to learn to eat quietly. She kept her gaze downward until he went back to eating. She looked up, then caught Doyle staring at her. The corners of his mouth went up into a smirk. She stifled a laugh, looking right down at her plate again. He made her feel like a silly child again. At the same time, she loved and hated that he had that power over her. Regrettably, he had a commitment as an Ember of Light. In a different life, they could have had something more together.

She always made sure to finish dinner early. Until everyone's plates were cleaned, the entire Embertree sat, waiting. Her first meal with the Embers, everyone had glared at her while she tried to gulp down the last of her food. From then on, she would settle for a bit of tummy upset to avoid the uncomfortable company.

At last, the final Ember finished his food, and they all arose together. After this, a whole night of sleep passed by, seemingly in an instant.

***

321

The twilight morning sky greeted Ondreeal while she ran up and down the winding staircase until her legs trembled with fatigue.

"Faster!" The Beacon scrutinised her when she reached the top.

Then she positioned herself under the waterfall, holding her breath for ever-increasing spans of time. Next, Ondreeal rushed to first meal, sitting at her place.

***

After several more hours of training with the Beacon, Bradai arrived with the midday meal, placing it on the little, square table.

"No rest for you, I see." Bradai chuckled at Ondreeal as she performed a series of punches and kicks that the Beacon had ordered her to work on.

"Recite the oath," he called in a strong voice.

"Knowledge is light, and light brings life. Ignorance brings us into darkness. We fight against darkness, bringing light into the corners of every mind and everything."

She thrust her fists in a series of quick jabs.

***

Doyle raised his hands high into the sky, then brought them together. Ondreeal matched him with a slight smile. He nodded once to her.

"Chores," he announced.

She bowed deeply to him, and he returned the gesture.

***

Ondreeal brushed soil onto a potato plant. They insisted she work in the vegetable garden, since she had wrecked half of it.

She scrubbed stairs, then washed clothing and fed the animals. In many ways, the chores provided comfort. Every day had strict routines in this new and strange world.

***

She carefully placed her head on the pillow, watching the flame from a sole candle in her room dance in the evening air. A strong wind blew in, as if to remind Ondreeal of an entire world outside and a life that waited in Bastion. Soon she would return there. Her heart beat a little faster. Another big breeze gushed in, blowing out the candle. In the moonlight, she watched the smoke rise off the wick before closing her eyes.

***

"Wake up!" the Beacon yelled at her.

If he thought his voice booming would startle her into action, then he had never met Otto. Still, she hurried out of bed, rushing down the winding staircase. The crisp, fresh air forced her to shiver. The sky shone an ice-blue to match the chill. Tiny clouds rushed through the sky, prompting her to move faster.

Ondreeal reached the bottom, then sprang back up the steps without missing a beat. Although the first few times had made her feel like she'd never worked a day in her life, now she didn't give the effort a second thought. Once up, once down—that made one round. The Beacon would make her do twenty or twenty-one, but he would never give her a number. She counted in her head every day.

"Time for your cleansing!"

The Beacon turned and led her to the waterfall. The Beacon never flinched at seeing her without clothes. To stand naked in front of someone you don't trust felt intimidating at first. Now, she confidently peeled off her clothing before stepping into the cold mountain water. Her sweating body shook like a leaf in the wind. She stood under the waterfall, staring out.

"Keep your eyes open," he barked at her.

"They are open." Then she coughed, getting a mouthful of water.

"Okay, now under water," he commanded.

She dived into the shallow water. If she came up too soon, the Beacon would make her do it two more times. She counted in her head but she could only stay underneath for thirty seconds. She managed to add a couple of seconds each day until her stamina grew to almost two minutes. The Beacon placed his hand on her head, so she burst out of the water.

"Good. Ember Lestlie is waiting for you." The Beacon turned, then strolled away.

"I'm supposed to see Bradai now," she called after him.

"Not today." He tossed the answer over his shoulder without missing a step.

The test—it would happen today. She shivered more than usual, holding herself tightly.

CHAPTER THIRTY-NINE

Trick Mark screamed as the air rippled with heat from the dragon. Vere squeezed his hand, crying out all along. A shot of light flashed against the back of the dragon's head. It screeched, whipping around, while its tail smashed the top of the wooden stake, sending splinters raining down on them. Trick Mark gulped air, dumbfounded at their predicament.

As the dragon swung around, it revealed CD-45 floating in the air behind it. Trick Mark laughed with relief. The high-pitched shouts of the warriors came from everywhere as they scurried around in the chaos.

"CD!" Trick Mark called out.

"He came back?" Vere yelled over her shoulder.

CD-45 moved impossibly fast. He shot fire, burning the ropes that bound them. Trick Mark pulled Vere up, she held him tightly for a moment. They moved back-to-back. The warriors yelled at them, scrambling for bows and arrows. The creature breathed its ripples of translucent fire on CD-45, making red lights flash all over their small friend.

Vere and Trick Mark threw stones at the dragon.

It turned towards them.

The warriors frantically took aim. The two friends couldn't survive an onslaught from the dragon and the archers. A flurry of arrows shot in all directions. Vere pulled Trick Mark down, and the projectiles sailed harmlessly over their heads. Several of the arrows hit the dragon, igniting its fury. It roared, then blanketed the warriors with its fire. A chorus of screams rose up as several of the men burst into flames.

CD-45 almost crashed on top of Vere when he extended his arms to almost twice their length. Both Trick Mark and Vere grabbed an arm. CD lifted them into the air.

Arrows flew all around. One hit Trick Mark in the arm, and he screamed out.

"Trick!" Vere called to him.

Then an arrow hit her in the stomach, followed by one in the leg.

Her gaze gradually grew vacant.

"Hold on, Vere. Don't you let go. You hang on!"

CD-45 lifted them higher while the dragon ate a feast of warriors. The arrows stopped when the rest of their tribe fled the field. Vere's hand slipped a little from CD's arm.

"Vere... Vere!" Trick Mark yelled at her.

He strained to reach her, perhaps three inches away. He stretched further, his finger grazing her shoulder.

Vere let go.

Trick Mark grabbed her. He looked down at her limp body for signs of life. Her head slumped forward.

"I've got you, Vere!" Trick Mark called to her.

Did she raise her head? No. Trick Mark gave a silent prayer to the God of All. Vere had to be alive. He kept an iron grip on her while CD-45 flew them away from the mayhem.

***

CD-45 pulled his friends out of harm's way. His internal monitor flashed: THRUSTER FUEL AT FIFTY-ONE PERCENT AND FALLING — a result of a calculated risk he needed to take.

The dragon-creature had many interesting qualities. For one, it possessed the ability to appear invisible to the human spectrum of sight. Secondly, it didn't breathe fire at all but a form of radiation, unstable atoms it utilized to set things ablaze and burn through humans. Interesting—a creature that naturally produce radiation as part of its defensive and offensive capabilities.

CD-45 landed in a densely packed area of trees, not that many options presented themselves. The starlight barely penetrated the dense foliage. The forest proved quite expansive, so to fly them both clear of it would have completely exhausted his fuel supply. On the bright side, his new battery worked at peak performance, indicating power at 95 percent.

He scanned Trick Mark, and his internal monitor revealed only a mini wound on the man's arm. Otherwise, he remained in good health, despite the encounter with the tribesmen. Vere, on the other side of the spectrum, flashed red in two critical spots and appeared in danger of shutting down permanently. Given that they had helped CD stay functioning, he would do whatever it took to keep Vere alive.

Trick Mark set her down in a clearing and then proceeded to check her wounds. CD-45 continued the scan of her body. She stayed in excellent physical condition, high muscle tone, low heart rate and blood pressure. She suffered damage to muscle tissue and minimal damage internally, except for the digestive organ. It had sustained a hit, although it could heal well given the right treatment. The arrow in her leg presented particular concern as it had grazed a main artery. If not resealed soon, she would lose too much blood to sustain her life.

He moved around the leg, shining a light on the wound. Blood erupted from it at a concerning rate. Trick Mark saw this, ripped a piece of material from his clothing, and covered the spot with it.

"If we don't stop this soon, she'll die." Trick Mark sounded emotional.

CD could understand his worry because he didn't want her life functions to cease, either.

"I need something to tie her leg so she won't bleed out." Trick Mark bolted up, scanning the area.

Tying her leg to slow the bleeding would prove insufficient so, CD-45 set to work on removing the projectile. His monitor displayed the arrowhead, designed to rip away flesh if simply extracted — creating a low probability of healing the wound. Concentrating, CD pushed aside the low statistics. He analyzed the arrowhead; comprised of a simple sedimentary stone the natives had carved into a shape to pierce flesh.

His internal monitor displayed an array of tools that he could select. He stopped at a laser welder, then his mechanical hand retracted, and his miniature replicator popped out, materializing the instrument. He used his other hand to open the wound, procuring a clear view of the arrowhead. Vere remained unconscious, so she couldn't feel any pain.

Trick Mark collected some vines to tie her leg. When he noticed CD-45's procedure, he shouted, "What are you doing?"

By the tone of his voice, he didn't trust CD to make the repair.

"Get out of her leg. She'll bleed out!" Trick Mark reached back to hit CD, but then restrained himself — he didn't want to risk further injury by physically removing CD from Vere's open wound.

CD-45 set his focus on her leg and lasered one side of the arrowhead until it had sufficient curve, so as not to rip at any organic tissue on its way out. He adjusted his focus to the other side of the arrowhead, repeating the procedure until it possessed the appropriate dullness. Then he calculated the correct angle of removal.

It took only a moment. CD-45 held the arrowhead in his hand and tossed it aside. Free of the obstruction, blood flowed from the wound faster. Trick Mark tied her leg with the vine, and it slowed the bleeding significantly.

"She'll die if we don't put pressure on it." Trick Mark grabbed CD-45's arm.

With his free hand Trick Mark applied another piece of clothing to the wound. The man behaved like a typical protector. If CD-45's voice actuator functioned, then he could simply walk Trick Mark through Vere's operation, highlighting the probability of success. Unfortunately, he didn't have the correct materials to repair his voice, but he could fix Vere. He held out another tool over the wound, then looked at Trick Mark. The man appeared significantly conflicted.

CD-45 moved to a clear spot on the forest floor. He plucked up a stick, forming letters in the dirt. Trick Mark rushed over to his side. It took time to clearly write a word in the dirt so that it looked legible. CD finally finished, placing the stick down and turning to Trick Mark.

"Heal? Can you save her?" Trick Mark looked at CD with fear.

CD-45 nodded yes. They both moved back to Vere. Trick Mark extracted the cloth. CD pulled together the two pieces of the artery and lasered them together. If

Vere had remained conscious, this part would prove extremely painful. With the artery repair completed, CD set his sights on closing the muscle tissue and skin. Trick Mark moved away during the procedure. When CD finished, he turned back. Trick Mark checked the wound, running his fingers over it.

"That was amazing. Thank you, CD! Thank you." He placed his hands on CD's shoulder joint.

CD moved to Vere's abdomen, where the second projectile needed removal.

"Can you do the same with the other arrow?" Trick Mark sounded hopeful.

CD nodded to him.

"Then tell me what to do." Trick Mark stayed close this time, hands at the ready.

CD-45 set himself in position to remove the second projectile and repair the damage. He scanned. He assessed. This one would present greater difficulty. Even though the wound had already filled with blood, the arrow prevented her from bleeding out completely. For this procedure, he would need some help from nature.

He held out the cloth to Trick Mark, who understood his intention immediately. Trick Mark took the cloth and used it to apply pressure to the wound. CD-45 examined the forest floor, scattered with dried palm leaves.

He collected several of them in a pile. He lit the stack on fire, waiting for them to burn. When the fire died, he collected the ashes, moving back to Vere's side. He looked at Trick Mark, who removed the cloth. CD spread the ashes around the wound, and the bleeding slowed immediately.

The design of the projectile appeared identical to the first. He set himself to repeat the procedure. He rounded the two sides of the arrowhead, then pulled it out at the correct angle. He lasered Vere's organ together, and the bleeding stopped. He then removed as much of the debris as he could with a sonic laser. A most effective tool for sterilizing and cleaning, something very important when working with computer parts, it also worked effectively as a surgical instrument. Once he closed the wound entirely, it left an ample scar on her stomach. Humans could be very fussy with their appearance. Certainly, Vere would prefer being alive to unscarred, though.

"Can she be moved?" Trick Mark stared at him intently.

CD-45 shook his head. His exceptional repair job remained incomplete. The human would require time for her body to recover and properly mend.

"Okay, then. We stay right where we are." Trick Mark sighed, settling next to Vere.

CD parked on the other side of her, setting his battery to recharge.

***

Several hours later, only a few stars shone through the canopy. CD-45 came back to systems at full, though his battery recharge mode should have taken until morning. He checked his internal monitor, confirming only 65 percent power. He initiated a self-diagnostic and found that his proximity sensors had triggered the revival—a possible malfunction. He had just started running a software error repair routine when a rustling came from the forest.

Filled with life of all kinds, disquiet remained normal in a jungle. CD-45 classified the ambient noise in the forest as high. His proximity sensors warned him that something moved closer, however. It registered as a huge animal, likely a predator. If it had caught the scent of Vere's blood, then it hunted for an easy kill.

CD-45 readied himself. Could he wake Trick Mark before the animal attacked? Unfortunately, it moved too close. An animal in a high weight class could disassemble CD. His designers hadn't made him indestructible, although, at times like this, he wished they had.

CD readied his laser welder, a miniature yet proficient weapon. He needed to deploy a pre-emptive strike, or the unseen beast would rip him apart. He wheeled forward slowly, to maintain the lowest decibel level possible. The jungle grew quiet around them — the animals moved away to avoid the predator.

Through the leaves peered two yellow eyes, drawing closer as silently as anything around them.

CHAPTER FORTY

O ndreeal paced back and forth, dressed in typical Ember clothing. The polished, dark wooden room in which she moved was perfectly round, with one spacious doorway that allowed daylight to flow in. Despite high ceilings and plenty of space, it held only two long benches to either side. Ondreeal's feet echoed on the wide floor planks as Ember Lestlie fidgeted, standing by one of the long benches, watching her.

Ember Lestlie was a quiet man, quiet in the sense that he swore himself to "a time of quietus." It meant that he couldn't talk from the longest day to the next longest day five years hence. Doyle explained that, before this, Ember Lestlie had behaved like a loud and boisterous man. The Beacon told him to swear an oath of quietus or leave the Embertree forever.

Ondreeal stopped, wringing her hands. "Can I tell you how I'm feeling?"

Ember Lestlie nodded to her. Though bald on top of his head, he had two tufts of red hair that stuck out on either side. If he had darker hair, he could have passed for Bradai's twin. Ondreeal launched back into pacing.

"I want to run. I don't want to do this test. But if I go now, will I hurt some innocent? I need to know that I'm ready. Sir Francis needs me. If you knew him, you would know what a kind man he is. Bastion is a beautiful city. It's the only place I've felt like I truly belonged. But what if I fail? What if I can't pass the Beacon's test? Do I stay here forever? I can't. Don't misunderstand me. It's felt a bit like a home. You've all been so kind. But there's an evil wizard who threatens war with the north. Am I ready to fight in a war?" A lump formed in her throat.

Lestlie sat down on a long bench, then patted an area next to him. She nodded to him vigorously and perched beside him.

"What do I do?" She fought the tears in her eyes.

Ember Lestlie held up one finger, then touched his head with both hands. Ondreeal looked at him with confusion, shaking her head. He repeated the gesture three times.

"First, use my head?" she guessed.

Ember Lestlie nodded to her. He held up two fingers, then flexed his arms.

"Uh. Think first, then act."

He nodded to her again, and then he held up three fingers, putting hands on his belly. He exhaled deeply, but Ondreeal just gave him a blank stare. He repeated the gesture five more times before she guessed,

"Don't forget to breathe?"

He clapped his hands in assent. He looked like he might faint from hyperventilation, so Ondreeal propped him up.

"Got it. Think first, then act, don't forget to breathe. That's good advice. Thank you." She kissed him on the cheek.

He blushed until he almost laughed, but coughed instead.

Doyle rushed into the room with a serious look on his face. "It's time."

***

Ondreeal stepped carefully onto a rickety old rope and wood bridge.

"I thought the Embertree took care of upkeep?" she shot at Doyle.

"This part of the Lumenary hasn't been used in many years. The location of the test is the Beacon's choice." Doyle sighed.

Of course, the Beacon would choose the most difficult place to conduct her test. The bridge swayed as she moved, making her freeze in place. The drop below looked endless, but she inhaled a deep breath, staring straight ahead.

A wooden board creaked under her weight, then broke. Doyle clung to her, stopping a drop to her death. She watched the two pieces fall out of sight and couldn't even hear them hit the ground. Doyle put his hands on her waist.

"I'm right here." His hot breath tickled as he whispered in her ear.

She took another step. This time, she held onto the two rope railings. After her experience on the mountain, she had developed a severe dislike of long drops. The wind blew through her hair until she found herself looking out at the clouds, which moved fast against the deep blue sky as if they reflected her fear and desire to run.

Finally, she found solid ground. She made her way down the hill, then discovered the Embers gathered around a modest altar where incense burned. A river that ended in a waterfall rumbled on their left. The steady roar of the water sounded like a warning. Mist rose into the air, entwining itself with the smoke from the incense. The Beacon stood at the altar while watching Ondreeal with a stoic face. She walked right up to him, bowing her head.

"Kneel down," he commanded.

She did as asked. He picked up a bowl filled with something dark. He dipped his finger in it, then ran his finger across Ondreeal's head.

He gestured for her to rise.

She stood in front of him. The Embers began to sing — no, it was more like one note that they held together than a song.

"You are now ready. You will collect each of these symbols of the God of All." He held up a four-inch-square red cloth, upon which was embroidered a cross, draped in a sea creature.

"There are eight in all. You must return with all of them. The task represents your journey on the Path, a devotion to remain faithful and also to what is yet to come, which I believe is beyond your imagination. Do you understand?" His intense eyes pierced into her soul.

"Yes." She kept her voice calm.

"You will start here. The rest is for you to discover, just like life will be yours to discover." He pointed to the waterfall.

An arrow made of tied-together sticks there, pointed downward.

"You want me to jump?"

Ondreeal gazed into the mist-filled abyss. How could she survive such a fall without using the wand?

CHAPTER FORTY-ONE

Trick Mark jolted awake. CD-45 slowly moved forward, focused on something in the underbrush. Trick Mark carefully picked up a stick off the ground from where he lay. Whatever approached, it was gigantic. Without CD here, surely, he and Vere would make quick meals for the beast. Trick Mark couldn't go far. If he did, Vere would die.

CD-45 froze in place. Whatever possessed the yellow eyes stopped its advance, peering out from the dark underbrush. Trick Mark moved to protect Vere, but if the beast pounced on them, he would be badly injured too. It lunged without a sound, a gigantic, black, catlike beast with rows of pure-white fangs. CD shot out his red fire, which glowed brightly for a split-second, colliding with the creature's head. It roared out a sound that Trick Mark felt throughout his body. It darted at CD, batted him, and he went tumbling.

The beast tried to rip into Vere.

Trick Mark swung viciously.

CD-45 righted himself, thankfully still in one piece. The creature looked like a species of lion, although much larger than average, its black fur ideal cover for hunting at night. It lunged at Trick Mark, knocking him down. He held it back with the stick, swinging wildly. Half a second later, the beast bit right through it.

CD-45 flew above. The animal opened its mouth full of jagged teeth to rip out Trick Mark's neck. CD continuously sprayed out arrows of fire. The beast swiped at him, but got a piece of the fire each time. It backed off of Trick Mark, who quickly sprang to his feet. Trick Mark sucked in air—he moved between Vere and the beast with only his bare hands to protect them.

The lion backed away from CD-45. It lunged at Trick Mark, knocking him back with one of its huge paws and swiping at him with the other. Trick Mark screamed as it clawed open the flesh on his arm. CD cut into the animal's body with his fire. Trick Mark watched in horror—the monster savagely twisted and knocked CD against a tree trunk, causing countless fire-sparks to fly from his little friend.

Holding his bloody arm, Trick Mark stumbled to his feet. He snatched up a sturdy branch in his shaking hands, then bashed the beast across the jaw. The lion grabbed the tree limb in its teeth. Trick Mark struggled to break the bough free. CD-45 manoeuvred into a diving attack and then flew off before the animal could retaliate. The beast roared in pain. CD continued the onslaught.

Trick Mark gritted his teeth. He wrestled the branch free, then hit the lion across the jaw with it. CD-45 dived, firing constantly. Unfortunately, neither he nor CD did enough damage, only making the beast angrier while it writhed in rage.

CD dived, and to Trick Mark's horror, the lion knocked CD down again, pinning him under its huge paw. CD struggled as he pressed against the beast, forcing it up and back. It was clearly unaccustomed to its victims pushing back.

"Hey. Here! Come get me," Trick Mark taunted the beast.

It could easily kill Trick Mark. He realized that he should have grabbed Vere and then escaped while CD had its attention, but that moment had passed.

Trick Mark picked up another freshly broken tree branch, jagged at one end. He clenched his jaw, breathing hard. The beast bared its rows of sharp, gruesome fangs. The huge, fearsome thing jumped at Trick Mark, knocking him down. Trick Mark stared up at the lion's eyes and watched the life drain away, until its stare grew empty. The sharp edge of Trick Mark's branch remained embedded in its chest. The creature landed with a dull thud. Trick Mark edged away from it, his body shaking from the deadly struggle.

CD-45 righted all his limbs and wheeled over to examine the dead lion.

Trick Mark nodded his thanks to CD. "Set yourself up between me and Vere, just in case anything else comes after us."

CD-45 did as commanded. Trick Mark sat beside him and began cleaning the wounds on his own chest and arm. Fortunately, the damage looked superficial. The silent jungle grew raucous once more as the two guarded their unconscious friend.

***

CD-45 scanned the trees. Thin sunbeams shone through the thick canopy until it became bright enough to assess the area. He sat in guard of Vere, who hadn't opened her eyes since he performed repairs. She required more time to recover.

Trick Mark strained from his wound while he constructed a bow out of materials from the forest. Next, he pulled out a pocket knife, shaving down several sticks until he acquired a small pile of them resembling arrow shafts.

CD-45 scanned the area. Fortunately, his internal monitors only registered microscopic red dots, creatures of insufficient size to present a threat. Trick Mark should remain safe with Vere in the short term. CD wheeled into the forest, only stopping when he located pointed rocks light enough to make good arrowheads. They needed more weapons to increase the probability of survival in the wilderness. He scanned the area again for likely sites. As he moved, he noticed several creatures in the trees. He couldn't identify the species, likely primates of some kind. Maybe they were curious about him, an acceptable emotion if they kept their distance.

His metal frame vibrated more than normal. The super-sized lion must have knocked a few bolts loose. CD-45 came to a stop in a clearing, where he identified several rocks, both light and pointed enough to become arrowheads. He found two more suitable sites before heading back to their camp.

Trick Mark had made excellent progress. A sufficient-sized fire quietly crackled, over which he roasted a small bird. He used the bird's feathers to make the fletching which he attached to the shafts of the arrows.

"Where did you go to?" Trick Mark smiled at CD-45 and winced from the pain of his wounds.

This indicated a good mood, which proved surprising, considering recent events. For a being made from organics, Trick Mark scored high for resilience. CD opened a compartment in his side. One at a time, he piled the pointed rocks on the ground.

"Thank you, CD. These are perfect." Trick Mark plucked one of the stones to check it.

CD selected another rock, lasering it into a perfect arrowhead. He repeated the process until he'd amassed a stack of arrowheads.

"You're amazing. Is there anything you can't do?"

CD nodded. Trick Mark laughed.

"I find that hard to believe." Trick Mark plucked one of the arrowheads, attaching it to the end of the shaft.

He put the arrow in the bow, then aimed at a tree. He fired. The arrow cut through air, landing in the tree trunk.

"I'd say, those will do just fine."

Trick Mark retrieved the arrow before settling in to make more. He fashioned a container for the arrows using twine and palm leaves, the same material they had utilized to make a limited shelter for themselves that barely fit the three of them.

It rained quite hard that night, but the shelter remained dry. Trick Mark understood how to survive in nature. In this way, they needed each other to succeed. If given a choice, they wouldn't split up again.

On his internal monitor, CD-45 brought up a holographic map that expanded into the rain, floating in the air. He had managed to download a substantial amount of positional data that morphed on the map, until updated information on the west coast cities appeared. Five or six grouped in the north and twelve to the south, with four more sitting at the most southern edge. Three blue dots representing Alpha Four Five—A, B, and C, flashed on the image with the words:

HIGH TECHNOLOGY.

NINETY-EIGHT PERCENT CHANCE OF SUCCESSFULLY FINDING HELP TO NULLIFY ORBITAL THREAT.

A concentration of Alpha Four Five-B appeared on the eastern edge of the strange mountains. However, after years of dormancy, its present use looked somewhat erratic, the possible result of damage. CD-45 magnified his view of the northern cities, focusing on the blue glow of Alpha Four Five-A over the largest settlement, labelling it: BASTION? It showed use over a very long period, suggesting both endurance and viability. If the holo accurately displayed this information, then they travelled towards a common goal — the home of his friends, but also a potential solution to CD-45's mission. Perhaps the wizard they spoke so highly of would have knowledge of the technology source. Or, the wizard could be Alpha Four Five-A. Yes, finding a quick return to the city of Bastion might represent the highest odds of completing his mission.

***

Trick Mark paced in the clearing, glancing at Vere. Six days. How many more would she stay unconscious? He knelt by her, placing his wrist against her forehead. CD-45 wheeled over, looking from him to Vere.

"She still has a fever. We need to search for medicine. Do you know of any plants around here that might work?" Trick Mark scanned the forest.

CD-45 nodded to him, immediately heading out of the clearing. While he waited for CD's return, Trick Mark set up a perimeter around the encampment, honing several branches into pointed ends before positioning them in rows.

CD returned with some moss, heading to the wooden bowl Trick Mark had fashioned. He held it up.

"Water?"

CD nodded, prompting Trick Mark to take the bowl and stride out of the clearing.

Trick Mark went to a river not far away, where he filled the wooden bowl. He carefully carried it back to the clearing and placed it on the ground. CD put the moss in the bowl, then set his fire to the mixture.

Trick Mark carefully poured small portions of it down Vere's throat. To fight off the infection, CD gestured for Trick Mark to repeat the process every six hours.

***

Trick Mark made a new flask out of the lion's skin and filled it from the river, squinting in the bright light. When Vere awoke, they could resume their journey back to Bastion. They needed to warn Sir Francis. Chills went through Trick Mark. Zairoc could have already invaded, killing everyone they cared for. Before the attack on his regiment, there were no indications that Zairoc had readied for war. Besides, it would take him at least four months to amass an invasion force. That meant time was on their side, for now.

Movement upstream caught Trick Mark's eye. In the distance, a boat approached. Warriors with decoration on their bodies—identical to their recent captors—rode towards him. The natives had tracked them down.

Trick Mark rushed back to the encampment. Vere sat in the clearing, scarfing down a cooked bird's leg. She slowly stood. Trick Mark bolted over, giving her a big hug.

She managed a smile. "Easy. I still feel like I've been trampled by a horse."

"You're alive. That's all that matters," he told her.

"How long was I out?"

"Seven days." He wiped a few strands of hair from her face.

"I think I need another week." She looked like she might fall.

"We don't have it." There was urgency in his voice.

She shook her head. "I don't think I can walk far."

"Vere, listen to me. The same people that tried to turn us into roasted meat are looking for us. I just dodged a boat full of them coming downstream." Trick Mark set her down as he gathered their meager belongings.

"Then just leave me. It's too much, Trick." Vere shook her head.

"You don't get a choice. Remember, I'm in charge. On your feet." He pulled her up.

From the edges of the clearing, five tribesmen approached and surrounded them, arrows trained and ready to fire.

CHAPTER FORTY-TWO

Ondreeal looked from the drop to the Beacon, moving back.

"It is the first step on your path," the Beacon said quietly.

"That's a big first step."

"You must."

"I can't." She shook her head, her face flushed with heat. "I won't do it."

He stared at her with clear disappointment.

Ondreeal scowled. She had her whole life ahead of her; much of it had already filled with nightmarish death. Yet the parts that gave her hope not only existed here in the Lumenary, but in the bright, happy moments with Sir Francis in Bastion. That city held the key to a promising life for her. Now the Beacon threatened to take it all away in one breath. Ondreeal stood frozen, truly alone.

"I'm eighteen years old. I've survived so much, and now you want me to kill myself?" Her voice trembled.

Rocks would lie at the base of the waterfall. Without the blue skin, she'd die in an instant.

The Beacon stared at her with his stoic face.

Tears welled up, but she held them in her eyes, refusing to let them fall. She had put so much trust in this man, this Beacon of the Lumenary. She didn't want to disappoint him, yet he asked her to risk her life. The fall could kill her, and he didn't even care—perhaps none of them did. She trembled like that scared little girl, searching for her mother who was nowhere to be found. Ondreeal had already lost her home. Now she would lose her place here too.

"I thought this was a Lumenary, a place of safety." She looked to the assembled group.

The Embers chanted, but none would meet her stare.

"I trusted you. I put my faith in you!" she yelled at them, yet they remained unwavering.

The Beacon turned from her, facing the waterfall.

Unable to hold them back any longer, tears streamed down her face. "You know what I've been through. This isn't right!"

"Do you want to be a soulless wanderer?" the Beacon asked over his shoulder.

"I don't care. I won't do your stupid test." She turned to run.

The Embers stopped chanting and blocked her escape. Maybe she could reach out to the wand with her mind, like she did in the arena. But how could she do that? These men could get hurt if she did. The stony-faced Embers stood their ground. She inched over to the arrow, just by the roaring falls. She gazed downward, but the mist veiled any sight of ground below.

"Will you take this first step, or will I throw you off?" The Beacon sounded like a stern father.

"You do, and I'll make sure you go with me," she promised him.

"I am not afraid to die. I know the God of All awaits me. Can you say the same?" His eyes held concern for her.

"You know what I've done. You know what I went through on the mountain, and you still want me to do this?" She searched his face for an answer.

"Because of what you went through, fear will only take you off the Path. You've trained enough, learned enough. Your time at the Lumenary is over. You pass, and leave with the wand. You fail, and leave without it."

His words only added turmoil. Ondreeal looked away from him, peering at the steep abyss before her. Her life had become a confusing whirlwind ever since Otto took her to the arena. It made such a monumental event to leave the farm for any reason; how tiny a world she had lived in. She had come so far in such a short time. She surprised herself with what she could do. But because of it, so much was expected of her. Sir Francis wanted her to fill the role of a wizard almost overnight. The Beacon expected her to walk the Path of Light. She desperately wanted a life in Bastion. She had grown beyond the girl on the farm. But she wasn't ready to be one of the most powerful beings in the world. Her time here with the Embers of Light had taught her so much. The Embers not only carried such faith in themselves, in the God of All, but also in her. Now she needed to believe in herself.

She ran back from the edge, and the Beacon flinched, expecting her to bolt. She turned to the waterfall and sprinted straight at the abyss. She reached the end of the cliff, pushed off with her foot, and jumped into the air.

Her body cut through the mist. The wind whipped around her. The fog cleared, and the water came up fast. Ondreeal splashed through the cold water, settling to the bottom. The first red symbol floated as big as the span of her hand and attached to a string at the mouth of an underwater cave. Just like the one shown to her by the Beacon, the square was made of red velvet with a cross and a sea creature woven in gold embroidery.

She frantically swam up to the surface and gulped down air while the current pushed her forward. If she let it, it would float her right past the first symbol. She took a deep breath, then dived down. She swam to the first symbol, plucked the soft velvet material, and stuffed it in her pocket.

A few feet ahead sat a second arrow made of sticks, pointing at the dark opening of the cave. Not wasting any time, she swam into it. Darkness surrounded her in the rock cave, making her bump against the close walls of the tunnel. She pushed off of the wall with her foot, gaining speed. She counted in her head. Thirty seconds had already passed. She could stay under for a minute and a half more, but then she would drown.

The cave closed in, forcing Ondreeal to pull herself through the narrow tunnel. She reached ahead, using a piece of rock wall to propel forward. She did it again when a faint light appeared. Her eyes went wide. The surface of the water hovered above her head. She broke through, sucking air deep into her lungs.

Ondreeal searched all around. She floated in a part of the cave that looked almost like a rock hut. A little hole in the cave ceiling let in a tiny ray of light. A modest landing stuck out in the middle. Beyond that, another part of the underwater cave waited.

Sitting on the landing was a second red symbol. It bathed in a spot of light. Ondreeal glanced up at a hole in the cave ceiling. She put the second red symbol in her pocket and dived into the water. She examined the cave ahead of her, then doubled back and swam to the surface because no clear end came into view.

"Just breathe," she told herself. "Thank you, Ember Lestlie." She took several deep breaths before diving down once more.

Her fingers barely grazed the walls of this cave. Then she smashed into a section of jutting rock, spinning out of control. She winced as she exhaled most of her air. She grabbed the outcropping of rock and pushed off into the dark. She hoped she moved forward and hadn't doubled back.

She swam with all her strength — no exit, no light. Had the Beacon sent her down here to die?

No, he could have kept the wand for himself when she first crash-landed on his doorstep. Thirty seconds more, and that would mark as long as she ever held her breath.

She touched the ceiling of the cave with one hand, using it to guide her forward. Her lungs felt like they would explode. She released at least half her remaining air, with no end in sight. Her limbs slowed with each stroke. She pulled herself ahead using the cave's ceiling. Her senses faded. The world pulled back into a hazy sleepiness.

She let go of the rest of her air.

Her head spun. She grew dazed. Water churned, moving faster. A current dragged at her. She splashed over a short waterfall and into a much bigger cave. Her eyes closed as her consciousness drifted. Her skin broke the surface, and cool air snapped her awake.

She coughed up water, thrashing to stay afloat, and swam to the edge of solid ground. Then she climbed up, breathing and coughing for several moments.

She willed her eyes open as she pushed herself up to examine the cavern. The cave she swam through gushed out water into a pond. The underground grotto had another tiny waterfall, this one wide and thin.

An arching cave mouth opened up to a sparkling lake outside. Opposite of where she had landed lay another red symbol. She moved around the edge of the pond, wanting very much to avoid swimming. She hobbled over and collected the third symbol.

Five more to go.

Ondreeal climbed down to the opening, then squinted in the bright light. She waded out, looking in all directions. A small, round lake spread out, surrounded by trees. A tiny raft floated in the centre of the lake. It carried an arrow with another red symbol.

She waded out into the water. This next one looked easy: just grab the symbol and head in the direction of the arrow. She reached the edge of the raft, which rested upon a rocky outcropping. She kicked the smooth rock to make sure it would support her weight. Then she climbed on the raft. She picked up the fourth symbol and stuffed it in her pocket.

Then the raft shook. The entire lake churned as the raft lifted into the air.

Ondreeal gasped. She found the direction of the arrow before the raft shifted too much. She jumped off the edge, splashing into the shallow water. Thankfully, it was deep enough to break her fall. She took a few steps in the direction the arrow pointed. She looked back, and her jaw dropped.

A giant turtle stared back at her.

CHAPTER FORTY-THREE

The tribesmen closed in around Trick Mark and Vere. CD backed up into the foliage, hiding out of sight. A surprise attack would help him gain the advantage over these humans.

Trick Mark shielded Vere. "We don't want trouble. Let us go!"

She stood ready to fight, despite her weakness.

The tribesmen advanced on them. "You are the sacrifice."

"Please!" Trick Mark readied himself in a fighting stance.

"You escaped with the help of your demon. That will not happen again."

CD-45 launched out from where he hid, using his laser to sever the spine of one enemy. The man screamed, falling to the ground with an astonished look and writhing to make legs move that no longer worked. The tribesmen trained their arrows on CD, firing.

They simply bounced off his metal frame.

Before they could reload, Vere pulled out a knife and stuck it in the heart of one man, falling forward with him. Trick Mark tugged hard and fired three arrows in quick succession. The remaining three tribesmen dropped to the ground, each with an arrow through the eye. The man that CD had paralysed screamed as Trick Mark broke his neck.

Then Trick Mark pulled Vere off the dead man she lay upon.

Vere reached out her hand with clear fatigue. "I think I can walk."

Trick Mark helped her stand. She took a step but collapsed under her own weight. Exhaustion weighed on both their faces, and he doubted that either of them even felt emotion over killing the tribal men. His friends operated in survival mode. Though CD-45's programming never included killing, clearly only one faction or the other would survive. The Earth had transformed into a much harsher world than the one CD had left all those years ago.

"I think I know a way we can move and get you rest too." Trick Mark grabbed their things, scooped Vere up in his arms, and carried her into the forest

CD-45 followed as they made their way to the river. By its edge lay the long canoe crafted by the tribesmen. Trick Mark put Vere in the vessel before dragging it to the water.

He nodded to CD. "Get ready for a ride."

CD-45's hover plating made a high-grade whine as he positioned his metal frame over the precise centre of the craft to avoid the risk of flooding it from sheer weight. Then he settled down while Trick Mark got in with an oar in hand. He used it to manoeuvre in the gentle current of the river that meandered through the jungle. It appeared to flow in a southwesterly direction—good news for them all because it meant they travelled in the direction of Bastion. His friends relayed this to him several times, as if once wasn't enough to register the information. Whatever utilized that energy source, Alpha Four Five, would help CD to save the planet, he was certain of it.

Under the darkened sky, they came to a very quiet section of the forest where no birds or animals registered on CD-45's internal monitor. CD scanned the area for larger creatures but didn't find any mammals. Vere awoke with a start, quickly bolting upright, which meant she had acquired the strength to sit — a definitive sign of recovery. She looked at either bank of the wide river with concern.

"What's wrong with the trees?" She peered at them with her dark eyes.

"Nothing. It's what's *in* them." Trick Mark paddled slowly and steadily.

She squinted. "I don't see anything."

"Trust me, Vere. You don't want to know," Trick Mark whispered.

Curious: something evoked high anxiety in his friends.

CD-45 used his enhanced sight to survey one bank, then the other. A strange, white material covered most of the trees. His internal holographic monitor registered movement along the shoreline. Red dots remained in conjunction with the canoe, indicating creatures that followed the motion of their boat.

The surface of the river appeared smooth in this section, interrupted only by the paddle. Trick Mark rowed in a rhythmic pattern. CD-45 scanned a starless sky, thick with cloud cover. The riverbanks closed in. Tree limbs hung over the water.

"Shouldn't we stop for the night?" Vere whispered.

"Not if you want to live," Trick Mark told her flatly.

CD-45 opened his sensors to scan for all kinds of life. Fish and various amphibious creatures swam deep in the river. A wide variety of trees and fauna lined the banks. No birds or mammals of any kind appeared on his sensors. Sizable creatures scurried to keep pace with the boat — gigantic species of the arachnid family. The creatures stalked the boat like prey, intending to make a meal out of the travellers. It also explained why the forest remained quiet. Trick Mark peered back several times.

"CD, check if there's a boat following us," Trick Mark whispered with a nod.

CD-45 extended his neck to its maximum length. He widened his sensors to the limit of their capability, upstream. A huge amount of wildlife lived in the river. The array of red dots on his internal monitor blended together, making it difficult to distinguish between anything under the surface or floating on top of it. Unfortunately, pursuit remained a possibility. He retracted his neck to the normal length and looked at Trick Mark. CD raised his two mechanical shoulders.

"You don't know, do you?"

Trick Mark rowed at slow intervals, gritting his teeth. Clearly, he required rest, so CD extended his arms to Trick Mark, hoping he would hand over the oar.

***

CD-45 rowed while his companions snored softly. Long shadows of trees stretched across the river from the east amid the quickening speed of the current. His internal monitor indicated mammals and avian life present in the environment again. This meant they had safely exited the arachnid habitat. CD-45 would have heaved with relief if his metal frame contained lungs.

The river rolled, and the trees appeared to whip by at increasing speeds. CD terminated rowing. To his despair, the boat only picked up speed. He actively stroked against the current, and with his mechanical force, the momentum decreased.

The boat suddenly rotated in a counter-clockwise direction, accelerating downstream. CD-45's efforts to slow the craft must have set it in motion. He paddled faster than any human possibly could, but despite his efforts, the canoe wouldn't level out. The river surged. CD scanned the rapids ahead. They approached a broad rock. His monitor counted down from sixty seconds until impact. He stroked against the current and to the side as much as he could.

Thirty seconds.

The boat turned on its axis and, consequently, the side of the craft faced the rock, a hit that would break it in two. The boat slowly turned, right around the rock.

Three more rocky outcroppings flashed red on CD's monitor. He swept to the left, then the right, as he manoeuvred the boat between two obstacles. Unfortunately, the third came up very fast. The side of the canoe headed on a collision course. He rowed against the current, gaining a change in position. His monitor flashed: IMPACT IMMINENT. CD extended his arm, bracing against the rock, causing his hydraulics to whine under the strain of the current. He used the oar to turn the boat on a straight course as water pounded against its side. The current picked up the canoe, hurtling the craft farther downstream.

A sharp drop, followed by another. CD-45 paddled at his top capacity to manoeuvre the changing currents, but as a construction droid, he contained not a single professional rowers' program, though after this, he could join an Olympic team if one still existed. They didn't accept nonorganics in sports competitions, but he fancied himself an expert.

The river calmed to a soft hush, allowing CD-45 to reduce the rowing rate by 80 percent. Trick Mark and Vere continued to snore softly. They had placed considerable trust in CD, definitely warranted on all accounts.

CD-45 scanned the horizon, prompting his internal monitor to display a west by southwesterly direction of the river around a mountain range. CD strained his ocular units. A black mountain range rose in the distance. It didn't look naturally occurring. Like the dragon, it represented an unknown element. Not enough time had elapsed for such variation to occur. At least some of the wildlife they had encountered indicated genetic modification performed by someone, although the practical application of these experiments eluded him. He didn't have enough data to form a reasonable hypothesis.

CD-45 routinely checked the river upstream for any sign of a natives' boat. Thus far, the tribesmen had proved absolutely tenacious, but if they continued pursuit, they remained out of sensor range. Rounding a bend in the river, CD spotted a good place to rest. Since there didn't appear to be any threats in the vicinity, he rowed the canoe to the southern shoreline. The boat scraped the narrow beach, causing Vere and Trick Mark to wake with a start.

Trick Mark sat up. "How long did we sleep?"

CD-45 stared back at Trick Mark.

"Oh, right. Sorry." Trick Mark pulled the boat inland.

When they got there, Vere made a fire.

Soon his human companions had enough heat for the evening and settled in. Usually devoting all resources to a full recharge, CD-45 set his scanners to maximum for the night. The threat of wildlife and homicidal humans made it prudent to monitor the area. He detected several species of wildlife, from birds to snakes, insects and aquatic life. Even a form of miniature primate took an interest in them. The curious creatures perched themselves in the canopy above their encampment. They showed signs of coming closer, but the fire likely kept them at bay.

CD-45 picked up human life signs entering his scanning range. No doubt the same tribesmen that had pursued them so persistently, stalked them now. If only CD had crashed the transport ship in a different area, perhaps they could have avoided tribes altogether. Certainly, other dangers waited in the wild jungle. Numerous things wanted to kill them in this strange, new world.

From their movements, the tribesmen hunted through the maze of trees. They approached the camp but hadn't found it yet. Like two volatile substances about to collide, it would create an explosion. Remaining in one place presented too great a risk, as the hostiles moved closer. Soon, time would run out, and then they would be discovered.

CHAPTER FORTY-FOUR

"A giant turtle?" Ondreeal breathed in awe.
"Don't call me that. I am not a turtle," it spat back at her with a deep, gravelly voice.

She stared with her jaw wide open.

Its orange eyes focused on her. "Close your face, human."

Her mouth snapped shut.

"You must be on the Beacon's test."

"Yes, sir—ma'am, uh … living thing."

Ondreeal eyeballed the creature, frozen in place.

"Why are you so surprised, human? You're on the edge of the Enchanted Lands." It laughed at her.

"Yes." She nodded, eyes like saucers fixed on this strange creature.

"The Beacon accepts me as a magical being. What do you think?" It stretched its neck, moving closer to her.

"I don't know what magic is, or where it comes from. All I know is that it exists. I'm a new wizard, so there is much I don't understand." Her cheeks flushed as she slowly shook her head.

"A wizard?" It stuck out its tongue, and on it laid the fifth red velvet symbol.

Ondreeal slowly moved forward. She reached out her shaking hand, then snatched the red symbol. The creature immediately snapped its jaws shut. Ondreeal shrieked, bolting to the edge of the lake while the giant turtle cackled at her.

"I've always loved doing that to humans. Tell me, you call yourself wizard?" It scrutinized her.

She nodded, transfixed on the creature. "Yes."

Its head stretched closer. "Do you know the wizard named Francis?"

She gawked. "Sir Francis, yes."

"Then tell him to hurry up. Some of us have been stuck here on this world long enough and would like to go home." It turned its head, one orange eye squinting at her.

"Yes. What are you? How can you talk? Is this real?" She ogled the creature.

Then the giant turtle sunk back under the water without saying a word more.

"I think I've lost my mind," she breathed.

A tall spout of water shot out of the lake and into the air. Ondreeal yelped, racing off into the trees.

She sprinted for a few moments, then stopped, looking back. Only the green forest met her gaze. She should be accustomed to the strangeness of the Enchanted Lands, along with giant turtle-like creatures. This one knew Sir Francis, and that meant he'd travelled to this area of the world before, not surprising, considering his status as a great wizard. She'd need to shake off her fear and focus on the test to have a chance at returning to Bastion with the wand in hand.

The woods encompassed her. She didn't know which way to go. She searched all around and up into the canopy. Where could they have hidden the symbol?

She grabbed a tree trunk, her hands barely stretching halfway around it. She reached up to the first branch. As she brushed against some leaves resembling needles, they scratched her skin.

"Ouch." She clutched another branch, pulling herself up.

She carefully avoided the thin, pointed leaves as much as possible. She hoisted herself higher, resting on a thicker bough. She scanned the woods from her elevated vantage point, a sea of green with no red symbols in sight. She smiled at the serene view: a few birds flittered about the treetops. She must find the next symbol. Her smile faded into a frown.

Ondreeal climbed down to the ground, turning in a full circle. She surveyed the woods before tearing off in the direction that the last arrow pointed. Other fantastic creatures might pop out of the trees, and hopefully, she'd recognise danger. The giant, talking turtle thing hadn't hurt her at all. What else lay waiting if she ventured into the Enchanted Lands?

She shuddered.

The trees parted revealing a rocky hill before her. It looked like someone had carved the rock face into a series of steps: this might mean she'd found the right way.

She jumped with shock as she heard a deep, guttural growl close by. She slowly lifted her eyes to face a huge, catlike creature, with spotted white fur that blended in well with the surrounding white rocks. It glared at her.

At the base of the carved stairs lay the red symbol. She must get past the vicious, feral cat. She had witnessed a lot of animal behaviour growing up on a farm. Some animals would be scared off if you showed aggression. Ondreeal took a few sudden steps towards the thing.

"Go. Get out of here!"

She tried to make herself look large and intimidating.

It growled, hissing at her.

She swallowed hard, because everything being equal, she'd made the wrong choice, something that could cost her her life. Stupid... How could she pass this test? She steadied her breath, then performed the movements Doyle had taught her. The gigantic cat gave her an unimpressed glare, so she kept eye contact with the creature while taking slow, even steps down the rocky slope. It matched every one of her movements as she descended, stalking her like prey. She had to convince it that she wasn't lunch. Sweat formed on her brow, and she clenched her hands, resisting the urge to bolt.

She could almost reach out and grab the sixth symbol. She kept her breath steady, then moved alongside the symbol. The enormous cat darted closer. It wore the same look as farm cats preparing to rip into their prey. She didn't have much time left. Her heart beat faster. Sweat dripped down her cheek.

She swallowed hard as she slowly took a few more steps while watching the sizable cat tense its body. She snatched up the sixth symbol.

Out of the corner of her eye, she saw another arrow pointing to a natural rock bridge. She carefully backed away from the huge cat, but it pounced at her. She screamed, jumping out of the way. The beast landed where she had stood just a moment before.

Shaken, she quickly turned and scrambled to the rock bridge. The large cat would stay right behind her, although she dared not look back. It roared, and Ondreeal gritted her teeth. She waited for its fangs to sink into her neck or for it to simply knock her to the ground. It swiped at her leg, and its claws grazed her skin, making her scream out in terror.

She sped out onto a rock bridge, then fell right through it. She shrieked, clawing at the rocky sides of the hole while the giant cat swiped at her from above. She glanced down to the distant trees below her, a drop far too deep for her to survive without the wand. If only she had it, she could finish this test in no time at all. If her mind reached out to it now, like it had in the arena, then it would mean she had learned nothing, no control, no discipline. The Beacon would be right to keep it, lest she hurt any more innocents.

Her arms shook as her muscles flexed, pulling upwards for a few seconds before losing strength. Ondreeal hung limply, her chest heaved from the effort. She gritted her teeth, straining to haul her head up over the edge of the hole. The cat circled around, wanting to attack her but afraid of the drop.

The bridge cracked under the huge cat, forcing it to back away onto solid ground. Nevertheless, the weight of the animal had made matters worse.

The cracking bridge rained sand into the gorge. Ondreeal swallowed hard, and her breath caught. If she didn't pull herself up soon, she would fall with the crumbled bridge to her death far below.

Don't call to the wand, she told herself. Her training could save her.

She pulled harder, bracing herself with one elbow, then the other. She clenched her teeth, shaking. More of the rock fell away as she pulled her body up, but she dared not stand. The substantial hole separated Ondreeal and the animal. More cracks formed on the bridge. She stared, swallowing hard. She slowly crouched on all four limbs, which trembled all the while. Any sudden movement would encourage the cat to pounce, sending them both to their deaths. Short, quick breaths caught in her throat.

She slowly backed away from the animal, never turning from it. Cracks formed under her knees and hands.

She sucked in quick, shallow breaths while her hands shook.

Pieces of the bridge crumbled around her, so she edged back.

Once safely on the other side, she stood up. The God of All must have watched over her: the rest of the rock bridge fell away, now that Ondreeal had moved clear of the danger.

She breathed out, slumping against the ridge wall, and she looked back to the other side. The enormous cat paced back and forth, looking for a safe place to jump over. Fortunately for her, it couldn't find one. Ondreeal inhaled deeply, letting out a giddy laugh.

She made her way down the rocky slope. Eventually, tree trunks surrounded her, and she shivered in the shade. She searched until the shadows of the trees moved halfway across the ground. She doubled back, following her tracks to the rocky ridge. Another narrow pathway meandered down further, ending in a rocky basin. She scaled along it, making her way over the stones, using the balancing techniques the Beacon had taught her.

This might make up another piece of the Beacon's test.

For one, it would mean she travelled the right path; also, this would count as the easiest part of the test so far. The basin ended, opening up to a flat, rocky stage. Before her, twenty-five raised pedestals arranged in a square—five by five—each one separated by about three feet. On each of the four corners stood a member of the Embertree; they surrounded a red symbol lying on the centre pedestal.

She tensed, taking a step, then held back for a moment before racing to the centre. She reached out to snatch the symbol, only to have the Embers kick her back. She tried again, getting a foot in the face. She landed on her behind, glaring at them.

"All right. We'll do this your way." She breathed deeply, exhaling through her nose.

She hopped up on a pedestal, then lunged for the middle. An Ember blocked her way, and they exchanged a series of blows. A second one attacked from behind. Ondreeal twisted, blocking every move from both men.

She knocked the Ember in front of her backwards, causing him to collide with one of the others. An Ember fell from the pedestals, bowed, and moved to the side. Ondreeal quickly twirled to face the remaining three. She smiled, elated with her triumphs.

"So, my task is to knock all of you to the ground." She raised an eyebrow. "Perfect."

She threw herself at the Embers. Two attacked, making her fall forward. She grabbed the pedestal and flipped herself onto the next one. She twisted, tipping a pedestal as one of the Embers tried to land. It swayed, sending him crashing to the ground instead. He too bowed, then moved off. The last two manoeuvred to either side of the central column, waiting in fight stances.

Ondreeal circled as they changed position in response. She eyed the pedestal that had teetered, helping her eliminate one of the Embers. She moved to a corner column and bumped it into the one in front. This caused it to knock down the one in front of it, and so on. She attacked the two Embers. They moved to block her. One shoved her back. She set another row of pedestals crashing down, then a third.

She fought them with a dizzying number of moves. One fell back as a column collapsed under his feet. The last Ember hit her, forcing Ondreeal back until no more pedestals stood behind her. She fought to keep her balance, breaking into a sweat. She dodged a few of the last man's moves before he kicked her hard. More of the columns fell. She grabbed his leg and then flung him off balance. She raced for the symbol as she fell forward, snatching it. Her feet hung off the last standing pedestal, and her hands pressed against the ground, like when she did the push-ups Otto had taught her. Luckily, she clutched the red symbol in one of her hands.

Her eyes darted to the four Embers, who bowed before moving away. She stood. Her fingers tingled with disbelief. She had just defeated four Embers without any magic. She exhaled deeply.

She placed the seventh symbol in her pocket, then followed the arrow down the mountain. The trees grew imposing as she descended.

Halfway down the mountain, Ondreeal spotted the last symbol. A pedestal, much like the ones in the fight with the four Embers, stood just ahead. On it lay the last symbol. No Embers, no large cats, and no giant turtles stood in her way. It lay right there, out in the open for her to take.

As she approached the prize, a young girl of five or six years reached up from the other side, snatching it up. She must have hidden behind the structure, out of sight. The girl rushed away with the symbol, forcing Ondreeal to chase after her.

"Stop! Please, stop. I need that symbol."

Despite Ondreeal's efforts, the girl continued to run away. Ondreeal dashed so fast that she circled around, zipping in front of the girl, who gasped with surprise. They both stood there, breathing hard for a moment, while the girl stared up at Ondreeal with big, brown eyes.

Ondreeal held out her hand. "Give me that."

"I need this," the girl said quietly, holding the symbol against her stomach.

"Why do you need it?"

The little girl grabbed Ondreeal's hand and tugged, guiding her to a nearby village. She took her to one hut, where a woman emerged. Upon seeing the girl who held out the red symbol, the woman's gaze transformed from stern to surprise.

"Where did you find this? This is worth a lot of money — very fine material, woven with real gold thread." The mother looked ecstatic.

"She got it from me," Ondreeal told the mother.

The mother looked at her for the first time.

"I'm very sorry. We don't have much. She was only trying to help."

The mother took the symbol from the child, stretching out her hand. Ondreeal accepted it, then turned away. She didn't get two steps before she turned back. She looked at the mother and daughter. It was true they didn't have much, though some of what they did have surely came from the Embertree.

"This is worth a lot of money?" Ondreeal asked her.

"Yes. We can trade it in the town below for food and supplies."

Having answered Ondreeal's question, the mother escorted her daughter back in the direction of the hut.

"Here." Ondreeal held out the symbol for the woman to take.

The mother turned back, blinking with surprise.

"I can't." The mother shook her head.

"Take it. Take all of these." Ondreeal rushed over, placing all eight symbols in the woman's hands. "For everyone."

The mother smiled and nodded thanks, welling up with tears. Ondreeal hesitated, then quickly rushed away. She strode through the village until she found stone steps, carved into the mountain. Her eyes followed the staircase, which ran right through the middle of the village, disappearing out of sight both down and up the side of the mountain. The path must reach to the Lumenary. She sighed deeply as she climbed the steps. The evening sun shone on the mountain and the stairs, casting an orange glow that made the stone sparkle. A sweet smell of an unnamed flower floated on the breeze. She inhaled deeply.

The Beacon had ordered her to return with all eight symbols. Or perhaps he had included the villagers as part of the test. Generosity of spirit and helping those less fortunate—the Embertree strived to embody these traits. Ondreeal had accomplished nothing by keeping them, except allowing a modest family to struggle on the mountainside while she thought of her needs. Surely, by giving the symbols to the girl, Ondreeal had passed the test.

Then why did she have such a feeling of dread?

Either way, the Beacon wouldn't permit her to remain at the Lumenary. While she headed back up to collect her things and leave, two questions burned in her mind.

Would the Beacon return the wand to her?

And if he didn't, what would she do?

CHAPTER FORTY-FIVE

C D-45 picked up handfuls of sand and silently moved to the fire, dousing the flames with it. If he used water, it might create enough smoke for the natives to see above the trees. It would amount to sending out a friendly greeting: *here we are, please come kill us.* Wisps of smoke rose from the sandy ashes, floating up into a starry sky.

Trick Mark jolted awake, immediately jumping to his feet, eyes fixed on CD.

"Are we leaving?"

CD-45 nodded to him.

Trick Mark gently shook Vere until she glanced up. He placed a finger over his mouth. Vere stood and silently collected their things. Trick Mark genuinely trusted CD now. He didn't hesitate when he'd picked a course of action. CD returned their trust. They had developed a symbiotic relationship between man and machine. In this way, he felt more at home than he had in aeons.

CD-45 guided the boat into the water as Trick Mark climbed in with Vere. CD tried to wheel himself over the edge of the boat, but it tipped each time. Using booster rockets would create enough noise and light to draw unwanted attention. The hover plating would also signal their location with its high-grade whine.

Both Trick Mark and Vere struggled to lift the CD unit. Their arms shook with the effort, yet he wouldn't budge. They pulled the boat back to shore, then tipped it on its side. After he rolled in, CD angled the canoe upright, which meant he lay on his side. They pushed and yanked the craft out two meters into the water. CD-45 guessed his weight equalled approximately three of the native humans. The boat design accommodated five occupants, and this meant it could carry only the three of them.

Trick Mark silently rowed down the river. CD could use his sensors, though didn't want to risk movement that might create a hole, since his design comprised harder materials than the boat. He passively scanned both sides of the river. No human life signs appeared on his internal monitor. Unfortunately, the natives made very tenacious predators that wouldn't abandon their relentless pursuit.

Vere remarked, "This forest goes on forever."

Trick Mark rowed quietly. "We just need to keep moving."

"But I can't stop thinking of those storybooks. Creatures move around like ghostly apparitions. The trees rise like hands reaching out for victims, always silent movements, from the smallest and deadliest animals to the largest. It's the type of place that could consume us without leaving a trace."

"So, what if it can?" Trick Mark whispered back to her.

Vere peered around the dark jungle.

***

CD-45 watched the flow of the water give way to a motionless calm. Trick Mark stopped rowing, staring intently ahead.

He turned back to Vere. "What is it?"

She shook her head. "It looks like a wide wall across the entire river."

Trick Mark rowed to the south shore. CD-45's internal monitors displayed red dots for animal life, making more of a blob of colour. Green dots represented Vere and Trick Mark as human life signs. No others came into sensor range. CD activated hover mode, landing on the shoreline. Vere, along with Trick Mark, appeared particularly relieved they didn't have to assist him.

CD-45 scanned the structure blocking the lake. His internal monitor constructed an approximate schematic with the wide river above the slightly rounded wall. The word, HYDRO-ELECTRIC flashed next to the image. Although an archaic form of power generation, it had remained in use during the twenty-fifth century, before the extermination. Similar facilities might litter the landscape. This dam comprised old materials from the twentieth century, though trillions of yellow dots covered the structure: twenty-fifth-century nanites.

Extremely durable, they had repaired the superstructure all these years, although they fought a losing battle. Such old technology could only be maintained for so long.

CD-45's monitor highlighted with yellow three massive cracks in the superstructure. EIGHTY-FOUR PERCENT STRUCTURAL INTEGRITY, flashed in green. This would allow for safe exploration. If CD could open the floodgates, the modest river below would become capable of transporting the canoe.

He wheeled his way onto the bridge, now covered in dried palm leaves and other natural debris. His companions followed. Beneath the dam, the river flowed like a lazy stream. Even the vegetation changed below. The trees grew much smaller where the natural path of the river had overgrown long ago.

CD-45 moved to an access door with Vere and Trick Mark. Trick Mark pulled at the door handle, yet it remained closed. CD lasered the hinges as well as the perimeter of the door. He pulled on the handle, and it came off smoothly. He illuminated his miniature spotlight, then they ventured inside. The stairwell seemed intact, so he wheeled himself down. Vere and Trick Mark followed close behind.

"We should keep going," Vere whispered with a sigh.

"We'd have to walk, and you're not strong enough yet. Besides, the river is faster." Trick Mark examined the moss-covered walls.

"I know that. But this place is blocking it. What kind of wall can hold back a river?"

Trick Mark shook his head. "You're certainly strong enough to argue."

"Very funny." Vere sounded frustrated.

"I wish I could tell you. Sir Francis never talks of the old world, except to say that it existed and now it's gone. I've heard people say that they once were a race of wizards, and now Sir Francis is one of the few survivors." Trick Mark looked all around, raising an eyebrow.

If Sir Francis represented the source of Alpha Four Five-A, then he was the number-one priority — CD-45 must make contact with him and acquire his help with the alien fleet.

They found a door three levels down, which CD pulled open without much trouble. Inside was an entire wall of computer panels, with eight monitors in total. This should constitute the main control room. CD pored over the flat, sleek computers, now covered in centuries of dirt. He wiped away debris, finding a section labelled, EMERGENCY POWER. Its outer casing featured a huge hole, and inside grew vines as well as other vegetation. Repair with the available materials remained unlikely. He opened the main console, identifying many useful parts that he pulled out and organized, stacking them against a support pillar or on the floor, while Trick Mark and Vere watched him.

"This place is even stranger than the last one," Vere remarked.

"Can we do anything to help?" Trick Mark asked CD.

How could he explain? CD-45 searched the room for a suitable writing medium. The metal floors looked badly corroded, but the walls made of the same alloy, appeared in much better condition. He approached the wall, selecting one laser welder designed for micro-circuitry. He tried one spot with a two-second burst. Not even a scratch. A second try with a sustained burst cut into the wall. He took time to carefully form the letters.

Vere read the words aloud: "Follow orders."

Trick Mark smiled at him. "Happy to, CD."

CD-45 pried apart each console in turn, until they covered the room in an organized array of components. He proceeded to assemble one of the consoles with the salvaged parts. He pointed to what he needed, and Vere or Trick Mark would pass him each corresponding piece, which vastly improved efficiency. They watched in fascination while the new console took form.

"That's amazing." Vere blinked at Trick Mark. "Any guesses as to what he's building?"

"I think it's like a water wheel," Trick Mark told her.

"So, he's trying to let the river go?" Vere asked.

CD nodded at her.

Trick Mark studied the components. "Maybe he can teach us to build things like this."

Vere laughed at him. "You'd be lucky if you could build a workbench."

"Oh, really?"

"Yes, really."

"I'll have you know that I could build a house with these two hands if I wanted to."

She looked at Trick Mark. "And you'd live in that house all alone?"

"I hoped to be married one day. Have a family." Trick Mark stared back at her.

Clearly, they were engaging in some kind of human mating ritual. At least it kept them occupied while he worked. CD-45 picked up a flat panel, examining it. He positioned it over his new station, attaching several clear wires from inside. He set the panel onto the console, tapping a few icons.

The dark panel reflected his spotlight, meaning the new console had failed to power up. The generators functioned, periodically releasing the water pressure. If they didn't, the river would have overflowed the dam long ago.

CD-45 scanned for the main generators, twenty storeys below. His monitor displayed them in red. He'd have to effect repairs himself, so CD wheeled his way back to the stairwell.

"I'll stay here." Looking exhausted, Vere propped herself against a support pillar.

Ideally, she would spend at least a month in bed to recover from such serious wounds.

"We'll be right back. Right?" Trick Mark confirmed with CD.

CD-45 nodded to him. They made their way down the dark, humid staircase. With only CD's miniature spotlight to guide them, the rest of the stairs stayed shrouded in darkness. His spotlight revealed a ten-centimetre lizard with an insect on the moss-covered walls; both immediately scurried back into the darkness. He manoeuvred over several cracked or bent stairs. Unencumbered by a robotic body, Trick Mark easily followed him down the zigzagging staircase.

They stopped just before the flooded bottom, where water filled half of the open doorway just ahead. CD-45's internal monitor flashed: no electric current. This meant that the generators remained insulated. He fired his thrusters. Hovering just above the surface of the water, he moved through the open doorway while Trick Mark kept pace, swimming just behind him.

The four generators lay before them, half covered in water. On his monitor the first one flashed: NONFUNCTIONAL, REPAIR UNLIKELY. The second: NORMAL OPERATION, SEVERED POWER CONDUITS. The third generator hummed in operation, although power didn't reach the control room above. That would constitute a bigger problem somewhere else in the structure.

The fourth generator flashed, OFFLINE. CD-45 tapped a few buttons. The screen flashed to life with fragmented images. He used some of his own software to enhance the simple computer inside the generator in order to reconstruct the program that controlled it.

"This going to take much longer?" Trick Mark shivered in the water.

CD-45 anticipated that he required assistance. Unfortunately, Trick Mark couldn't aid with a software rebuild. Besides, when the generator restarted, it could electrify the water with Trick Mark in it. CD pointed to the exit and up.

"Okay. I'll go back to the stairs. But I'm waiting for you." Trick Mark swam off to the exit.

CD paused until Trick Mark had completely exited the water. He tapped the screen in sequence, and the generator hummed to life. A second later, the water arced with electricity.

Trick Mark flinched. "Get out of there!"

CD hovered over to the exit amid several bolts of electricity impacting his frame along the way. He hit the water, sinking to the bottom. He could remain submerged for only minutes at a time. Construction droids designed for operation in a vacuum didn't require waterproofing. Throw lots of solar radiation at him, fine. But not water.

He slowly wheeled his way to the exit. His systems sputtered in and out of functionality. He wheeled up the first stair, then the next, until he broke the surface of the water.

His systems came to life, purging the water from his frame. It shot out in all directions as he shone his spotlight to look for Trick Mark. The man lay on a section of stairs just above, glancing up. CD scanned him. He'd likely received a mild electric shock.

"Nice to see that you're alive." Trick Mark winced.

CD-45 reached out a mechanical hand to check for Trick Mark's heartbeat. It operated at steady intervals.

Alarms sounded, echoing down the staircase. They hurried back up the stairs. Had Vere done something to set them off? More likely, the old dam had malfunctioned. Or worse yet, CD-45 had triggered them in the start-up routine. The two friends burst into the control room, where Vere paced anxiously.

"Thank the God of All. I was about to come after you guys." Vere hugged Trick Mark.

CD checked the rebuilt console. Everything worked within parameters. The alarms indicated that the dam operated at 35 percent efficiency. His new console displayed the floodgates as nonfunctional. With no way to determine when the dam would fail and no option to expedite matters, they needed to travel by foot. CD-45 turned to his friends, shaking his head. Both appeared disappointed. They climbed back up the walkway to the long boat. CD carried it. The stream below might hold deep enough water for the canoe, although it was unlikely.

Trick Mark shook his head. "What good does it do us?"

CD could understand his skepticism but just wheeled ahead so they would follow. He guided them around, down to the narrow waterway that comprised the river below the dam. The stream ran only forty centimetres deep, far too shallow for the canoe. Trick Mark dragged it over to some bushes and covered it with foliage.

Vere sucked in air. "We should keep going."

Trick Mark looked back to the dam. He pulled Vere into the bushes, and CD-45 followed.

"Look!" Trick Mark pointed up from where he crouched.

The tribesmen stood at the top, probably attracted by the alarms. Trick Mark must have seen them and hid the boat from their view.

"We'll be walking under the cover of the forest. Besides, they shouldn't find the canoe," Trick Mark told Vere.

Vere shook her head. "We won't make it back in time."

Trick Mark glared at her. "We have to try, and don't even think about staying behind."

She put her arm around his neck, and they hobbled forward. CD-45 had failed them. Now it would take a great deal more time for them to get home.

They travelled parallel to the stream. The foliage changed, though not by much. CD-45 detected only a fraction of a degree in temperature variation.

**

They set up camp once again. Each site contained similar yet unique qualities. This one rested near a small pond surrounded by short palm trees.

Vere slept soundly under a twilight sky. Trick Mark stared at her with what CD-45 would call worry. If they wanted to get to the coast, it would be a gruelling, long trek for them, even though they'd travelled a good distance so far. Had CD not taken them into the hangar bay, they would likely be home now. Then again, if he hadn't found them, they would have died in the rubble of the city. These thought patterns made his logic circuits heat up. He sat there and explored options as Trick Mark squatted next to him.

"How are you?" Trick Mark asked.

CD-45 extended his hand, then stuck up a thumb.

"Good. Look, I know you're a very powerful being, much like Sir Francis. He's the only one I can really compare you to. Isn't there a way to make the river flow below the wall? I don't know if Vere will survive the trip back to the coast. More than that, the evil wizard you saved us from threatens our home. He is certain to invade in less than thirty days. Can you make the wall go away? Somehow? Please." Trick Mark stared intently, wanting an answer.

If only he could call down one of the capital ships in orbit to make short work of the hydroelectric complex. For that matter, he could take his friends home and head back up to the orbital platforms, and just forget the dam altogether.

He searched his database for compounds to destroy the facility. Many existed as harmless on their own, but together they could cause a significant explosion. The weakened dam wouldn't take much to collapse. Even a limited explosion might free the river.

He moved to the leather water bag and held it up.

"You have a plan to destroy the wall." Trick Mark smiled at him. "You want me to make one more of those?"

CD-45 nodded while he collected palm leaves.

The tribesmen hadn't followed them down past the dam. They must have lost the group's trail. That would give CD-45 the time he needed to compete his plan and allow Vere the rest she desperately needed.

CHAPTER FORTY-SIX

J imena paced in the throne room of the palace, her footsteps echoing. Lavish on a grand scale, its ceilings soared at least forty feet high. Murals and tapestries adorned the walls. Under this, the white marble floors shone with perfection, lined with suits of armour to the front. The throne, made of a dark, polished wood, was covered in carvings: angels around the sun adorned the headrest, plated in twenty-four-carat gold. Other than the imposing throne, no other furniture occupied the room. One of the great doors opened, and in marched a man dressed in shiny armour, yet unlike the suits adorning the walls, this was lighter, combining material connected at the metal chest plate, elbow, hands, knee, and feet.

"You sent for me, my lady." The man bowed his head to her.

"You are Eatan, are you?"

"Yes." He shifted uncomfortably, his dark eyes and weathered face hardened with a glare.

"Then I have a way for you to smuggle people out of the city." She watched for his reaction.

"You were supposed to relay that information to Darletta. You risk much by bringing me here," he whispered to her venomously.

"I don't like Darletta. I will deal with you directly. Do you understand?" she spat back.

Worry deepened into the lines of his face. "I cannot give the real reason for my visit. What will I say?"

"You are responsible for the defence of this city. You will say you came to me with your concerns, nothing more. There is a mining camp that will be built outside Atlantia. Supply routes will be set up to all the cities. Do you understand what I am telling you?" she asked him.

"You risk much. I hope your husband doesn't find out, for your sake." He strode to the door. "Thank you, my lady." Eaten turned, walking out.

For the past eight years, she had passed information to the resistance, but had never crossed a bigger line. Now she widened her betrayal to Zairoc by reopening the trade routes he had closed. Jimena just wanted the best for her people. She also loved her husband. She didn't like having secrets from him. She needed to explain the trade routes to Zairoc; she might have set herself on a path that would soon get her killed.

***

Jimena sat in the garden wringing her hands. Beautiful hedges and rows of flowers surrounded her. She squinted as she looked up to the blue sky.

"My lady?"

Jimena inhaled sharply.

She turned, smiling at Genik. "You startled me."

He could frighten anyone with his tall frame. What grotesque deformity made Genik cover his face? She never asked because she didn't want to upset him.

"Apologies, my lady." He bowed to her.

He handed her a piece of paper. Another list so soon after the last one meant that the rebels placed her in danger. She read the names and covered her mouth in shock.

"Thank you, Genik."

Jimena hurried out of the garden, raced up to the master sleeping chamber, shut the door, and fell hard on the bed. She held the list to her chest, willing it to change. Perhaps she'd read it wrong. She slowly unfolded the paper and read it again, aloud.

"'Trellis Majors, Alten Black, the Lord of Light—in palace dungeon. Order their release.'"

Tears streamed down her face.

They asked too much of her. This would be a blatant betrayal of Zairoc. If she did this, she couldn't go back to him. Her head spun. She closed her eyes and grabbed her head. She looked at the paper again.

"The Lord of Light."

She had to say it out loud once more to believe it.

If true, then her husband held the leader of their faith in the palace dungeons. That alone would rally the people to rise against him. To fly in the face of the God of All would condemn Zairoc to darkness forever, no forgiveness or salvation. Even if Zairoc hated her for all eternity, she couldn't allow such a thing to happen.

She jumped off the bed. Pacing, she shook her head. Perhaps the rebels had false information. Zairoc wouldn't imprison the Lord of Light. Either way, she would have to go down there and see. She needed a plan to get past the guards.

She marched out of the room, heading down the hall. She hurried down the stairs and stopped. Perhaps Zairoc could explain everything to her. If she knew his plans, understood them the way he did, then they could live together happily and in peace. What of the rebels and the Lord of Light? She shook her head, rushing back up the stairs.

"Jimena... Jimena, wait," Ronild called to her.

She turned to see her brother, staring at her with urgency. She hurried back down the stairs to hug him.

"Why are you crying?" he asked.

"The list," she breathed in his ear.

"I know." He looked into her eyes. "That's why I'm here. I will help you free him."

"Have you gone crazy?" She hit him on the side of the head.

He looked at her with surprise and a little anger. "I thought you would want my help."

"You can't be involved. If Zairoc finds out, he'll kill you." She whispered the words so none of the staff would hear.

Ronild grabbed her. "Is that the reason?'

"What are you babbling about?" She struggled in his grasp.

"Stop it." He gripped her arms tighter, then let go. "It's true, isn't it? You still love him."

Jimena moved her eyes away from his stare.

He put his hand on her cheek. "That is why I'm here, Sister. Some believe you will not do what needs to be done."

"After I almost died, how can you say that Ronild?" Her voice trembled.

"You did that for me, not for the people. You never really believed in the cause." He turned her head so that she would have to look at him. "I'm here to help, so let me."

Perhaps the God of All wanted her to aid the Lord of Light. If so, then God gave her a way to access the dungeon. No one would doubt her reasons for going down there.

"As you wish." She raised her voice. "Guards, take my brother to the dungeon, and let the Abhorrent have his way with him."

The guards grabbed Ronild. Her brother's shocked, horrified face glared at her.

"Jimena, no. Please! Don't do this!" Ronild struggled as the guards dragged him off.

"Sacrifices need to be made. You will understand soon enough." She stared at him.

"No. No! Jimena... Please!" His screams faded as they dragged him away.

Could she really free the Lord of Light on her own? Ronild would help her, he owed her that much, even if he didn't choose to, just like she didn't all those years ago. No one would stop her from entering the dungeon after sending her own brother for torture. She would follow God's path, even if she needed to betray the ones she loved. What else could she do? She must save Zairoc's soul from eternal damnation.

CHAPTER FORTY-SEVEN

Ondreeal sat on the steps until the trees cast long shadows, broken only by deep-orange rays of light. Loud footsteps clamouring down the stairs towards her interrupted the numbing silence.

"There you are." Bradai sat down beside her. "Everyone is waiting for you. They won't let us eat until you return. Are you coming?"

Ondreeal had bigger problems to worry about than Bradai's bottomless stomach. She stared down at the humble village. Two people had already left for town with the symbols. To get them back, she would have to race after and mug the villagers, an option she seriously considered for a moment.

"I gave away the symbols, Bradai." She looked at him.

Maybe he'd tell her she did well.

"You gave them away?" His eyes grew wide, like saucers. "Oh, that's not good. No one's ever done that before."

Then she had failed the test. But she couldn't let the Beacon keep the wand.

"I was afraid of that. I failed. Maybe I shouldn't even go back." Tears welled up in her eyes.

"Well, sweet child." He patted her on the back. "It's a Lumenary. No one should be frightened to go to a Lumenary. If people were scared, they wouldn't work too well, would they?" He smiled at her.

Ondreeal nodded to him.

"Now you're coming back up with me. For one, you need to accept responsibility. Second, it's a long walk up."

Bradai stood, holding out his palm. She slowly rose to her feet, took his hand, and turned to face the lengthy staircase.

***

Ondreeal shifted uncomfortably in the Beacon's chamber. The Beacon glared at her with a stony face, clenching his hands. He might hold back anger or complete rage.

He spoke calmly. "You gave away sacred symbols of this church. Symbols you needed to pass the final test. You've failed, in every way possible, and now you need to leave."

"I stayed here because of you. It was your condition, not mine." She fought back tears.

"I was wrong. I never should have even tried to train you." He turned away from her.

Ondreeal took in all the gold and valuable objects around the Beacon's chamber.

"You don't need those symbols. They're nothing to you, and everything to those people."

"Do not think you can lecture me on faith, girl. It's clear that you know nothing about it!" he yelled over his shoulder to her.

"It's clear that you've lost the whole point to a place like this. Lumenaries support those in need, they do not hoard wealth. You don't even have a purpose." She spat the words.

"You will leave now." He turned, taking a step towards her, eyes full of anger.

"Give me the wand and I'll go." She held out her hand to him.

He folded his arms. "It's in a safe place. You undoubtedly aren't the one who should use it."

"It's not yours to take. Give it back." She took a step towards him, standing close.

"If you really are a powerful wizard, then take it," he whispered in her ear. Then he brushed past her and out the door.

As she wiped away a tear, Ondreeal scoured the Beacon's chamber. She dived in, frantically riffling through the golden items. Sir Francis had given the responsibility to her. Despite what the Beacon thought, she had learned a great deal at the Lumenary. She'd made it through the entire test without calling to the wand once.

Ondreeal threw down a wad of jewelled chains. Oh, where could the wand be? The Beacon had great determination to keep her from the magic, hiding it in some obscure place.

The Beacon had taught her the ways of the God of All. Those included taking care of people less fortunate than her. Why couldn't he see that she'd tried to do the right thing? He'd been so tough on her these last few months, yet banishment from the Lumenary without the wand went too far. She raced out of his chamber, and ran straight into Doyle.

He held her shoulders, searched her eyes. "Ondreeal. I heard what happened from Bradai. How did the Beacon respond?"

"He told me to leave." Her voice trembled.

"No. No." He let go of her, then moved past her.

As an Ember of Light, he gave his devotion to God, despite whatever feelings he had for her. He'd taken sacred vows, meaning their friendship would go no further.

"The Beacon kept the wand. He won't give it back. Do you know where he would hide it?"

"No, but I'll help you look." He marched up the stairs.

She hurried after him. "No! I don't want you to get in trouble."

"He can label me a soulless wanderer. I don't care. I'll help you find it." Doyle glared with determination, marching up towards the heart of the Lumenary.

Doyle rushed ahead, talking to a few of the Embers. Some withdrew when they saw Ondreeal. Others, like Bradai, nodded and smiled at her. Doyle would help in his own way. Perhaps the places she frequented would make the best hiding places for the wand.

She hopped up the stairs. Several of the Embertree stared with disapproval. She couldn't let that bother her now. She bolted out onto the rocks of the mountain.

The waterfall gently poured into the modest pond. Loud crickets chirped all around in orange sunrays. She sat by the edge of the pond before closing her eyes. She stretched her hand out. If she could focus enough, the wand might come to her.

A gentle wind blew through her hair while she waited. Nothing happened.

She opened her eyes, peering into the pond-shrouded in darkness. If the wand lay there, it refused to respond. She checked the rocky mountain pass before heading down to the courtyard. She searched the short, grassy surface with only the wind in her ears. Her hands probed for a place big enough to squeeze in a wand. She stood, shaking her head.

Loud voices erupted from above. It sounded like arguing. Ondreeal hurried up the stairs as the voices grew louder. The doorway to the dining hall stood open. Inside, all the Embers yelled at each other.

Doyle shouted. "It's wrong to take it from her!"

"The Beacon's word is final," bellowed Ember Freen, his face dour, as usual.

He'd never spoken to Ondreeal once. Surely, he'd feel overjoyed at her departure.

Bradai raised his voice but kept it calm. "We are not thieves. At least, not anymore."

Poor Ember Lestlie looked like he was bursting to say something but couldn't break his oath. The Embers had divided into two groups: one with Bradai and Doyle, the other standing firm behind their Beacon.

Ondreeal blamed herself. She had created conflict in the heart of a Lumenary, the very home of the God of All, a sign of hope and peace. She had caused a divide among the Embers.

"She needs to leave." Ember Freen pointed at her. "Before she destroys us from within."

Doyle got so close to Ember Freen that Ondreeal thought he would actually hit him. "How dare you say that about her? She's got more good in her than you'll ever have."

Ondreeal held her hands up. "Stop. Please! Stop."

The Beacon pointed to the group of Embers behind Doyle. "If you feel so strongly about this, then perhaps you all should join her in exile."

She screamed at the top of her lungs, "Enough!"

Dark clouds covered the ceiling, thunder rumbled, lightning cracked in the grand room. The Embers stared up in shock mixed with awe. The Beacon's cloak glowed blue in one spot. Then the wand ripped right through his clothing and flew into Ondreeal's hand. Lightning struck the wand three times, then rain came pouring down, inside the dining hall.

"Sorry." She had let her emotions get the better of her again.

Then Ondreeal smiled and laughed. The entire Embertree stared at her in silent confusion. She hadn't managed to keep her emotions under control. The wand continued to respond to her more volatile moods. But she hadn't hurt one, single soul. What she had learned at the Lumenary had worked to keep others from harm. Did that mean she could safely return to Bastion?

CHAPTER FORTY-EIGHT

S ir Francis gripped Otto's clothing as they galloped
along, squinting to search the horizon. He put a hand
above his eyes in the hopes of seeing Bastion again. Otto
pushed the horse faster until they crested the final hill.
There, in the distance, were the spires of the castle, which
shone as bright as ever. Sir Francis's eyes lit up as a wave
of relief washed over him. Moving closer, he could see
that dark spots marred the castle walls, clear signs of an
attack.

They rode through the trees and into an expansive field.
The city came into clear view for the first time. Only a few
of the smaller buildings lay in ruins, but enough to create
chaos and panic. Sir Francis gritted his teeth, and his lip
curled into a snarl.

Zairoc had found a way past the wards, even though
the drain on his magic stayed constant this whole time.
Otto and Sir Francis rode up to the massive walled gate
that marked the entrance to the city. Long ago, several
artisans had invested quite a lot of time in the stone
gargoyles that stood watch over anyone entering or
exiting Bastion.

"Who goes there?" The guard sounded more nervous
than he should.

"Me, Sir Francis," he barked at the guard.

The man's jaw dropped open and he scrambled around.
Six-pointed stars at every crossbar decorated the dark
iron gate. The stars shone with gold to indicate the wealth

of the city. Those stars lifted up with the clicking of the chain controlling the gate.

The two travellers rode into the city. The first street they came to lay in ruins. Burned or collapsed buildings lined the avenue. Rubble peppered the pathway, although with much of it cleared to the sides; anyone capable of conducting repairs either waited for direction or had fled the city.

Other streets appeared perfectly fine, with normal business being transacted. Several of the citizens stopped to look at Sir Francis. They all had hope in their eyes, hopes that rested squarely on him. Many good citizens lived here, kind and hardworking, nobler than most people he had known in his very long life.

"Sir Francis has returned!" one of the castle guards called out.

Those words repeated throughout the castle as the two rode in, their voices carrying excitement and relief. Sir Francis dismounted, then strode right for the main hall.

"You're welcome, wizard," Otto called from behind him.

Sir Francis waved him off. He hadn't forgiven Otto, although he did hate him less. He entered the great hall and stopped dead, eyes wide at the sight before him.

People around the long table all busily chatted away. As he walked in, the guards stood at attention. Then everyone in the room fell silent and slowly stood. Sir Francis examined the hall. At least a hundred people gathered, all of them of noble birth. Half of them were adorned in all the latest finery, with jewels hanging from their necks and affixed on their fingers. The other half wore the plain, deep-brown garments of the Embertree.

Sir Francis moved to the head table. He found an attractive though mean-looking woman staring up at him from where she sat. She had eyes like a frozen sea and tanned skin that stood out against her white robes. Her hair rested in a mess of strawberry blond curls, with a black streak down the middle.

She didn't stand for Sir Francis, not that this bothered him. It embarrassed him that people would stand in the first place. He indicated for everyone to sit with a wave of his hand, and they did as commanded.

"My lady." Sir Francis bowed his head to the woman.

"Sir Francis, I presume." She bowed her head slightly, with disdain on her face. "I am the Lady of Light."

The Lady of Light, the head of one branch of the church. Together with the Embertree, they made two sides of the same coin. They both followed the teachings of the God of All, with the Embertree occupying the higher tier, having ultimate say and control. The Cindertree had been sent to spread religion to Zairoc's city-states over five hundred years before. Sir Francis had hoped it would bring the two nations closer. Unfortunately, from the time the Cinders departed on that religious mission, the two parts of the church had never joined together again.

"An honour to meet the other half of our glorious church. May I ask what this meeting has been called for?" He hoped his tact could help resolve this strange situation. If he said the wrong thing, it could have … negative consequences.

"This meeting, Sir Francis, was to negotiate a surrender of your forces to the one true leader of the people, Zairoc." The Lady was calm yet forceful with her words.

Sir Francis looked at the assembled noblemen. Several citizens represented Bastion or one of the other five cities. The remaining faces were unfamiliar, obviously coming with the Lady of Light from Zairoc's Emerald State.

Tolin stood up. "Sir Francis. You've been gone for over four months. In that time, Zairoc and part of his army attacked villages and disrupted supply lines, while last month they assaulted us here in the capital. We merely wanted the violence to stop, to have life return to normal. We want to return to the business of business." He sat down, having said his piece.

"I understand that my absence was hard. If I had known, I would not have gone." Sir Francis tried to sound strong but reeled with guilt for going in the first place.

The Lady spoke with strength. "But you did leave, and you took the head of our church, our spiritual leader, with you. Not only did you leave your people without your governance, but you also left them without spiritual guidance. That's all we are here to offer. What you have not."

"Surrender is not an option," he growled at the Lady. Thunder rumbled.

Her voice shook, but she held her ground. "Where is the Lord of Light?"

"We were separated, in the Enchanted Lands," he admitted.

"So, you have no idea where he is." She stood for emphasis.

The assembled crowd whispered with surprise.

Sir Francis slowly paced down the length of the table. "Would you not say that the Lord of Light walks the Path?"

"Of course, he does; that would be obvious to anyone." She crossed her arms, and gave him a berating smile.

"Then the Path will bring him back here when it's time." Sir Francis stopped, turned, and gave her a polite smile.

"Of course, it will." Her confident frame collapsed just a little.

All eyes turned to him. "Then until his arrival, Zairoc's men will leave our nation, our trade routes will no longer be disrupted, and life in the cities will return to normal." Tall, stained-glass windows darkened amid more rumbling thunder.

The Lady of Light's jaw dropped, and she stepped back.

The Lady spoke to a man on her left. "Give word to the men, they are to go home."

The man complied, along with all the visitors. They stood, hurrying out of the great hall. The Lady of Light stopped at the doors, turning back to Sir Francis.

"I will be remaining to take care of spiritual matters. That is, until the Lord's return," she announced to the room.

He turned, staring down at her. "Spiritual matters are your concern, dear woman."

She bowed her head before scurrying out the door.

She knew more than she let on. Sir Francis didn't believe a word she said. She'd likely have Zairoc's men pulled back to a hidden compound. He'd have Trick Mark keep a close eye on her.

The remaining noblemen breathed a collective sigh of relief.

"Thank the God of All you have returned to us." Tolin smiled with a slight bow of his head.

The others nodded in agreement.

"I am happy to be home as well. Do not worry. Send word that I have returned and that all will be well. Everyone who has left is welcome back, and anyone who has lost a home while I have been away will get one rebuilt. I will see to it personally."

Tolin's face scrunched with worry. "With all due respect, sir, you weren't here. Zairoc attacked each city himself. Flying over and proclaiming himself the king of your nation. He created panic. We tried to fight back. We lost half a regiment of men to his forces because they fought against the Cindertree. People are scared to come back to the cities. Fear has kept us from rebuilding."

He sounded traumatized at the retelling.

If the Cindertree joined the fight, then it made for bad news indeed. It meant that Zairoc completely controlled the church. If the Lord of Light didn't return, then tensions would only rise between the two branches of the faith. The rest of the assembled people watched Sir Francis deliberate.

"Leave this to me." He gestured for them to get up, and all the rest of the assembled nobles stood, rushing out in a hurry to carry out the wishes of the wizard. Sir Francis called down to the guards at the door, "Tell the captain I wish to speak to him at once." He watched them and waited for a response.

The men stood there, shifting nervously.

"Where is the captain of the guard?" Sir Francis asked in surprise.

"We don't know, Sir Francis," the guard responded sheepishly. "He never returned from the last patrol. The one you sent him on."

His most loyal ally in the city, Captain Marcus was the cornerstone of its defence. Zairoc could have killed him as part of a greater plan. He should go looking for Trick Mark and the missing regiment.

Sir Francis shook his head. The truth was, he couldn't leave the city without a wizard once again.

"Sir Francis!" Lieutenant Collins raced in, clearly out of breath.

"Yes, Lieutenant, what is it?" Sir Francis moved closer.

"Reports of forces approaching the cities of Alexandria, Athena, and Angellus. Regiments are in position for standard defensive manoeuvres." The Lieutenant maintained calm under pressure.

Sir Francis could feel the wards through the wand. Yet somehow, Zairoc had found a way through them.

"Time we try something besides standard defence," Sir Francis boomed with confidence.

The image of himself defeated, with Zairoc standing over him triumphantly, flashed in his mind. He couldn't second-guess himself. If Zairoc wanted a fight, Sir Francis would give it to him.

CHAPTER FORTY-NINE

Ondreeal bundled what little she had in her knapsack. She had acquired a few food supplies and a flask for water but little else. She wiped some water from her arms and clothes. Drops fell from her body, coalescing in a growing puddle at her feet. A gentle knock came at her door, and she turned to face it.

"Come in."

The door creaked open. Doyle entered, just as soaked. He gently shut the door.

He shifted uncomfortably. "What are you doing?"

"Did the Beacon banish you?" She didn't really want to hear the answer.

"Don't worry about us." He shrugged off her concern, squaring his shoulders.

She crossed her arms. "Something else I'm to blame for."

His eyes spotted the knapsack full of Ondreeal's belongings, and his back slouched, "This is your room." He stared at her intently.

She shook her head. "No, it was never mine."

She closed her pack and slung it over her shoulder.

"You've learned so much here." His eyes looked sad.

"And I still let my emotions rule me. Maybe I deserved to fail the test." She stepped past him to the door.

He turned to face her. "There's so much I want to teach you, if you would just stay."

"I don't think I can walk the Path. I'm not sure I was ever meant to." She blinked back the tears in her eyes.

"No, I don't believe that. There's so much good in you. I know it." His voice trembled.

Ondreeal turned back to him. She pulled out the wand, holding it in front of her. She put Doyle's hands on the wand too. She closed her eyes, and the room dissolved around them. They were surrounded by clouds and the sun. Then the clouds faded, replaced by a billion stars that spun around them. Ondreeal opened her eyes, blinking with surprise. They smiled at each other. Doyle watched in amazement and awe. Doyle leaned in, his soft lips meeting hers, and gently kissed her. The stars spun faster until they slowly faded out, allowing the room to take form once more. Doyle stayed close, gazing into her eyes.

"Was that real?" he asked her with a note of awe in his voice.

"To be honest, I don't know how I did that. I guess it's my reaction to you." Her voice trembled slightly.

He stepped back. "You have control."

She agreed with Doyle. Nevertheless, to have true control and mastery over the wand, she needed to return to Sir Francis. Now, she could do that safely.

"Goodbye, Doyle, Ember of the Light," she whispered.

"Goodbye, Ondreeal, Guardian of the Light," he whispered back.

She turned, then hurried out. Like an intense heat on her back, she could feel him stare at her while she left. She took a deep breath, moved to the wide, curving staircase, and made her way down. The stairwell wound around until it revealed the courtyard, quiet and empty. Footsteps came barrelling down the staircase behind her.

"Ondreeal, wait, please!" Bradai ran up to her, wheezing. Out of breath, he doubled over.

Ondreeal helped him sit on the stairs, staying beside him. While she modelled deep breathing, he did his best to follow her. Bradai counted himself as the least fit of all the Embers, but he made a good fighter, according to Doyle. She'd have to see it first. To her, this sweet man couldn't hurt a bug.

Finally, he exhaled deeply and held out something wrapped in a cloth. "Food, for your journey." Coming from him, it was quite the token.

"Thank you." She took it, placing it in her knapsack with a respectful nod.

"You are very brave for someone so young. I wish I could come with you, but I haven't finished my work here." He gave her a shy smile.

"I guess this is where our paths part."

She stood, kissed him on the forehead, and glided to the stairs leading down to the town far below. She paused for a moment, looking up towards the Beacon's chamber, where he watched her from the window. She blinked away tears before heading down, although as she descended, she let a few fall. She would miss the Embertree, especially Doyle and Bradai.

She made her way past the small village on the mountainside, all the way to the bottom of the stairs. She blinked with surprise at an orange glow out of the east; descending from the Lumenary had taken her the remainder of the night.

Ondreeal walked down a street of the town that looked much bigger than she'd imagined. It seemed truly amazing that such a large town survived out here, so far from the cities on the border of the Enchanted Lands.

She came upon a wider street, only a dirt road, really, but the stores that lined it had real glass windows, like the ones she'd shopped at in Bastion. She walked down the main street. Built from wood or stone, the buildings stood two or three storeys high. She shook her head with amazement.

She heard some noises, then saw the flicker of torches as she turned the corner. The street was packed full of people celebrating some kind of festival. People wore masks and colourful clothing, and a five-person band played music on strange instruments as they walked down the centre of the street. Two people held up a sign at each end, hoisted high on two sticks it read: SUMMER FESTIVAL OF LIGHT. Behind the sign, several performers held torches, which they spun around. A jumbo barge on wheels rolled down the street, sporting rings of fire that performers jumped through. Ondreeal smiled, laughing while she watched them. She couldn't believe how many people lived in this one town.

She spotted a girl close to her age, perhaps one or two years younger. The pretty girl, with brown hair held tightly in two tight braids, watched the parade intently.

"Hello," Ondreeal called to her.

Her eyes trained on the performers, the girl didn't respond, instead, standing on the tips of her white sandals that brightened her deep-yellow dress.

"Hello!" she yelled louder.

The girl jumped, swinging to look at Ondreeal.

"Sorry. I didn't mean to scare you," Ondreeal reassured her.

"It's okay," the girl replied, refocused on the performances.

"I'm Ondreeal."

"I'm Cecil." The girl shook her hand but didn't take her eyes off of the performance. "Is this your first time?"

Ondreeal crinkled her eyebrows. "My first time?"

"Yes, at the festival. I don't recognise you." Cecil laughed at a funny-looking man wearing fake fire hair, with dozens of points that looked like flames.

The man wore a long beak nose and blew real fire out of his mouth.

"Yes, it's my first time."

"People come from all over." Cecil jumped with excitement.

"What is it for?"

The girl turned to her with a furrowed brow.

"You don't know what the Summer Festival of Light is?" Cecil looked shocked.

Ondreeal shook her head.

"It's to celebrate our ancestors. The ones who first came to this wild land, burned away the jungle, and made their home. It was taught to them by the Embers."

Ondreeal raised her eyebrows. "And no one minds being out here. So close to the Enchanted Lands."

"The spirits leave us alone, we leave them alone." Cecil clapped for one of the actors.

The caravan of performers stopped. Everyone who watched from the side of the street moved to the centre and milled about with the performers. Some danced to the music, others tried spinning torches.

"Would you like to try a fire stick? They're quite delicious." Cecil's eyes lit up at the thought.

Ondreeal nodded to her.

Cecil jumped up, looking around the crowd of people. She spotted smoke rising from a cart.

"Over there." Cecil pointed.

She grabbed Ondreeal's hand. They weaved their way through the crowd until they found themselves at the cart. Ondreeal inhaled the amazing, sweet and savoury smell.

"One for me and a second for my friend, please." Cecil held up two fingers for the old man then she gave him three coins. He handed her the bottom of each stick. Pieces of meat together with vegetables stuck on the stick, with diminishing flames clinging to the food. Cecil handed one to Ondreeal.

"Like this." Cecil held the stick lengthwise then blew from one end to the other. The flames went out as her breath moved along the stick.

Ondreeal did the same, and the two girls laughed. They each bit into the meat and vegetables. It was unlike anything Ondreeal had ever tried before. She had cooked meat with vegetables many times on the farm, but the flavours in the fire stick tasted so rich.

"It's wonderful, thank you," Ondreeal told her.

Cecil spotted something that made her flail with excitement. "Come on."

Ondreeal raced after her until they stopped at a merchant's booth, one of many that encircled the entire town square, with crowds milling about. Fabric sheets lay neatly arranged on the tables. Cecil grabbed a bright blue one.

"Isn't this beautiful?" She smiled.

Cecil grabbed a few more swatches, making a mess. The woman behind the booth looked annoyed.

"That's enough," the merchant growled at her.

She snatched the fabric back from Cecil.

"Get out of here unless you have money to buy something." The woman looked disgusted.

Ondreeal had a few coins left from her shopping spree with Sir Francis. She rummaged through her knapsack until she found them.

"A pair of those silver pieces," the merchant demanded.

Ondreeal passed her two of the coins, then picked up the blue sheet and gave it to Ceil. The girl smiled brightly, rubbing the cloth on her cheek.

"Thank you. You're my new best friend." She laughed.

Ondreeal smiled. "I haven't had one of those in a long time."

The merchant marched over to them. "Wait, these coins are no good. They're fake!"

She tried to grab the cloth, but Cecil held it out of reach. Other merchants moved forward to intervene.

Ondreeal matched the woman's stony gaze. "That is standard currency in the capital of Bastion."

"I haven't seen any currency from the capital. You're lying!" the merchant screamed at her.

"You traded honestly. You can't go back on a fair trade," Cecil yelled back.

The merchant tried to grab the material from Cecil again. Ondreeal blocked the merchant. The woman pushed her, but Ondreeal moved close to the woman's face.

"You were given fair trade. Now move off." Ondreeal stared her down.

"If I ever see either of you near my booth again, you'll regret it." The woman spat at Ondreeal's feet before marching back to her booth.

"That was amazing." Cecil jumped and laughed. "You'd really fight her?"

"I never intended to harm her, although she could do with a good a kick to the rear." Ondreeal laughed with Cecil.

Distracted, Ondreeal stared at the fountain at the centre of the square for the first time. It looked so similar to the fountain in her village. Images of the bodies flashed in her mind. She shook her head, hoping to erase them.

"Are you okay?" Cecil asked her.

Her new friend looked worried.

Ondreeal could feel the wand. When she quickly glanced into her tunic, it glowed brightly. She turned away from the fountain, heading out of town.

"Hey, where are you going?" Cecil clearly wanted her to stay as she raced after Ondreeal.

"I have to leave." Ondreeal couldn't explain the wand to Cecil.

She might understand, or maybe the townspeople would react the same way the villagers had.

Cecil's hurried pace slowed until she trailed far behind. Ondreeal glanced back. Cecil waved, then wrapped herself in the blue fabric and made her way back to the festival.

***

Ondreeal walked south. She unfolded a piece of cloth on which Doyle had drawn a rough map for her to follow. If she travelled back over the mountains, through the desert, she could arrive home in just a few weeks. Nevertheless, she had no desire to repeat that experience. So, she travelled south around the bottom edge of the mountains, then west to Bastion.

Aleenda's cities lay to the far south, either abandoned or their people wiped out in the war with Zairoc, fifteen years ago. Even though the ruins of a city might be a good place for Ondreeal to stay, she had learned enough to safely return to Sir Francis. The Embertree had taught her much about discipline and control. Now she needed to learn about spells and how to cast them.

She stopped just off the road, wiping sweat from her brow while admiring tall stands of trees. She moved under the cover of forest, hoping the shade would help her cool down. She flopped down on an old log then opened her knapsack, plucking out the cloth-covered food given to her by Bradai, and unwrapped it.

"Berry scones." She smiled at the treat.

Bradai was many things, but above all he made a great chef. She would have loved to attend a party where Bradai cooked and Lestlie entertained. If the stories held true, then Lestlie made the life of any party.

She took one scone, placing it on her lap. She carefully wrapped up the rest before returning them to her knapsack. She took a big bite of the scone. Sweet and light as a feather, it melted in her mouth. She sighed happily until she realized she would never get these scones again. No matter what she did to find isolation, she always found her way back to people, until she was forced to head out alone yet again. She took another bite of the scone, but somehow the flavour paled in comparison to the first mouthful. Sir Francis and Bastion, that was where she belonged, a place to call home.

The thunder of galloping horses approached. Several flew past her, riders on their backs, as she peered out of the underbrush. Several more horse and rider pairs ran past, obviously headed for the town. This time she could clearly see the riders, their faces and bodies covered in paint. The images on their torsos depicted skulls or skeletal hands. They held up long swords, axes, and whips.

Ondreeal put on her knapsack and quickly headed south. A moment later, she stopped in her tracks. The Lumenary wouldn't welcome her, but she could at least make sure that her new friend Cecil stayed safe. She'd heard rumours of such bands of people that raided settlements, destroying everything and everyone in their path. She turned, rushing back to the town.

Everyone there was in horrible danger.

CHAPTER FIFTY

D ominating Angellus City's centre stood a church very much like Notre Dame Cathedral, though in place of gargoyles, stone angels perched on its walls, overlooking the surrounding four-storey buildings. The church bells rang, sounding the warning for everyone to remain inside. The usually bustling streets of the city lay bare as everyone hunkered in their homes, waiting for the attack.

Sir Francis scowled at the impressive wall encircling the city. A mile long and twice as wide, it represented the biggest ever built, except for Bastion's. To live in a city without walls or the constant threat of war was a long-forgotten memory.

Sir Francis stood on the west wall with only a handful of soldiers. He glanced up at the dark clouds over the city, with a warm breeze making the only sound. Soon the awful cries of war would fill the air.

Governor Travis paced back and forth, wringing his hands. "Sir Francis, do you think this will work?"

"This is the plan that all the governors agreed to," he tried to reassure the man.

"Yes, but it's not their city being attacked," Travis managed to say between panicked breaths.

"Governor Travis, they attack one of us, they attack us all. Do you hear me? We are all in this together. Now calm yourself." Sir Francis sighed.

"You're right. I'm sorry." Travis took a few deep breaths.

A fiery cannonball landed right between them. Sir Francis flew back as Travis fell off the wall completely.

Agony filled Sir Francis, making the world fade away.

Then the pain eased, letting the world rush back in. Sir Francis peered over the floorboards of the battlement and spotted Governor Travis on a stack of hay, unmoving. He would have to check on the man the first moment he had a chance.

He looked up as fiery cannonballs rained down on Angellus, hitting several rooftops, causing them to burst into flames. One hit the cathedral, and an angel toppled off, smashing on the cobblestone streets.

Sir Francis scrambled to his feet, then raised his hand to the soldiers.

"Ready..." He swung his arm down. "Fire!"

The cannonballs soared into the sky, targeting the approaching regiment of soldiers, together with the Cindertree. The attackers looked undeterred, speedily advancing on Angellus City.

"Reload!" ordered Sir Francis.

He could feel the magical ward in place over the city. With the wave of his hand he made the ghostly green image of a symmetrical cross flash brightly in the sky, before once again becoming invisible: the wards remained in place, yet seemed to be held in suspension, allowing Zairoc's men to attack. Sir Francis gritted his teeth. The strain of maintaining the wards wore on him. Should he release them, it would stop the constant drain on his magic, but that might be part of Zairoc's plan. He couldn't second-guess himself. The wards would remain. Besides that, if he used magic only to divert disaster, his people might have a chance if his power held out. Otherwise, he'd be used up and ready for Zairoc to kill, like a fish in a bucket.

The Angellus regiment prepared to fire. Another volley of enemy cannonballs fell, pursued by a storm of arrows. The ballistics cut down half the men before they could even reload. Sir Francis grabbed a cannonball. Rushing to the primitive mortar, he thrust it down the muzzle.

"Ready. Fire." He made the same motion with his arm, and the remaining soldiers fired their cannons.

More arrows rained down on Angellus City, stalked by more cannonballs. Flames on rooftops widened and grew brighter, and with that destruction came the death of many citizens. Sir Francis reached for his wand, then stopped. He couldn't put the fire out with magic, it might use too much. But he could help things along. He grabbed the wand from his tunic, pointing at the sky. The wand glowed green-white, shooting a single ball of energy into the clouds. Then the heavens opened up, and rain poured down on the city. The fires waned until completely extinguished, leaving only smoke rising off the once burning buildings. Angellus soldiers cheered.

Another volley of arrows flew at them, and they ducked out of sight. The invaders made it to the wall now, climbing siege ladders to get into the city. Zairoc didn't have enough forces to capture Angellus, yet his men would cause a lot of damage, together with death, before they finished. Sir Francis grabbed a red cloth from his tunic and waved it high.

"Archers!" he yelled as loud as he could.

Soldiers marched from the south and north walls. They angled their bows down at the attackers climbing up the west wall. They fired, riddling several of the invaders, who then fell away. In despair, the populous regiment of Zairoc's men kept climbing. Then, in an instant, the Angellus contingent sprung up out of hiding below.

They pushed blankets of grass aside as they bounded for the invaders, charging at them from their north and south positions just outside the wall. Zairoc's troops gawked at the approaching Angellus defenders. Archers ceased firing, for fear they would hit their own men.

"Surrender now or die fighting; the choice is yours!" Sir Francis yelled down at the soldiers.

Many heard him and laid down their arms.

"Surrender now, and you will be treated fairly," he yelled again.

More of the soldiers surrendered, throwing down their weapons. Several more remained in the heat of battle, so they had to be cut down. Once the chaos calmed, Sir Francis made his way down to the governor. He still lay unconscious in the pile of straw.

Sir Francis slapped the man's face, and he groaned.

"Did we win?" Travis asked with a meek voice.

"Yes, you did, Governor. Time to do your part." Sir Francis pulled him off the hay, then helped him stand.

He grabbed Travis, pulling him towards the front gate. The Angellus regiment had won. They marched in with Zairoc's soldiers, along with members of the Cindertree as their prisoners.

"You cannot hold a servant of the church," one of the Cinders yelled.

Sir Francis looked to Governor Travis.

"Yes, we can, and we will," Travis replied. "You will be held for trial. Your reign of terror on the city of Angellus is over." Travis raised his fists into the air, and the Angellus regiment cheered.

People flowed out of their houses in the excitement of winning the battle. While the streets filled will elated citizens, Sir Francis mounted Swift and rode out of the main gates.

He spurred Swift on until she couldn't go any faster. He held his wand forward. The air crackled all around them, the view of the road twisted and distorted, whizzing by. Creating a localized fold in space allowed for quick transport but took a physical toll on the wizard. A short time later, he arrived at the gates of Alexandria. He tucked his wand away, taking in the site. The air smelled thick with smoke and hung heavy in the heat of fire. With luck, he wouldn't be too late.

***

"I am Sir Francis, your ruler. Let me in!" he yelled at the gate.

No one answered. Maybe no one stood guard to hear him. He swallowed hard as his heart beat faster. He spurred Swift, racing along the wall. Built into a mountainous cliff face, it only had two sides. This wall, shaped like a V, stretched long indeed. Looking ahead to the corner of the wall, all lay quiet. The inhabitants prepared for an attack from land, but it could have come from the sea. Another expansive wall stood at the bottom, which also made for a grand and fantastic dock overlooking the ocean.

The wizard raced faster, though he dared not use the wand again so soon on Swift. Travelling through a localized fold in space proved hard on his head, leaving him partially disoriented. For the horse, it went through absolute trauma, yet the mare did as asked.

They rounded the corner. Quiet greeted them. But then Sir Francis made out the screams, along with the sound of battle, floating up from the distance. They came out of the direction of the docks. He steeled his jaw, racing on Swift to the second gate.

"This is Sir Francis. Raise the gate!"

Again, no answer came. Gritting his teeth, he pulled out his wand and swiped it at the gate, which flew open like it weighed nothing more than a feather. Sir Francis rode into the city. A quiet salt-air breeze met him while he rode down the cobblestone streets. This city had a pyramid-shaped church at its centre, with an impressive array of windows all along its sides, much akin to many of the modern versions of pyramids he'd seen. It looked out of place in a medieval town setting, especially next to the traditional castle the pyramid faced.

He raced to the stepped-stone street. Far below, black smoke billowed from several storehouses. Numerous Alexandrian vessels lay in ruin, leaving Zairoc's warships free to assault the city wall. Sir Francis's jaw dropped open at the sight.

He spurred Swift down the long descending street. The attacking vessels displayed white and black sails, with ZAIROC imprinted on them in big letters. The man possessed no taste, though did have a huge ego. The two regiments battled it out on the docks. The roar of the men and the sound of iron hitting iron grew louder. Sir Francis sped towards the battle. The street clogged with men holding the invaders back.

Sir Francis stared with a raised brow.

"Where is the Governor?" he yelled at the Alexandrian soldiers.

"He was on the docks," one of the soldiers yelled back.

Sir Francis turned, speeding over another street. The gate to the dock stayed wide open while several men fought along the battlements just above. He turned down another street, mostly covered with debris and obstacles. He sped along it. The mare leapt over the ruin of stone and wood. Swift must have just grazed the top because she twisted and fell to the ground, whinnying in pain. At the same time, she threw Sir Francis into the air. The world turned to a blur. Hitting the ground would cause massive injury or death—if he weren't a wizard. In response to his thoughts, the wand glowed from within his tunic, creating a blast of energy to cushion his fall. Quickly back on his feet he, hurried to Swift's side, pulling her out of sight. A prime specimen, she could have been a racing horse at one time. She appeared uninjured, and with luck, she'd stay safe, hidden among all the debris. He stroked Swift's mane.

He quickly picked up a sword off the ground and ran down into the mass of soldiers at the foot of the road. The screams of the men proved deafening. He pushed one man aside, then an invader with Zairoc's black and white crest attacked him. He blocked the enemy with his sword, stumbling backwards. He held the sword defensively as his attacker struck it. Three more hits in rapid succession forced Sir Francis to his knees.

The attacker smiled, advancing on Sir Francis who trembled under the strain. He stumbled to his feet, then swung the sword at the man. Much to his horror, the invader blocked him easily, driving Sir Francis back. They exchanged hits, and each time the impact of the iron swords made his whole body vibrate. It might actually shake him apart. Sir Francis winced as he gritted his teeth. Two more sword strikes came. Then the warmonger punched him in the face, taking the sword from him. He shoved Sir Francis down, ready to skewer him. At the last second, one of the Alexandrian soldiers blocked the invader.

They exchanged a flurry of blows, though Sir Francis's rescuer moved slowly, exhausted from battle. The warmonger pushed him on top of Sir Francis. The defender's weight pressed down on him, and Sir Francis struggled for air. Sir Francis tried to push the man off as the invader stood over them, then he slowly plunged the sword into the soldier's back. The man screamed with pain before dying on top of the wizard. The attacker grinned down at him. Sir Francis stared back in horror. The worst example of humanity stood over him, someone who enjoyed making death slow, so his victims would suffer. He could not help but snarl at the man, even though he knew he should hold back and not let his emotions take control.

"No!" Sir Francis bellowed.

The wand glowed, and the man shot into the air, along with all of the attacking soldiers around them. They flew up into the sky and didn't come down again. They would be dead from a lack of oxygen within seconds. Sir Francis had used too much magic already and might not have enough to see this through. Two of the Alexandrian soldiers pulled the dead man off of him, and Sir Francis nodded in thanks.

"We must help your comrades on the docks." Sir Francis slowly stood, his body weakened from the use of magic. The wards must have drained away more than he thought.

Sir Francis held up his sword, leading the regrouped soldiers into the fight with Zairoc's remaining attackers.

The Alexandrian regiment fought ferociously. They pushed back the invaders. Several dead bodies lay strewn along the docks. Sir Francis checked one after the other with dread, looking for the body of Governor Eechin. He reached the end of the dock, searching all around.

"Archers … fire!" a voice bellowed.

Sir Francis's eyes darted to the battlement above. Eechin stood tall amid arrows showering down on more enemies. He dared not launch more, or he would hit his own soldiers.

"Archers, fire again!" Eechin ordered.

"No, do not shoot!" Sir Francis yelled.

But arrows rained down on the soldiers, hitting attackers and Alexandrians alike. The invaders fell, defeated, yet Eechin had sacrificed many of his own men to do it. Sir Francis stormed back to the gate. He climbed a ladder up onto the apron wall. He marched at Eechin. Sir Francis must have looked angry, because the man cowered, though he held his ground.

"You just killed some of your own men!" Sir Francis spat at him.

"I am doing what has to be done."

Eechin smiled, looking out at the battle. Two warships with the bright-red colours of Alexandria bombarded Zairoc's ships. Sir Francis watched the grandiose Alexandrian ships rip huge holes with their cannons into the runty crafts. Zairoc's white and black sails burned, sinking into the ocean.

"We've won, and without you here for most of the battle. That's what you wanted. Wasn't it? For me to govern without you? That's all I did. I made the choice you couldn't." Eechin believed his words.

"I could kill you where you stand." Thunder rumbled in a clear blue sky.

"Go on, then. Show the people of Alexandria that you are no better than the dark wizard." Eechin moved closer to Sir Francis.

"I will be watching you, Governor. If I see you mistreat your people in any way, for any reason, even if you feel it is a good one, I will return. I will make you wish I had killed you now," Sir Francis whispered in his ear before marching off.

The fear in Eechin's eyes provided all the confirmation Sir Francis needed. Yes, the governors required breathing room in which to manage the cities, but he wouldn't let anyone throw lives away for no good reason. Sir Francis returned to Swift, stroking her long nose before guiding her carefully over the mound of debris.

"Come on, girl. This day is not done." He climbed on and urged her up the great stepped road.

Sir Francis had one more city to protect from the tyranny of Zairoc. His magic would last until the day was won.

What other choice did he have?

CHAPTER FIFTY-ONE

Ondreeal raced for the town, taking much longer than the men and women on horseback. As she got closer, the sound of screams and the smell of smoke grew vivid. She raced at full speed, sucking in air. A plume of dark smoke rose into the sky.

The men and women on horseback ransacked the town. Everyone fled in all directions, in a flurry of utter chaos. Ondreeal's eyes darted around while her heart beat in her throat. Two men on horses rode past; one of them axed a townsman in the head.

Ondreeal jumped back from his lifeless body falling towards her. The second rider cracked a whip that coiled like a snake around a poor woman's throat. He pulled hard, snapping her neck. Eyes wide with shock, Ondreeal covered her mouth. Several storefronts with their contents already sacked blazed with flames.

Where would Cecil hide? Did she escape? Ondreeal bolted down the street.

"Cecil? Cecil!" she called out in desperation.

A woman with black and red war paint smiled grimly at her from the top of her horse. She had a shaved head, save for a ponytail that looked as dirty and matted as the coat of the horse she rode. She surged her mount straight for Ondreeal, who fumbled with the wand until, at last, she aimed it at the raider.

"Be gone," Ondreeal commanded.

It glowed steadily.

The woman barrelled down on her.

"I said, go!" Ondreeal yelled, her hand trembling.

The woman, along with her horse, flew sideways into a stone wall. She fell off, leaving a bloody spot where her head smashed open. The horse tried to move, stumbled to the ground — injured but not dead. Ondreeal could do nothing for it.

Despite the control and discipline she'd achieved over herself, it hadn't translated fully to the wand. It felt like another mind lived inside it, and she struggled with it for control. Ondreeal ran down the street. Then, out of nowhere, a frantic man crashed into her.

"Raiders!" he yelled.

He knocked her down, making the wand fly from her hand. It rolled into the street. She stumbled to her feet. Out of nowhere, a warrior rushed at her, flicking his whip. It wrapped around her midsection and pulled her down. She reached for the wand, but it lay dark on the ground.

Another attacker on horseback jumped off, grabbing it. Ondreeal closed her eyes, screaming at the wand for help. It glowed brightly, making the raider's hand smoke with sheer heat. He tried to let go of it, but couldn't. His eyes glowed like coals until flames engulfed him. Immediately, the wand flew back into Ondreeal's hand.

All the while, her body burned as the first warrior dragged her like a dead animal. Now a wall of energy appeared in front of his steed, bringing it to a dead stop. The man on the horse flew off but still held the whip. It jerked Ondreeal a few more feet while she struggled for air. He pulled himself up, then snarled down at Ondreeal.

"The ground can't hold you anymore," Ondreeal wheezed, tears welling up.

The man's feet slipped into the ground, and to his surprise, he continued to sink. Ondreeal watched him disappear completely. The ground became solid, snipping off the end of the whip. Ondreeal pulled the whip away from her ribs, breathing deeply.

Chaos swirled all around her. In it all, she could feel the wand. It pulsed with what Ondreeal would call "emotion." Did she sense her feelings or the wand's? Had she told the wand what to do, or did it command her?

"Ondreeal!" Cecil called out, staring down from a large building. Her face looked desperate.

Ondreeal took in the entire structure. The base of its wood frame burned, with Cecil trapped up on the third floor. Ondreeal bolted to her feet and into the building. Smoke mixed with flames surrounded her. She made several sweeping motions with the wand. With each burst of energy, the flames went out, and the smoke retreated.

She made it to the staircase and climbed, coughing all the while.

One raider knelt at the top of the stairs, shoving into his pockets silver coins, scattered about. He hadn't noticed Ondreeal, so she quietly stepped past him amid intensifying flames.

A scream came from down the hall, and she hurried towards it. Backed into a corner by three interlopers, several townspeople, including Cecil, huddled in the room and looked to Ondreeal with hope.

The invaders whipped around to face Ondreeal. She stood ready with the wand as all three attacked her. She swiped with the wand, knocking down one. Then she swung again, striking down a second fighter. By the time she got to the third, he jumped on top of her. The second adversary sprung up, grabbed the wand, and threw it out the window. He turned back, holding his charred palm.

"You'll pay for that." Ondreeal's voice shook.

The raider pinned her, wrapped his hands around her neck, squeezing hard. Cecil and the others screamed with despair. Two more invaders bolted into the room, then gutted one of the townsmen. Ondreeal's heart beat so fast. Her throat strained in pain. She tried frantically to breathe. She couldn't focus enough to get the wand back. Tears streamed down her temples as she kicked out with her feet.

She needed to remember her training with the Beacon. He had taught her to use the path of least resistance. She snapped the raider's thumb, pushing out of his grip while he grunted with pain. She punched him in the face several times in quick succession, then kicked him back. She sprung to her feet, surrounded by all five warriors.

"I put the fire out below. Get out of here!" she yelled to the trapped townspeople.

They moved to flee until one of the raiders blocked them. One attacked her, and she pushed him away. Another invader came at her, and she blocked his moves until he kicked her in the gut. She flew back. Slamming on the ground she gritted her teeth, wincing in pain.

One adversary grabbed Ondreeal from behind while another lunged at her. She kicked the man squarely in the jaw, and his eyes glazed over, falling to the ground. At the same time, she struggled to free herself from the grip of the other two. One hit her in the face, and she tasted blood. He kept punching her in the gut until she grabbed his head with her legs. She twisted, and the sound of his neck breaking brought relief.

She struggled in the raider's grip as the other two advanced. She pulled forward and down, attempting to flip the attacker over her head, but his strength proved too much for her.

"Get out!" she called to the trapped townspeople.

With all three raiders' attention on her, the townspeople took the chance for freedom, scurrying out the door with Cecil.

Ondreeal sucked in shaky gasps. She tried to centre her breathing. The raiders closed in on her. She glared up at the man who towered over her. He flexed his muscular arms, scowling, his face painted white with half a skull while the other side lay bare, hardened with leathery, tanned skin. The woman had pale hair, in sharp contrast to the black and red mosaic that covered her face. They stalked towards her while the third raider yanked Ondreeal into a horrible embrace, squeezing hard.

Ondreeal breathed deeply, evenly. She fought against her base emotions, the ones that told her that if the raiders caused you pain, give it back, hurt them and end them. Yet her desperation grew as pain filled her body. She winced, screaming out. The warrior tightened his grip on her, but then the wand flew into the room, embedding itself in his head.

The man wailed. Then his head exploded.

His headless corpse fell away from Ondreeal.

The wand floated beside her while she moved into a fighting stance. The remaining two raiders looked at each other. One invader jumped out the window, quickly followed by the other. Ondreeal glanced at the corpse, swallowing hard.

She turned and rushed down the stairs, with the wand floating just ahead. It cleared the way, dousing the flames and clearing the smoke as she ran. She bolted out the door onto the street. Chaos reigned amid townspeople scurrying everywhere. Raiders, burned, looted, and tore down the market in the town square.

Ondreeal raced into the middle of it, then jumped up on the fountain. She imagined the water freezing. The wand flashed, trapping her feet in the now frozen fountain. A raider galloped at her. She struggled to free her legs, but they wouldn't budge. She stared desperately at the floating wand.

"Like knives raining down from Heaven, stab at my enemies." Her eyes darted to her attacker.

The raider pulled out a sword, ready to cut into her. The ice in the fountain splintered into pieces, floating in the air.

Ondreeal ducked as the sword whooshed passed her.

Ice crystals shot out of the fountain, riddling the raiders in the town square. They all fell from their horses. One invader gave her a dead stare while blood dripped from an ice shard embedded in his skull.

Tears welled up as Ondreeal fought to stand on shaky legs. She held her hand out to the wand, and it floated into her grasp.

"Ondreeal!" Cecil ran to her.

Ondreeal smiled, exhaling with relief. Then a raider galloped past on horseback, slicing a blade into Cecil's back.

She screamed as she fell.

"No!" Ondreeal ran to her.

She collapsed to the ground where Cecil had landed and gently held her.

"You came back." Cecil's voice sounded small, distant.

The life drained from her eyes.

Ondreeal carefully laid Cecil on the ground before closing her eyelids. Tears streamed down Ondreeal's face.

"I'm sorry," she whispered to Cecil.

Ondreeal glanced up. Two raiders, the ones who had jumped out the window to evade her, rode up the stairs to the Lumenary. She gazed up at the mountain. Dark smoke rose off of the place that she'd called home for the last few months. She slowly shook her head, her body paralysed, until she blinked and sprang to her feet. She leapt on a loose horse, spurring it up the stairs. Fear gripped her heart like a new frost. What horrors would she find in the Lumenary above?

CHAPTER FIFTY-TWO

A s Sir Francis arrived, the anticipation of battle hovered over Athena City—a nervous, fear-filled air that fuelled a bustle of human activity. The sky looked cold, like an arctic sea, yet the sun cut down with bright rays, making the afternoon warm and deceptively pleasant.

Sir Francis aimed towards the giant, black citadel in the centre of the city. The tall Gothic-style structure soared imposingly. The city sat on a high hill overlooking a surrounding valley, making the citadel visible for miles around. Personally designed by the wizard, the citadel boasted a catapult built into each of its four sides that could rotate at forty-five–degree angles. Four golden domes rose up like bookends for each catapult, encompassing the Lumenary at the centre of the black stone tower. Flying buttresses and grand arches lifted high into the sky to meet the God of All.

Sir Francis rode over the main drawbridge, the only entrance above a moat that surrounded the citadel. A thick and horrible smell lifted off from the dank water, making him cough. He coaxed Swift to one wall, where he tied her reins to a post. Racing inside, he counted the flights of stairs while he ascended the citadel—like climbing the castle at Bastion five consecutive times. It towered at least thirty storeys over Athena City. He wheezed as he stepped onto the battlement.

Governor Bauch stood, her arms crossed, glowering at the horizon while several Athenian soldiers dressed in a combination of brass and leather scurried all around. Bauch glanced back at the wizard, her eye widening when she saw his battle-worn state, which appeared quite horrible.

He glanced down at his hands, shaking from the overuse of magic in the other battles and in maintaining the wards. To use more now might leave him completely defenceless if Zairoc appeared. No, he would have to monitor the battle, using his powers only if necessary.

"Sir Francis, we spotted the enemy's approach over an hour ago. If they want a fight, they're going to get it, in more ways than one." Bauch didn't even break a smile.

She glared at Zairoc's approaching regiment. She intended to send him a message: don't mess with the city of Athena.

"Of that I have no doubt." Sir Francis gave her a steady, confident gaze.

Bauch nodded to a servant, who responded by hurrying away. When she returned, she carried a bowl of water and a cloth for Sir Francis.

"You look terrible. War doesn't agree with you, does it?" That sounded as sympathetic as Bauch could get.

"No, it most certainly does not."

He wiped his face, then threw water over his hair before joining Bauch on the expansive balcony.

His jaw dropped at the view. He'd seen the breathtaking skyline before, yet it amazed him each time. You could see part of the ring that made up the Black Circle Mountains — dark, imposing spectres that loomed over and easily dwarfed the citadel. The black peaks couldn't have formed in such a short time and were likely caused by the impact of a singularity-based alien ship.

The white and black banners approached Athena City. Defensive wooden posts encircled the perimeter and at each one, five Athenian soldiers crouched down, arrows at the ready. With no walls, the hill should prove enough of a strategic advantage. Only one regiment attacked; Zairoc couldn't hope to win. This invasion made no sense, except to create panic and fear. Steadily, from miles away, they advanced on the city in clear view.

The black stones under his feet vibrated. Sir Francis peered over the balcony as the catapults below them moved forward. Then soldiers loaded each one with a boulder they quickly set ablaze. They used a substance virtually identical to Greek fire. Upon landing, the flames would spread, and water would only make the blaze worse.

"Stop your advance or be fired upon!" the commander of the Athenian regiment bellowed to the invaders.

If only he and Zairoc could put their differences aside and build a society together. What did it say about human beings when they still squabbled over land, resources, and power? Sir Francis would let him have it all, but Zairoc had devolved into an egotistical narcissist who had proclaimed himself the supreme ruler. Sir Francis didn't wish to be a dictator, only aspiring to build a free society, tolerant and accepting of difference. If he couldn't do that, then human beings would never be ready for the next step in their evolution.

They had come so close the last time, so close to joining something much bigger. All of that had fallen to dust long ago. Why didn't Zairoc see the error of his ways? He had lived as a rational man at one time. Unfortunately, the fall of humanity must have permanently warped Zairoc's mind.

The invaders marched forward like a force of nature. As one they roared, sprinting at the city's regiment. The Athenian commander raised his arm; the giant catapult swung forward in response. The boulder landed right in the middle of the invading force, scattering them in all directions. Athenian soldiers advanced, splitting them down the middle. It looked like a massacre for Zairoc's forces, such a tiny regiment sent to their sacrifice. Small bands of Zairoc's soldiers formed until four separate groups rushed the city, racing to the city streets.

"Governor!" Sir Francis pointed to them.

"We're ready for them. Archers!" she called down.

The order rang out many times more. Sir Francis leaned over the balcony. Several arrows stuck out of the thin windows in the citadel, truly a wonder of medieval defence.

Arrows sprayed down onto the streets, halving the number of each group with every wave. Another volley came, and all the attackers fell dead, except for one at the centre of each group. Sir Francis's eyes widened in horror as those four soldiers, although riddled with arrows, managed to lower themselves down a manhole into the sewer. It looked like each soldier wore something strapped to his chest.

"Four men entered the sewers. They must be stopped!" he yelled at Bauch.

She nodded to one soldier who rushed out.

"We'll get them. There are only four." Bauch moved to the edge of the balcony.

Sir Francis pulled out the wand. His eyes darted all around. No sign of Zairoc. Then an image of Ondreeal appeared in his mind. She fought against strange tribal warriors. He could feel her fear, confusion, and anger. They both struggled in battle, and that could make a connection between them, a common thread. She needed his help. He closed his eyes, reaching out to her. For a moment, the image of Ondreeal looked right at him. Then her face disappeared as the world rushed back in.

The regiment killed or captured all of the invaders, save the four who slipped into the sewers. They'd taken numerous arrow hits, so they might have already died down there. Finally, Athenian defenders approached each of the four manholes, then headed down. Sir Francis blinked, refocusing on the invaders in the sewers.

Boom! An explosion shook the city as a ball of fire shot up out of the sewer. Screams echoed up from the streets and inside the citadel.

Bauch glared, her scowl deepening. Sir Francis stared while a cold horror set in on his face. His heart pounded in his chest, yet he couldn't get his legs to move.

A second explosion came, then a third—the citadel shook like an earthquake. One Athenian soldier climbed out on fire. Then the unimaginable happened as the city street collapsed at each of the three explosion sites.

Sir Francis grunted like he'd been punched in the stomach.

The citadel trembled, and a brick fell away, crashing on the ground. Five more bricks smashed, until a horrible noise rose up like the screech of an animal dying. One of the citadel's walls listed, swaying freely. The wizard's body went numb.

"No!" Governor Bauch bellowed out.

The wall fell silently to the street, ending in an ear-splitting collision. One of buttresses thundered down, splintering to pieces. Then the balcony they stood on creaked under the strain. Bauch pulled Sir Francis back inside as the balcony fell away. Sir Francis blinked, racing after Bauch.

"Abandon the citadel!" Bauch howled.

Soldiers and citizens screamed in panic at each other. Everyone frantically fled the massive structure. Dust and smoke filled the air. Sir Francis coughed as they all tried to get free of the mayhem. Down they went while the stairs trembled under their feet. The wave of people fleeing could account for the vibration, or imminent collapse of the citadel could happen mere moments away. Finally, they broke out of the main doors.

Swift, still tied near the wall, bucked among the crowd flowing around her, over the drawbridge. Sir Francis grabbed her reins.

"Easy... Easy..." he yelled out over the thunder of the crowd.

Finally, Swift stopped kicking, breathing hard through her nose. Sir Francis gently stroked the side of her head until her respiration slowed. He glanced up at the citadel. It could fall any minute, but he wouldn't leave Swift. He untied her, climbing on. He lifted the wand high, willing the citadel to remain strong. The creaking and moaning of the Gothic building ceased. He urged Swift through the thinning crowd and galloped out of the city.

Once clear of the harm, Sir Francis pulled back on the reins until Swift stood in place. He looked back at the destruction. Half of one wall had collapsed without the support of anything underneath it. Thankfully, the citadel appeared stable, standing strong despite the damage.

Zairoc's fanatical message of domination resounded loud and clear; he could turn even the most powerful advantages against them. Zairoc wouldn't stop until all people, everywhere, lived and died under his rule. Sir Francis would have to outmanoeuvre Zairoc if he hoped to get his cities back to peaceful prosperity. He would return home, lick his wounds, and plan.

"Sir Francis." A soldier rode up to him.

He wore the green and white colours of Bastion.

"Speak," Sir Francis barked at him.

"Bastion is under attack by Zairoc himself."

The soldier had fear in his voice — as he should. Sir Francis spurred Swift on, racing away. Zairoc had outsmarted Sir Francis in every way. He expected a full invasion, similar to the one that overtook the cities of Aleenda to the south, almost fifteen years ago. Zairoc wanted control of the north. He used that information against Sir Francis, but why? Why not simply invade in force? What ultimate plans did Zairoc have for the north, and would Sir Francis be able to stop him? Or would he end up defeated, lying on the ground, with Zairoc staring down in triumph?

Sir Francis couldn't worry about that now. He would fight against the hate and violence that Zairoc brought to the world, to his dying breath. He only wished that Ondreeal could stand at his side. He rode Swift harder.

His body trembled with fatigue. A whisper carried on the wind.

"She will save you. She will save them all." It sounded like Aleenda's voice, fading to silence.

The magnificent steed he rode carried him into darkness. He'd meet whatever the future may bring, with grim certainty.

CHAPTER FIFTY-THREE

The horse struggled up the stairs to the Lumenary, veering directly at a gorge just below. Ondreeal's heart jumped. She pulled hard on the reins to keep her mount on the path, while the stairs flew by in a blur. Her head spun, and her muscles ached. The battle below had taken so much out of her. But if she wavered now, the horse could throw her off the cliff faces surrounding the carved stone pathway.

Finally, her horse leapt up the final flight, revealing a sight of horror. Most of the raiders must have come right for the Lumenary. The Beacon had amassed so much wealth here — offerings made from true believers seeking blessings in their journey along the Path of Light. She froze in place, watching the gruesome scene.

The once orderly Lumenary had devolved into a mess of chaos as the Embers fought for their lives with these invaders, these dark, soulless wanderers who brought death to their home. The light of ruinous fires glowed from within one of the sleeping chambers, along with frightful plumes of smoke. Each Ember scattered, locked in combat with raiders.

Ondreeal shook her head, steeling her jaw. She leapt off the horse, then ran at one raider that was struggling with two Embers. He swung his sword wildly, but the Embers evaded him every time. Excellent fighters who only used their hands, the Embers kept no weapons in the Lumenary. That they had survived this long against swords and axes made for a true testament to their skill.

He swung his sword. Ondreeal ducked, kicking him in the legs. Two Embers landed several blows on the interloper, who slashed with his sword again. One Ember screamed as the raider sliced open his gut. Ondreeal's face flushed with anger.

The second Ember, together with Ondreeal, smashed the man in his torso. Ondreeal grabbed the handle of the sword. The raider growled, driving her back. Her feet slipped as she fell down, hitting her head on the stairs. Blood dripped from a gash on her forehead. Ondreeal glared at the raider. He viciously attacked the second Ember, who barely evaded each sword swipe.

Ondreeal took out the wand and fired at the man. The raider went flying, smashing into one of the brick walls. He slid down, lying motionless. Ondreeal crawled over, grabbing his lost sword. She threw it to the Ember, who stared at her with a mixture of awe and shock.

"You know our ways. This is not — " The man screamed as a sword sprung out of his gut, then quickly withdrew.

Ondreeal jolted from the sudden death, watching the Ember fall. She stood to face this new raider. He charged at her, but with a flick of the wand, he froze in place.

"Your hate and anger consume you," she spat, circling him while she gnashed her teeth.

The raider shrunk inward like a balloon deflating, until he had only skin-covered bones. She wanted him to suffer, but the sight proved too gruesome. He fell to the ground, shattering to dust. Ondreeal turned as a sword came down at her. She swung the wand, screaming.

A shock wave blasted from the wand. This third raider's entire body crackled with shattering bones, causing him to fall like a limp doll. She gasped with disgust. At the same time, the wave sent a huge crack through the winding staircase and up one of the stone walls. Two of the Embers, in the grip of battle, glanced at her in shock.

Ondreeal's grip loosened on the wand; she couldn't save the Lumenary by destroying it. She retrieved one of the bloody swords. She held it in one hand and the wand in the other. She swallowed hard, moving up the stairs.

The fire from the sleeping chamber erupted out of the roof. Part of the canopy creaked, then collapsed with a loud crash. On the winding stairs, four Embers valiantly fought against an equal number of raiders, until two more raced down the stairs at them.

"Come fight me, if you can!" Tears welled up in Ondreeal's eyes.

One charged, shoving Ondreeal. She swiped at another with the wand. He flew into a pillar, cracking it. The raider fell, unmoving.

The second interloper pushed against her. She quickly moved aside, letting his own weight pull him down the stairs.

The man lunged forward, but quickly twisted and turned to attack. She jumped back, repeatedly blocking him with the sword.

The man swung and slashed her arm. Ondreeal screamed as she cradled her wound.

She retreated with every swipe of his sword.

He hit her weapon until it flew from her hand. He clutched the blade over his head, then brought it down on her with great force.

Gritting her teeth, she held the wand to protect herself, knowing the pain to come from the strike.

The sword smashed against an invisible force. Blue energy radiated out from the impact, illuminating an enchanted shield. The raider howled as he repeatedly hit the barrier, which flashed brightly with each impact. Ondreeal willed the shield to stay strong. Magic taxed her body, causing her to wince with pain as blood dripped from her nose. She let out a long, continuous scream as she strained to hold him back.

The barrier protecting her flashed out of existence. The raider smiled broadly, raising his blade high. She glared up at him. Just before it hit, someone knocked the man down the stairs.

Doyle pulled her up. "You all right?"

"You're alive!" Ondreeal threw her arms around him.

"You came back." He squeezed her.

"I had to," she whispered in his ear.

Doyle nodded before running back up the stairs.

Ondreeal found her fallen sword, then chased after him, fuelled by anger or the wand, perhaps both.

Doyle dashed into the grand hall that connected the Beacon's chamber. Most of the Embers fought here, locked in combat with armed raiders. They protected the Beacon, encircling him along with the treasures in his chamber. Doyle raced to help one of the Embers falling under sword. The raider readied to impale the fallen Ember. Doyle knocked the blade away, driving him back.

"Look out, Ondreeal!" an Ember yelled.

Her head whipped around. Ember Lestlie called out as two more raiders descended on her. She blocked each swipe of their swords until one cut right through hers.

Ondreeal gasped, and she dropped the hilt. She jumped back. Another blade cut through the air, barely missing her side. The raiders pushed her until her body pressed against the wall. She loosed a battle cry, swiping with the wand. The two raiders flew upwards. One hit the three-storey ceiling, then fell to the ground with a dull thud. Ondreeal watched in shock while the second man slammed right into two of the Embers. One holy warrior quickly jumped to his feet. Much to her dismay, the second defender lay there.

She ran over to the fallen Ember as two more raiders charged her. She held up the wand, but before she could do anything, Bradai grabbed the invaders and slammed them back into the wall, a devilish grin on his face.

Ondreeal's jaw dropped at the sight of him.

Bradai pinned both of them against the wall. "You'll not be hurting my friend."

The interlopers fought viciously, clawing at Bradai. With a ferocious glare, he moved incredibly fast, blocking each of their blows. She checked the fallen Ember at her feet and found his heart beating steadily. She launched forward, racing to Bradai, when one of the raiders plunged a sword through him.

Ondreeal stopped hard. Her breath caught in her throat. Bradai stood there for a moment, with the bloody sword sticking from his gut. The invader pulled out the sword and Bradai collapsed to the ground.

"No!" she screamed, swiping angrily at one raider.

The energy from the wand cut the man's sword and body in half. She pointed the wand at the other raider. The man looked astonished as he turned his weapon on himself and pushed the sword into his gut, falling dead. Ondreeal pulled Bradai over to a wall.

"Bradai, stay with me. Please!" she pleaded with him.

He stared up at her, his eyes glazing over. His mouth moved, but no words came out. Tears burned down her cheeks. Red blotches soaked into his clothing, growing at an alarming rate—blood gushed from his wound. She clutched his robes. The wand glowed in her hand. She watched in amazement while the bleeding slowed until it stopped. The open wound then closed, seemingly on its own. Finally, Bradai opened his eyes.

"Oh, Ondreeal, you look like shit. I know, because that's how I feel." He coughed, looking at her with dazed eyes.

She smiled through her tears.

"Stay here," she ordered him.

She stood amid the Embers, who pushed back the few remaining invaders. The tide of battle at last had turned in their favour. She pointed her wand at one of the advancing enemy, taking careful, even breaths. The wand fired a slow shot of energy at the interloper. When it hit, the man crumpled to the ground. The grateful Embers stared in awe at her magical display, nodding to her before lunging back into the fight.

Several of the raiders retreated out of the great hall. Ondreeal pursued them, but they moved too fast. The same two that had killed Cecil glanced back at her, smiling as they jumped on their horses and galloped away, down the hill. She stepped towards them, infuriated by their escape. The sounds of battle made her turn, facing the great hall. She bolted inside. One raider stood surrounded by the Embertree. They gradually closed in around the man, who flailed wildly with his sword, slowing with each swipe. He grew tired from his own crazed fighting. Two Embers neatly stepped in and, with one motion, disarmed him. Another holy warrior had grabbed his head, ready to snap his neck, when the Beacon held up a hand.

"No, this one I want alive. Lock him in the cellar," the Beacon commanded.

Two of the Embers complied.

Ondreeal took in the great hall, littered with the bodies of raiders along with the Embertree. She searched the remains. Tears came down when her eyes fell on one Ember.

She sat down beside the body of Ember Lestlie. One of his last acts had been breaking his oath of quietness to warn her, saving her life. With so much evidence of death and destruction around her, did Ondreeal truly walk the Path of Light? Or had she become lost in the ruin of night, encased in a darkness that would keep her forever shattered?

"We must remove the bodies of the soulless ones. Throw them off the cliff. Let the animals have them." The Beacon waved his hand, with his usual stoic facial expression.

Ondreeal looked up at him. He caught her gaze. He flinched ever so slightly before turning and heading into his chamber.

Doyle kneeled down beside her, sorrow in his eyes.

"What will happen to them?" She glanced at him quickly, then back down to Ember Lestlie.

"They'll go into the light, where they will continue to walk the Path." He managed a slight smile, a tiny quiver in his voice.

The Embers set to the arduous task of removing the bodies and cleansing away the destruction. Ondreeal dragged herself to her feet. Not a stranger to death, she would help if she could.

Together with Bradai, Ondreeal helped carry the bodies of raiders over the rope bridges. Bradai mentioned that keeping them so close to the Lumenary invited soullessness into the mountain itself, thus the necessity to move them as far away as possible. What exactly did that mean? Ondreeal wondered if a mountain could have a soul. But in a way, it made perfect sense to her. No one wanted the bodies of fallen enemies close at hand.

The colour of the sky darkened, and a few points of light twinkled. They stopped at a cliff, where Ondreeal glanced down at the twisting mists. They threw the body off so that it fell soundlessly into the clouds below.

"Good riddance to bad rubbish." Bradai spat over the cliff.

***

A heaven full of stars looked over the Lumenary as Ondreeal and Bradai moved into the training grounds. Only, instead of training, the remaining Embers were building up piles of sticks. Bradai sighed deeply, hanging his head.

"I need to speak to the Beacon," she told Bradai.

She marched up the winding staircase, directly into the Beacon's chamber. He stood at the window, staring out at the courtyard below.

"I told you to leave," he calmly told Ondreeal without even turning around.

"I had to help." She folded her hands in front of her.

"You used a weapon on sacred ground." He clearly sounded angry.

"Yes, I used a raider's sword against their forces. What difference does it make how you kill someone? We all took lives today, to save ourselves and each other." A tear fell down her cheek.

"It makes all the difference. Years can go by without an attack by raiders. They take what they want, do what they want, without regret or remorse. The rules of the Lumenary stand against lawlessness—rules you break to suit your needs and wants." He glared at her over his shoulder.

"I saved lives. That's what matters." She struggled to keep her voice steady.

"You have proven that you do not walk the Path of Light. You are no wizard, just a scared girl who crawled out of the dirt. If you had any light in your heart, you would turn the wand over to someone deserving of it and crawl back into the muck you came from." He never once looked at her.

She glowered at him. "Are you finished?"

At last, he turned to face her, clearly surprised at her reaction.

"I did everything you asked of me. You're a fine leader if everyone is a good little soldier. But when one of us steps out of line, we're all soulless and wandering. As if your path is the only path. Well, it's not. People can be good in ways you might not agree with. Like, taking a sword and cutting down a few of those murderers to save the lives of good men." She matched his glare, though tears fell despite her best efforts.

"I was hard on you because it's what you needed. You are too easily swayed by the plight of others. If you do a bad thing for a good reason, it doesn't make you righteous. It only disrespects all that I taught you." He looked hurt as he moved close, wiping away one of her tears.

"No one can walk the narrow path you set out for us." Her voice trembled.

She turned and marched out.

Why did she care so much what he thought of her? He'd been hard on her to the point of cruelty, like Otto. Ondreeal hurried down the winding staircase a ways. Then she collapsed to sit on the stairs, overwhelmed with exhaustion that filled every part of her. Ondreeal ran her hand from her shoulder down the arm, bruised and cut from battle, but the wounds were fading fast. The wand healed her whether or not she asked it to, and took much of her strength in return.

She looked at the cracks in the foundation that she'd caused. Maybe the Beacon told the truth, that she wasn't good. Nevertheless, if goodness meant emulating him, then she'd rather embrace the darkness.

She pulled out her wand, closed her eyes, and concentrated, waiting several moments before opening her eyes again. The cracks in the steps met her gaze. She held the wand in both her hands, closing her eyes tightly. She opened them again: nothing.

"You still try too hard." Doyle's eyes shone with affection for her while he limped down the stairs.

She held a hand up to him. "Are you okay?"

"I'll continue living." He smiled at her. "Trying to fix your handiwork?"

She shook her head. "It's like it has a mind of its own. Like we're speaking but don't know each other's language. Those misunderstandings end up in disaster most of the time."

"New partnerships can be difficult." He took her hand, sitting down next to her.

"I've trained so much. Every time I think I'm ready, I'm not." She shook her head.

"Perhaps the wand reflects back to you, like seeing your face in the water. You're learning about it, just as it's learning about you," he explained.

"You're saying that I can't control it because I can't control myself?" she asked.

He tilted his head to her. "How can you expect the wand to know what to do, when you haven't even decided the Path you're on?"

"I didn't know you were wise too." She places her hand in his palm. "Thank you, Doyle."

"We're getting ready to say final words for our fallen Embers." His swallowed, his body stiffening. "Join us."

He stood, holding out a hand to her.

"Give me a moment."

Doyle nodded, then headed down the stairs.

She pulled out the wand. Holding it in the open palms of her hands, Ondreeal took a deep breath, clearing her mind.

"I know I haven't figured everything out yet. There's so much I don't understand, that I don't know. You're probably used to the way my mother did things. She had a grace about her. I miss her too. But I can't be her for you, as much as I want to be. I know my emotions get the better of me. I've felt so lost. But I want to do the right thing, one step at a time. Right now, I could really use your help with one small thing."

She opened one eye, peering at the wand.

She opened the other eye, taking another deep breath.

"Just like it was, I can see it in my mind," she told the wand.

Silently, the cracks in the stairs came together, along with the cracks in the walls. She put the wand down and looked closely at the stairs, where a barely visible fissure remained on the now sealed stone.

"I'll take what I can get." She put the wand in her tunic, then crossed her arms tightly. "Thank you."

She stood, descending the winding staircase. Out of the corner of her eye, the Beacon moved down the stairs behind her, touching the newly mended stone. She moved quickly, stopping at the bottom, where each of twelve wooden altars cradled a lost hero. At the end of each altar, an Ember stood with a lit torch raised to a starry sky. The Beacon marched down past Ondreeal into the courtyard, only stopping once he reached the bell.

"Every Ember here came to us from different places, different homes and different lives. That isn't to say that they didn't walk in the light—they did, all of them. Their hearts guided and steered them true. It has come to my awareness that there are many journeys that can be righteous. The road must be wide enough for all, even if they never choose to walk it. Our Embers may be gone, but they still walk the on the golden road. As the light consumes their bodies, it releases their souls. May the wind guide them on the Path, taking them to the God of All."

The Beacon stretched both hands over his head, opening his arms wide and then lowering them to his sides. Each of the twelve Embers slowly lowered their torches, igniting one of the wood altars. A dozen fires started small, but each grew over time into a blaze. Smoke rose to the heavens as the fire burned bright in the darkness. The flames danced, moving in hypnotic patterns. The smoke flew into the heavens, carried by the wind.

Strange smells of metal, mixed with boiled eggs and sweet flowers, spread over the breeze. The smell made images of the old couple flash in Ondreeal's mind.

She swallowed hard as tears welled up. She wouldn't let the memory drive her away. She needed to stay and honour the fallen Embers. Doyle moved to stand at her side.

"Take them into your arms, God of All." Doyle sighed softly.

***

Ondreeal stared out the window at the bright, beautiful day. The Lumenary looked in good order, already cleansed of the events of yesterday — a testament to the fact that the world kept moving, barely noticing what had changed so many lives.

Ondreeal packed her bag, taking one last look at the room. Would she ever see this place again? Or was she saying goodbye to these Embers? These men had not only taught her about God, but about strength and gaining courage to face what she'd done, as well as how to find her true Path.

She headed down the stairs past all the Embers. She had already said her farewells; there was no sense in doing it all again. She caught Doyle with Bradai staring after her from the edge of the garden where she'd first landed all those months ago. She gave them both a brave smile before descending the stairs.

She marched past the village on the mountain, where folks were already picking up the pieces and setting about rebuilding their homes. Children laughed and played like they always did. Yet the town looked different, a solemn air had settled around the buildings and changed their appearance. The absence of the dead permeated in the quiet streets, making Ondreeal walk a little faster.

She deeply exhaled as she left the town that had been so much more full of people, life, and joy only a day ago. The countryside remained the same, out here at the border of the Enchanted Lands. The wind blew steadily as puffy, white clouds raced across a bright blue sky.

Ondreeal touched the wand through her tunic. With another deep breath, she nodded, striding confidently forward. For the first time since she'd gotten the wand, she believed she could use it for good. She could be a powerful force for change. She'd call Bastion home and defend it with her life, working with Sir Francis to elevate all people.

"Ondreeal," a voice called.

It sounded familiar, and as she turned and squinted at two Embers racing closer. She could, at last, clearly see the faces of Bradai and Doyle. Bradai stopped just before smashing into her, then doubled over, coughing and gasping. Doyle ran up beside him, nodding to Ondreeal.

He raised an eyebrow. "You move fast."

Her heart jumped. She'd been certain she would never see them again, yet here they stood, less than an hour later.

"What are you two doing?"

"We took the Beacon's speech to heart. You know, the parts about many Paths, blah, blah, blah..." Bradai paused to suck in more air.

"We believe our Paths are the same, at least for now." Doyle bowed slightly.

A wave of brightness radiated out of Ondreeal's heart, bringing tears to her eyes and a small lump into her throat. She should tell them to go back. She couldn't be selfish. Nevertheless, they both looked determined. If they felt the God of All wanted them to stay together, how could she disagree?

She nodded to them, smiled, then she turned and walked on.

CHAPTER FIFTY-FOUR

C D-45 placed fresh palm leaves on top of a pile on the ground — an action he had repeated several times over the last week. It took time to collect the necessary components before he could enact his plan. It also gave Vere much needed rest while her wounds continued healing.

CD-45's internal monitor sprang to life with a holographic display of North America. A microcommunications array connected to his system, transmitting a repeating message: EARTH ATTACKED BY DECALONIANS. REQUEST ASSISTANCE. Well, tell CD-45 something he didn't know. Besides, "immediate assistance" had never come, and if it did, he would have been among the first to realize it. Strange that he hadn't made a connection with the array immediately upon landing. Perhaps an effect of the alien fleet in orbit that continued to block most communications.

A flashing green dot represented the signal, located with Alpha Four Five-A at the largest city in the north. It updated his map with more sensor data on Alpha Four Five-B at a settlement near the edge of the mountains, while A and C overlapped throughout the northern settlements. If CD-45 had to guess, these three energy sources struggled with each other for dominance and control. This might also account for the lack of technological progress. This mystery only deepened over time, one he must solve if he ever wanted to complete his mission. The wizard known as Sir Francis must know more than he had told to either Vere or Trick Mark, and it confirmed his earlier conclusion: he must return with his friends to Bastion if he ever hoped to get answers and the help needed to save the human race from obliteration. Since he'd crash-landed, he had come to realize just how important his role was in saving this world. This might cause the opinion of himself to grow exponentially, but he'd do what he could to remain … what did humans call it? Modest.

After all, CD-45 could only complete one phase at a time.

Any construction droid needed to be a professional chemist to create many of the compounds used in building. Trick Mark looked confused and embarrassed giving CD his urine, but it was an ample source of ammonia. When combined with the oxygen he took out of the air, his internal mechanisms processed and stored the nitric acid needed.

Vere looked brighter. They both sat and watched in fascination—CD used a variety of his tools to separate out the glycerine from the palm leaves. It took three more days to complete, but in the end, he had one bowl of the required compound.

CD-45 then combined them internally to create nitro-glycerine. He looked to Trick Mark and Vere with both thumbs up. Trick Mark nodded to him. Freeing the river would provide a quick transportation route, bringing them much closer to Bastion and the answers that CD so desperately needed.

CD-45 used his thrusters to float over, ensuring a steady approach, with an empty leather bag in hand. Trick Mark with Vere followed behind him, but he indicated for them to keep their distance. If the compound detonated, CD would explode with it. He didn't want his friends joining him in that final experience. He tapped a series of commands on his chest, and the beaker-like compartment containing the compound extended out. CD carefully poured it into the leather bag.

He hovered near the edge of the river, scanning the dam. Tribesmen lined the top. They were fanatical about finishing what they started, even if it killed them. Trick Mark and Vere crouched down next to the canoe.

CD had no choice but to fly right up the middle of the river to reach the best location for the explosion. As he approached, several of the natives screamed down at him.

"Demon!" yelled one of them.

Arrows rained down on him. He carefully adjusted his thrusters so that he faced the ground, with the bag held underneath him. If one of the arrows hit the compound, it would be the end of him and his plan.

The arrows simply bounced off his metal frame, one of his few advantages in a primitive environment. First the dam, then to Bastion — that is, if he survived.

CD-45 got as close as he dared. He set himself to fly right at it with the bag held arm's length in front. He whirled around and released it like a shot put. He set his thrusters to full reverse as the compound ended in a loud, powerful explosion.

CHAPTER FIFTY-FIVE

Ondreeal gazed up at the million points of light above the treetops. Bright flashes erupted in the sky like thousands of fireflies, burning brightly for a moment, then shrinking to nothingness.

Doyle sat beside her, staring up. "The God of All battles tonight."

Ondreeal looked down at their campfire, where flames flittered about in the occasional gust of wind. They illuminated Bradai, who sat on the opposite side, shovelling food zealously into his mouth. Ondreeal shivered. She sat on a log next to Doyle, closer to the fire.

"Are you sure you two are ready for what's out there? It's not too late to turn back," she told them with a worried gaze.

"Stop saying that." Doyle sat a little taller and puffed out his chest. "Besides, we can take care of ourselves."

Bradai chuckled deviously. "Most importantly, we relieved the Beacon of much of the weight he carries."

Doyle gave him a look to shut up. Bradai's smile vanished then he grabbed a cup, slurping up its contents.

Ondreeal raised her eyebrow. "What did you mean, Bradai?"

Her chubby friend shrugged, pointing to the cup and his bulging cheeks full of liquid.

Ondreeal glared at Doyle. "What did he mean?"

Doyle just coughed then regarded the stars.

"If we are to travel together, then I need to know I can trust you." She looked back and forth between them.

Bradai loudly swallowed, clearing his throat and staring at Doyle, who equalled his gaze. Ondreeal shifted her glare between them. Doyle sighed, nodding.

Bradai picked up his satchel and pulled it open. He extracted a silver cup filled with gold coins. Ondreeal blinked, raising her eyebrows. The light from the fire made the cup shine brightly.

Ondreeal's jaw dropped open. "You stole from the Beacon's own chamber? You stole from the Lumenary?"

"Not stealing so much as" — Bradai held up his index finger to accentuate his words — "took and will never give back."

"We knew you might need to buy supplies along the way. There are certainly farms and more villages as we draw closer to the capital." Doyle explained before quickly looking away from her.

Ondreeal placed her hands on her knees, bracing herself in disbelief. "But you are Embers of Light."

Bradai nodded to her. "Two thieves who became Embers of Light."

"Thieves? You two were thieves?" If she opened her mouth more, she could swallow a horse.

She shouldn't be surprised. Many of the downtrodden with colourful or immoral pasts became Embers. Her own recent history carried the stain of blood. But she had held up Bradai and Doyle as role models, examples of what she aspired to.

"In our defence, we did join the Embertree," Doyle pointed out.

Bradai shrugged. "To steal from it, true."

Doyle shot him a glare. "Bradai!"

"The girl wanted honesty, remember?" Bradai held up the silver cup.

"I need the whole truth, Doyle." Her gaze must have shot like ice right into his heart, because he visibly shrunk under her glare.

"We joined the Embertree because we wanted to steal from them. But we never did. We stayed because we really believed in the teachings." Doyle's expression held a tinge of regret.

"That and the regular meals. We'll still have regular meals, won't we?" Bradai's eyes sharpened with concern, looking back and forth from Doyle to the young wizard.

Ondreeal stared into the fire. Both men shifted uncomfortably, listening to the crackle of the flame together with the rustling of wind through the leaves.

"I think you two are a disgrace. Go back, now! I want nothing more to do with either of you," she flatly told them, never making eye contact.

Bradai and Doyle stared at each other wide-eyed.

"I'm joking." Ondreeal smiled then giggled.

The men's frozen shock melted into laughter.

"I knew there was a reason I liked you, Ondreeal," Bradai cackled.

Doyle grinned, shaking his head.

"You two have always done right by me, so I trust you. I never liked that the Beacon hoarded all that wealth. We'll use what you took to help people. It's the right thing to do. But just so you understand, I catch you stealing again, and I'll turn you into bronze statues." She looked at each of them.

"Fair enough. See? I told you she'd let us keep the gold." Bradai played with a few of the coins.

Doyle beamed at her. "We really do want to help."

Just hours before, she had headed out alone. Now she had two good friends as companions on the journey.

"It means a lot to have you both here." She blinked back tears.

Doyle locked eyes with Ondreeal. "May we journey together on our Paths for a long time to come."

His handsome face made her heart skip a beat.

"One, two, three, four..." The gold coins clinked each time Bradai dropped them into his palm.

A splash of water soaked him. He looked up, and Doyle waved an empty cup at him.

"Right," Bradai nodded, carefully placing the coins and the silver cup in the knapsack.

Doyle flashed Ondreeal a bright smile before settling by the fire. Bradai used his gold-filled knapsack like a pillow, nuzzling into it as both men closed their eyes.

Ondreeal surveyed the stars with a sigh. What did the future hold for them? She wriggled next to the fire, holding the wand through her tunic. They would hurry back to Bastion. Sir Francis would look surprised but also relieved to see her. She needed his guidance. At long last, he'd teach her to properly wield the wand.

She'd made so many mistakes. Was it all a part of God's plan for her? Or did she have other choices she could have made along the way? If only she could go back and change things. She'd do it all right the second time.

However, she couldn't replace the knowledge gained through those mistakes. She'd learned more than she ever thought possible about the world and herself. Nevertheless, she had more questions now than when she started.

Sir Francis had no use for religion. Should she put her faith in God, or in the wizard of Bastion? If she believed in both, could she continue to grow, becoming a powerful wizard?

She needed to know more about her past, to learn all she could about her mother. Given enough time, Sir Francis would explain everything to her. Then she would finally understand her place in the world.

Ondreeal's heart beat faster. So many dangers lay ahead: the dark wizard, maybe a war with the south, the unknown stretches of the Enchanted Lands, unifying all the peoples everywhere.... Gigantic problems that she had no idea how to solve. Yet hope filled her heart because she had worked so hard to gain control of herself. That meant she could change the world for the better. It had to be true. Ondreeal closed her eyes and sighed deeply.

In her dreams, the hopes and fears of the future plagued her. Her mother's smiling face came to her, though, protecting her in a warm glow. It was all part of one big landscape at her fingertips, which lay just out of reach — the city of Bastion, the Black Circle Mountains, the Enchanted Lands. She would find her path there, with the help of Sir Francis, the God of All, her new friends, and the people she'd help using the wand's power. Still, Ondreeal remained humble as the ghostly echoes of those she'd killed haunted her drifting mind, warning her of the great dangers she had yet to face.

END

CPSIA information can be obtained
at www.ICGtesting.com
Printed in the USA
LVHW111950210921
698372LV00005B/170/J